CONFETTI CONFIDENTIAL

They Do,

I Don't

AVAILABLE FROM SUSAN MURPHY

CONFETTI CONFIDENTIAL: THEY DO, I DON'T

SUSAN MURPHY

Confetti Confidential: They Do, I Don't by Susan Murphy
Copyright © Susan murphy 2022

First Published in 2015 by Harper Collins Au
Republished by Susan Murphy in 2022

Version: 1 August 2022
Print ISBN: 978-0-6455863-0-5

Susan Murphy

is a marriage and funeral celebrant turned author from Adelaide, South Australia. With almost two decades as a celebrant, she's had the pleasure and blessing of conducting ceremonies all over the country including weddings, baby naming's, commitment ceremonies, funerals and anything else that has been requested by a client. The stranger the better!

With a passion for telling the stories of people, Susan crafts marriage ceremonies, eulogies and writes books that tell those stories. From love and hardship to life and loss and everything in between, Susan has the unique opportunity to see and be a part of the most special and important moments in people's lives.

Her past writing includes the Confetti Confidential series, Annabel's Wedding, Aloha Love and A Moonta Bay Christmas and she was also the Writer in Residence at the SA Writers Centre. With a Bachelor of Writing and Creative Communication from the University of South Australia, Susan hopes that, like her idols, she will be able to write stories that move people and take them to new and exciting places.

"Writing about weddings came naturally to me. I'd been a part of that world for so long and seen everything there was to see – good and bad. But there had to be humour. Coming from a large Irish family there was no way I could write without the laughs. I drove my family nuts giggling away to myself while writing this book."

Connect with Susan at susanmurphyauthor.com

Acknowledgement

Thank you to every person who listened, read pages and put up with my incessant ramblings about this book.

A special thank you to my family and especially to my sisters who provided so much content for this book, even when they didn't realise they were doing so.

CONFETTI CONFIDENTIAL: THEY DO, I DON'T

CHAPTER 1

The End

*H*ey sexy, wot you up to, I'm at a party tonite call me if you can get away, was the first thing I saw when I opened the messages on Peter's phone. My legs buckled and gave way as I slid to the floor. I took a large swig from the wine bottle I was clutching.

When you came into the ofice today I saw you lookin at me. Trust me youll want what I got.

I felt sick. She couldn't even spell. I stood up with a wave of determination and dialled the number.

"Heeeeey," she made a pathetic attempt at a sexy voice.

"Who the hell is this?" I screamed down the phone that shook in my hand. The gasp she expelled before she hung up said more than any words could have. I rang again, my heart pounding louder than the dial tone. No answer. Pressing again and again with frantic fingers, I knew full well she wouldn't pick up, but

I needed her to know that I was onto her. I dialled until my fingers hurt.

Fury and rage ignited every cell of my body as adrenaline pumped through my veins so forcefully that I could have lifted a car. Could I lift a car and throw it through the bedroom window onto Peter?

Inhaling deeply, I straightened in an attempt to compose myself. My thoughts went to the kids. Natalia was working a night shift at the café and the boys were away at a soccer training camp. I marched to the bedroom and switched on the light.

"Who is she?" I asked in the calmest voice I could muster, determined to get as much information as possible before I killed, or at least maimed, him.

Peter's eyes squinted against the sudden bright light. His mouth dropped open as his eyes adjusted and he saw the phone in my hand. When he didn't answer I threw the phone onto the bedside table next to him, feeling satisfied when it sent the lamp crashing to the floor. I stared at the pieces, feeling as broken as they were. It felt good to hear it smash. What else could I break? I turned my attention to the expensive aftershave bottles, feeling satisfaction as they too fell to the floor in pieces.

"Answer me you gutless bastard. Who is the woman sending you filthy messages?"

Peter pulled himself up to a sitting position. "Someone from the office."

Someone from the office? "Who from the office?"

"Daniella. She's one of the payroll girls," he muttered.

"There are only four girls that work in the whole place, and you had to start screwing one of them?"

"I'm not screwing her, we've just been flirting - that's all."

"You expect me to believe that?" Holding up the phone, I began reading aloud the sordid exchanges between them.

"I'm telling you," Peter pleaded. "I know it sounds bad, but we haven't done anything. It's just been messages and flirting."

"I don't believe a word you're saying, you lying piece of shit. After everything we've been through together, our kids." The last word caught in my throat as I thought of our three children. "How old is she?"

He was silent.

"How fucking old is she?" I hissed, the force burning my throat.

"Twenty-two," he mumbled.

I launched myself onto the bed with waving arms, thrashing and growling, primal sounds rising from the depths of my darkest places. Peter was yelling for me to stop. He grabbed my wrists and brought my arms in tightly, restraining me easily. I knew I looked like a lunatic. Even in the throes of the deepest anger and rage, I was actually wondering how I must look. Is that normal? I was distracted momentarily, long enough for Peter to look at me with a puzzled expression, wondering why I had stopped.

"Calm down," Peter pleaded. He increased the pressure to hold me off. Exhausted and out of breath, I slid back off the bed and onto the floor.

Peter's stunned face stared at mine. I wondered if he thought I was losing it. Was I? The air in the room seemed to thicken and I gasped to fill my lungs. My chest heaving, I leaned back against the sliding mirrored door, utterly defeated.

The gravity of what he'd done was beginning to sink in. My

shoulders felt heavy. "Twenty-two, Peter? Natalia is nineteen! How can you even look at her and not see someone who's your daughter's age?"

"I know," was all he could say.

"And what about the boys? They're sixteen. How the hell are you going to explain this to them?"

He wouldn't even meet my eyes.

I suddenly had a thought. "Don't tell me that this is where all that money's been going?" Peter had been making a lot of unusual cash withdrawals lately, but when I asked him about it, he always had some excuse. "Have you been using our money to buy her gifts or flowers or to pay for motel rooms? I swear to God, Peter."

"No, I haven't. I haven't bought her anything."

"So where has all the money been going?"

He was shaking his head, "I can't".

"Can't? What do you mean you can't?" I demanded through clenched teeth.

"You'll hate me even more."

I let out a hideous snort. "Are you serious? How could I hate you any more than I do right now? You might as well get it all out so that at least I know what I'm dealing with."

His silence was intensifying my already bursting frustration.

When he finally spoke, it was little more than a whisper, "I've been gambling."

"What? What did you say?" I stepped back.

"I've been gambling. That's where the money's been going. I haven't been working late into the middle of the night, I've been going to the pub to play pokies."

I felt like I had been hit by a ten-tonne concrete block. I slumped back to the floor, stars circling before my eyes as my lungs emptied. Breathe, keep breathing.

"You've been gambling?" I asked quietly, not sure I really wanted to know any more.

"Yes. Pokies, and sometimes the dogs."

I winced as he spoke, trying to shield myself from his words.

"When I first started losing, I borrowed from people so you wouldn't find out, but then I had to pay it back. I was getting depressed and so one of the guys from work got me something to make me feel better, but it only lasted for a while and then it started making me moody. I haven't been able to sleep."

Now he was on drugs too? Who the hell is this person I've been married to for the last nineteen years?

"That's when Danni noticed I was missing things at work and that I looked stressed and wired all the time."

Danni? Is he actually shortening her name right now?

"She asked me straight out what was going on, and for some reason I confided in her." He shrugged, as if it meant so little. "After that, she was the only person who knew what I was doing and what I was going through."

My limbs felt numb. A strange calm had taken over my body, I felt resigned to the fact that there was no going back. "You need to leave now."

"Please, just listen," he begged, sobs making him gasp.

But I couldn't. I couldn't listen to any more of his betrayal, or look at his pathetic face. I marched out of the bedroom and, grabbing the bottle of wine from the kitchen bench, I went to sit on the patio swing in the dark. Tears streamed, staining my cheeks, but I stayed still, upright, not giving in to the temptation to crumble.

"All I can say is that I'm sorry. I'm so, so sorry, Viv." Peter stood in the frame of the back door, the light behind him casting an odd shape on the ground. "I love you and I always have, but I felt lost."

Shut up! Just shut the hell up.

"When some of the guys from work were gambling and partying it looked like fun, a way to just let go. It got out of control, and to be honest, I sort of stopped caring about anything else."

This was actually making him feel better, clearing his conscience. Absolutely not!

"How did this happen? How the hell has this happened to us?" My voice sounded detached, as if someone else was speaking and I wasn't really listening. Peter's shrug in reply made me wonder how I'd stayed married to such a feeble idiot for so long.

"So, all of those times that I tried to talk to you," I went on, "asking you to tell me what was going on, and you screamed at me to leave you alone, and made me feel like it was all my fault – you were running to her and telling her everything?"

"It wasn't like that. I just didn't think you'd understand."

"Understand? I've done nothing but try with you, Peter. Time and time again you closed off and shut me out. Don't put this on me. You made the choice to turn to someone else. I looked away from him, staring straight ahead. "Just leave. NOW!"

"Viv, please. It's not what you think."

"It's exactly what I think." I hissed, turning back to him. "I don't care if you slept with that girl, what I care about is that you gave her everything that I have been begging you to give to me -

your time, your confidence, your care, your interest. You lied to me over and over again. You spent time talking to her and trusting in her to help you with your problems." Peter was avoiding my wild glare. "Look at me!" I demanded. "You made me believe that I wasn't good enough, that I was making you miserable. I might have been able to get passed you having a one-night stand or a brief encounter, but to have given her the parts of you that I was so desperate for, and to treat me with contempt and annoyance the whole time, that is unforgivable."

"I just wanted to—"

I cut him off before he could say anything else. "I honestly can't listen to any more right now, Peter. Please go."

I curled into a tight cocoon, my chest heaving as I listened to his car leave. Hours passed until the colours of the rising sun broke over the distant hills, beautiful, even through the haze of my red, swollen eyes. Its burning intensity, eased by streaks of pink and amber, was perfect in the midst of my desolation; beaming with fierce determination as if to insist that there was still beauty in the world.

Tea. I needed tea. Inside, the house was still and quiet, I was completely alone with only the sound of the bubbling kettle. I jumped when my mobile phone came alive, vibrating and chirping to announce an incoming email.

milly& jake@lovenet.com

Hi, my name is Milly. My fiancé and I are getting married in August and we'd like to meet up with you if possible, to see if you would be the right celebrant to perform our wedding.

I hit delete. "Go away, Milly. I am not the right celebrant for you right now, trust me."

Love felt like a crock of shit. I'd spent nineteen years trying to make Peter happy, sacrificing so many parts of myself and my own dreams just to be a good wife – and where did it get me? damaged, sad and alone. There was no way I could possibly look at yet another pair of love-struck romantics thinking they had their whole lives ahead of them and that they'd live happily ever after like some fairy tale.

I clicked on the next email.

tom.kelly@yourperfectpic.com

Hey Hun, just checking that we're meeting at 1:30 on Saturday at Stockport Botanical Park for the Allington wedding. I'm shooting the groom in the morning and the bride at her house from 12–1. Meet me half an hour before at the cafe and we'll grab a quick coffee. Xx Tom

I clicked Reply and typed:

Hi Tom, I wish you would literally shoot the groom in the morning, and the bride, because if I even make it to this wedding it will be a fucking miracle. I can only actually think of a handful of people who have managed to stay married longer than ten years, and even some of them had an affair or had to deal with their partner having an affair. And are they happy? Have you seen anyone that has been in a long marriage that looks happy? NO. NO is the answer, Tom.

I marched to my office, yanking and swearing at my cluttered, crooked filing cabinet until the drawer flew out and landed on the office floor. "Shit!"

I scooped up the pile of white folders and laid out all of my current clients' files. There were ten. Ten couples that had already submitted their paperwork and paid their deposits. Ten weddings that I would have to honour.

> *I'm done with this, I typed to Tom. I have ten couples already booked and when I get to the last one, that's it. No more. I'm done with all of it and I'm giving up being a celebrant. I intend to find a job that doesn't require me to have to see or speak to anyone. See you tomorrow. Viv xx*
>
> *P.S. Peter's had an affair.*

Pulling out my calendar, I checked each of the entries. Tomorrow was the wedding of the CC's – "Just like the chip" Cadence had proudly announced when she and Christian seated themselves in my office for our first meeting. The sweet blonde pair had come up with that all on their own. Between the two of them, they had actually fewer brain cells than a bag of chips. "He's my soul mate" Cadence had giggled, squeezing Christian's hand while he admired his reflection in the glass of my framed practising certificate.

I grabbed a piece of blank paper from the printer and made a running sheet.

1. January 25 Cadence & Christian (The chips)
   @ *1:30 - Stockport Botanical Park*
2. February 1 Sharon and Jason (The Harley fanatics)
   @ *1:30 – At their house*
3. February 8 Nina & Chad (Needy)
   @ *1:30 – Jangar Farm*
4. February 21 Albert & Dinh (The old cheapskate)
   @ *1:30 – Creaser Memorial*
5. March 1 Mary & Chuck (Crier & big head)
   @ *12:30 - Stockport Botanical Park*
6. March 15 Erin & Jimmy (Warring fathers)
   @ *1:30 – Blockade Community Centre*
7. March 22 Kimberly & Brad (Shorty shorts & Gym junkie)
   @ *1:30 – Private Garden - Gawler*
8. April 5 Dee Dee & Max (Sweet older couple)
   @ *1:30 – Location TBC*
9. April 13 Anastasia & Rocco
   (The Greek & the Italian – Romeo & Juliet)
   @ *1:30 - Solero Winery*
10. April 26 Charlotte & Barton (Masquerade Ball)
    @ *1:30 - Carlo Santino Reception Centre*

By May I'd be all done. I closed my calendar, pleased that there was an end in sight. But as with any decision I've ever made in my life, uncertainty quickly took its place. Was this really what I wanted? Would I feel better, or just more useless? I'd been a celebrant for over ten years.

I sobbed, sinking into it again. I hated Peter for this. For all of it.

I stood still under the water of the shower as my mind retraced and relived everything he had said. I couldn't recall exactly where it had all started to go wrong. We didn't have the best start, deciding to marry sooner than either of us would have liked, but with Natalia on the way, it was better than any of the alternatives we could come up with. Once she was born, we'd settled into married life pretty well. Peter wasn't the perfect husband by any means, but then I wasn't the perfect wife either. He was never very attentive or giving with his time or affection and I threw myself into my work and being a mother. After the twins were born, we barely made time for each other and we started to grow apart. There were times that I felt lonely even when Peter was sitting beside me, but we were raising the kids and working, so we made it enough. Had it gotten so bad between us that he couldn't confide in me at all? Every harsh word between us returned with a painful sting as I sorted my way through the last twelve months, recognising the lies and betrayal that I had missed. The times he had blamed me and called me names and left early in the morning because "one of us had to earn the big bucks". My heart ached. The family barbecues when he had been texting or taking a call about "work", he was talking to her. He was talking to her while surrounded by his children and all of the people that loved him.

"Mum, are you okay?" I hadn't heard Natalia come in. "I picked the boys up on the way home from work." I had completely forgotten that the boys were coming home from their soccer training camp today.

I quickly wiped my face. For a brief moment I thought about covering up, lying to protect them, but they would see through it, my face and voice would give me away. "I'll be out in a minute, honey. Can you get the boys? I need to talk to you all. Make some tea?"

When I came into the kitchen they were sitting at the table. "There's something I need to talk to you guys about, and it's hard for me to find the right words," I began. "You're all old enough to be told the truth, so I'm just going to say it."

"You and Dad have had a fight, haven't you?" Adam had never had any tact or sensitivity, but at 16 like most teenage boys, he was hopeless.

"Adam, shut up!" Natalia elbowed him. "Go on, Mum."

"Well, we have had a fight, but it's a bit more than that. I've asked your dad to leave. He has some things to work through, and we can't be together right now." I swallowed hard, pushing back the urge to cry.

"Oh Mum, I'm so sorry," said Natalia. "What's been going on with him? He's been so weird and cranky all the time. He barely says a word and then blows up over nothing. I know how hard you've tried with him lately. Maybe this will make him realise." She put her hands on mine, but I was stunned into silence.

Had we been that transparent? I felt guilty for not realising that Peter's behaviour was affecting them as much as it was me. I thought I had done a good job of hiding how desperately hurt and lonely I felt from them. Maybe they had heard our arguments when I thought they were asleep, or me begging Peter to talk to me.

It was Jack's turn. "Mum, we're here for you. Where will Dad go?"

I shrugged. I wasn't sure. Maybe he'd go to her, or to his mother's.

"Well, I'm sorry, Mum," Adam added, "but Dad kind of deserves it. I agree with Natalia, he's never happy anymore and he's always growling at everyone. He never used to be like that."

I wanted Peter to suffer, but I prayed they wouldn't find out all of what he'd been up to. For their sake.

Covering my face, ashamed of my inability to hold it together, I sobbed. I truly had no idea they'd had any inkling of what I had been going through and that they'd been feeling it too.

"I'm so sorry, guys. I love you so much and I had no idea that all this was hurting you too."

"Mum, stop worrying about everyone else and think about yourself for once," said Natalia.

"You guys are everything to me," I said. "I hope that you can show your dad as much support as you've shown me. He needs you too right now and he loves you all so much." I lied about him needing their support – he needed to rot in hell – but I was saying it for their benefit. Natalia and Jack both nodded in agreement, but Adam rolled his eyes.

Peter would have a lot to explain to them if he was going to earn their forgiveness. He would never get mine.

CHAPTER 2

Sisters

When the phone rang, I contemplated ignoring it.

"It's just me, thought I'd ring and see what you're up to. I'm kinda bored, I was thinking of heading out for coffee. Can you come?"

My older sister, Annabel, was a horrible liar.

"Natalia called you, didn't she?" I said.

"Yeah, okay, she did, and I'm worried about you. Come and meet me so we can chat, I can do some tapping on you," she offered.

Dear God, have I not been through enough?

"I heard you roll your eyes. I know you don't think that this stuff works, but just let me try," she insisted.

Annabel was a Reiki master and currently studying EFT. "It's not Electronic Funds Transfer" she had explained. "It stands for Emotional Freedom Technique." And yes, it was as kooky as it sounded. EFT involved her tapping on different pressure points on your body while making you recite some mumbo jumbo like, "Even though my husband is a cheater and my life is in ruins, I deeply and completely accept myself".

I groaned something that sounded like, "I suppose so."

"Great. Meet me at Carmello's in an hour."

Carmello's was a sweet little cafe where my sisters and I met for coffee once or twice a week, when we could manage it. I hung up, already dreading the tapping and positive affirmations I would be forced to do in public.

"You heading out?" Natalia appeared in the doorway looking far more innocent than she was.

"Yes." I shot her a knowing look. "You know that Annabel's new age crap drives me crazy."

"I know, Mum, but she's been through a lot, and look how good she is now."

How could I argue? Annabel had been through one of the most traumatic marriage breakups any of us had ever had the displeasure of witnessing. Kim, her husband for over 25 years, had been leading a completely double life. It all came out when he was caught in a compromising position with a client's wife. The fall-out was monumental and led to the client withdrawing all of his money from Kim's investments, sending him broke. Annabel went from owning thirteen properties, including their own mansion, to moving in with one of her daughters. Even worse was that the client had threatened to hurt Kim and his family. Annabel's newfound life philosophies had kept her sane, so as long as she wasn't rocking in a corner somewhere, we were all happy to go along with it.

It was a short drive to Carmello's, nestled quietly on the edge of a lake in a housing estate, north of the city. They built the houses around the tiny cafe when the owners refused to sell to make way for the estate. Its bay windows and chequered table-cloths added a warm charm to the harshness of the Lego-style houses that surrounded it.

By the time I turned into the tiny car park behind Carmello's, my swollen eyes burned. The car rocked in time to my sobs brought on by one stupid eighties song that blared from the radio with perfect timing. *Alone,* by the group, Heart, used to be one of my favourites, but now, as Peter took yet another thing from me, it mocked me with every word. I wiped my face with a tissue and sat up straight in my seat. "Shit, pull yourself together."

Grabbing my purse, I wound my window up and checked my reflection in the rear-view mirror. Horrifying. As well as eyes that were as red as a ravenous vampire's, it was at least 38 degrees out and my damp hair clung to my forehead.

"Bloody hell." I pushed it back, failing in my attempt to make it look neat, and blew cool air upward into my eyes. I spotted Annabel waving at me enthusiastically through the window of the cafe.

You can do this. Yes, there will be pitying eyes and sighs of "Oh, you poor thing", but you don't have a choice. Suck it up and get it over with.

Carmello was rolling out dough and waving his hand angrily at a new waiter, yelling profanities in Italian as I made my way to the table. As it came into view, I groaned. For goodness' sake! Annabel had called in the cavalry. Sitting at the table with her were my other two sisters, Julia and Carrie, all looking at me with their pitying eyes. I forced a fake smile.

"Oh, stop looking at me like that," I demanded.

"Like what?" Carrie asked. She knew exactly what I meant. Carrie was the black sheep of our family. She had a history of only ever dating old men - and I mean old, like almost dead. None of them would have any hope of attracting another woman, let alone have an affair, which meant she had no credibility to comment on my situation.

"Are you okay?" Julia leaned in, her eyes searching my face.

"I'm fine. I don't know why Annabel hauled you both down here, I'm dealing with it."

"Yeah, looks like it." Carrie pointed to some tissue that was stuck on my face. I wiped it away and poked my tongue out at her.

"Let's order coffee," Julia suggested, getting up. Her Indian-inspired skirt jingled as the tiny bells that lined the hem clanked together. She'd never moved on from the eighties. Carrie grumbled as Julia pulled her up and dragged her away to the counter.

"I hate you," I scowled at Annabel once they were out of earshot. "Why did you do this to me? Don't you think I've been tortured enough already?"

"You need your family around you right now," she said in a gentle, somewhat grating voice. "You need support, and to know that we're all here for you."

I grunted. I loved my sisters, but as the youngest, they always thought they knew what was best for me.

"Right, now let's do some EFT before they get back."

I groaned, louder this time, as Annabel grabbed my wrist and began tapping on it.

"Now repeat after me," she said. "Even though my husband has done some horrible things and hurt our family, I deeply and completely accept myself."

Squeezing my eyes shut I concentrated on trying not to scream. It had already taken everything I had in me to keep myself together enough to come here, let alone being forced to recite how much I loved and accepted myself.

"Don't think about it, just try it. Trust me, it works," Annabel added gleefully, with a cheesy smile.

I'd rather have burned my eyes out with a hot poker, but instead, I took a deep breath. "Even though my husband has done some horrible things and ruined our family, I deeply and completely accept myself." My voice was already wavering.

"Again," Annabel insisted.

"Even though my husband..." I could feel a lump beginning to rise in my chest, and in an attempt to hold it at bay, a loud snort escaped.

Why not add public humiliation to my long list of soul-destroying moments?

The lump rose higher. "... my husband has done ..." Snort, snort. "... some horrible things and ruined..." Snort, lump rising. "... our family, I deeply and ..." Huge snort, wail beginning to escape my lips "... completely ..."

And then it came out, like a rush, with such speed and ferocity that spittle landed all over the table "... hate my pathetic life. That stupid son of a bitch! I feel like ringing his neck."

The tears returned, accompanied by wailing.

"How could he do this to us, with a girl young enough to be his daughter?" I dropped my face into my empty plate and sobbed uncontrollably.

"What the hell have you done to her?" Carrie exclaimed as she and Julia hurried back to the table.

"Nothing. I was just getting her to say some positive affirmations and she lost it."

Lifting my head from the table I looked at them. Their expressions of pity only fuelled my despair and I began to wail even louder. Carmello made his way over.

"Is she okay? Do you need something?" He was looking around nervously at his customers who were obviously wondering what the commotion was as I continued to cry into the porcelain.

"Just our coffees, thanks, Carmello," said Julia. 'We'll sort her out."

"Right, Viv, pull yourself together," Carrie said sternly, under her breath, the way a mother would to a naughty child having a tantrum. "You are in a public place, and everyone is looking at you,"

I lifted my head, rather annoyed that she wasn't being more concerned in my hour of need, but she was right; this was a little too much drama for strangers to have to deal with over lunch. I adjusted myself in my chair and used a napkin to clean my face.

Our coffees arrived, brought by Carmello himself.

"Sorry, Viv," Annabel said. "I was just trying to help."

Poor Annabel, she meant well, as she always did. I felt a little guilty for ruining her attempt to do something nice for me.

"No, I'm sorry, Bel, it's just not the right time for 'deeply and completely accepting myself' yet."

"So, tell me what the dickhead's done." Carrie said.

"Hasn't Annabel filled you in already?" I asked. There was no way she would have been able to resist.

"Yeah, but I want to hear the details. Who is she?" Carrie said.

I hesitated. Carrie would go to the ends of the earth for me and she was a good person to have in your corner if a spot of revenge was ever needed, but I knew it wouldn't help. I wanted him to hurt, but I knew he would be already and being vindictive would only lead to hurting the kids too.

"She works in the office," I said. "But you know what? Peter's the one at fault; it's him I'm angry at. He's the one who has a wife and three children, and made promises of sticking it out through the good and the bad." My lip was quivering again and Annabel put her hand on my arm to calm me. Apart from being instinctively caring and intuitive with emotions, she was desperate to avoid another scene.

The conversation continued around me as my sisters discussed what a sod Peter was and how he should pay for what he'd done, but I found myself staring into my coffee, unable to participate any further. I felt drained and lifeless, I just couldn't string any more thoughts together. Lifting my coffee cup to my lips was about all that I could manage. I gazed past Carrie's head out the window behind her. Summer was my favourite season. Despite the dry, searing heat, it was all worth it just for the summer evenings. Daylight Savings meant that it didn't get dark until nine o'clock, giving me hours of time after work to take a stroll on the beach or just eat ice cream on my swing in the backyard. Peter and I used to sit outside on summer nights. He would cook some meat or fish on the barbecue and drink beer, while I sipped red wine and chatted aimlessly about nothing. I smiled remembering how good that felt.

"See, she's smiling," Annabel gloated, dragging me back to the present. I couldn't bring myself to tell her that it was because of the memory. The distraction, though fleeting, had the effect of lifting my mood a little, at least enough to re-join the conversation and finish my coffee.

"Look, I appreciate you all coming here and supporting me, in your own 'special' way." I nodded at Annabel. "But I think I just need to take some time out and process all of this. I'm not going to fall apart. I think that in some way this has been coming for a long time."

There. I said it. Out loud. The thoughts that had been bouncing quietly around in the back of my subconscious had finally made their way to the surface. I hadn't the guts to even think about them fully, let alone say them.

"Peter and I got together when we were so young that we never got to experience all the things that most people do, like having other partners, or dating and flirting and travelling aimlessly around the world. We were both kids for God's sake."

All three of them were staring intently, studying me, looking for clues to my sudden composure. Annabel spoke first.

"Yes, I know that, but it doesn't mean that you can't feel bad for what has happened. You're allowed to grieve for what you've lost. Just give yourself some time."

"Look, Viv," Julia added, "you are the strongest person I know. We've all run to you so many times with our problems and you've always fixed them, no matter how big, but this time you need to stop being the hero and just let us take care of you for a while."

The tears were welling again. This was exhausting, I wished they would stop making me cry.

"Yes, well, I think there's been enough moping for one day," said Carrie. "And lucky for us it's Friday! Why don't we have a girls' night out?"

"No, Carrie," I answered with the sternest tone I could muster, "I don't feel like it. And anyway, I look like hell. I'm just going to go home, put on my pyjamas and watch TV."

"No." She was holding her hand in front of my face in a 'talk to the hand' gesture.

"No? What do you mean, no? You can't force me to go out," I protested.

It was time to put my foot down. I was geared up for a self-indulgent mope tonight, and not even the good Lord himself was going to change my mind.

Carrie slumped back into her chair, clearly defeated. "Okay, but I'm giving you one month, do you understand? Four weeks from today we are hitting the town and I don't want any whining or arguing."

I nodded my head in agreement.

"I'll pick you all up," Annabel announced. She was the only one out of the four of us that didn't drink, so she was usually the designated driver.

"Promise?" Julia squeezed my hand.

"Yes, I promise," I lied. I had no idea how I would feel tomorrow, let alone in a month.

I headed home, leaving them there to talk about me as I knew they would. The phone was ringing in the house when I pulled into the driveway. It would be my mother. She was the only person who would call home rather than my mobile first. She and Dad were away on a cruise, but she called every time they docked or had mobile reception. I was not in the right frame of mind to deal with her at the moment. The relationship we shared was somewhat strained. Maybe strained wasn't the right word; "Pull your hair out in frustration" was possibly a better description of how spending time with my mother often made me feel. I'm sure that my own behaviour and overreaction to almost everything she said was just as much the problem, but I preferred to blame it all on her. It was easier that way.

The phone stopped as I reached the front door, but my relief was short-lived. My body stiffened at the sound of a car coming to a halt in my driveway. I stood there, rigid, holding the door-knob and praying to God that it wasn't Peter or another family member, particularly any of his.

"Hey!" Tom grabbed me in a big bear hug before I could even utter a word. And then came the tears.

How could there even be any tears left? Tom led me gently through the door and onto the couch.

"I'll make you some tea," he said with a gentle smile. I had never been so glad to see him.

"Now, what was up with that email? And all that stuff about you giving up being a celebrant?" he asked.

"Peter's..." I couldn't say it, not to his face.

"It's okay, you don't have to talk about it right now. Annabel's mostly filled me in."

"Jesus, is there anyone she hasn't told?"

"I'm so sorry, Hun." Tom had called me that since the day I met him, 22 years ago. He had been standing in a tiny bookstore that I liked to go to, tucked quietly away in the back corner of a busy shopping strip. I had a habit of spending hours loitering in book shops. I had just picked up a text on the history of photography when Tom decided to introduce himself and give me a history lesson. He'd studied Art and Photography, and worked as a freelancer. We'd been best friends ever since.

He handed me a cup and sat beside me on the couch, his large, heavy frame sinking the seat so low we were almost at eye level.

"I just want you to know that I'm here and I love you. And if you need anything at all, you only have to say so," he said.

I screwed up my nose. "Are you really sorry?"

Tom smiled. "Well, I'm sorry that you're hurt, not sorry that he's finally gone."

He'd despised Peter since the beginning. I'd only known Tom a year when Peter and I met, but they had instantly disliked each other. I tried on so many occasions to find some common ground between them, but nothing worked.

"He was a self-absorbed prick, Viv, and he never deserved you."

I scooted closer and wrapped myself around his arm. "Thanks," I said, sipping the hot tea.

CHAPTER 3

The Wedding of Cadence and Christian (The Chips)

"Where the hell are you, Viv? Everyone's waiting."

"Tom, I'm stuck on Direk Rd behind the slowest drivers in the world. I'll be there in ten minutes."

"Jesus, the groom's freaking out and his mother is having a fit."

"Oh, bloody hell, hang on – *Mooooooooove*," I shouted out the window, waving my fist. "Why the hell are they all looking at me like I'm a crazy person? They are seriously driving so slow. It's ridiculous."

Silence filled the phone line as my breathing increased to a pant.

"Viv? You there?"

"Oh no, oh my God, Tom, I'm going to hell."

"What? What's wrong? Don't bloody hyperventilate while you're driving," he said.

"Oh Tom, I'm going to hell. Those 'idiots' I've been swearing and waving my arms at..."

"What? Was there an accident?" The pitch of his voice had elevated.

"No, it's a funeral procession, and I just cut off the hearse!'

I heard him gasp.

'That's it, I've had it!' I declared. 'Cancel the wedding. I'm not coming because I'm going to throw myself off the nearest bridge. Tell them I died."

"Okay, deep breaths, calm down and just get here when you can," he pleaded. "I'll cover for you, I'll make something up. Just relax, you're heading for a nervous breakdown." His tone was stern but gentle. "I'll be right here with you. You'll be fine, we'll get through it."

"Okay," I grunted. Everything wouldn't be fine. I wasn't fine.

"No stops on bridges," he insisted "I'll be here waiting for you."

To my relief, the bride was running 40 minutes late anyway. Tom had calmed the groom and his mother by explaining that I was merely in the car park rehearsing my ceremony and awaiting the bride's arrival. He calmed me when I got there with a swig from his hip flask.

"I love you," I said, downing the amber liquid that soothed my tingling nerves.

When the pink and white Cinderella-inspired carriage drew to a halt at the top of the path, Cadence's arrival was met with gasps from the gathered guests. Christian was already bawling his eyes out.

"She's here," I said with a little clap, trying to get him to pull himself together.

As the music began and the carriage doors opened, the gorgeous Cadence emerged smiling. The gasps, however, soon turned to shrieks of horror as she lost her footing on the carriage step and planted face-first into the fake grass. Christian, giddy with nerves and fright had to be seated on one of the chairs as everyone else rushed to poor Cadence's aid.

I watched, holding my breath. She bounced back to her feet and I clasped my hand over my mouth. You're awful, what an awful thing to do, to laugh at the poor girl falling, I told myself. But I couldn't contain myself. I'd always had trouble not giggling when someone fell over or banged into something. I patted Christian and then headed to the drinks table to get him some water.

My eyes immediately sought out Tom, who was helping the unfortunate girl's father brush her off. Stunned and slightly bleeding from the bridge of her nose, Cadence took her position on her father's arm. By the time she reached Christian, she had composed herself and dabbed the blood from her grazed nose. I had to give her credit, she was one tough cookie. Christian on the other hand was a complete mess.

"Do you, Mr Chips ..." I couldn't believe they were actually making me say that out loud. "...Take Ms Chips to be your lawful wedded wife?"

"I do," he sobbed.

"And do you Ms Chips, take Mr Chips to be your lawfully wedded husband?"

Cadence hesitated for longer than expected. As she looked into Christian's eyes, her smile fading, I wondered if she was seeing the life that she would have with him. He hadn't rushed to her aid when she fell from the carriage, he'd taken care of himself first. And there he stood, crying like a baby. I watched as the implications of what she was about to do seemed to consume her. Would he care for her? Would she end up just having to do everything for him like a mother instead of a partner? Was she remembering past loves, men who had made her feel safe, and wondering if she had chosen wisely?

Cadence looked at all the loving friends and family that had gathered to support them today, and as she turned her attention back to Christian, her expression told me that she had made her decision.

"I do," she beamed, squeezing Christian's hands.

I let out the breath I had been unintentionally holding, feeling bad for secretly hoping she would walk away. I wondered where I'd be today if I'd walked away. I would have travelled, definitely, and probably gotten a degree. But I wouldn't have had the kids, and I wouldn't change that for anything.

As the guests swarmed on the happy couple to offer their congratulations, Tom and I fell to the back and swigged from the flask.

"Did you see that face-plant?" He laughed. "I nearly had a heart attack."

"That poor girl." I tried to maintain a serious face, but as Tom flicked through the photos on his digital screen, the images of poor Cadence's contorted face as she lost her footing brought tears of laughter that refused to be stifled.

"No more, it's so mean and I'm going to wet myself," I warned Tom, which, of course, only made him laugh more. "I'm glad she was okay. She was so courageous, I really like her. Most would have cried and made a big scene, but she just got on with it."

"I give it a year," he waved, as he set off to take thousands of happy smiling pictures that would get stuffed in a drawer somewhere and never looked at. Mine were in a box in the shed. Fitting really.

I packed up and headed to the car. Adam had called and left a message.

Mum, will you be home soon? We're trying to pack for camp, but Jack can't find his backpack and I can't find my soccer shorts.

My heart sank. Adam and Jack were heading off again for a school-run bonding camp before the start of the term. I dialled Adam's mobile.

"Honey, Jack's pack is in the hall cupboard and your shorts are on the line. I'm on my way home anyway so get the bags out and I'll sort it all when I get there."

"Thanks, Mum," he replied.

"Is Natalia Home?" I asked.

"Nah, she's studying at Jude's."

They still need me. At least I have that, I thought. I hung up the phone feeling conflicted. I didn't want them to leave, they only just got home. One week, it's only one week, I reminded myself, but deep down I knew it was the beginning of them leaving me. Natalia was hardly ever home these days. Between studying a law degree and working part-time, she was in and out. She'd even opted to do summer school in the holiday break to complete her degree faster, but I missed her and the time we used to spend together. The boys were beginning to make their own lives too. When they weren't playing soccer, they were out with friends or had their noses buried in their mobile phones. Pretty soon I would be living in that house alone and sad. At least I don't have cats. Yet.

"Mum, where's my shin pads, the green ones?" Adam called as he pulled everything from his cupboard when I got home. The house was already a pig-sty.

"Adam, stop making such a mess. Let me look," I said. I pushed him aside and found them in the first drawer I opened.

"Thanks, Mum," he smiled, kissing my cheek.

Jack looked worried.

"What's up, mate?" I sat beside him on the bed. "You okay?"

"Yeah, I just hate leaving you right now, Mum. I feel bad. Maybe I should stay and Adam can go."

I wrapped my arms around him. He had grown into the body of a man, but he was still my little boy.

"You know, when you were little, you'd never leave my side. Adam would run off and play with the other kids, but you'd be holding onto me for dear life. You always made me feel so loved and needed, Jack, but this is your time now. You have to let me stand on my own two feet. I want you to go and let me learn how to be me again. I need to."

His blue-green eyes had filled with tears. "I love you, Mum."

I squeezed him tight and stood up. "Right, let's get you

packed." I needed to get them organised before my facade broke and my resolve shattered.

"Hey, Natalia," Adam said when the phone rang on the way to the school. "Let me put you on speaker."

"Have a great time, guys," she said. "Sorry I can't get there to see you off, but you can tell me all about it when you get back. Kiss, kiss."

The school car park was packed with kids and their families.

"Hey boys, all ready?" Their soccer coach, John Lane, gave them both a pat on the shoulder.

"Look after them, John," I said. I was glad that he was chaperoning.

"Haven't I always?" He smiled. He had coached the boys since they were six years old. His own son, Henry, was the same age, so every time Henry went up an age group, so did the boys, and so did John.

"How are you doing?" he asked, pity filling his voice. Word of my split with Peter had obviously gotten out. Before I could answer I spotted Peter approaching. What the hell was he doing here?

"Oh, Mum, I'm so sorry," Jack whispered. "Dad called to say he'd come and see us off. I forgot to tell you."

"Honey, it's fine. What are you sorry for? Don't be so silly."

It wasn't fine. I wanted to scream. I didn't want to see Peter, not yet.

"Hello, Viv," Peter said carefully. He leaned in to kiss my cheek.

My skin crawled. What on earth made him think that I

wanted him to even come near me? I looked at the boys who were watching us closely.

"Hi, how are you?" I smiled for their benefit as Adam ran off to speak to a friend and Jack relaxed his tense shoulders.

"I've been better," said Peter. "It's been pretty hard."

Did he honestly think I gave a hoot about how hard it was for him? *Hard?* Hard is finding out your husband is a cheating, lying bastard. Hard is having to be the one to tell your children that their parents are splitting up. Peter ended the conversation, taking the hint from my seething expression.

"Can we talk?" he said. His tone was less sickly-sweet once the bus had pulled out.

"I don't want to talk to you, Peter. I don't even want to stand here next to you."

"Please, Viv, I need to get some things off my chest."

"I'm well aware of the fact that this is all about what you need, and to be honest, our whole life together was all about what you needed, so nothing's changed."

"Five minutes is all I ask. Please," he begged.

I relented and followed him to a nearby cafe. The coffee tasted as burnt and bitter as I was feeling, but I drank it anyway as I waited for Peter to return from the bathroom. I watched him slot into the booth across from me. It had been a long time since I'd really looked at his face, taken notice of his features. He was unshaven but clean, and despite being a total wanker, was actually still attractive – at least on the outside.

"I want you back. I want to fix this," he said, taking my hands in his.

I pulled them away. "You have got to be kidding me, Peter.

I thought you wanted to talk to me about the house and our finances."

"Keep the house. You can have it all, just give me another chance, please. I've made a horrible mistake, several, but I swear I'll change, and I'll be the best husband you could ever want. I'm going to see a counsellor."

Acid burnt my throat as it rose from my stomach. Why was he saying this crap now? He's the one who broke us.

"Peter, it's only been a few days, you just haven't come to terms with it yet. This is better for all of us. We haven't been happy for a long time. We hardly even speak to each other."

The truth, and we both knew it, was that little things we once loved about each other had turned into things we despised. Even the way Peter chewed his food and sniffed continually was enough for me to want to throw myself across the kitchen table and strangle him.

"Yes, but it was all my fault, Viv. You tried, I know you did, but I closed off. I can change. We'll take the trip to France you've been talking about for years, and spend some time together." Tears were running down his rough, bristly cheeks as he reached for my hands again. "I swear to you, we can fix this. We can be happy again."

I didn't have a single thing to say. I was frightened of being alone and terrified at the thought of having to be single and one day meet someone new, but how could I go back? I studied Peter's sad face. His big, soft brown eyes – the same ones that had made me fall for him the first time we met – pleaded with me.

"I have to go," I said, standing up. "I can't think about this right now. I'll speak to you soon."

It was harder than I expected to walk away. We had been together for half of my life, but I had no choice. I could feel him drawing me back.

The house was quiet again when I got home. I poured a glass of wine and sat on the couch. Could I seriously consider the possibility of forgiving him?

I remember hearing someone say that the definition of insanity was to do the same thing over and over again and expect a different result. I had scoffed at the time, giving it little consideration in the scheme of my life, but it seemed oddly relevant now. It confirmed what I already suspected; that I was definitely, no two ways about it, an absolute lunatic. I had either subconsciously, or in conscious denial, been doing the same things repeatedly for so long that I didn't even have to think about them anymore. My routine was so ingrained, so automatic, that it was like I was on autopilot. Yet, for some strange, deluded reason, every single day when I woke up, I hoped with eternal optimism that somehow things would be different. *I* would be different. Peter would magically develop an understanding of what it was to be a good husband and partner, and everything that was wrong in our lives would just work itself out. Ever the optimist, but always disappointed, it was obvious that I was actually insane, or at least well on my way there. I poured another glass. "Screw it all!"

***

Sticky and sweaty, I opened my eyes. The smell from the Shiraz that had spilled and soaked into my shirt was burning my nose.

Sitting up, I blinked my vision clear and peeled the melted block of chocolate I had been devouring, from my chest.

My phone buzzed and vibrated. When I checked the screen, there was a stream of text messages.

> Carrie: *Viv, call me or I'm coming over there. Natalia says you're wallowing.*

> Julia: *Do you need anything? Haven't heard from you since Friday. Call me.*

> Peter: *Viv, call me. Have you thought about what I said?*

I threw the phone onto the couch. God, I wish they would all just leave me alone!

According to my phone, it was Tuesday. I'd barely seen poor Natalia, who was busy with work and study, but her absence had worked in my favour. It had allowed me to wallow in my misery. When she did come home, I would straighten up and look like I loved being alive. She was usually only checking in and heading back out, so I didn't have to keep up the facade for long.

I rolled off the couch onto the floor, lying in repose as if I was a corpse in a coffin. I was beginning to like this misery, it seemed so much easier than trying to please everyone.

"Go away, I don't want any company, or your lectures," I yelled when the doorbell rang. I didn't care who it was.

"Well luckily I'm not here for any of that then," Tom called through the door. "I just missed you and wanted some company."

I huffed, but felt slightly pleased that he actually still wanted to spend time with me, despite me being a drunken, washed-out hag.

"Have you eaten?" he asked after I'd let him in.

I held up the melted, family-size block of chocolate in response.

He shot me a look of disapproval. "Well, you need to eat something a bit more substantial. Go have a shower while I order some Chinese. I've brought a movie to watch."

I groaned in protest but followed his instruction. The shower had a strange cleansing feeling, not just on my body, but on my miserable mood. I had meant it when I said I didn't want company, but now that Tom was here, I felt utterly relieved to have some.

"Did you order the entire shop?" I asked, pointing to the large array of dishes spread out on the coffee table, along with chopsticks, wine, and cushions on the floor. Thank God there was wine.

"I know I've been awful lately and I'm sorry," I said. "But I can't get myself together at the moment. I appreciate you being here though."

He smiled. "What are friends for? Now eat up, and let's get this movie started."

Tom's movie of choice was *The First Wives Club*. Perfect, only a man would think to get a recently dumped and traumatised woman a movie about a bunch of other women who have been traded in for younger versions. I wondered if it had been a random choice or if he'd deliberately chosen it, given that the women get their own back in the end. He was so enthusiastic that I didn't question his motives. Instead, I settled back and drank some more, and at some point, after gorging on Chinese food and prawn crackers, I fell asleep.

Restless from the wine, but dozy and comfortable, I snuggled into the warm flesh beside me and leaned my face against the rough stubble of Peter's cheek. I kissed him, just inside the nape of his neck, trailing his jaw line gently until my lips met his. I wrapped one leg over his and stroked his forehead, letting my fingers push through his hair. His hand came around me, finding the back of my neck. It stopped there for a moment and then trailed lightly down my back onto bare skin. My lips pushed harder against his before I remembered – Peter was gone!

"Tom, I'm so sorry." I jumped off of the couch, losing my balance and landing on the floor.

"What?" He was half asleep and completely confused.

I got to my feet and backed away further. "I'm so sorry, I thought ... I don't know what I thought". I buried my face in my hands, disgusted with myself. "I thought you were Peter," I said, unable to meet his eyes.

Tom swung his legs off the couch and sat upright. "It's fine," he assured me with a big smile. "You're under a lot of stress. Don't go getting all upset and crazy. We were half-asleep, don't worry about it."

I turned away and walked into the kitchen. This is your best friend and now look what you've done. Why do I have the uncanny ability to screw everything up? I loved Tom, but I didn't love him like that.

Tom followed me into the kitchen. I forced a smile, "Sorry," I whispered.

"You're being ridiculous, I don't want you worrying about

this. It was a mistake, whatever, it doesn't matter. We've been friends a long time. Something as tiny as this isn't going to change that."

"I know, I know," I lied as my stomach churned, but it wasn't as simple as that. Our relationship had always been clear. Peter and I were married, and Tom was my best friend. I just didn't want this changing anything or coming between us.

"I'm not going to say I didn't enjoy it," he joked and rubbed the top of my head. "You're not bad when you're delirious."

CHAPTER 4

The Wedding of
Shazza and Jason
(The Harley fanatics)

"I'm taking your car," I said, nudging Julia with my foot.

She was passed out on the lounge room floor. There was no food in the house. I hadn't bothered to shop with the boys away and Natalia hardly ever home, but after my sisters had converged on me for a 'cheer-me-up' drinking session the night before, the house was a shambles and there was nothing but carrots and a half-eaten salami stick left. A trip to the supermarket was well overdue.

"I'll come with," Annabel chirped in a pitch that hurt my brain. I admired her for her abstinence. She had already showered, dressed and tidied the kitchen.

Carrie groaned from the boys' bedroom. "Get some Berocca. And food."

Donning Adam's sports cap and a black tracksuit, I grabbed

my purse and headed out the door with Annabel behind me. "We'll have to make it quick. I've got a wedding this afternoon and I need to prepare the paperwork."

I whizzed through the aisles, head down, and not making eye contact. Of course, as luck would have it, Peter's cousin, Daphne, pulled in right behind me at the checkout. There was no escape. No backing up or attempting to do a runner. I was stuck, and Daphne began her interrogation.

"Geez, you look like shit, maybe dumping Peter was a bit hasty," she sneered.

I smiled, refusing to stoop to her level.

"Aunty Gina's devastated you know. She thought you might have called or come to see her to explain why you threw Peter out."

My legs started to shake. Was she for real? It was typical of Peter's mother to assume that I had done the wrong thing. Her baby boy could never put a foot wrong. My face burned with fury. I had assumed that Peter would have at least told her that he'd made some mistakes rather than let me take the blame. Daphne was waiting for an answer.

"Look Daphne, what went on between Peter and me is private. If he doesn't want to tell his mother the whole story, then that's his business, but if Gina wants to talk to me, then my door is open. She can come and visit her grandkids any time."

Daphne's mouth hung open. In all of the years I'd been married to Peter I had been polite, even sweet to his family. I took my bags from the trolley and walked away as the checkout girl called out to give me my change. I kept walking, leaving Annabel to chase after me.

"I don't need this shit," I complained when she finally caught up. "Setting his stupid family on me! I always disliked Daphne anyway."

***

When Shazza and Jason said they were having their ceremony at home, I had envisaged lovely trees, perhaps a pond or a pool, and some pretty coloured hanging decorations. As they stood at the end of their concrete driveway with the car door open, CD player blaring, and random chairs and old car seats set in a semi-circle, I realised that I clearly had the wrong end of the stick.

"Mum's gonna watch through the window cause she's too big to get up now. Is that okay?" Sharon asked. She was a sweet girl despite her yellow teeth.

"That's fine," I smiled, setting up my table with crisp, white linens and a very out-of-place feathered pen.

"How's it goin'?" Jason asked. "It's okay that I've had a few beers, ain't it?"

A few? What was a few? "It's fine as long as it's only one or two. If you've had more than that, you may not be of sound mind to legally consent to the marriage."

"Oh, I consent, don't fucken worry 'bout that," he said, grabbing Shazza's rear end. His bride smiled back, clearly pleased with his enthusiasm.

Much to the pleasure of the guests, Jason recited his personally written vows. "You's all know how much I love my Harley, and if there was any way I could marry my bike, I'd stick Sharon in the shed instead and just ride *her* on weekends." I cringed as Jason's mates cheered and the bride slapped him adoringly. "Since you can't marry a bike, Sharon's the next best thing, so, I Do."

Sharon's vows weren't much better. "In the words of Forrest Gump, life is like a box of chocolates, you never know what you'll get, but I know what I got. Tough and dark on the outside, sweet and soft on the inside, and a huge, hard middle," she said, grabbing his crotch.

How had I ever thought they were sweet? I said goodbye and made my escape amid pleas for me to stay for a drink. By the time I reached the end of the drive way, a sculling competition between the bride and groom was in full swing. Eight more, just eight more.

It was Sunday and I could have done with a sleep-in, but I wanted to cook the boy's breakfast. They'd returned home from camp yesterday and I hadn't had a chance to hear how it went. They were completely exhausted and had showered and gone to bed early. I made pancakes before waking them.

"Thanks, Mum." Adam smiled, pushing his messy hair away from his face. He was looking more like Peter every day.

"They're great," Jack added, his mouth already bulging.

"So, how did it go? Did you have fun?" I asked, grabbing a pancake from the rapidly decreasing pile.

"Better than I thought." Adam laughed, eyeing Jack, "It was actually pretty fun."

Jack rolled his eyes. "Only because he asked out Tahlia Montgomery on the first day and they spent the rest of the time behind the equipment shed."

"Adam!" I wasn't as surprised as I made out. Adam had grown into a tall, handsome boy, they both had, but Adam was much more confident than Jack. "You were supposed to be getting to know your classmates, not spending all your time with a girl."

"Not just any girl mum, Tahlia. She's gorgeous," he smirked, "It was much more fun getting to know her than the rest of them."

Jack rolled his eyes again, "Well I got to know people. I actually met a few cool people to hang out with this year."

Adam shoved in a final piece of pancake and got up from the table. "We've got a soccer pre-season session at ten, Coach said he'd swing by and pick us up."

Jack followed, taking his and Adam's plates to the sink, "First game's in a few weeks and coach is organising a few sessions and professional players to come out and show us some strategies."

"Well, have fun and give me a call if you want me to pick you up after. I'll be home most of the day."

When they were gone, I slumped down on the floor of my office and pulled out a box of photos and papers that I'd been meaning to sort.

There was a knock at the front door.

"What are you up to?" Julia said following me back to my office.

"Sorting through a bunch of stuff I've been storing up and avoiding. I didn't expect to see you today."

"Steve's away again." Julia's husband Steve was an engineer who flew in and out regularly from various mines where he worked as a consultant. "As for the kids, Jackson's still in Europe and Ava's flat-out settling into her new place," she explained.

I picked up a picture of Peter and me from the pile. "Was I not a good wife, Julia?" I asked, "I tried to be. I'm well aware of my own failings and I know can be difficult to live with. But overall, if you look at the bigger picture, I've always been there for him, picking him up and dusting him off every time he didn't succeed at something, haven't I?"

Julia sat on the floor beside me.

"I was the first to encourage him to go further, be better, try harder," I went on, "and you know I managed absolutely everything in this house – the finances, the kid's stuff, the family holidays, everything."

"I know, babe, but people take the ones they love for granted all the time. It wasn't you, it was nothing to do with you, it was him. *He* was lost, *he* was confused and *he* made the mistakes. The sooner you understand that the better."

"He was a good father though," I sobbed, "at least he tried to be. And there were good times. I can't pretend it was all bad. Even if he was always working and tired, he provided for us and made sure the kids had everything. In his mind, that was his role. It breaks my heart."

"He still is a good father. He might not be great at showing it, but he loves the kids and having an affair doesn't take that away. Sure, he's hurt them and he has to make up for that, but he's still their dad."

I pulled a brochure from the pile and waved it in front of Julia's face. "What a fool I was." I had been planning to organise a renewal of vows ceremony for our twentieth wedding anniversary this year. I felt ashamed of myself for being so naïve and stupid. "Somehow in my completely blind and gullible mind, I thought that a renewal of our wedding vows in front of all of you and our friends would give our marriage a new lease on life." I had fantasised about us getting things back on track and one day being able to visit our grown-up children and grandchildren.

Pangs of anguish constricted my chest as Julia hugged me. "I can't believe he would throw us away for a little girl, after everything that I've sacrificed for him, after everything we've created together. And now every memory, happy and sad, is tainted. I hate him for that, Julia, I hate him."

Anger welled up inside of me. I stood and marched to the bedroom. Within minutes, Peter's clothes, shoes, caps and everything else of his I could find was landing on the floor, one on top of the other. I stuffed them into garbage bags in no particular order.

"Here," Julia threw me Peter's shirts as she stripped them from their hangers. "This is good," she smiled. "Cathartic."

We dragged the bags to the front door, and I texted Peter.

> *You've got three days to collect your crap before it goes to Good Will.*

He replied immediately.

> *I need some time to sort everything out. Please don't make any decisions now. Give me a chance.*

He clearly wasn't going to give up that easily.

"Have you seen this?" Julia asked, returning from the kitchen with coffees and an envelope. She handed it to me, but I already knew what it was, I recognised the gold logo.

"It's from the Bridal Industry Awards," I said. "Tom and I got tickets ages ago, but I'm not going."

Julia snatched it back and ripped it open. "You've actually been nominated for an award, Viv, Celebrant of the Year," she announced, as if I should be excited.

"I don't care, Julia. I don't want to do this anymore. I can't do this anymore." I tried to explain, "I used to love being a celebrant and I loved being part of such an important day in people's lives, it felt like a privilege. Now it feels like a curse. People planning their weddings don't need the added burden of a cynical, frustrated celebrant who doesn't even believe in love anymore. It's time for me to give it up."

"Well, I think you're being too hard on yourself," Julia argued. "If your clients think enough of you to nominate you for this then you must be doing something right."

"They nominated me when I was still nice and liked them," I laughed. "Next year I'll be up for the 'worst and crankiest celebrant ever' award."

Tom didn't share my desire to give it a miss when he turned up an hour later. "You have to come with me. I've bought a suit and I've been nominated in the category of..." He checked his ticket, "Most Creative Wedding Photographer."

I stamped my foot like a stubborn child and pulled my saddest face. "I don't want to go, Tom. Please don't make me."

"Fine. That's fine then," he sulked, "but how many times have you dragged me to things that I didn't want to go to?"

I had forced Tom to accompany me to many events over the years that no man should have to attend, including a Tupperware party. There was no choice. I owed him. I would be going to the stupid awards.

Natalia squealed with delight when I told her.

"I'm so glad, Mum, you need a night out. I'll help you pick out something to wear."

If only it was that simple. Find a nice dress and have a night out, and all would be right in the world.

***

Monday morning, I decided to start getting ready. With the awards on tomorrow night, it would require at least two days of preparation. Despite my initial reluctance, I was getting a little excited.

The shower door rattled as I stepped out. The last drop of water, still warm, rolled slowly down the small of my back before disappearing between the two slightly oversized cheeks that jutted out below my waist line – or *waste land* was a more accurate description. I dried off and pulled on my track pants, the size 14 waist noticeably tighter. With an open hand, I wiped the steamy mirror. Was that really me? I looked older. Sadder. Saggy stomach, deflated boobs, and desperately in need of a wax, and not just a bikini wax. I yanked and tugged at a rogue eyebrow hair that was longer than all the rest until it came out with a sting.

I slapped a line of foul-smelling hair removal cream across my top lip, chin and eyebrows and plonked down on the hard edge of the bathtub to wait for it to work its magic. Life had chewed me up and spat me out. Where was my reward for all the hard work I'd put in? Nineteen years of marriage, and squeezing out three extra-large-headed children with no pain relief. I felt like a stretched, saggy, shrivelled-up old prune.

"I'm off, Mum," Natalia's voice came from the hall.

"What time will you be home?"

"Late probably, so don't wait up." Her face appeared in the doorway. "I've got a cram session tonight. I'll see you in the morning," she said, screwing up her face at the hideous sight. "Geez, Mum, is all that really necessary?"

"Do you want me to actually go to this stupid award ceremony tomorrow night or not?"

"Yes, I want you to go."

"Well then, it's necessary." I declared.

Getting to my feet with a groan, I recoiled as it reminded me of the way my mother sighed every time she got up from sitting anywhere. My backside felt numb and sore and my back muscles screamed in protest. I'd probably be in for a hip replacement soon. It's not all bad, I reminded myself as I cleaned off the cream that was now burning my face. Lots of red patches, but the hair removal was an improvement at least.

I stepped back from the mirror and looked down at my legs. In my twenties, I had taken tap dancing for a few years, which had really strengthened my calves. So below the knees I looked pretty good.

Moving back to the mirror, I ran my finger over the now faint scar that started at the top of my forehead and disappeared beneath my hairline. It was a constant and lasting reminder of one of the many nights I had again been led astray by Carrie. A smile forced its way onto my lips as images of falling into the doorway of The Irish Club on St Patricks Day came back to me. I puckered my lips and sucked in my cheeks. Shit, that's not helping.

I stepped back and took a good look in the mirror. There was no denying it. It was time to make some changes.

"I need to get myself in shape!"

On the other end of the phone line, Carrie found it completely amusing, of course.

"What do you mean get in shape? And why are you calling me? I'm no personal trainer. Have you seen my arse?" She laughed.

"I mean in shape as in cleaned up, you know – some makeup, a push-up bra, new hairstyle, that kind of thing."

"Oooh, now that I can help you with." Carrie loved nothing more than a makeover project. She'd been dressing me up since I could walk. Most of the time it had been horrifying, but as we got older, she had, on many occasions, worked wonders.

***

"There's no way I can convince you to let me stay home?" My pleading never worked on Tom.

"Would you like some cheese with that whine?" He teased, "You look amazing."

"You don't look too bad yourself," I smiled, giving him the once over.

"You're not trying to seduce me again like the other night, are you?"

Carrie emerged from the bathroom and was grinning like a Cheshire cat. "Hi Tom," she smiled.

He had just given her a nice juicy bit of gossip. By the time our car tyres hit the road, she would be on the phone to Annabel and Julia.

"You suck," I said under my breath, while Tom opened the front door and led me out.

"I didn't know she was there," he protested when I slapped him playfully on the arm. It appeared to be much funnier to him that it was to me.

"You wait, I'm telling Caroline that you want to take her out," I threatened in retaliation.

"Don't you dare, Viv, she's a nutcase and you know it."

Caroline from 'Styles for your Event' had a thing for Tom. She always seemed to manage to book weddings where he was the photographer and then she would follow him around like a stalker. To Tom's utter horror, she was the first person we saw when we entered the ballroom.

"Oh, bloody hell," he griped, spinning around to face me, "she's waving at me."

"Let's go say hello. We can't be rude now, can we?"

Caroline was jiggling about like a hyperactive chimpanzee, trying to get Tom's attention.

"Hi, Caroline, nice to see you." I flashed her my sweetest smile as I pulled Tom by the hand.

"Oh, hi," she grunted, looking passed me to find him.

Caroline was in her forties, single, and desperate to get married. She hated me.

"What the hell are you doing?" She spat when I sat on the chair beside her, "I was saving that seat for Tom."

"Sorry, I didn't realise," I apologised, moving to the next.

"Your seat is *that* one," she said, pointing to the other side of the table.

Tom saw his opportunity and planted himself quickly on the chair allocated for me, "That's fine, I'll take this one."

Caroline smiled at Tom and batted her eyelids before giving me an 'I'm going to get you for this' stare.

"You're so mean," I said to Tom when she left to go to the bathroom. "Thanks a lot. Now she's going to hate me even more. She's probably plotting against me right now you know."

Tom rolled his eyes, "I don't give a shit about Crazy Caroline. Let's go," he said, grabbing my hand, "the bar's open."

The Scotch helped my stiff, stressed muscles to relax. "I'm sure everyone knows Peter's left me for a 21-year-old play thing," I moaned, downing another.

"No one knows anything and nor do they care, Viv. Stop being so self-absorbed and let's have some fun."

I squinted my eyes to an evil slit in response to his insinuation. My mobile buzzed in my purse and Annabel's name appeared on the screen.

"Hi," she said when I picked up. "It's just me, thought I'd check in on you and see how you're doing?"

"I'm fine, other than the fact that Tom is forcing me to suffer this award ceremony. You can come and save me if you like."

"He said that you were whingeing about it."

"Did he? And when did he say that exactly?" There was dead silence on the other end of the phone. I shot Tom another warning glare.

"Annabel...? Tell me."

"There's someone at the door, I'll ring you tomorrow." The

line went dead. I considered yelling at Tom, but the warmth of the alcohol was beginning to have a calming effect. I was starting to feel good.

"Check out Gordon," Tom laughed, "he's gone for the slick look."

Gordon, another celebrant, had been cursed with the most awful hair. His long mullet with its natural kinks, would frizz out and then semi-curl at the bottom. It was exceptionally ugly. Tonight, he'd gone for the slick back and sides, with the frizz back.

"Business in the front, party in the back," Tom teased, demonstrating.

I laughed and tossed back another Scotch. "Gordon's lovely, you have to admit, but who on earth would want him to marry them and risk having that hair in their photos?" I asked.

"He still lives at home with his mother, you know," Tom added, leaning in as if he cared that people might hear him. I knew he didn't.

"Don't make eye contact," I warned, spinning around to face the bar. Gordon liked to get drunk every year at these functions and start telling tales of his escapades with lady friends.

"Vera's here, shall I buy her a drink?" Tom joked. He was being mean.

"Vera's a sweetheart, leave her alone," I scolded. "You know that if she even smells a drink, she'll fall down."

At every event, someone would give Vera a drink and she would begin to stagger around and giggle like a psychotic hyena. She would flirt with all the young guys and eventually end up passing out on someone's lap.

The lights dimmed and the music got louder. My foot began to tap. Was I actually having fun? Don't show it, don't let him win. I gave Tom a scowl that he pretended not to notice.

"Why don't you just give her a chance?" I asked, gesturing to Caroline who was waving her arms at him wildly.

"I may have gained a few kilos, but nothing would make me want to take a dip in that crazy pond."

Tom had gained more than a few kilos, and he hadn't had a girlfriend in over five years.

I'm sure she's not that bad, once you really get to know her." She looked like a mad stalker right now. "Let's get back to the table before she passes out from all the waving," I said.

"I'm going to the loo," Tom called, avoiding Caroline's line of vision.

I made my way back to the table with wobbly legs. I didn't usually drink Scotch, but I loved how quickly it was loosening me up.

"Where's Tom?" Caroline glared as if I had eaten him or hidden him away in my handbag.

"He's gone to hide from you, actually. Is that okay?" I shot back.

She stomped off in a huff, in search of Tom no doubt, as the director of the awards took to the stage.

"What did I miss?" Tom puffed, returning to his seat.

"Why are you out of breath?" I mouthed across the table, pouring him a wine. His smirk gave the explanation and Caroline trotted in behind him looking furious. He'd obviously been trying to give her the slip.

"This is it," he said, squirming in his seat as the category was read out.

"For best Artistic Photography, the winner is..."

Tom's eyes were on me, his knuckles white with tension.

"Jonathan Milaros."

Applause filled the room while I watched Tom's heart shatter. He had wanted this so much. I went around the table and squeezed in beside him.

"Next year, Hun, you'll get it."

"You know what?" He smiled, desperately trying to hide his disappointment. "I don't know why I even wanted it. Photographing weddings pays the bills, but you know it's not what I really want to do."

"I know it's not. You have to start believing in yourself though. Apply for one of those Arts grants or—"

Tom shushed me with a wave. "You're up."

"What? I don't even care." I said, receiving glares from other celebrants for my far too loud dismissal.

"In the category of Best Marriage and Civil Celebrant..."

Tom squeezed my fingers.

Please not me, please not me.

"Genevieve Athilodi..."

Another wonderful gift from Peter, a surname that no one could ever pronounce. I'll be changing that back.

I smiled despite the fact that I wanted to crawl under the table and die.

I don't want the stupid award; I don't even want to be here.

"Viv, get up there, move it," Tom prompted when the clapping became awkward.

Why? Why? Why?

I accepted the ridiculous figurine and headed straight back to my chair.

Someone get me a drink.

Tom appeared with another Scotch on the rocks. He often read my mind, or just knew when I was about to have a breakdown. I downed it as a dozen or so celebrants cast their jealous eyes in my direction. After three more Scotches, I didn't care about any of them. In fact, I felt like dancing.

Swaying my hips seductively, I made my way onto the crowded dance floor with Tom in tow. I can do this. I've still got it. Peter will regret cheating on me.

I spotted Mary, my favourite florist, and waved at John from 'Cool Kat Car Hire'. The fluoro's dimmed, but the beautiful array of coloured fairy lights on the ceiling shone as I closed my eyes against their brightness. When I opened them again, the ceiling of my bedroom was all that I saw.

CHAPTER 5

The Aftermath

My body felt like it had been run over by a truck. What happened? How did I get home? A bolt of fear shot through me. I threw back the covers, relieved to find that I was wearing my nightie, although it was on backward. Think, think. We were laughing at Gordon trying to get it on with some young girl who was looking at him like he had leprosy, and Tom and I were dancing. I said hi to Mary, the florist and hot John from 'Cool Kat Cars'. The fairy lights were the last thing I remember.

"Shit," I groaned, trying to get up. The pain was excruciating. A stranger wouldn't have gotten me changed. Had Tom done it? Shit, shit, shit. First, I slobber all over him in my sleep, and now he's probably seen my bits.

I tried again to get out of bed, but as soon as I attempted to swing my legs around, pain ripped through my back like it was being torn apart.

"Is anyone here?" I called out, hopeful someone would come

to my aid. No answer. I couldn't even reach my phone, which was sitting on the dresser. Breathe. "Fucking hell. Shit. Stupid shit, I hate this!"

Mid-rant, my bedroom door opened and Tom peeked in.

"You okay?"

I closed my eyes tight and started bawling.

Tom sat down on the bed beside me. "Settle down, I've got some pain killers for you and I've organised an appointment with the physio in an hour."

I took in a deep breath and considered holding it until I died, but gave up after only a few seconds. Typical, I never finish anything I start. Peter always went on about my lack of commitment and inability to see anything through. How dare he hate me for something so petty after all the bullshit I put up with from him?

Tom snapped his fingers in front of my face. "Earth to Viv, are you with me?"

"Tell me what happened," I demanded, in a voice that sounded like the possessed girl from *The Exorcist*.

Tom opened his mouth to speak.

"No wait, I don't think I want to know," I jumped in. "Should I know? Do I need to know? No shut up, I don't want to know."

Tom put his huge hand over my mouth "Shut up for a second, will you? Do you remember anything at all?"

I shook my head. "The last thing I remember was us dancing and the pretty fairy lights."

Tom sucked in a deep breath. It must be bad.

"Well... we were dancing, but you were more like... sauntering around. I think that maybe you were being seductive?"

I lowered my head in shame. I vaguely remember trying to inconspicuously get John's attention, although my definition of inconspicuous was probably a little off given that I was completely drunk.

"I think I remember John from 'Cool Kat Cars' dancing with me," I offered, suggesting that perhaps my attempts at being sexy had paid off.

"He did actually come over and start dancing with you, but unfortunately your, 'sexy moves' were a bit too much for him and when you attempted to lunge into his arms, he dropped you and you did your back in."

I cringed. "Oh, bloody hell Tom! This is all your fault. Why did you make me go and why did you let me drink so much?"

Tom raised his eyebrows. "I hope you're kidding."

I wasn't. "How embarrassing, what happened then?" I wasn't sure I wanted to know.

"Well, John took off like a rocket and I picked you up off the floor, seeing as you couldn't move, and brought you home."

"Mmm, well at least you got me out of there, I suppose. Thanks."

"There is a little bad news though."

Bad news? Wasn't that bad enough?

"Unfortunately, by the time you did your Dirty Dancing lunge at John, everyone had already gathered to watch."

"No, don't. Don't go on."

"Some," he winced, "filmed it on their phones."

***

I put the pillow over my face and screamed.

"As of this morning you're a YouTube star," he added quickly, as if delivering the blow at a faster pace would somehow lessen its impact.

"Get me the laptop," I muttered.

Seconds later, Annabel and Julia walked in with the computer. I shot Tom a death stare.

"Before you kill me," he said, "I called Julia to come help me last night to get you into bed. I didn't think you'd want me to undress you, and to be honest, you were so out of it I could hardly carry you."

"Mmm," I said, retracting the stare. Thank God.

Annabel plonked the computer in my lap. "Now, before you watch this," she warned, "I want to remind you that this is just one little incident and it does not define you as a person. You are so much more than that and we all know that you aren't great when you drink too much."

I pushed her hands off and turned the computer around, hesitating and then pressing Play. Julia turned her back to me and began laughing before the video even started.

"Oh, sweet Jesus." It was mortifying.

The video was blurry at first, but soon cleared, showing me throwing myself around the dance floor like some freaked out, overgrown turkey, arms flapping, butt sticking out, doing what could only be described as a pathetic, desperate, mating call. The look on John's face was a cross between horror and fear. He tried to run, but when one of his friends pushed him back onto the dance floor, he looked completely stunned.

Stop, don't watch anymore, I told myself. But I couldn't stop.

It was like passing a car accident. You know you shouldn't slow down and stare, but you just can't look away.

I watched the horror unfolding. I had wrapped my arms around John and, from what I could see as the camera bounced around, I began to recreate 'that' scene from *Dirty Dancing*. John was clearly looking for an escape route while the audience cheered. When I attempted to throw myself into John's arms, I landed flat on my face on the floor with my skirt above my waist.

I gasped in horror and slammed the laptop shut, my hand instinctively covering my mouth to prevent the scream from escaping. I looked up at Annabel and Tom whose sympathetic eyes were watching me. Julia was still facing the wall. I opened the screen with shaking hands. I had to see the end.

Tom had rushed to my side as I lay on the floor, bottom exposed, moaning and clutching my lower back. It was bad. Really bad. I shut the laptop again and looked up at their faces, including Julia, who had finally managed to compose herself enough to turn around. They waited for my reaction.

"Thirty-three thousand hits already. Wow, that's good," I said.

Julia looked at Tom and Annabel, who were looking at me with puzzled expressions.

"Well, I guess that's that then." I closed the laptop and pushed it aside.

"What's what?" Annabel looked worried.

"My life is over. I'm completely cursed. The Universe or God, or whatever is out there, is clearly out to get me. It's probably payback for that bloody funeral procession. I told you, Tom, didn't I?"

Annabel looked at Julia to see if she had any clue what I was talking about.

"Viv," Annabel insisted, "we all do stupid things now and then, we just have to get back up and dust ourselves off. One silly mistake does not determine who you are as a person. I've done plenty of stupid things."

"I don't recall you ever attempting to put on a drunken floor-show for your colleagues, before falling flat on your face, arse in the air, and having to be picked up and dragged away."

She had nothing to say.

"I also don't recall the most hideously embarrassing moment of your life being uploaded to YouTube and beamed around the globe for the entire world to see," I cried.

Julia burst out laughing. "I'm so sorry, Viv," she apologised, "but it's so funny."

Annabel leaned in and hugged me. "I know this is bad, but all I can say is that we love you and we are here for you, aren't we, Julia?" She gave Julia a stern look.

"Of course we are, although don't tell anyone we're related," she giggled.

I threw the pillow at her. Why? Why? Why was this happening to me?

When Tom and I arrived at the physio's office, I was in absolute agony.

"Take me back to bed," I moaned.

To add to my discomfort, my stomach was churning. Given the excessive amount of alcohol I had consumed, I was suffering from what my father liked to refer to as "mud guts". It was a delightful term he often used to describe uncontrollable gas caused by way too much alcohol, that smelled worse than a rotting carcass left in the sun. I just wanted to go home and crawl back into bed and wallow in my own pain and self-pity.

"Genevieve?" the therapist called, as Tom took my arm to help me to my feet. He had practically carried me in, given that I could hardly move without excruciating pain.

No, no, no! I was greeted by one of the most handsome men I had ever seen. Tall, with a strong build and dark hair, his fabulously white teeth shone through a wide, gorgeous smile. I smiled back, immediately aware of how much I resembled a homeless person. I smoothed my matted bed hair and straightened out my faded tracksuit pants that hung around my backside like a pair of 80's MC hammer pants. I still stunk of alcohol.

"Hi Genevieve, I'm Dean," he said in a deep, masculine voice.

"Hi," I managed. "I don't always look like this, sorry."

Dean gave me a sweet smile. Was that sympathy or pity? I couldn't tell.

"We all go through hard times," he said gently, as he led me through to the examination room.

Hard times? What the hell does that mean? Does he think I'm an alcoholic or something?

"Just hop up on the table and let's see what's happening." Dean put his large, manly hand on my elbow and helped me up onto the table. They felt strong and warm. "Just remove your shirt and lie face down. I'll give you a moment," Dean offered, closing the door behind him. Once I was laying down on the table with my face in the little hole, Dean returned and began to rub his oily hands across my back with just the right amount of pressure.

"Does that hurt?" he whispered.

Did I imagine that he whispered?

"No, that's fine. Can you go further down, a little lower?"

As Dean's hands travelled down my back, I felt a tingling sensation as they pressed against my skin.

"Right there," I said, flinching in pain.

"Ahh, yep, I can feel it. I'm just going to work on that for a bit and then we'll see how you feel."

Perfect Dean rubbed and oiled, propelling me into an ecstatic mixture of pleasure and pain. He went lower and began running pressure points on my buttock.

"Oh, yeah." Crap, was that out loud? I waited for a second to see if Dean had heard it, but he carried on without noticing. My back was actually feeling looser, but laying on my stomach was making me feel sick.

"I'm just going to use a little more pressure," Dean said, as he pushed down harder on my tailbone. I tensed, but before I could stop it, a loud, gurgling sound escaped. Dean's hands stopped dead and I stopped breathing.

It was as if time stood still as the rotting smell wafted into the air. There was no hiding it, there could be no cover-up. We both stayed completely still, until Dean, lovely, perfect, gorgeous Dean, broke the silence. "I'll just go out and write up some notes and then we'll see how you feel."

When the door shut, I swung my legs around and hopped off the bed. A moderate pain shot through my back, but I didn't care. I was getting the hell out of there before he came back. I dressed hurriedly and opened the door a crack to check the hall. No sign of Dean. Tip-toeing at first, I launched into a brisk pace as I passed the reception desk.

"I've had an emergency, could you please send me the bill. Thanks," I called as I ran for the exit.

By the time Tom looked up from his newspaper I had passed him and was already out the door.

"Do I dare to ask what happened in there?" he said when he caught up with me at the car.

I shook my head. "I wouldn't," I said, "but I blame you."

"You bloody well blame me for everything! I'll have you know that keeping up with your string of disasters is exhausting." He smirked, getting into the driver's seat. "Does your back feel any better at least? You got out of there pretty fast."

"Much better, thanks for organising it," I answered, in a tone that warned him not to push it.

When he pulled into my driveway, Tom asked, "Do you want me to help you inside?"

"I'll be fine, but thank you. I mean it." I really was thankful. Tom put up with a lot from me.

Natalia met me at the front door. "Hey, Mum. Are you okay?" she said, noticing my discomfort.

"I'm fine, baby, just exhausted." It sounded unconvincing, even to me. I wasn't fine.

"I'm making dinner. Just for the two of us," she beamed, leading me inside. "The boys are at John's and I feel like we've hardly seen each other lately."

We hadn't, but right now I just wanted to crawl into my bed and never come out.

"Mum, I want you to know that even though I'm in and out all the time, I'm here for you if you need anything."

"I know, sweetheart, I just need some time, that's all." I pulled her close. She always wanted to make everything right in the world. "I want you to concentrate on your studies and let me take some time to get through all this. I promise that I'm fine."

"Okay, but Dad came just before."

Thank God I wasn't here. "How was he?" I didn't care.

"He looked pretty awful, like he hadn't shaved, or ironed his clothes."

Satisfaction enveloped me. Good, he's suffering. "Did he take his things? I had them packed for him near the front door."

"He took some of it, but he said he'd get the rest later. I'm worried that he thinks he's coming home soon." There was a slight quiver in her voice even though she tried hard to cover it up.

"Did you talk to him?" I asked.

She was avoiding my eyes. "Sort of," she responded, without looking up from the stove. "I will, but I just can't bring myself to be nice to him right now after what he's done to you, to us."

I felt the familiar pangs of guilt. "Honey, despite what he and I are going through, he loves you all so much. It doesn't change the fact that you're his kids. He was there for all of those years, going to sports and school events and tucking you into bed. He always tried to do absolutely everything he could to make sure you all had what you needed."

"Except running off with a child," Natalia spat. Hurt and anger were spilling over in her words. She'd obviously been speaking to one of my sisters.

"Yes, well, not one of his finest moments, but it doesn't erase all of the other good memories, does it?"

"No, I guess not," she finally conceded. "I'll give him a call tomorrow. Now let's eat."

Dinner was fantastic. Natalia's cooking, trained by her YiaYia, Peter's mother, was to die for. Another item on the long list of things she was amazing at.

I'd so missed chatting and laughing with her. Why do they have to grow up? It felt good to be together, even if she thought my epic YouTube video was horrifying, but hilarious.

"Nan left a message on the voicemail saying that they get in Thursday week," Natalia winced. "She wants you to pick them up."

My body tensed. I couldn't bear the thought of listening to Mum's marital advice. She adored Peter. He cut her lawn and built her a chicken coop and that was enough to make him perfect in her book.

"That's fine, I'll sort it out." I smiled, deciding which one of my sisters would be coming with me.

"Let's watch something funny. I hired Billy Connolly, stand up." She was waving a DVD in the air. Natalia knew how much I loved Billy Connolly, and I appreciated the effort. We sat, drinking tea and laughing, and for a few short hours of blissful contentment, I forgot about all of the disaster that had gone before.

CHAPTER 6

The Wedding of Nina and Chad (Needy and Fancy?)

*D*ress *fancy*, the email said. Needy Nina had decided on Thursday night that her wedding on Saturday would be fancy dress.

Ninasweetiepie7@live.com

Hi Genevieve, Chad and I have decided (I know it's last minute, sorry) that we'd like fancy dress style for the wedding. I hope that's okay. We'd love it if you dressed up too. Thanks. Nina

What the hell could I go as, with two days to prepare?
I hit Reply:

Hi Nina and Chad, it is a little bit late notice. Is there anything in particular you'd like me to wear?

What the hell were they thinking? Nina had irritated me from our first meeting, with her sickly sweet, passive/aggressive nature. Behind her innocent smile and flower-print dress, she was not to be crossed.

"We just want everything to be perfect," she had beamed, her smile so wide that pink gums were visible. "You can make sure that it's perfect, can't you?" she asked.

What she was really saying was, "Screw this up, lady, and I will end you."

She had followed that meeting with 38 emails in total, checking every single detail over and over and making change after change to her ceremony, constantly wanting my approval for every decision, while daring me to defy her by suggesting it wasn't a good idea.

Chad, who really did seem like a sweetheart, barely uttered a syllable. He did manage to ask if the wording to his vows could be changed slightly, but soon retracted when Nina's beady eyes attempted to penetrate his skull and explode his brain, all while maintaining her perfect composure. I predicted she'd end up murdering him. With poison, and then move on to the next husband victim.

My email tone chimed.

Ninasweetiepie7@live.com

Hi Genevieve, nothing in particular, whatever you think is fine. We are so excited and can't wait for Saturday. I can't believe it's finally here! Don't be late. Lol

There was no 'laugh out loud'– it was an evil cackle, and a warning. What the hell was I going to wear?

"Natalia!" Her bedroom was next door to my office.

"What's up?" she called back.

"I need a costume for this stupid wedding on Saturday," I moaned, throwing my hands in the air for dramatic effect as I burst through her door.

"Costume? For a wedding?" She laughed.

"This woman has decided, two days out from the wedding, to make it fancy dress. Have you got anything?"

"I've got Wonder Woman from my 18th."

We had thrown a huge fancy dress party for Natalia at home for her 18th birthday. It was a great night and was probably the last time I remember us all having a fabulous time together as a family. Pain cut through my chest as I remembered how Peter had gone off to get bags of ice and taken so long, we had to call him to check if he was all right. I bet he'd gone to her. Nausea hit me like an ocean wave.

"Mum?"

"Sorry." Was it ever going to end? Or would every memory end up being tainted with the realisation of what he had been doing? Everything good was gone, except for the early years maybe, but who knows?

"Come look in my cupboard," Natalia prompted, realising I was lost somewhere sad. "Here, it's this one." She pulled a blue cape, gold belt and red suit from the hanger.

"There's no way I'll fit into that! Where's the one that I wore? Little Bo Peep."

After some searching, she yanked a heap of blue and white

material from the cupboard. "I think the hook thing is in the shed."

It definitely wasn't perfect, but it would have to do. It wasn't like there were any other options.

***

"Are you shooting the whole wedding, or just the 'before' shots and the ceremony?" I asked Tom when he called on Saturday morning.

"Just before, at their places, and then throughout the ceremony. They want a few immediately after, but that's it. They've got a videographer doing the rest."

"Did they tell you to dress up, too?" I hoped he would look as ridiculous as I did.

"No, I didn't even know it was fancy dress." He sounded worried.

"Well, Needy Nina only emailed me on Thursday night about it. I feel ridiculous."

"What are you wearing?" I could tell he was smirking.

"None of your business, you'll have to wait and see," I teased. "I'm packing the car, so I'll see you there."

I packed my ceremony gear into the boot of the car and adjusted my white hat. I should have told them to stick it. I'd been a celebrant for thirteen years and conducted over three hundred ceremonies, yet here I was, dressed as Little bloody Bo Peep.

Seven more after this, then that's it, just get it over with. I buckled my seat belt and headed to Jangar Farm.

The sign at the entrance to the private road leading into the farm sent a chill up my spine.

'Caution, Llamas roaming.' Roaming? Why the hell were they roaming? And what was the caution for? To be careful not to hurt the llamas, or to be careful *of* the llamas. Were they likely to attack?

I stopped in the driveway and googled llama on my phone. Aww, they're cute and fluffy ... Eww, hang on. I flicked through a few more pictures. Weird, cranky faces and big teeth. Are they just roaming around here? I checked Wikipedia. Under 'Behaviour', it read:

> *Fully grown, they can reach 1.8 metres. When mature, they will begin to treat humans as they treat each other, which is characterised by bouts of spitting, kicking and neck-wrestling.*

Neck-wrestling? What the hell is that? And why are these idiots breeding these crazy, spitting beasts?

I threw my phone onto the passenger seat and planted my foot on the accelerator. If I could make it to the house, I might survive without being neck wrestled to death.

"Are you going to be here soon?" I whispered into my phone as I unpacked the car.

"Why are you whispering?" Tom asked.

"There are apparently llamas here, and they like to neck-wrestle people."

Silence. "What are you on?" Tom said finally.

"I'm serious! There's a sign out the front that there are llamas."

"You're killing me, you know that, right? I'll be there soon. Just get set up, and if you see one get in the car."

Tom was laughing, but it wasn't amusing. It would be just

my luck to get neck wrestled by a fluffy, buck-toothed llama while dressed as Little Bo Peep. I didn't need a second YouTube sensation.

I tiptoed down the stone pathway and through the vine covered arch that opened onto the garden area. The guest chairs and umbrellas were already set up, along with a decorated signing table and lectern. Fabulous, I didn't have to go back to the car and get mine.

"Genevieve?" I heard Chad's voice from behind me.

"Hi Chad," I said, turning around to find him dressed in top and tails. The look of horror on his face frightened me. I scanned the area to see if there was a llama approaching.

"What are you wearing?" He seemed upset.

"I'm Little Bo Peep. Nina said it was fancy dress and to wear anything."

"Dress fancy! Like black tie, that kind of thing. FANCY!" His voice had risen to a high octave.

I had nothing. Dress fancy! Who says dress fancy? Why didn't she bloody well say BLACK TIE!

Chad stomped off, leaving me to the strange looks of arriving guests who were in full-length gowns and tuxedos. When Tom saw me, I thought he was going to die.

"I've been trying to call you!" he said between gasps.

"My phone's in the car. What the hell am I going to do? That witch will curse me when she sees me dressed like this."

Pity filled his eyes. "There's nothing you can do, just smile and get it over with."

I inhaled the deepest breath my lungs would allow and took my place in front of the lectern, beside the squirming Chad.

Whispers of, "What is she wearing?" filtered up and down the rows of guests seated in front of me, but when Nina's eyes landed on me, her face screamed "You'll pay for this."

She stared me down for the entire walk down the aisle, glancing only briefly at Chad, who was shaking, before looking back at me. She was calculating; weighing up her options. Throw a fit and ruin everything she had worked towards? Or pretend it was all part of the show and try to pull it off? I waited, breath held tightly in my throat, as she approached on her father's arm. He kissed her cheek and joined her mother and the other guests. There was silence.

Nina reached for Chad's hands and turned her eyes back on me. Squinting and tightening her lips, her look warned me this wasn't over. Then she flashed her full gummy smile at her groom and the guests. I breathed, for the first time in what felt like minutes and began.

"On behalf of Chad and Nina, I'd like to welcome you here to celebrate with them as they publicly pledge their commitment to one another in marriage."

Nina had smiled throughout the ceremony, until we got to the exchange of rings. "Chad, take Nina's left hand in yours and repeat after me. Nina, this ring I give you. My personal ... llama." There was a damn llama approaching.

"Get on with it," Nina hissed at me under her breath.

But there's a friggin' Lama coming! Why isn't anyone running?

Tom was making round circles in the air at me with his hand. "Keep going," he mouthed, as I shifted nervously away from the approaching beast.

"My personal gift, my promise to be loving and faithful, for the rest of my life," I continued.

The llama was behind me now. What was it doing back there? What if it launched into a neck-wrestle right here? How would I escape? Would anyone even save me?

"Nina, please take Chad's left hand in yours and repeat after me." I tried to look to see where the beast was now, as Nina repeated my words. The llama was huge – taller than 1.8 metres, and approaching as I shifted on the spot.

Go away. Go away. I willed it.

I looked at Tom with pleading eyes, signalling him to shoo it away.

"I now pronounce you to be husband and wife. You may kiss your bride!" I announced, skipping the end part I had beautifully written for them. It wasn't worth being neck-wrestled over.

Seeing the llama's quickened movement from the corner of my eye, I dropped to the floor, commando-style, as the guests rose to their feet with applause, and the llama, spooked by the noise and motion, hissed and spat viciously at the horrified guests, before casually walking off.

"Are you okay?" Nina's father asked, helping me up.

"Yes, thanks, the llama just spooked me. I'm so sorry about everything. Nina is furious."

"You leave her to me, honey. She's been a total crackpot organising this wedding, driven us all mad. But it's done now, and it's time for her to pull her head in," he said.

Really? Thank goodness. What a wonderful man. A sigh of relief exited my lips. "Please accept my apology, and I hope it's a wonderful reception. Llama free!" I joked, gesturing to the ugly beast that was baring his big yellow teeth at us from across the paddock. I felt terrible for the misunderstanding and for upsetting Nina after she'd worked so hard to make sure every detail was perfect. Even if she had been behaving badly, she still deserved to have a wonderful wedding day.

Tom grabbed my arm. "Are you free after this? Can we talk?" he asked, as the guests were congratulating the couple.

"Sure, what's wrong?" He sounded serious.

"Nothing's wrong, I just need to talk to you about something." He wasn't going to give in.

"Okay, but I need to change, unless you want to talk to Bo Peep?" Tom didn't laugh. "Okay, do you want to meet me at the Somerton pub at six? We can have dinner?"

He nodded. "Sounds great."

It wasn't great. Something was wrong, I could tell.

***

The Somerton was just outside the city and much closer to Jangar Farm than my house. Instead of going home, I decided to stop in at the nearby shops and buy a new outfit to change into. It had been ages since I'd bought myself anything new anyway.

My phone buzzed. It was Peter.

> *Hey Viv, just wanted to see how you are. Can we talk? I miss you. Please.*

Ughh, go away. I hit Delete.

Much to the delight of small children, Little Bo Peep made

her way to a boutique in the top end of the mall. I plucked a few pieces from the sales rack and headed into the change room. The costume hadn't been easy to get into, and was even more difficult to get out of. The poor teenage store assistant had to help me out of the dress and bloomers.

I tried on a few pairs of pants, a striped full-length skirt, and several coloured and frilly tops, all of which were either too tight, too short or too Lycra. Nothing sat right or fitted where I wanted it to.

I called out to the sales girl and she came back over to the change room.

"I'll take these," I said, passing her plain black pants and a blue knit top. "But then can I have them back? I need to wear them now."

My phone buzzed again. Go away, Peter, for goodness' sake. But it was Tom:

Waiting at the pub, where are you?

I checked the time. It was already six. Tossing the phone in my bag, I frantically searched through the pieces of the Bo Peep costume. Where the hell was my bra? Shit. I picked up every single item one by one. Where the hell is it?

My phone beeped again.

Are you coming? Should I leave?

On my way, sorry. Wait for me. I sent back.

The bra was gone. Stuff it. I threw on my new knit top,

grabbed my bag and sprinted bra-less down the mall holding my chest.

When I arrived at the pub, Tom was sitting at the back and waved to me as I staggered in, still red-faced and panting.

"What the hell is wrong with you?" He laughed as I plonked down onto the chair across from him. "Viv, is there any reason you have a large, bright red bra hanging from your back?" he asked casually.

"Well, obviously not, *Tom*." I frantically grabbed at my back, making more of a spectacle than I had already created. Jesus, is this ever going to end? "Get it off for goodness sake," I ordered.

"It's a never-ending circus with you, honestly," he grinned, as he retrieved the bra, and I stuffed it into my handbag.

"That's a nice look by the way, I like it." He pointed to my boobs, that were hanging like potatoes in a stocking.

I crossed my arms. "Get me a bloody drink, will you," I sighed.

Tom stopped a passing waitress and ordered me a glass of wine.

"Anyway, I don't care," I declared. "Bra or no bra, nothing could be worse than the last few weeks of my life, so I'm just going to stop caring and enjoy myself. From now on, I'm going to try and see the bright side. Like today. Despite the humiliation, that stupid llama didn't try to neck-wrestle me, so that's a win."

Tom was silent as he stared into his beer.

"Are you okay?" I asked. "What's wrong?" Something was up.

"I'm glad you're feeling positive," he replied. "Because I have something I need to tell you."

"Oh God, what?" My heart was pounding. "You're not dying, are you? Jesus, Tom, tell me," I begged, grabbing his hand.

"I'm not dying, Viv, it's good news really."

I snatched my wine from the waitress and took a gulp. Thank goodness it's good news. Does he have to be so dramatic and give me a heart attack?

"So, what is it?" I asked, my wired nerves calming only slightly.

"I've been offered a photography fellowship. It's a prestigious appointment, and an opportunity to really learn from the best."

"That's fabulous." I held up my glass in a toast, but Tom hesitated. "What's the matter?"

"Nothing's the matter, but there is a catch."

My heart began to thud again.

"It's for three months, and it's in England."

I swallowed against the large lump that had formed in my throat. "England? As in the other side of the world?"

Tom nodded while my heart sank.

"When do you leave?" I asked, staring into my glass.

"Monday week," He delivered the news hesitantly. "They only just made the decision, and I haven't got much time to get over there and get set up before I take up the position. I'll be back in no time, I promise. You'll barely notice I'm gone."

Did he really think I wouldn't notice his absence? Didn't he realise how important he was to me? How could he go and leave me like this? Abandon me in my hour of need?

There had never been silence between us, but neither of us could find the right words.

"You're not saying anything, but I know you, you're upset with me," Tom said finally, breaking the silence. "Just tell me. I'd rather you be honest and say how you feel, than pretend it's okay and freeze me out."

Tears filled my eyes. "I don't want you to go. I need you, I need you here keeping me sane," I sobbed, knowing how selfish I sounded.

How could he have hidden this from me? He must have known for weeks that there was a possibility of leaving. At least since he applied.

"I know," Tom said. "But you're strong, Viv, and you're finding the path you're meant to be on. And as much as I like you needing me, I absolutely know in my heart that you don't *need* anyone." He gently put his hand under my chin and lifted my face. "Do you honestly think that you're not smart enough, strong enough, funny enough, or beautiful enough to make it on your own? To make a life for yourself without Peter?"

I didn't answer.

"If you were being honest with yourself, Viv, you'd realise that you've been doing it alone for a long time. Peter may have been in the bed beside you, but when was he truly there for you? When did he ever really listen? Or care, or even ask you anything about what was happening in your life? In your heart you must see that he's been emotionally absent for a long time."

I thought about his words. It was true, Peter had merely been a physical presence in my life, especially over the past few years. He had been a constant source of worry and anguish for me and he'd shown little interest in me on any level. I had relied on other people for my self-worth my whole life, and it was time to change. I had to learn to find worth in myself from the inside. But I still didn't want Tom to go.

CHAPTER 7

The Return

"Is your back feeling better?" Annabel asked when I sat down.

"Mmm, yes," I muttered, waving to Carmello to bring coffee. He responded immediately, the cafe was always quiet on Wednesdays. I hadn't seen my sisters since before the physio, and I'd been deliberately vague in my text messages and calls. Carrie had sent me regular updates of the views on my YouTube video, Annabel had sent daily affirmations for me to practise, and Julia had left a goody basket full of chocolate on my doorstep.

"Thank you for all of your lovely thoughts, but I'm fine."

"Well, you don't look fine."

Carrie always had to point out the obvious. They were all very good at picking up when I was hiding something. I didn't answer her.

"Is everything all right?" Julia asked. "You seem down. Are you still upset about the awards night and the video?"

"No," I said. "It just feels like everything I do in my life ends up a complete disaster. I'm like a daily comedy routine, a magnet for bad luck," I sulked.

"Oh honey, has something happened since last week that you're not telling us? Is it Peter?" Annabel was looking at me with her eyebrow raised.

Should I tell them the whole story? I'll hear about it for years if I do, but I needed to tell someone. I let out a deep sigh and hesitantly relayed to them, blow by excruciating blow, what had happened with gorgeous Dean. I watched as they cringed, their faces contorting to indicate both horror and pity at the peaks and troughs of the story.

When I finished, no one spoke for a few moments, until Julia and Carrie both burst into laughter and Annabel covered her face with one hand and put her other hand on mine. "Oh, you poor thing, that's awful," was all she could manage before she lost it, too.

The three of them were killing themselves at my shameful admission, but as they laughed, and Carrie made fart noises, my misery evaporated. Annabel's snort pushed us over the edge into a full fit, tears and all. The entire cafe was glaring at us as we doubled over in agony, and Annabel continued to impersonate a pig.

Carmello quickly made his way over to our table.

"Everything all right here, ladies?" he said playfully, gesturing his hands in a downward motion for us to be quiet. "You girls are turning into troublemakers. First crying, now laughing like you're crazy or something. Pazzo!" He muttered, making little circles beside his head with his finger.

Carmello's Italian accent made us laugh even more. Giving

up, he threw his hands in the air and returned to the counter. My stomach hurt and my back was aching from the strain. I looked at the others, Annabel with black eyeliner running down her cheeks, Carrie with swollen red eyes, and Julia trying to clean her tear-streaked glasses.

"Despite the fact that you are all rotten, I love you and I feel so lucky," I said, gratitude overwhelming me in the moment. No matter what happened, I could always count on my three sisters to make me laugh. This is what we do, how we cope – tease each other and joke about the most terrible things in order to go on.

"I can't believe you had two of the most awful and embarrassing moments imaginable, and within the space of 24 hours," Annabel kindly reminded me.

Thanks for that.

"You know, Viv, you're so lucky to have Tom,' she went on. "I wish I'd had someone like that to rely on, especially after Kim left."

Annabel was forever trying to recreate her own version of the television show *Will and Grace* and had tried to recruit numerous gay men to become her best friend, to no avail.

"He's so good, isn't he?" Carrie chimed in.

"He's great," I said. "I couldn't have gotten through this without him."

It warmed me to think about how much support he had given me. But my smile turned to a frown as I recalled our last conversation, and the fact that he would be leaving me.

"What's wrong, did you and Tom have a fight?" Julia asked, picking up on my sudden change of mood.

"No, but he's leaving," I said.

Annabel waved to Carmello for refills. "What do you mean? Where's he going?" she asked.

"England, apparently. For a photography thing." I pushed out my bottom lip. "I'm happy for him. This is what he's been working towards, and he's fed-up doing wedding photos. But I'm just sad. I don't want him to go. It's for three months."

"He's got the hots for you, you know that, don't you?"

"Shut up, Carrie, he does not. You just like to turn everything into sex," I argued. "We've been friends for years and he's just there for me as I would be for him, that's all." I gave her a stern look, warning her not to dare tell them about the kiss. I was shocked she hadn't already.

"I know you've been friends for years," said Carrie. "But he's loved you from day one, it's obvious. I know he's a bug guy, but he's pretty cute," she added.

I couldn't believe she was actually saying that to me. I wanted to strangle her.

"I can't believe you would even think that," I returned. "I would never judge Tom, or any person, by their weight. But besides, Tom is not in love with me, he loves me as his friend and that's it. He may have had some feelings initially, decades ago, but he never acted on them and we both moved on. I've been married for nineteen years, if you hadn't noticed!"

"Look," Carrie said, her tone gentle now, realising how irate I was becoming, "I know you would never judge him like that. What I'm trying to say is that it's natural for you not to be attracted to him in that way. But if he had made a direct advance, and he wasn't quite so overweight, I think something may have eventuated between the two of you."

I shook my head in defiance. "You're wrong. He's my friend and even if he was the most muscled, gorgeous guy on earth there would be nothing between us other than friendship."

Would there? Was I not attracted to Tom because of his size? Carrie was getting into my head. No, I liked bigger guys. I'm not attracted to Tom because he's my best friend and there's no spark between us. I could never risk our friendship. I had to stop listening to her.

Carrie put up her hands and sat back in her chair gesturing defeat.

Julia interjected to ease the escalating tension. "Look, regardless of what either of you say, you're lucky to have him, Viv."

"How did the farm wedding go?" Annabel asked.

The snorting started up again, much to Carmello's annoyance.

"Wrestling llamas?" Annabel didn't believe me.

"Honestly, I'm telling you, look it up," I insisted. "They've got big, ugly teeth and weird, tiny little heads, and if they decide to take you, they spit and then neck-wrestle you to death."

It was no use explaining further, they were hysterical.

***

For the first time since Peter left, I felt happy to enjoy the silence of my empty house. I ran a bath and made a cup of tea, which I sipped slowly while soaking. It felt good to force my mind to be quiet for once and relax in the steaming water. I concentrated on the floating sensation and how light it made me feel, refusing to allow myself to obsess about anything – including how fat my legs looked.

"I am at ease with the Universe, all is well in my world," I chanted, channelling my inner Annabel. I needed to be mentally strong and prepared for my mother's arrival home from the cruise tomorrow. She would grill me, offer advice, try to take over, and probably attempt to get Peter and I back together. Her lawn needed mowing, afterall.

I was at total peace with myself when I heard the front door slam. "Mum, you here?" Natalia called.

"I'm in the bath, sweetheart."

"Everything all right?" she said through the door.

"Fine honey, I'm relaxing. How was work?"

"Busy. I'm exhausted, but I've got some study to catch up on." She sounded tired. She was overdoing it with working so many shifts and studying.

"Do you want to order in some food?" I suggested.

"I'll order pizza,' she said. 'And Adam called, he said you didn't reply to his message." I'd been keeping my phone on silent to avoid having to deal with Peter's incessant texts.

"They're over at a friend's, gaming or something. Adam said they'd get a lift home before ten," said Natalia.

"Thanks Hun."

"Mum," she paused before continuing, "Dad called today. He wanted to organise for us to get together for dinner tomorrow night. Me and the boys, I mean."

I got out of the bath and wrapped a towel around me before opening the door. "I think you should go, it'll be good for all of you," I smiled.

She looked unsure, but it would be better for them to see him on their own before the twins' birthday on Sunday. I was dreading it, but I would have to see him. For their sake.

***

My stomach ached and my head pounded violently as I waited for the ship to dock. I wasn't sure if it was Tom's impending departure or my parents' return that was causing it. I spotted them in the disembarking crowd with their roller-bags and over-sized cases. Mum was out in front, as usual, and was hollering something back to Dad who looked utterly miserable.

"Dad looks happy," Julia joked, getting out of the car. I had forced her to come with me. There was no way I could do this alone.

"Honeeeeeey," Mum smothered me with her embrace. "Grab these, my back is absolutely killing me." She thrust her luggage into my hands.

"Hi, love," Dad said, kissing my cheek. He looked exhausted or defeated, I couldn't tell which.

The entire way home, Mum gave an excruciatingly descriptive account of their trip. Every gory detail, including when her and Dad both ended up with diarrhoea after eating tacos on a shore stop. Dad winced beside her.

"So how did you find it, Dad? Did you enjoy yourself?" Julia tried to steer the conversation in a more positive direction.

"Great, yes it was lovely. Drop me off first, love?" he added, giving me a terrified look in the rear-view mirror.

My parents lived in separate houses, and had done for the last fifteen years. They had separated due to their inability to live together, but they couldn't live without each other either. As soon as Dad was out of the car, Mum launched into a rant.

"Honestly, love, I don't know what's wrong with him. He's so moody, it's like I can't say anything right," she wailed.

I knew exactly what was wrong with him, it was being stuck on a boat with her. I nodded and agreed, shooting Julia a smug grin.

"So, Mum, did you have any fun at all?" Julia teased. She knew how to handle Mum better than I did. She refused to allow her to dictate or interfere in her life, as did Carrie, who would tell her to stick it if she even tried. Annabel and I were the ones that suffered.

"Other than putting up with your father's crappy moods, it was fantastic. But what I really want to hear about is you."

Please let her be looking at Julia. I peered into the rear-view mirror. Her eyes were firmly locked on mine. Glassy and penetrating, they demanded answers. Oh well, tell it like it is. You're a grown woman, what can she do?

"Well, Peter's left and I'm trying to move on with my life." I was matter-of-fact.

"And what about your marriage, your children?" she fired back. "He's their father"

Obviously! Does she think I don't know that?

"What exactly would you like me to do, Mum? Forgive him? Just forget that he had an affair and has been lying to me for God knows how long?"

"No, I don't think that, but I do think that you should at least talk to him. Go to counselling, try to work it out," she insisted.

How did she know I was refusing to talk to him? I looked at Julia, who was shaking her head to indicate that she wasn't the dobber. I bet it was Peter. Mum must have called him!

"Mum, have you been speaking to Peter behind my back?" I demanded, refusing to let her away with it.

"No, I have not."

Yes, she had.

"Not behind your back," she went on. "You never asked if I'd spoken to him. In fact, you never took any of my calls while we were away."

I pulled into her driveway faster than I should have and slammed on the brakes. How could she do this to me? What about loyalty. I'm her daughter.

"I can't believe you," I spat, yanking her cases from the boot. I was determined not to let her reduce me to a blubbering mess.

"You and Peter need to try to sort things out," said Mum. "You don't just throw away nineteen years of marriage without at least trying to fix it." Her voice was getting higher and louder. "At least Peter wants to try. Kim ran off with that girl and never looked back, leaving poor Annabel to pick up the pieces. You owe it to yourself and him to at least talk. No marriage is easy, but you don't just give up."

I got back in the car and reversed out, my anger giving way to doubt. Maybe I have just given up.

"Don't listen to her," said Julia. "She's manipulating you to do what she wants. You have to do what's right for you."

"But what is right for me, Julia? Maybe she has a point. I haven't given Peter a chance and he is trying. He said he's going to counselling."

"Viv, all I'm saying is that it's for you to decide, not for Mum to bully you into. If you end up giving Peter another chance, then we'll all support you, but don't do it for her," she pleaded.

"You know, it's the twins' birthday Sunday. I'm going to have to see him."

"Well then talk to him and see how you feel. Do you want my honest opinion?" she asked.

"Of course I do. Why are you even asking me that?"

Julia had always been the most rational of the four of us. She gave good advice and never tried to sway me one way or the other.

"It's too soon and you're an emotional wreck. You were married for a long time. You haven't even found your feet yet."

She was right. With work, the kids, and all my recent disasters, I hadn't had a chance to think about anything. Who the hell am I? What do I want for myself in this life?

"Viv, you need to live a little," said Julia. "You've never experienced being on your own, going on a date, or sleeping with someone other than Peter, for God's sake. Just think about it before you make any decisions. Because if you go back now and then change your mind, it'll be harder on everyone, including the kids."

I hadn't been with anyone else. Peter was the only real boyfriend I'd ever had. Did I settle? Had I given up on myself in order to be Peter's wife? Ugh, I can't take this.

"Let's go to the pub," I decided, not giving Julia a choice, as I pulled into the carpark of the Black Jack Tavern.

"Get me a Scotch on the rocks," I called as I found us a comfortable couch.

My phone, still on silent, buzzed in my bag. It was Peter.

Hi Viv, just seeing if we're doing anything for the boys' birthday on Sunday? Family barbecue? I'd really love it if we could. I miss you all.

My fingers hesitated over the delete button, Mum's voice playing in my head. I have to. I have to try and at least make the effort. I clicked Reply.

Sounds good. About six.

I took a large mouthful of the Scotch and relaxed back into the couch. "He's coming Sunday for a barbecue."

Julia sat beside me. "Great. Is it just you guys, or are you inviting the rest of the family?"

"I'll ask the boys when they get home, but I think just us. They've made plans to meet friends at the soccer club after, I think, so at least I'll have an excuse to finish up and get Peter out of there early."

"See how it feels to have him there," said Julia. "See if it feels different, weird. You'll know pretty quickly if you can't stand being around him." She smiled, holding her glass up. "Cheers?"

I clanked my glass against hers, wondering what there was to celebrate. I wanted to tell her about Tom.

"A few weeks ago," I began, "Tom came over. We had a few drinks and watched a movie." Julia's eyes were wide, sensing something big was coming. "We both ended up falling asleep, so nothing happened." I hadn't realised she was holding her breath until she exhaled heavily. "But I did kind of cuddle into him, and kiss him, accidentally."

"How do you accidentally cuddle and kiss someone?" she probed. "Do you have feelings for him?"

"No, nothing like that. I was fast asleep and I thought he was Peter."

"So, were you wanting Peter? Or maybe subconsciously wanting Tom?"

"I don't think I wanted either, I was just sleepy and confused." I think.

"Look, you're seeing Peter on Sunday and Tom is leaving Monday. There are too many emotions flying around right now, so just relax."

I swallowed another mouthful of Scotch.

"We need to go out and have a bit of fun like we agreed," said Julia. "Get this weekend over with, and then next weekend we'll hit the town, see what's out there and flirt a little. You're a single woman now, you need to have some fun and loosen up a bit," she added, nudging me with her elbow.

A fun night out with my sisters sounded good, but this time, I would be staying relatively sober.

CHAPTER 8

Falling Back

"It was brilliant, Mum." Jack was beside himself with excitement. Their coach had organised a soccer clinic day with some big-name players and the boys had both spent the day with their team learning skills and having fun. "They even gave us pointers on what the scouts will be looking for when they come to games." They hadn't stopped talking since I'd picked them up.

"These are all dirty." Adam handed me every item from his bag.

"Fabulous. Thanks!" Taking the pile with a screwed-up nose as Jack added his. "I'm glad you enjoyed it," I said, peering over dirty shorts.

"I'm starving, what's to eat?" Adam was always starving.

"The fridge is full, so go for it."

I'd stocked up knowing they'd be ravenous when they got home. I put on a load of washing and sat on the couch beside Adam.

"I know we were going to have a quiet dinner for your birthday tomorrow, but Dad would like to come over and have a family barbecue. Is that okay with you both?" It would be so much easier if they said no.

Jack looked at Adam for the decision, as he had done since they were babies. Adam often spoke for both of them. "It's fine, Mum, as long as you're okay with it."

I had to be, for their sake.

"But we're still heading to the club after to meet up with the guys and play pool."

"That's fine. We'll do the barbecue in the afternoon." I gave Jack a squeeze, "I can't believe my babies are going to be seventeen." Tears filled my eyes.

"C'mon, Mum, don't start with the waterworks," Adam moaned.

Jack hugged me tightly. "We'll always be your little boys, Ma," he whispered.

I watched them from the kitchen as they spread themselves out in front of the television. They were so big and so grown up. All those years I spent delirious from lack of sleep, putting up with tantrums, dirty nappies and fighting, were a distant blur. I thought of Peter. He'd given up these moments and all for a fling with a stupid little girl. I hope he realises what he's missing.

When Natalia got home, she immediately set to work cooking her famous Moussaka. We listened intently as she raved about the 'brilliant' lectures she'd attended, with guest speakers who had prosecuted high profile cases. Jack and Adam enthusiastically gave us a blow-by-blow rundown of the soccer clinic, and I provided an edited version of my physio 'incident', minus the reason I hurt my back in the first place to shield the boys from the horror. I hadn't seen them laugh so hard since they were small. We did the dishes together and squished into our small lounge room with pillows and blankets to watch a movie.

Sitting there, tucked tightly between Natalia and Jack, with Adam at my feet on a bean bag, I couldn't have felt happier or more loved. How could I ever feel alone in this life?

I was awake when the sun rose the next morning. I'd had my first full night's sleep in weeks. Rested, even invigorated, I threw on a tracksuit and sneakers, deciding for the first time in my adult life to go for a jog. By the end of the street my feet felt like concrete blocks smashing against the pavement.

I'm so unfit, I puffed, as the acid burned my throat and the fat on my legs and bottom bounced up and down. I didn't care. The morning air was cool and fresh, and the world was still, except for a slight swaying of the trees. I stopped and took in a deep, cleansing breath that filled my lungs like a magical tonic, awakening them from some deep, dark sleep. I gave up jogging and walked briskly instead. My mind felt clear and the heaviness that had burrowed deep into my chest lifted, leaving me light and free.

When I returned home the kids were still sleeping. I made a cup of tea and some toast and sat out on the swing in the now beaming sunshine to read the paper. But I soon ended up on the 'Singles' page.

"Go on some dates, have a fling." Carrie's voice echoed in my head. I flicked to the 'Men seeking Women' column.

Single man, Kevin, seeking a woman. As for me am cool and lonely. Athletic build, mentally stable, physically fit.

Lucky he's mentally stable. Who puts that in?

Rikko: I am 24 years boy, my name is Rikko, I hear for date girl, may go for long term relation or casual relation cant determine from beginning. but with honesty.

Rikko had some issues with grammar and sentence construction, but at least he had honesty. That was something.

Jonno: I likes to laugh.

I likes to laugh?

I am a generally happy person, I never demand anything from people. I like the little things in life and I appreciate what a smile is worth these day's. I like to act so being spontanous is in my nature and I have a good sense of humor. Actions in daily life is what it is all about with me. I'm interested in friendship with the possibility of a serious relationship.

Why did they all have such terrible grammar? Is that what I had to look forward to? Reading the menu out for my date? Jonno didn't sound too bad. At least he claimed not to be 'demanding'. What did that even mean?

Sonny had it in the bag. The women would be lining up to date him. Simple yet effective self-promotion.

Sonny: Single; Seeking a woman. My name is sunny and I am a normal man.

Finally! Someone that's normal. I folded the paper up and threw it onto the table. Were any of these people normal? I picked up one of the books I'd brought out with me, one of the many that remained unfinished on my nightstand for months. One by one, Natalia, Jack and Adam emerged, fussed about, came and then went as the sun heated to a burning gold. It was lovely to have the whole weekend off. No weddings, no appointments, and no one to annoy me, at least until Peter arrives for the barbecue. I was finally beginning to feel like me. Genevieve.

***

"Hi, Dad," Natalia said opening the front door.

He's early. Bloody hell.

Peter appeared in the kitchen and placed an armful of shopping bags on the counter.

"Hi," he said, kissing me on the cheek.

Why does he keep doing that? Let it go, he's just trying to be nice.

"Hey, Dad," Adam called from the lounge room.

"Hey, Adam. Jack? How's things?" he asked, noticing Jack's hesitance. "I've got something for you both."

He pulled two envelopes from one of the bags and handed them each one.

"Awesome, Dad, thanks." Adam was impressed.

"Thanks, Dad," Jack smiled. He wasn't as easily won over.

The separation was affecting all of them in their own way, but Jack wasn't dealing with it as well as the others. He didn't let go of hurt easily, which worried me. Peter could see it too.

"What is it?" Natalia asked, snatching the envelope from Adam. "Great, better watch out with these two on the road." She handed me the envelope.

He'd actually made some effort and bought them driving lesson vouchers. Impressive. Peter had never bothered to buy anyone anything. He hated shopping and left all of the gift buying, even for his mother, up to me.

"Jack, help me take all this outside and get the barbecue going," Peter said, trying to connect with him.

I watched them from the kitchen window, Jack shifting awkwardly from foot to foot. His arms were crossed defensively. Peter was talking and adding coals to the barbecue, and then turned abruptly to face Jack and embraced him.

What is going on? I waited to see if Jack would pull away or get angry, but he didn't. He wrapped his arms around Peter and my heart ached for him.

I quickly ran to the sink and washed the lettuce when Jack came in the back door. "Mum, Dad needs the tongs," he said, rummaging through the kitchen drawers. His eyes and his tone were brighter, and happier somehow.

"Third drawer, honey," I pointed. "Are you okay?"

"I'm good, Mum." His smile had returned. Whatever Peter had said, it was exactly what Jack needed to hear.

Maybe he had actually changed, or was this just a way to try and get back into everyone's good books?

I grabbed two beers and headed outside, ignoring the ringing phone. Between our home line and the boys' mobiles there had been a constant stream of chimes all day. First my mother, then my sisters, Tom, and of course, Peter's mother. I was thankful to have dodged that bullet. Jack had answered.

I handed one of the beers to Peter. "Thanks, Viv." He was smiling. "Just like old times."

No, not like old times, because in the old times I still loved and trusted you. In the old times we sat out here with our children and we were a family. Now ... I don't know what we are. I smiled back. It wasn't the time or place.

The smell of the fresh lemon on the ribs wafted through the warm afternoon air. Jack and Adam passed a soccer ball back and forth to each other, balancing it on their feet and lifting it into the air, while Natalia and I watched on. Peter put down the tongs and tackled Adam for the ball. He passed it to Jack before they all fell into a heap on the grass. If only I could forget all of the hurt he caused and erase it from my mind. But I couldn't, no matter how much I wanted to.

Peter was smiling at me, wanting me to feel the love and the family we had built, and I could feel it, but it was shrouded with hurt and deception. I had loved him with everything in me once, but it had slowly seeped out, with every birthday that went by without a card, and every anniversary that passed without celebration. I knew it was normal in long marriages and relationships, but it wasn't the way he looked at me that cut the deepest, it was the way he didn't. What I could see in his eyes, in this moment as he sat on our lawn, I hadn't seen for years. He wanted to be here. With us. With me. He needed me, and I was once again an object of his desire. The only problem was that I wasn't sure I wanted to be anymore.

Peter seized his opportunity while the kids packed up the plates and loaded the dishwasher. "Can we talk a minute?" he said, handing me another beer.

Don't ruin a perfectly good evening. But what choice did I have?

"I've been seeing a counsellor," he began, "and as part of that process, there are some things that she wants me to do."

He had my attention.

"Firstly, I need to own everything that happened and accept responsibility for my actions. I need you to know that I know what I did to you and to the kids."

"Peter, I..."

"Let me finish," he butted in. "The mistakes I've made in the last year, pale in comparison to the ones I've been making for years. I've taken you for granted, Viv, and the kids. I've put work first and my needs before all of you, but I can't go back and change that."

Tears streamed down my cheeks as Peter took my hands.

"I'm not going to push it right now, because I know how much damage I've caused. But I'm committed to seeing this counsellor, and I hope that when you're ready, you might agree to coming along and speak to her, too."

It was so much easier to hate him. Taking responsibility and acknowledging what a complete twat he had been was harder to deal with. But wait, why do I have to go to counselling?

He read the confusion on my face. "The counsellor wants to see you so she can explain my issues and hopefully help you understand why I behaved the way I did. Say you'll think about it?"

"I will," I agreed, as the kids returned with dessert and coffee. Natalia looked worried when she saw me wiping away the tears. I flashed her a warm smile, easing her concern as we sang "Happy Birthday" and devoured the double chocolate cake.

Adam got up from the table. "I hate to end the love, but we have to get to the soccer club. Natalia, can you drive us?"

She nodded. "I have to go straight to work after, Mum. Are you okay to clean up?" She was really asking if it was okay to leave her father here with me alone.

"I'll give her a hand," Peter volunteered.

I nodded, assuring her that I was fine.

We waved them off, giving the usual parental warnings, and then went back into the house. "Do you want another drink?" I asked, while Peter filled the sink. He's actually doing dishes! I'd never seen him clean a dish in his life.

"Sure, if that's okay."

"It's fine." I hated to admit it, but maybe my mother was right. Had I been too hasty assuming it was completely over?

"I was a bit upset when Mum told me that she'd spoken to you behind my back," I confessed. I needed to get it off my chest.

Peter smiled. He knew too well the relationship I had with my mother. "She called from the cruise and wanted to know what was going on. She said you weren't taking her calls."

"Ugh, she's a liar," I scoffed.

"I told her that I'd left and I was trying hard to sort myself out. She asked if I'd seen you and I told her that you weren't keen to see me right now. Sorry if I did something wrong."

"No, you know what she's like, though. She bloody well drives me nuts."

"She's always loved me," he joked.

I picked up the tea towel and dried while Peter relayed with humour how much he hated living back at his mother's house.

"You liar," I teased, flicking him with the corner of the towel. "You'd be loving having your bed made for you and your dinner waiting on the table when you get home."

He turned to face me. "I hate it, Viv, I really do," he said, stepping closer to dry his hands. He smelled nice, a mixture of sweet and salty. The short goatee he had grown suited his long face, making him look strong and masculine as his eyes locked firmly on mine.

Is he going to kiss me? Before I could even think, his warm, full lips pressed against mine, soft, but intense. He pulled me in tight against his chest and kissed down my neck.

Only hours ago, I hadn't even wanted him to touch me, but now, as his mouth met mine, I was on fire.

Shit, my legs are hairy and there's rib meat still stuck in my teeth.

Peter pulled back and met my wide eyes. "I'm sorry, I didn't mean to do that. I know that you need time and I need to prove that I've changed."

Stop talking! Why is he talking?

He picked up the beer I had opened for him, and took a sip. "I'm serious about winning you back, Viv, but I know I have to earn it and sort myself out first."

What the hell are you doing? You can't just start that and then pull away.

"Of course," I replied. "You're right, we just got carried away."

"Walk me out?" he said, setting the bottle down. "Actually, do you mind if I quickly grab a few things?"

Who was this person with his manners and gentlemanly behaviour? The Peter I had been stuck with for the last nineteen years did what he wanted, when he wanted, and rarely considered my feelings. I would definitely be visiting this shrink of his. I wanted to see what crazy, magical treatment she was practising.

The bareness of the wardrobe startled us both. Peter sat on the edge of the bed and stared at the empty shelves. We hadn't been in this room together since that night. "It feels weird." He seemed as if he was saying it to himself.

I sat beside him. "The thing is, Peter, while I'm still so angry and hurt by what you've done, I almost knew it was coming. We weren't happy, we never smiled or laughed or enjoyed each other's company anymore. Whether it happened this way or some other way, we were always going to end up here."

Was I saying that out loud? Actually admitting some of the responsibility? My mouth kept moving. "We grew apart and neither of us did enough to hold onto it," I said, my voice finding a gentleness it hadn't expressed in some time.

"I just wish I'd seen it before it was too late you know?" He brushed a tear from his cheek. "Why didn't I see what we had and what I was risking?"

I looked away. "C'mon, I've got some of your things stuffed in these drawers and the rest are in the garbage bags by the door."

As he packed a few clothes and shoes into a shopping bag, sadness filled me. There was still some love between us, deep down, we had just forgotten it and let life take over. Neither of us had tried, or really made the effort to change things. I wanted to make it all his fault, but we were both to blame. Peter had just acted on it, while I'd buried it.

"I'll see you soon then?" he asked, as he left with his shopping bag.

"Sure. It's Natalia's birthday in a couple of weeks, so maybe we can do this again."

"Give me a call if you need anything, I can come and fix up the yard for you, mow your mum's lawn if she needs," he offered.

Won't she just love that?

"That'd be great." I smiled as he drove away.

The house was quiet again.

CHAPTER 9

Leaving

"Now don't get upset," Tom said, while I threw items in my shopping basket, holding the phone to my ear with my shoulder.

Telling someone not to get upset before you say what it is, is usually the best way to make them upset.

"I don't want you to come to the airport today," he said.

"What? Why not?" I *was* upset. I put the basket on the floor and snatched the phone.

"I don't want it to get all emotional, Viv. I'm going to come around in about half an hour and see you before I head to the airport."

All emotional? What does that mean? What was happening to the men in my life? It was like they were role reversing.

"Well, I'm at the shops, so make it an hour." If he was going to act like he didn't care, then so would I. But I did care. Why was he being like this?

I packed my shopping bags into the car and headed home, but Tom had beaten me to it. His car was in the driveway. Good. I wanted him to think that I hadn't rushed back just for him, even though I had. I got out of the car and walked past him without a word.

"I get it, you're mad, but please don't be," he said, following me in, "not when I'm leaving."

I put my handbag and keys down and headed back out to collect the shopping, with Tom trailing behind me.

"I'm sorry if what I said sounded mean, it wasn't meant to." He took the shopping bag out of my hand and turned my shoulders to face him. "This is hard for me. Leaving you is hard for me. I don't want to be looking at you when I walk away." His tone had softened.

"Well, it's hard for me too you know." My chin was pushing upward, squashing my lips against each other.

"You make me want to be a better person, Viv, and I need to do this for myself, for both of us."

For both of us? How the hell does this help me? I'm so selfish, bloody hell.

"Please?" He pleaded.

I relented, and we settled inside and made tea.

"How did it go with Peter yesterday?" Tom asked.

Bloody Annabel, she could never keep her trap shut.

"It was fine. He was happy to be here, and it was sort of nice us all being together like we used to."

"Have you already forgotten what he's done to you?" said Tom. "He's treated you badly for years and now one barbecue and he's forgiven?" He was getting flustered.

"I didn't say he was forgiven. Why are you being like this?"

Tom's face was turning pink as his blood vessels expanded. "I'm not being like anything. I just don't want you to make another mistake."

"Another mistake? Which one are you referring to, because there have been so many?" I hissed. "Why don't you tell me which one you mean?"

Tom shook his head. "For years you let him use you as a housecleaner, cook and parent to his children. You might say he's been a good father, but being a provider and making sure they have everything, doesn't make up for really being there. He rarely ever took you out, gave you flowers, or even remembered your birthday. I just don't want to see you go back to that after finally breaking free."

"Breaking free? Is that what you call it?" I was on my feet. "I didn't break free of anything. My world fell apart and I have been trying to pick up the pieces the best way I can. For myself and for my kids." My finger was pointed firmly at Tom's face.

"I'm sorry," he apologised, backing down from his high-horse. My reaction had shaken him. "I don't want to fight. I just care about you, and I'm worried." He gestured for me to sit back down.

"Tom, I'm doing the best I can, but you judging me only makes everything worse. I've always thought I could count on you, no matter what." Tom had been there through everything. From pregnancy emotions to being a Godfather to all of our children, but he was being unfair.

"I know." He met my eyes. "Just promise me you won't make any major decisions while I'm gone. It's only three months, Viv.

You need that time to re-establish yourself and find out who you are."

Have I been so dependent on him that he thinks I can't make a reasonable decision without him?

"If I need to make a decision, I'll make it," I declared. No one, not even Tom, was going to dictate to me anymore. "But I have your email and we're connected on Facebook. I promise I won't do anything rash."

The conversation with my sisters the other day at Carmello's ran through my mind. If Tom had feelings for me, then why would he leave? But it would explain why he was so upset about me letting Peter back in. Maybe it's just concern, as a friend. What if he's gotten the wrong idea from what happened between us on the couch? Why is everything so damn difficult?

"Viv?" Tom waved his hand in front of my face.

"Sorry, I was just thinking."

He swallowed the last of his tea and took the cup to the sink, "I have to get going. I need to be at the airport in an hour."

"I still don't want you to go." Tears were welling in my eyes. "But have fun, and good luck, I suppose."

"I'll message you when I get there." He pulled me in tight and kissed my cheek. "Be good. Promise?"

I nodded my agreement.

"And don't let those sisters of yours lead you astray!"

I was sobbing by the time his car left my driveway.

***

No new messages. Tom had been gone two days and I was already missing him. He had sent an email from his hotel saying he'd arrived and would be busy working for the next few days, but there had been nothing since.

I closed my email when the doorbell rang.

"Hi, Albert. Chinh, it's nice to meet you," I greeted the couple who would be getting married on Saturday and had not completed their documentation yet. I had met Albert previously to draw up most of the necessary paperwork, but Chinh hadn't arrived from Vietnam. She nodded and smiled as she entered, leaving her shoes at the door.

"Chinh only got here on Friday, so I'm sorry we left it so late," Albert apologised. He ushered his young bride to a seat in my office.

"Well, Chinh, I'm Genevieve and I'll be performing the ceremony on Saturday."

She nodded.

"I have all of your documentation ready, so if you have your birth certificate, we can get it all finished."

Again, a nod in reply.

"I have it all here." Albert fumbled in his plastic folder for the papers.

"Albert told me you have good English, Chinh. Did you learn at school in Vietnam?" I was determined to make her talk.

"Yes."

Hooray! "Are you excited about the wedding?" I persisted.

She looked to Albert. "Yes, we both are," he answered for her.

"I'll need you to sign these documents to say that you understand what your commitment means, and that all of the information you have given is correct." She looked to Albert again as my concern increased. According to her birth certificate, Chinh Dinh was 23. Albert was 55.

"That's fine," he said. "She knows."

"Albert, can I have a look at your driver's licence? I need to verify your identity." Please let him have left it in the car. I wanted to speak to Chinh alone.

"It's in the glove compartment, I'll pop out and get it."

As soon as he was out the door I pounced. "Chinh, I need to know that you understand what's going on here. That you are legally marrying this man. Do you understand what this means?"

Her soft, brown eyes darted quickly to the door. "Look," she whispered, "I know that he's old and I let him make all the decisions, but I need this. My sisters are all living here, and I want to live here, too." She continued with clear English, "Albert's cool. He's old, but he's nice and he buys me whatever I want. I'll take good care of him like a wife should. We help each other." Her broad smile beamed at Albert as he returned to the table.

I was stunned.

"Everything okay?" Albert asked, trying to understand why I looked like I'd just been hit by a bus.

"Um, yes." What could I do? It wasn't illegal for two people who find each other mutually beneficial to marry. Chinh wasn't lying about who she was or what she wanted, and Albert was pretty pleased at gaining a 23-year-old wife.

"Sign here," I said, pointing to the declaration. It seemed like it was so easy for them to decide. Neither of them cared or even wondered about the motives of the other, or the practicalities. They knew the reality and what was expected of them and just got on with it.

Why was everything in my life so damn complicated? Why couldn't I just detach and let things go like these two?

"Any chance of a discount seeing as it's a small wedding?" Albert asked. It was the fifth time he'd tried to make me drop my price.

I wondered if Chinh realised what a cheapskate he was. He buys her what she wants now, but I suspected it might stop once they're married. Could be a deal breaker. She'll probably divorce him eventually and take him for all he's worth.

"I'd love to, Albert, but with things the way they are, you know, I just can't do it."

He looked disappointed.

"See you Saturday." I smiled, closing the door behind them.

I went straight back to my office and checked the run sheet. After this weekend there would only be six more to suffer through.

***

Chinh and Albert's wedding went off without a hitch. Only about fifteen people turned up, which prompted Albert to once again ask for a discount. His 32-year-old son watched on with a scowl as his new stepmother smiled gleefully while removing the likelihood of him ever getting an inheritance. Chinh's two sisters shone in shimmering dresses on the arms of their aged husbands. All in all, it was a lovely ceremony.

Now, it was down to business. Tom had given me his stern pep talk before leaving; no out-of-control drinking, no wallowing, and no living on chocolate, no hiding at home, and definitely no major life decisions, while he was away. Some of those I could keep, but others would be broken before the weekend was out, if Carrie had anything to do with it.

After four shopping expeditions, none of which had ended with a suitable outfit for our girl's night, I finally found the dress of my dreams. It accentuated my curvy hips perfectly and still managed to hide, or at least control, the bits that liked to jiggle around. I had shaved my legs, plucked my eyebrows and curled my hair when the doorbell rang.

"Hang on," I yelled. "I'm still getting dressed."

Moments later I swung the door open expecting to see one of my sisters, but instead it was Peter standing there.

"Hi, Viv," he said, forcing a smile. "Can I come in?"

"Sorry, Peter, I'm on my way out," I blurted. He looked sad. I stepped aside and let him pass.

"You look great," he said, as he followed me through to the kitchen.

Of course, now he thinks I look great. A few months ago, I could have done naked star jumps in front of him and he wouldn't have given me a second look.

"Why are you here, Peter?"

"I miss you, that's all. I thought I'd pop by and see if you were busy."

I heard a car in the driveway. Shit, I hope it's not Carrie, she'd probably deck him.

It was Julia who walked into the kitchen.

"Hi, Peter," she said. She awkwardly avoided meeting his eyes. "Everything all right?" She asked, signalling me to let her know if it wasn't.

"Everything's fine, Julia," I assured her. "Peter and I were organising a time to go over some things and he was just leaving."

He nodded and flashed me another forced smile. "Will you walk me out?"

Out at the car, he took my hand, leaning in to kiss me before getting in.

I had definitely given him the wrong impression. I had let him think that we might get back together eventually, but that wasn't true.

"Can I see you tomorrow?" He asked through the open window. "I thought after last weekend..."

"I'm not sure, Peter." I cut in, "I need some time." I had no idea if we would get back together or if I could ever love or trust him again. It was just one kiss in the heat of the moment. I felt awful.

"That was a bit awkward," Julia laughed when I came back inside. "Quickly, finish getting ready. Annabel just texted – they're five minutes away."

***

I hadn't been to the city in years, not to nightclubs anyway. We started at an upmarket place in the lobby of a fancy hotel, but our raucous laughter was far too distasteful for their clientele.

'Murphy's', an Irish pub, was much more suitable.

"I wanna dance, c'mon," Annabel begged, dragging me to the dance floor. I hadn't even tapped a foot since my *Dirty Dancing* re-enactment. Julia joined in, dumping her bag in the middle of the circle we'd made. Carrie downed her 'Cowboy' shot and made her way over. She never bothered with a handbag, she just stuffed everything into the back pocket of her body crushing, tight black jeans.

"You're an idiot," Julia laughed, teasing Annabel's Mick Jagger pout and duck-arse dancing.

"Shut up. Look at you!" Annabel fired back.

Julia was all torso, she looked like she was trying to spin an invisible hoola-hoop.

"You can both shut up, I don't even want to hear it," I warned them, holding up my hand. Ever since we'd been old enough to get into clubs, they'd made fun of the way I danced. Granted, I had no sense of rhythm or coordination, but usually once I'd had enough to drink, I could pull some moves together.

"I'm getting another drink," Carrie announced. She preferred to sit at the bar and drink, pointing and laughing at us from the comfort of her stool. She downed three more before she came back to the dance floor. "Let's go, this place is boring, I know a great new place that's opened up."

The 'new' place was dark, dingy and some idiot kept activating the smoke machine and choking everyone to death. Despite being unable to breathe, the music was pumping, so we found a spot on the crowded dance floor and dropped our handbags.

The floor was packed, a giant pit of thrusting, sweaty bodies, made worse when I felt a hand run up the back of my leg.

"What's wrong?" Julia yelled into my ear as I spun around to look. There was another group of women dancing behind us and a man standing off to the side of the dance floor. Could he have made it over here and back that fast? I scanned the room. Did I imagine it? Am I that desperate for a man to touch me?

"Nothing, I just felt someone rub up the back of my leg."

"Good for you!" she hollered back, giving me a thumbs–up. Her eyes were already bloodshot, it wouldn't be long before she was on a couch somewhere. Once Julia was drunk, she always found a place to fall asleep.

I felt the hand on me again, but this time it was on my back. I spun around, desperate to see who it was, but no one was even looking at me. By the time I turned back, Carrie was escorting Julia to the nearest couch and gesturing to me that all was okay.

My cheeks flushed from the alcohol and heat, but my body was tingling with excitement. Who is touching me?

Annabel pointed to the toilet and left me standing in the middle of the dance floor with all of the handbags, alone. Perhaps a little subtle seductive dancing will entice my admirer out of hiding. I swayed my hips and pretended to close my eyes, peeking through a small slit. What if he's horrible or creepy? I quickly opened my eyes wide and straightened.

I took a gulp of my vodka and lime and noticed a man – no wait, a woman – watching me. Annabel, hurry up. I scanned the room for the culprit, but he was nowhere to be seen. In fact, there weren't any men to be seen at all.

It was only at that very moment that I realised Carrie had brought us to a gay bar.

I bent over to pick up the handbags when I sensed someone behind me. I stood up abruptly feeling dizzy as I spun around. The woman who had been watching me smiled and held out her hand for me to dance with her. She seemed nice enough, so what the hell. We danced for a few minutes, laughing and spinning each other until she leaned in and asked me if I wanted to get a drink.

"I'm here with my sisters," I apologised, "I think we're leaving soon."

She smiled and leaned in close, "Are you sure?" She whispered in my ear.

I pulled back slightly and looked at her. Her eyes were dark green and rimmed with black liner. She had high cheek bones and gloss covered lips, but her leather jacket gave her a slightly bad, edgy look. She was definitely attractive. Did she think I was a lesbian?

Mt lingering gaze had obviously given her the wrong impression. She moved closer and kissed me softly. "Another time then?" She asked.

I flashed her my most pleasant smile. "Thank you, I'm flattered, and you are beautiful, but I'm straight, I think," I apologised. I turned away and marched through the crowd to Carrie who was pissing herself laughing at the bar.

"Didn't take you long, did it?" she said. "You've turned into a try-anything party animal."

I whacked her hard on the arm. "You bitch, you watched every bit of that. You are so nasty," I hissed.

"What did I miss?" Annabel's bright, sober eyes were studying us.

"Nothing." I warned Carrie with a stern look and a shin kick.

She held up her hands in defeat, "my lips are sealed" she laughed, making a buttoning action against them, "but yours aren't!" I knew she would tell them both as soon as I was out of earshot and they would all think it was hilarious! I stomped off to the bathroom to make sure she knew I was mad, not that she'd care.

The harsh lights above the mirror made me squint as I wiped the black from under my eyes. I felt my lips with my finger. I didn't hate the kiss. Her lips were so much softer than Peter's, than I remember any man's being.

It was kind of sensual. Unexpectedly gentle and sweet with melon flavoured lip gloss. Great, now I'm enjoying kissing women, what next? I was trying to uncomplicate my life, not further complicate it.

I skulked out of the bathroom and back to my sisters. Julia was up and about with water in hand to aid in the sobering-up process. Next stop, as always, would be McDonalds.

They giggled and gossiped at the table while I ordered coffee. "So, what was it like kissing a chick for a change?" Carrie gloated. "She was hot."

"Is this the way you cheer your little sister up?" I asked, taking my seat at the table.

Julia scoffed her meal and then laid her head on the table, groaning. "C'mon, Viv, spill it," she mumbled.

"This is ridiculous. Obviously, I'm not a lesbian, but it was alright I suppose. She was actually very nice and if I hadn't known it was a woman, I probably would have really enjoyed it," I declared in a flat tone, deliberately devoid of emotion.

"I've always loved kissing women," Carrie shared, unnecessarily and to Annabel's horror. Carrie often just blurted things like that out. "They're so much more sensual than men."

"You need to get back on that horse, both of you," Carrie gestured to Annabel as well. "Get yourselves fixed up, cleaned up, and waxed, and we'll go speed dating on Thursday night. I know a place."

We were too tired to argue.

"It's a date," Carrie cheered triumphantly.

CHAPTER 10

Let the Games Begin

When I pulled up at Julia's on Tuesday, Steve's car was in the driveway. He usually worked away and only came home every couple of weeks. Unlike my lying, cheating gambler, Annabel's double-life banker and Carrie's half-dead old man, Julia had chosen well. Steve was moderately handsome, in a nerdy sort of way, and he treated her like a queen.

"Hey, Viv." He smiled when he opened the front door, giving me a big hug. "She's out the back."

When I stepped out onto the back deck, Julia was puffing and panting as she slowed the treadmill to a walk.

"What's up?" she said. "I wasn't expecting a visit from you."

"Nothing, just thought I'd pop in and have a coffee," I lied.

"Don't lie to me, Viv, I've been your sister for 39 years." She grinned, jumping off the moving mat and onto the sides of the treadmill. "Steve, honey," she called through the open kitchen window, "could you make us a coffee?"

"No worries, love."

We took a seat under the multi-coloured pergola, wind chimes clanging in the breeze. Julia painted everything – plant pots, retaining walls, chairs, mirrors – and each in a different colour. Her retro outdoor setting had been restored to new and the seats were adorned with seventies-style cushions with peace signs painted on them, by Julia.

"I'm confused, you know?" I began. "I feel like maybe I've given Peter the wrong impression. Then there's the fact that I didn't exactly hate kissing that woman and Tom's taken off overseas." I sounded whingey. "I just mean that everything has changed so much. A few weeks ago, I was still married and thought I knew who I was and what was expected of me."

"Have you heard from him? Tom?"

My heart sank, "Only the email he sent on the day he arrived. But since then, nothing."

Steve appeared with coffee and a plate of cake and biscuits, giving Julia a kiss on the top of the head before leaving us alone again.

"Don't worry too much," Julia continued. "It was a huge move for Tom and he's probably still trying to find his way around."

I stared at the floor, I couldn't look her in the eye. "After what I told you happened with Tom, Peter and I sort of got a bit intimate after the barbecue for Jack and Adam's birthday too. And then when that woman kissed me it, kind of ..." my words trailed off.

"Turned you on?"

I cringed as she said the words. I hated talking about this stuff.

"You and Tom are close, it doesn't surprise me that after all these years, and you finally breaking up with Peter, that your feelings are all over the place. And as for "getting intimate" with Peter, well it's not exactly uncommon for exes to hook up a few times after they split."

"I suppose, but it's all so messy and confusing. I feel like I've led Peter on, driven Tom away, and I might be considering women as another option."

"Oh, stop that." She laughed, hitting my arm. "The kiss with that woman was something new and different, it doesn't mean you're interested in women. You're going through so many changes, things are bound to be weird and feel weird for a while," she reassured me.

I wasn't so sure, but I felt better. Julia was like my compass, pointing me back in the right direction whenever I messed everything up.

"This is what I think," she went on. "Don't keep looking for confirmation that you're okay or loved. You've been in a relationship for half of your life and I think that you need to learn to rely on yourself, to find love, happiness and pleasure from within."

My body language gave away my scepticism. That was easier said than done.

"Viv, you have all of these external factors confusing you and making you feel different things. They're dictating whether or not you feel happy, or confident or get pleasure. It's time for you to take control."

Her words were making some sense finally. That's exactly what I wanted. To take control for myself and not let my happiness be so dictated by all of the outside forces. "How do I do that?"

"Come with me on a little shopping trip and we'll get some things that might help."

"What *things*?" My defences prickled.

"Just some toys, self-pleasure aids, that sort of thing."

Sex toys? I had been envisioning meditation and long walks.

"Absolutely not," I shrieked in a much higher pitch than I had intended. "You're out of your mind."

"Look at me," she insisted. "Do you trust me?"

"Yes ... kind of." Not really.

"Well, then let me help you with this. I know it makes you squeamish, but you're a big girl now, a big, *single* girl, and it's time for you to take charge. Believe me, when you're in control of your own sexuality and pleasure, then everything else follows."

I'd never understood how touching yourself could be sensual. Isn't the whole point to have contact with another human being, not an inanimate object? It was all a bit weird and unsettling, really.

"Look, just come with me," Julia persisted. "I was going there tomorrow afternoon anyway to get some things for myself."

That was way too much information.

"I'll pick you up at three," she insisted

There was no getting out of it now.

***

Despite our lack of 'toys' in the bedroom, Peter and I had a reasonable sex life, up until the last few years. At least *I* thought so. Neither of us was particularly experienced in the beginning, but we had gotten better as time went on. Would I ever have intimacy like that again? Ever have someone who knows me so well? Probably not, it was just something else lost with Peter's betrayal. I miss him. No, I don't, stop it.

My stomach felt as if it was tied in knots as I thought about a decent place to hide whatever Julia might force me to buy. What if one of the kids found it? The most I had ever had in the house was massage oil and a g-string.

The text message tone chimed on my phone. It was from Mum.

Have you spoken to Peter yet? Shall I come over and help you do some cleaning? I've got eggs for you.

The phone chimed again, seconds later.

Are you ignoring me? Call me or 'm coming over.

Argh! I picked up the phone and called her. "No, I'm not ignoring you, Mum, I'm just busy," I growled when she answered.

"Well, it seems like you never call back when I leave a message." She was using her "feel sorry for me" voice.

"I appreciate the offer, Mum, but the house if fine. And I've had weddings and appointments, that's why I haven't called." I thought about my bank account. Was there enough money to send her on another cruise?

"Have you seen Peter?" she pressed on.

"Yes, I've seen Peter and he's fine. He came over on Sunday for dinner and we talked. It doesn't mean we're getting back together."

"It doesn't mean you aren't either. It's a good step," she said happily. "Do you think he would mow my lawn?"

Kill me. Just kill me now.

"You have his number, so why don't you send him a text and ask," I said, in the sweetest voice I could manage.

"I will. I'll drop the eggs off later," she said.

"Text me when you're leaving home and if I'm not here, you can put them at the side of the house." I wanted her to give me enough notice so I could make sure I got away before she arrived.

"Okay. Love you. Bye." She said before hanging up.

Every conversation with my mother left me feeling like heading for the nearest bottle shop.

I threw on my sunglasses and Jack's baseball cap and called out to Natalia that I was leaving. I waited for Julia outside.

"Have you taken up a secret career as a spy, Mum?" Natalia laughed when she came out the door to her car. "I'm off to work, where are you going dressed like that?"

My lips moved, but nothing came out. I couldn't think of any plausible excuse.

"Mum, you weirdo, are you alright?"

"Oh, shut up you, I'm fine. I'm just waiting for your aunt Julia."

Natalia stopped at her car door and looked back at me suspiciously, "What's going on? You're acting weird."

"No, I'm not Natalia, get going." She was on to me.

"Are you and your crazy sisters up to something?"

My cheeks burned, "As far as I recall, Natalia, I'm the mother and you're the daughter, so get going to work."

She hopped in the car, laughing at me like I was a naughty child. I felt so guilty.

Julia came flying up the driveway as always. She almost ran me over.

"Watch it, you crazy woman!" I yelled, much to her amusement. I hated driving with her, she was always speeding and hitting things.

"Why are you here?" I asked Annabel, who was sitting in the passenger seat and looked as wary as I did.

"Apparently I've been single way too long and I'm a prude," she said, casting an accusing glare in Julia's direction.

"You two may mock me now, but you'll both be thanking me later." Julia's smug grin stretched from one side of her face to the other. "You both look ridiculous by the way," she said.

Annabel was more disguised than I was. Her sunglasses were bigger than her face and she was wearing a scarf, in the middle of summer. We looked like we were off to rob a bank rather than buy a sex toy.

As it turned out, 'Beavers' wasn't as seedy as I had anticipated. Situated on a main road, it had taken us fifteen minutes just to get in the door, with Annabel refusing to enter until there were no cars passing.

"I'm going in," Julia had waved, leaving us hiding behind the wall at the side of the shop.

"C'mon, let's just do it," I tried to convince Annabel, but she wouldn't budge. Eventually I resorted to the, "Right, I'm leaving you here. See ya," method, I used on the kids when they were little. Annabel came running in behind me.

Inside the hot pink walls of the shop, the contents were terrifying. How had I reached 39 years of age and not been aware of any of this? I felt like a naïve child. There were so many different vibrators. Are vaginas that different? The 'King Kong' was the size of a rolling pin!

"Do people honestly use this stuff?" I whispered to Annabel, who was hiding in the corner, smelling edible underwear.

"What about this, Viv?" Julia called, waving around a silver "slim touch".

"Julia!" I used my warning tone. "For goodness' sake."

I grabbed the vibrator out of her hand and put it back on the shelf next to 'The Art of Oral'. "Are you crazy? Don't say my name and don't wave that at me in public," I scolded.

"Don't say your name? What are we, spies? Stop or I'll vibrator you!" She giggled like a schoolgirl. She found this experience much funnier than I did.

"This is all right," Annabel called from the back, signalling us to come over. All she had managed to find was a cute set of undies that were thrown quickly back on the shelf when she realised the crotch was missing.

"Right, you two, that's it. You are both grown women and you need to start acting like it. You're behaving like big babies. There's no shame in buying things to improve your sex life. We're all sexual beings, now get on with it. We're not leaving here until you have something." She grabbed a whip off the shelf and waved it in front of us.

We both sulked off to different parts of the shop to find something. Anything.

"What's in here?" I said to Julia, heading to a door at the back of the store.

"You don't want to go in there," she said, stepping in front of me, "I think this is enough for you today." Given her tone, she was right. I didn't want to go in there.

Annabel finally settled on some edible underwear – which

she would likely, unwrap and eat in front of the telly – and a small leopard-print vibrator, along with some other essentials. I had chosen a shiny new mini "friend" and *Becoming Orgasmic* DVD. I handed them to the little old bearded lady behind the counter.

"You'll like this one, love," she assured me, waving the DVD. "It really shows you what to do. Worked for me."

I hid my uneasiness with a smile. Why did people feel the need to share intimate details with strangers?

In the back of the car, I peeked into my brown paper bag. They actually used brown paper bags, how cliché. It felt naughty, but exciting. Julia was right; it was time for a new beginning, for me to be totally self-reliant. Annabel, who was holding her bag under her T-shirt for fear of someone seeing, didn't look so enthused. I'd give her two days until she resorted to eating the undies herself.

***

When I got home, I checked my emails again. It had been well over a week since Tom left and still no word. No response to my emails or pleas for attention. It was as if he'd fallen off the face of the earth. How could he do this to me? The coffee I'd already re-heated in the microwave three times, went back in for one last attempt.

Why isn't he responding to my emails? I thought. What if he's dead? He can't be dead, because I would have heard by now. He's probably just done with me; fed up with my continual descent into disaster. He's probably drinking cocktails and enjoying a break from the drama.

He couldn't be. We needed each other, we were like two peas in a pod. Everything felt so different without him, without his presence, his reasonable advice.

He's probably met someone and doesn't want to tell me. I felt sick at the thought. What is wrong with me? Don't I want him to find love and be happy? I do, but not in England and not if it means losing 'us'.

It's my fault, I know it. I had confused things between us and he probably decided to make a clean break.

Carrie's name flashed on the screen of my phone. I picked it up. "Yes, Carrie?"

"Just checking that we're still on for tomorrow night? Annabel's already trying to back out, so don't you dare," she warned.

"What about your husband, Carrie?" I groaned. I didn't want to speed date, I didn't want to date at all. "Doesn't he mind you 'speed dating' while he's at home alone?"

"Edward doesn't care about anything other than his dinner and his naps, Viv. I've organised him so he couldn't care less. Anyway, I'm only going for you two, not me."

Carrie's husband was ancient. I wish I could say she married him for money so that at least that would explain the attraction, but Edward wasn't exactly loaded. They'd been married for five years. Luckily, her previous husband had left her some money when he passed away. It wasn't a fortune, but it was enough to allow her an easy, carefree lifestyle. She had married Edward out of love, but unfortunately their relationship declined quickly until she was little more than his carer. Carrie had only ever dated old men. She'd been that way for as long as I could remember. Every decade she aged, so did they. We teased her that she'd be scouting out potential dates at the old folks home if anything ever happened to Edward.

"Anyway, he's had the flu," said Carrie, "so he's miserable and annoying."

"Okay," I said finally. "I'll go, but only if Annabel comes too. I'm not being tortured alone."

"Oh, I almost forgot," she said. "Tom called and said he'd tried to reach you at home, but you weren't there."

"What?" I said urgently. "What do you mean? When did he call, what did he say?" I had been home most of the week, except for a few trips to the shops and to pay bills.

"Calm down. He said he'd been really busy and that he didn't have good internet where he was staying so he hadn't been able to respond to emails. He told me to tell you he was heading out to do some work in the country and would be un-contactable for a couple of weeks."

Un-contactable? For *weeks*?

"Why didn't he try again, or ring my mobile?" I really wanted to talk to him. "Didn't he want to speak to me in person?" I seethed through gritted teeth.

"Viv, I don't know, he said he'd tried. Cheer up, he'll be back soon anyway."

I hung up the phone. Cheer up? How the hell am I supposed to cheer up? Why didn't he call my mobile or email or Skype me? Now he was going to be un-contactable for weeks. Tears dropped onto my chest. I grabbed a bottle of wine and a block of Old Jamaica, and settled in for a night of self-pity.

I fell asleep halfway through the bottle watching re-runs of *Everybody Loves Raymond*. The nothingness on the inside of my eyelids was a welcome relief from my paranoid delusions, until I was rudely woken by the clanging of pans in the kitchen.

"Mum, where's the frying pan?" Adam hollered.

"Where it always is, under the oven."

The smell of bacon and eggs wafted from the kitchen, making me feel ill. Jack came to sit at my feet and handed me a coffee.

"Geez, Mum, hard night? You do realise it's only Thursday," he grinned.

"Shut up, cheeky," I said, sitting up and smoothing my hair into a ponytail. "What are you two up to?"

"We've got a pupil-free day so we're making breakfast, then heading to the field for some practice games."

"Hey Mum," said Jack, "Natalia said you've decided to give up being a celebrant. Is that true?"

Was there anything Natalia didn't know? "Yes, I have. I think I just need a break from it all."

"Will you get a job?" He asked

" I'm not sure what I want to do just yet, but I'll find something else."

"Just remember, Mum," Adam chimed in from the doorway, flashing his cheeky smile, "this year's been tough for all of us, so when we finish year twelve, we all need a break."

It was typical of him to always be working some angle. He'd been dropping hints about an end of year trip to Europe for months.

"We'll see," I said, getting a towel from the linen cupboard. "You better talk to your father about it."

Over the sound of the shower, I could hear them making

plans, working out how to convince us that a gap year overseas was a good idea.

Good luck with that.

CHAPTER 11

The wedding of Mary and Chuck (Crier and big head)

"Excuse me, I think you might be in the wrong spot," I called to the woman who was clearly in the wrong spot, "I have a wedding booked here at 12:30."

"Well, this is where I was told to set up, and my ceremony is at twelve, so I guess that makes me first," she smiled.

"Well, where you're setting up isn't a designated area. I've been doing weddings here for years and there's either over there by the waterfall, or here under the rotunda," I said, holding out my arms. "You're only 50 feet from me." Thank goodness I'd arrived early.

"Well, I've already set up my table and my PA system," she shrugged. "And we did book well in advance."

Bugger! Guests for her wedding had already begun to arrive.

What now? I missed Tom, he should have been shooting this wedding. He would have known what to do.

"Well, I'm going to go ahead and set up. My ceremony at starts at 12:30, so if your guests can't hear, then I apologise in advance," I declared sweetly, unpacking my bag.

She didn't respond as she strode over to her PA system, eyes firmly on me, and turned the volume knob to full with a smug grin.

A tap on my shoulder stopped me from lassoing her skinny neck with the cord from my microphone.

"Is there another wedding right there?" Chuck's gigantic head was blocking the sun.

"Unfortunately, yes," I answered. "That celebrant claims she's in the right place and that it was booked well in advance."

I took a step back as pulsing veins bulged from Chuck's wide neck.

"They can't do that!" His nostrils flared like a dragon about to blow fire. "When Mary and I booked with the Council they said there was only one other wedding here today, and it was over at the waterfall." He was burning red.

"Where they're set up isn't even a designated spot," I added, taking another step back. "But I'm sorry, Chuck, there's nothing I can do. I can't force them to pack up and leave. We'll have to just go ahead, or delay the ceremony until they're finished."

Chuck's brain was ticking over as he contemplated his move. "Bullshit!" he hollered, striding over to his groomsmen.

Shit, all I need is a brawl. Why can't anything run smoothly anymore? I opened my briefcase and took out my feathered pen and folder. Where was my folder? The image of it sitting on my desk flashed in my mind. No! My chest constricted as the pace of my thumping heart rapidly increased. All noise disappeared, blocked out by the thudding in my ears. I checked the time, 11:45. I can't go back and get it. Shit! Shit! Shit!

Chuck was saying something to me, but I couldn't hear a thing. Guests were already beginning to arrive. In 45 minutes there would be approximately one hundred gathered in front of me and I had no ceremony, no notes. Nothing.

I turned to Chuck. "Why don't we just call Mary and let her know what's happened and see if she would prefer to delay the ceremony by half an hour?" I suggested. That would give me time to call someone and get them to bring me the folder.

"No bloody way!" Chuck shouted. "Those rotten bastards can delay their cheap-ass wedding. Mary will be furious."

It had been months since I'd met with Mary and Chuck, before Christmas actually, and Mary hadn't struck me as someone who got furious. She'd sat in my office with her legs crossed, holding on to Chuck for dear life. She'd burst into tears four times just planning the ceremony.

"Oh, it's so lovely," she'd cried, when I read out the options for their vows. "It's just perfect!" she'd exclaimed, when I gave her a copy of the introduction I had written. "I'm such a mess," she'd sobbed, as she walked from my front door onto the lawn in a practice run.

Chuck was wrong, Mary wouldn't be furious, she would cry. And cry. And cry.

"I'm going over there to sort them out," said Chuck. "They're not getting away with this," he insisted, heading straight for the groom.

I dug into my bag and rifled around for my phone. Chuck's voice was getting louder, as was the other groom's. I ducked behind the gazebo and dialled Natalia, she could bring me my folder.

"Mum, I can't talk, I'm at work," she whispered. "I'll call you on my break." Then the phone went dead.

Who else? Carrie! I'll get Carrie to bring it.

Carrie's phone rang out and went to voicemail. I tried again. No luck. Shit! The phone beeped with a message as I peeked around the gazebo to check on Chuck. He was now flanked by two of his groomsmen, and things were looking ugly. Maybe there'd be a fight? That would be perfect; it'd buy me some time.

What an awful thing to wish for something like that! I'm awful. Please God or the Universe, just let something happen so I can get this folder.

My phone buzzed with a message from Carrie.

At an appointment. Call you after.

Far out, what was up with her? She'd postponed speed dating Thursday night, claiming she had a migraine, and every time I tried to talk to her, she was busy. Speed dating was going ahead tomorrow night instead, so I'd bail her up there and find out what was going on.

I danced on the spot, trying to hold my nervous bladder and keep an eye on Chuck. As usual, Julia's phone wasn't even on, and Annabel was busy EFT'ing a client. I checked the time, 11:55. There was no way I could get that folder in 35 minutes.

Peter. I had to ask Peter, he was the only one who could get over there in time and had spare keys. What if he thinks I'm disorganised and hopeless as usual? Why did I even care what he thinks? There was no one else I could call.

"I'm really sorry and I don't like asking, given the circumstances," I said a moment later when Peter answered the phone. "But I'm stuck, Peter. I'm at the park setting up for a wedding and I've forgotten my ceremony folder."

"Viv, it's no problem, I'll get it for you. I'm glad you thought of me."

Well, I did try everyone else first. "Thank you, but please hurry. If I have to start without it, I'm stuffed. I'll meet you in the carpark."

Chuck was stomping back with his posse behind him. "Bunch of wankers," he griped. "We'll see how they like a bit of noise during their wedding. Did you see their suits?" He said to his two groomsmen who were standing either side of him. One of them was obviously related, probably his brother, given the similar head size. The other had to be nearly seven foot tall.

They reminded me of the Munsters. Stop it. You're so mean. This is why Karma is getting you! I told myself. I promise God, Universe, whatever, that if you just help me get out of this one, I'll try to be nicer. I'll do something charitable. I swear.

"Look, Chuck, let's just delay the ceremony," I suggested hopefully. Please Chuck, please. We have no ceremony anyway. "Then they'll be out of the way and we can take our time and have the place to ourselves."

He seemed to be considering it.

The PA system came alive with Celine Dion as bride number one appeared at the top of the laneway.

The celebrant, pleased with her win, shot me a sly smile.

"See, it's too loud," I said. "You need to call Mary right now and tell her to hold off an extra half an hour. Let's make it a 1:00 start instead?"

He was caving. Thank you, God.

"Here, you call her." He thrust the phone into my hand. "It's bad luck for me to talk to her."

I didn't want to call Mary. My nerves were already shot. "Hi Mary, it's Viv, the celebrant," I said when she picked up.

"What's wrong? What's happened?" she said anxiously.

"Nothing major, don't be alarmed." It was too late, she was alarmed. "We have a little bit of a situation with another wedding that has been set up right next to us, and they've already begun."

She was sobbing. Did her cat just die? Did war break out? Did I steal her taco? It's delaying a wedding ceremony, not a meteor speeding towards earth. "It's fine, Mary, but Chuck and I thought it best to delay the ceremony by just half an hour or so and let them finish up before we commence. What do you think?"

"What do I think?" she said between heaves. "What do I think?"

I waited with my fingers crossed.

"I think that this is ridiculous and the council are going to get a piece of my mind. It's totally unfair."

Chuck was right. She was furious. Technically we were both right, because she was crying and furious. I didn't think she had it in her.

"You are absolutely right, Mary," I soothed. "If I were you, I'd be asking for my money back."

The sobbing calmed. I was winning.

"And," I added to sweeten the deal, "I'm happy to stay as long as you need, at no extra cost, of course. This is so unfair to you and Chuck."

The crying stopped. *Hallelujah!*

"Is Chuck okay? How's he handling it? He has a bit of a temper."

"He's doing fine," I lied. "See you shortly."

Chuck and his two side-kicks were currently involved in a master plan to disrupt the other wedding. The big one was lying on the ground, behind the gazebo, slowly dragging his body between the bushes toward the PA system – to do who knows what – while Chuck and the other one made their way to the back of the group, laughing and making rude noises. Classy.

I hung up and signalled a thumbs up to Chuck. Please Peter, hurry!

"There's been a slight change of plans," I explained to the gathering guests. "We'll be starting a little later, due to ..." I gestured toward the other group, where the couple were pouring coloured sand into a jar as part of a unifying ritual.

I ducked behind the gazebo and called Peter for an update. "I've just left the house, I won't be long," he said.

"I'm heading up to the carpark now," I told him. "Just pull up when you see me and I'll grab it."

I headed for the bathroom, but heard the bride's car before I even shut the door. Half an hour! I told her half an hour.

I turned and ran for the car, "Hi Mary, you're a little early," I said, popping my head in the window. "They're just about finished. Driver, any chance you can go around the block once or twice? You know, to give the other wedding time to quieten down."

Mary's bottom lip was trembling. Oh, Mary for goodness sake. Enough already. Everyone is stressed here!

"You'll be married soon, don't worry," I smiled reassuringly.

Peter's car flew into the carpark as the bride's car exited. Tears of relief filled my eyes. "Thank you, Peter. You've saved my bacon. I was literally about to have a heart attack."

I took in a deep breath for the first time since I'd arrived, and noticed the sweet aroma of the blooming roses. It was going to be fine.

"No worries, Viv," said Peter. "I'm so happy I could actually help and do something positive. It means a lot that you called me."

There was no time for this now. "Okay, I've gotta run, but thanks."

I inhaled another deep breath, shaking off my wired nerves, and headed back to the park. I had only minutes before Mary would return. I rubbed my jaw which was sore from being held tight with the stress. I hadn't even made it to the bottom of the path when two police cars flew into the carpark, sirens blaring. Six officers ran past me while I looked back to see Mary, crying through the window of her limo.

Arghhhhh, crap!

At two pm the wedding of tear-streaked Mary and bleeding Chuck finally began, after police broke up the brawl between the two groups and had carted off one of Chuck's grooms-men, charged with assault. The ceremony was perfect, despite the couple being surrounded by the filthy best man who was covered in grass stains and Chuck's father who was filling in for the arrested groomsman. Mary's mother spent the entire time glaring at Chuck for spoiling her daughter's big day. Of course, Mary cried.

***

I didn't bother wiping away the steam from the mirror. It was a tough day, you can't expect to look fabulous, I consoled myself. I pulled on my suck-it-in knickers and bra and headed to the bedroom.

When I caught sight of my full-body reflection in the regrettable mirrored doors, I realised I didn't actually look too bad. I was heavier than I used to be, but still only a size 14 and the extra weight actually filled out the fine lines of my face, making me look a bit younger. I was feeling good until I noticed that tufts were hanging out the sides of my underwear. What if I met someone at speed dating? Or decide to have a one-night stand?

I called Julia, she waxed everything.

"Haven't you ever waxed it all off?" She laughed.

"No, I have not!" I replied.

"Viv, you need to grow up. Don't you even know what your body looks like?"

"Like everyone else's, I assume. Why would I even look, Julia? All I want is to get a wax."

"Well get a wax, but you should know every part of your own body. For yourself and for your health. Years ago, a reliable source – *Dolly* magazine – quoted some doctor as saying that every woman should, at some time in her life, get completely familiar with her body by investigating every part of it. Genitals and breasts included." She was so full of useless wisdom.

I don't even know why I called her. She was obviously deranged. I thought about my new resolution: *Rely only on myself.* Maybe she was right. I needed to know what I was dealing with.

Jack and Adam were out, but Natalia was home. I crept down to her bedroom. She was fast asleep after another all-night shift at the cafe. She'd be sleeping for hours. I stopped at the pantry and swigged a mouthful of Bailey's from the bottle. I'd been drinking far too much lately, I really needed to slow down.

I inhaled deeply and closed the curtains.

I was completely ready to embrace my femininity until I saw what it looked like.

I'm definitely not a lesbian, I decided. That was not attractive at all.

Panic stricken, I wrapped a towel around my waist and searched the house for the iPad. Is that how they're supposed to look? I found it and took another swig from the Baileys, before Googling to check. It was fine; they all kind of looked like that, give or take.

I changed the search to waxing styles. How can there be this many? There were pages of them. I flicked through until I found one I liked. The short strip down the middle was perfect. If I ever wanted to feel confident in my own skin or dare to have an intimate relationship with anyone, then I had to fix it. It was fixable.

CHAPTER 12

The Best Laid Plans

The instructions looked simple:

1. *Warm wax strip between palms and slowly peel apart.*
2. *Smooth onto skin in direction of hair growth.*
3. *Hold skin taut and firmly zip strip back.*

Sounds straight forward. Place in direction of hair growth? There was no direction. It was all over the place. I tried flattening it to one side, but there was no direction. What the heck are they on about? Maybe I should cut it first. I checked the box. It didn't say to cut it. With one leg on the bath tub, I warmed the strip in my hands and pulled it carefully apart. Step one. Done. Finally, we're getting somewhere.

I placed one strip over my left leg/bikini line, not that I could even see the line, and the other on the right, smoothing it down as instructed. This is easy. Please don't hurt too much. Deep Breath. I held the skin with flat fingers and yanked at the strip. Despite my screaming and thrashing about, the strip only came away on one end while the other hung on. One clump! All that pain and only one, tiny clump. I bent down to look. My poor red, raw skin was erupting with tiny little blood spots.

Shit, how do I get it off? I pulled gently at it, picking at the wax strip, but it was holding tight. It was like super glue. Why would anyone put this on their skin?

Grabbing a flannel, pain searing through my groin with every hair pinching move, I carefully moistened the area. Nothing. How the hell do you remove these things? I had broken into a panic sweat. Soapy water, hand wash and toothpaste, only added to the pain of my irritated skin. As I contemplated my next move, the doorbell rang. No! No! No! Go away. I stood completely still as the two steadfast strips hung from my lady parts.

"Viv, it's Mum and Dad," the horrifying voice called while the dead bolt on the front door unlocked with a clunk. I leapt, agonisingly, just reaching the lock on the bathroom door as her footsteps approached. I regretted ever giving mum a set of keys. "Are you here?" she called.

Stay quiet, maybe she won't find me. I scanned the room for the headphones Natalia sometimes used when she took a bath. I could say I was listening to something and didn't hear her. She was at the door.

"Viv?"

"Oh sorry, Mum. I'm in the bath. My head was under the water, I didn't hear you."

"You sound like you're near the door." She was a master at uncovering deception.

I jumped back and stood in the bath tub, "No, I'm just getting out. What's up?"

"Just came for a visit. I'll pop the kettle on."

What the hell are they doing here? Right now? They had to come right now! Scissors, I needed scissors. I rifled through the drawers until I found a pair. Nail scissors. Great.

Hacking at it, I tried to cut beneath the strip. I snipped and pulled, but it had actually glued itself to my skin in some places. I managed to cut away some of the plastic from the strip, but the pain was too much.

"Tea's ready," Mum called from the kitchen.

Sliding my tracksuit pants on, I carefully walked to the kitchen, "Bad back," I answered her questioning eyes before her mouth even moved.

I lowered slowly into the kitchen chair across from Dad, who was already scoffing mixed nuts from my 'healthy snacks' box.

"Any chance after your cuppa you can drop us at the train station?" Mum said, placing the steaming tea in front of me. I knew there was an ulterior motive.

"Your father and I are heading into the city and you know how I hate leaving the car there with all those..." she searched for the right word, "unemployed criminals."

Nailed it.

"I know it's not that far from here, but you know your father, he can't walk that far." Dad looked up from the nut box. He could walk just fine, in fact he walked his dog every morning. It was Mum who couldn't make her way around a shopping centre without sitting down five times. For a split second, he looked as if he was going to argue the point, but decided against it. We all learned long ago there was no point arguing with Mum. It wasn't because she was fabulous at making her case, it was because it went in one ear and out the other. It was a waste of everyone's time and energy.

I winced as the strips pulled uncomfortably. "Why don't you just take my car, Mum?" How am I supposed to drive with this crap stuck to me? The pain was unbearable.

"I'd rather you just drop us there, love, if you don't mind." It wasn't a request, "Oh and why is your hair dry if your head was under the water?" She had me. As usual, she had outsmarted my deception. She was a master. I excused myself to the bathroom for one last attempt.

"Honey, we need to get going," she called.

Damn you, woman!

By the time I got back from the station it had intensified to a burning pain. Nothing worked, they were completely stuck. I burst into uncontrollable, hysterical tears. Why doesn't ANY-THING, EVER, work out for me? How can I stuff up a simple bikini wax this badly?

There was no avoiding it. I swallowed hard and called Julia. She was helpful when she finally stopped laughing, "You need to either use baby oil, or the cleansing wipe they give you in the pack, and if all else fails, cut them out."

"Baby oil? Who has baby oil laying around with no baby?" I found the wet wipe sachet and tore it open. "It's the size of a bloody postage stamp, Julia," I screamed down the line.

The wet wipe was useless, with so much attached to the strip I couldn't even get near the sticky stuff. I picked up the scissors. There had to be a way.

"Jesus, Viv, only you. Honestly."

"Shut up. Do you think I don't know that? Why is it me? Why doesn't this stuff happen to you or Carrie or anyone else for that matter? The Universe hates me," I sulked.

I curled into a ball to see what the hell I was doing. "Have you got them off?"

"No, bloody hell. Wait a minute. It's bad enough without chopping something off!" I hacked away at it as carefully as I could, until finally one strip fell loose and then the other. "They're off!" I squealed, jumping to my feet and breaking into a painful victory dance. I was happy until I saw it.

"Shit, Jules, you should see it." My relief faded as horror set in, "I have bald patches and bright red bleeding bits."

I heard her snort. "The salon closes at five, you've got an hour. Go get it fixed."

***

The twelve-year-old beauty therapist gasped at the war zone that appeared before her stunned eyes.

"What the hell happened to you, honey?" she said as she moved her green chewing gum from one side of her mouth to the other.

"Home waxing kit," I muttered.

"You did this to yourself? I've never seen a wax job this bad," she declared, "Joanna, come check this out."

I wasn't aware that her fee included a running commentary on how badly I stuffed it up. Just fix it and shut your chomping mouth.

"Far out!" Joanna obviously hadn't seen one this bad either.

You know what? Stick it up your backsides. Whatever. Laugh away, because I'm over it. I relaxed back onto the pillow and concentrated on the tiny piece of web dangling from the ceiling. You won't break me. I've had far worse than you.

After numerous rips, yanks and sighs from the child, insinuating I had completely ruined her day, it was finally done.

"Now make sure you look after it and get it done regularly, so it doesn't get so out of control next time."

I left the salon and went straight home. Despite some redness and tingling it was baby smooth. Now this I can take speed dating.

**

"This is so embarrassing!" I sooked, pointing at the eager speed daters when we arrived that night. "These people all look like this is their last resort."

"Stop whinging, Viv, give it a chance." Carrie wasn't her usual self. She seemed tired or irritated or something.

"Well, I'm going to give it a go. I'm over being single and I want to find a man." Annabel was already signing us in.

"What's wrong with you?" I said to Carrie, "you cancelled on us Thursday and now you seem like you don't want to be here. You made us come, remember?"

"Yes, I know, now shut up and sign in," she ordered through a forced smile and headed to her usual place at the bar. Something was up. I knew my sisters inside and out and there was definitely something bothering her.

"You look lost, can I help?" I turned to see a handsome face with crystal blue eyes gazing down at me.

"No, it's fine. I'm just not sure why I'm here," I answered.

"You're probably here for the same reason as the rest of us," he said politely. "To meet new people and have a bit of light-hearted fun. That's why I come," he grinned, pushing his dark locks behind his ears.

Come? As in more than once? "How many times have you been to one of these? To be honest it seems pretty lame."

"I come all the time because I run it."

Excuse me a moment, nice man, while I extricate my over-grown foot from my very large mouth.

"Let me get you a drink. Believe me, it'll help loosen you up," he offered, heading to the bar and giving Carrie a hug.

Do they know each other?

"My name's Darcy," he said, returning with a pink champagne.

"Thank you, Darcy, I'm Genevieve. I'm sorry if I was rude be-fore, I suffer from eternal foot-in-mouth disease. I just find this all a bit uncomfortable." I swallowed the wonderful pink liquid and tried to relax. "I haven't had a date in 20 years." Oh, that didn't come out right. "Not that I couldn't get a date in 20 years, I could. If I'd wanted to. But I didn't. Because I was married. And had children. Three." Oh God, I'm rambling. SHUTUP!

I took another large mouthful and turned my attention back to the potential suitors before I managed to blurt out anything else ridiculous.

"Hurry up! Get over here, we're about to start." Annabel was waving her hand in frantic spasms.

"Aren't you participating?" I asked Carrie, who was already on her third drink.

"You two are the single ones. I told you, I'm just here for moral support. Plus, if I played, they'd all fall for me and there'd be none left for you two."

I poked my tongue out at her and sat beside Annabel. She was twitching and tapping and muttering about accepting herself. I quickly moved a seat down. I hoped no one saw me with her, she looked like a nutcase.

Robbo – according to his upside-down name tag – was my first "date". He plonked himself into the seat across the small table and gave me a wink. "How's it going, honey?"

Great, before you called me honey. "Fine thanks, and you?"

"Not bad, but pretty unimpressed with the talent here to-night," he said, gesturing to the other women seated at various tables around the room.

Talent? Most of these women, who were probably all very nice, had most likely spent hours preparing and talking them-selves into coming here tonight just to have to put up with dickheads like Robbo.

"Have a look at them," he went on. "They're all middle-aged and desperate. And that one," He openly pointed to a 40-some-thing, largish woman across the room, "she's got a moustache thicker than mine."

Did he own a mirror? Robbo was probably in his mid-forties, with grey hair, pulled back into a creepy ponytail. He smelled like a vile mix of Grecian Five Thousand and cigarette smoke. Robbo was not in any position to be casting stones.

"Well, we can't all be gorgeous, can we?" I replied. Five minutes was way too long to have to spend with each 'date'.

I shot an eye roll in Carrie's direction. Why did I even agree to this? Robbo was rambling on about something to do with dirt bikes as I smiled and signalled to Darcy that I needed another drink.

Relief swept over me like a cool summer breeze as the timer rang. "Bye, Robbo," I smiled, watching him move to the next poor victim. Relief, however, was short-lived as "Marco" took a seat opposite me.

Annabel was shaking her head and making faces at me. What on earth was she trying to say?

He had dragged his chair around beside me and was inches from my face. "How's it goin', darlin'?" He said in a husky attempt at a seductive tone. His breath stank. "I'm glad there's someone here worth my attention."

Tufts of black hair sprang out from beneath his bright-green tank top, unfortunately from the tops of his shoulders, rather than his chest. "Why's a decent lookin' broad like you, coming to a hole like this to meet a fella?"

Was he talking to his bicep or me? It was difficult to tell, given that he constantly glanced back and forth from me to his large muscle, flexing it, I assume in an attempt to impress me. At least he said I was decent looking. I'd take that.

I swallowed back the bile that rose in my throat and scanned the room for Darcy. Where the hell was my drink?

"Your drink Madam." Darcy's hot breath blew across my ear and down my neck, while Marco and his biceps moved to the next table. He leaned over me, placing a fresh glass of pink champagne on the table, the heat from his chest penetrating through his thin black shirt and onto my back. My skin reacted with the eruption of a million tiny goosepimples. I took a large mouthful of champagne and turned to him, our faces hitting as he leaned in to whisper again.

"Sorry," I apologised, taking in the sweet smell of his spice-scented cologne. "What are you wearing?" I asked, unable to shake the delicious scent from my nose.

"Isn't that what you normally ask on a 1800 line?" He joked.

"I meant cologne, what cologne are you wearing?" I laughed.

"Do you like it?" He grinned, touching my arm gently, while my next date, "Gordon" dragged the seat beside me back to its rightful position.

Go away, Gordon! I cursed, watching Darcy retreat back to the bar, his eyes on me. My arm still tingled from the sensation of his stroke.

"Hi, I'm Gordon," smiled the pimply redhead.

"Hi, Gordon," I managed, my eyes still drawn to Darcy. "What do you do for a living?" I really didn't care, but I had five minutes to kill before I could get Darcy to come back over here.

This could be it. My chance to let go and do something fun. Darcy's gorgeous and I have a fabulous looking vagina.

"Are you actually listening to me?" Gordon didn't look impressed. "Why are you even here if you don't want to talk to people?" he complained, as spittle flew out of his mouth and landed in tiny pools all over the table.

"I'm sorry, Gordon," I apologised, "I'm a little distracted."

"Everything okay here?" Darcy asked, saving me from Gordon's wrath. "Genevieve, I think it's probably best if you leave the dating tables, given that you are unable to give the dates your full attention," he scolded, flashing me a sly wink.

Gordon nodded, pleased that I was in trouble.

"Come with me," Darcy said sternly, taking my arm.

I met Carrie's eyes. She was watching us intently, her smile triumphant, as Darcy led me behind the bar to the office.

Shit! This is it. Relax. Go with it. You're a single, mature woman.

Darcy linked his fingers through mine and led me into the dark office.

"I can't see," I giggle. Every nerve in my body was standing on end as he backed me up against the wall. The computer screen was casting blue shards of light across the small room, enough to see his eyes looking intensely into mine as he pressed himself firmly against me. Then his lips came down on mine, moving in slow, circular motions. I gripped the back of his hair.

I'm on fire, this is amazing.

Darcy rotated his body hard against me, his lips moving from my mouth to my neck, while I filled my lungs with his delicious scent.

I want him. I want him.

I'd been cheated. I hadn't felt this kind of passion, ever. Peter and I had always enjoyed each other, but not like this. This was brilliant. This was what I'd been missing out on.

Darcy's hand rubbed sensually across my back and found the bottom of my shirt. He traced the line up my spine as my insides caught fire. God, take me. Take me! His hand made its way around to my breast, while the other one pressed the back of my head, holding my lips firm against his.

"Darcy, we need you out here," came a voice from outside the door.

No!

Darcy's lips pulled gently away from mine, his body making one final thrust against me.

"I have to get back out there. Can we continue this later?" he whispered.

Continue this later? When later? I was so hot and out of breath I couldn't respond. How could he leave it like this? I wasn't going to be able to go back out there.

Darcy leaned in and gave me one, final, intense kiss before leaving me there, flustered. If this is what single life had to offer, maybe I could get used to it.

CHAPTER 13

What really matters

By Thursday Tom had been gone for seventeen days and had still only sent one email and made one pathetic attempt to call. I hate him. No, I don't, I love him. But I hate him. Did he know how much this was torturing me? It was time to tell him.

genevieve.celebrant@yourperfectday.com:

Hi Tom, I thought I'd email you and see how things are going and let you know how much I completely and totally hate you right now. If I wasn't busy having so much fun, I would be mad enough to tell you to get lost. But I won't because you're my friend. I understand that you're busy and maybe things are going well for you there, but how can you just forget about me like this and not even bother to email or call more than once? I was pretty sad when you left, and I thought you'd at least care about how I'm doing. I care about how you're doing.

Anyway, I really do hope that everything is working out for you over there and obviously it is because if it wasn't you would probably have emailed or rang to tell me. So, have fun, and I suppose I'll see you if you ever bother to come back, or call, or Skype, or something!

From heartbroken, Viv.

Too dramatic? Maybe. Too bad. I wanted him to feel guilty. I missed him so much. I wanted to hear his voice. He's not coming back.

The phone interrupted my paranoid thoughts.

"Viv, it's Julia." Her tone sounded heavy and my throat instinctively tightened.

"What's wrong?" In the split second it took Julia to draw a breath, I imagined a hundred different scenarios, and refuted them all. If it was Mum or Dad, I was down as next of kin, so they would have contacted me in an emergency. Maybe it was Steve? He could have been hurt, but then it would probably be Annabel or Carrie calling.

"It's Carrie," she said, choking on her name, "she's in the hospital."

It was hard to make out what she said after that. Her words were inaudible, either from her crying or my inability to absorb what she was saying.

"Can you come here now? Annabel's on her way."

I dropped the phone and tried to move, but I felt heavy, my body not properly listening to the instructions my brain was trying to give it.

"Natalia," I cried out, grabbing at random things on the kitchen bench. I had no idea what to take.

"Mum, what's wrong?" Natalia took my arm.

"Can you take me to Aunty Julia's? Where are the boys?"

"They're in their room doing homework. Mum, tell me what's happened." Her eyes were full of fear.

"Carrie, she's in the hospital. I don't know ... Julia said she's sick."

"Sick with what?" She looked more frightened than I had ever seen her.

"I don't know, but Julia was crying and she said we have to go there now."

The words didn't even sound like mine. It was as if they were being spoken by someone else, across a noisy room. I got out a cup and put on the kettle.

"Mum, what are you doing? I'll tell the boys what's happening. Get your bag and let's go."

She was being practical, Natalia was always practical.

I got out the milk. "Mum, let's go!" she demanded, returning with Adam and Jack.

"Are you okay, Mum?" Jack asked, taking it from my hands.

"She's just in shock," Adam said with authority.

"Let's go, Mum," said Natalia. "It'll be fine. We just need to see what's going on. We don't even know if it's anything really bad."

It's bad. I knew it was bad. Julia would never react like that unless there was something terribly wrong.

"She's been weird the past few weeks, you know?" There was no emotion in my words. "She cancelled speed dating and then she was acting weird when we went the other night."

"It might be something simple, Mum, like an infection or gastro. Don't jump to conclusions until we know more."

Natalia was right. We didn't know anything, at least not until Julia opened the door when we arrived at her house.

"Carrie's got breast cancer," she sobbed, taking my arm. Natalia grabbed my other arm as my legs weakened.

"Natalia, can you take us to the hospital?" Annabel asked. Neither she nor Julia were in any state to drive.

"From what I can gather," Julia explained through stifled tears, "she had a biopsy last Saturday. She went back yesterday and saw the doctor for the results, and that's when they confirmed it was cancer. She has to have surgery."

Tiny butterflies filled my stomach. They made their way through my veins, causing my hands and feet to tingle as rage filled my mouth with a bitter taste.

"Why the fuck didn't she tell me!" I screamed, thumping my thigh. "Why did she keep this from me? From us. She knew. She knew and she didn't tell us."

That was the appointment she said she was at when I called from my ceremony. She hadn't called me back like she promised. She knew. And I felt betrayed.

"Viv, you know Carrie," said Julia. "She probably didn't tell anyone. I only found out because Edward called. Don't be mad at her right now, we need to be there for her. You can be mad later," she pleaded.

How could I not be mad? She had lied to me, to my face when I asked her at speed dating what was wrong. I should have pursued it. Why didn't I pursue it? Because I'm damn self-absorbed and worried about myself all the time. That's the problem. That's why. Cause I'm self-absorbed and I don't think of anyone else.

Annabel put her arm around me, "She'll get through this. But when we walk in there, we need to smile and help her be brave. If she sees us break down, she'll break down too, and she needs to draw on our strength right now."

I sucked in a long breath and dabbed my face with a tissue. "Lipstick on and a spray of perfume. Let's do this," Annabel said.

***

"How are you feeling?" Annabel asked when we arrived at Carrie's bedside. I could see she was tapping on her wrist.

She can't bloody help herself.

"I'm feeling fine, just a bit tired. The surgeon should be here in a minute."

My throat was already constricting and I swallowed hard.

"What time is the surgery?" Julia asked, leaning in to give her a hug.

Carrie sat up in the bed, her hair pulled back tightly in a ponytail. Her face looked pale, almost ghostly, against the glaring white of the walls.

"Fancy seeing you here," was all I could think of to say. Carrie smiled, but it was forced.

"Hi, Edward," I turned my attention instead to her elderly husband in the armchair beside her bed.

"I've brought you in some goodies from the kiosk," Natalia offered. "I'll pop them in your drawer. It's just some chocolate and a magazine."

"Thanks, honey," Carrie kissed the top of her head as she put them away.

"Mrs Cameron." A doctor came into the room, followed by

three students. "My name is Doctor Durbinder, and I'll be performing your surgery today."

Surgery today? Shit, this was really happening.

"We'll be taking you down in about an hour or so."

"What exactly will I be having done?" Carrie asked. Her voice was wavering.

My eyes filled as Natalia sat beside me. "It's okay, Mum," she whispered.

"We'll be doing a lumpectomy on your left breast, but unfortunately we have no way of knowing exactly what we are dealing with until we open you up and have a look. If we can just take the lump and some surrounding tissue, then that's what we'll do. But I do need to warn you that, if there's evidence it has spread, we may need remove some lymph glands, and in the worst case, the entire breast."

Tears were running down Carrie's face. I had only ever seen her cry a handful of times. Julia had hold of her hand while Annabel was tapping frantically on herself. The room seemed oddly still, the voices fading in and out as only some words penetrated the haze.

Helplessness flooded me. At least the others were doing something. I felt useless, no good to her at all. I didn't realise that the surgeon had left. In fact, everyone had left, except Carrie.

"Viv?" she said, bringing my eyes back to her. "Are you alright?"

"Where did everyone go?"

"I asked them to get some drinks and nibbles, seeing as they're insisting on waiting around until I go down."

"Go down where?" What the hell was she talking about?

"To surgery! Come over here," she said, patting the bed. "I can't do this if you're falling apart."

I sat on the bed.

"Am I strong, Viv?" she asked. "Can I beat this?"

"Yes." But I didn't know. Could she?

"You're upset with me, aren't you? For not saying anything?"

I had been, but now I didn't care about that.

"I didn't want to say anything until I knew for sure," she said. That's all, I promise. What was the point in getting everyone upset if it was nothing?"

"But it's not nothing," I choked. "I don't want this for you."

"Right, Genevieve." Her voice was stern. "No one wants this. I hate to say it, but better me than you or Annabel or Julia."

I straightened, pulling away from her. "What do you mean? That's not fair. Do you think you deserve this or something?" How could she think such a thing?

"What I mean is that all of you have children. You have people who need and depend on you."

"Well, I need you," I sobbed, leaning my head on her chest, "and I depend on you. Don't you dare ever say that to me again! I fucking love you!"

Carrie lifted my face. Her eyes were heavy with fear, I could see it. "I know you do, and I love you too. And those other two idiots." We were nothing without each other. Spaghetti without sauce, crackers without dip.

The moment was interrupted when my mother and father arrived, flinging the door open dramatically.

"Carrie, honey!" Mum cried, nearly pushing me off the bed. "Is there anything we can do?"

Dad shot Carrie a smile and made a face behind Mum's back. It said all he needed it to.

As the others returned, one by one, the room took on a strange feel. We joked and laughed as we often did in times of crisis, but there was something heavy looming, something we all knew was there, but were trying to pretend wasn't. At least until the orderly came to take Carrie.

My heart felt like it was ripping apart as I watched her slowly wheeled down the hall. When she was out of sight, I walked away from the room, from all of them, out into the fresh air. Please let her be all right. Please let it be contained.

I leaned back against the brick wall and dragged heavily on the cigarette a stranger had kindly given me. The butt shook against my lips while the smoke filled my lungs and made my head feel faint. My body easily remembered the habit, even though it had been thirteen years since my last cigarette.

Julia appeared and grabbed the cigarette from my hand, taking a long drag. "This feels so surreal," she said. "It doesn't even seem like it's happening."

"Mum's looking for you two," Annabel called from the entrance doors. "Are you two smoking?"

Here we go.

"You shouldn't be smoking!' Annabel shrieked. 'Honestly, here we are at the hospital with Carrie with c—" She couldn't finish, couldn't say the word as the realisation broke through the facade she had been holding onto so tightly. Darkness crept over her face.

"C'mon," I said, taking her arm, "let's go deal with Mum."

The dread of having to listen to Mum's whinging was making me clutch Annabel's arm tighter than I should have.

"Viv, you're hurting me," she complained, yanking it away with glaring eyes.

"Excuse me," a smiling brunette interrupted as we approached Carrie's room. "I'm your sister's nurse for this evening."

We all nodded at her.

"I just wanted to let you know that she's going to be down in surgery for quite a while. If you wanted to head home and have some dinner, I'd be happy to give you a call when she's on her way up to the ward."

Dinner? My stomach was rumbling, but whether I could eat anything was another matter.

"Thanks ... Annie," Julia said, leaning in to read her name badge. "I think that's a good idea. I'll go in and tell my parents."

Edward had disappeared and Dad was fast asleep in the arm-chair. Mum had already scoffed half of the chocolate Natalia had bought, but before I could tell her off, Natalia gave me a dismissive wave.

"We just saw the nurse outside," Julia announced. "She said it could be hours before Carrie's out of surgery. She suggested we head home and get a bite to eat."

"I think that's a really good idea," Natalia agreed, getting up. "We could all use a stretch and some food."

Mum poked Dad's arm, making him jump.

"What?" he muttered, before realising we were all looking at him.

"Dad, we're going to head home and get something to eat. You should go home too, and get some rest. You look tired," Annabel said, adding to Mum's annoyance.

"I'm tired too, you know. I've been running around all day." Mum needed to ensure that we were aware of her own efforts as Dad rolled his eyes and poked his tongue out behind her. They were worse than children.

"Drop me home," he said, getting up. "I'll come back and see her when she's awake tomorrow."

"Has anyone seen Edward?" Annabel asked.

"Hopefully he's taken himself off to the aged care ward," Dad scowled.

"Dad! Stop that," Julia warned, smacking his arm. "He's Carrie's husband, be nice."

"He went home to have a sleep," said Natalia. "He said he'll be back in the morning."

"That'd be right." There was no love lost between Dad and Edward, and he wasn't shy about it.

***

When we arrived home, Peter's car was in the driveway. "Why is your dad here?" I said to Natalia, with more annoyance in my voice than I meant her to hear.

"The boys probably called him. They would have been worried."

Jack was already standing on the porch. "How is Aunty Carrie, Mum?" he asked, as soon as the car door opened.

How could I answer? She's sick? She's got cancer? All of it would scare him. It scared me.

"She's in surgery, Jack. They have to remove a tumour." I

cleared my throat to disguise the worry creeping into my voice. "We've just come home to freshen up and have something to eat and then I'll head back in."

"I'll go with you," Jack offered.

"Honey, you've got school in the morning. And anyway, the hospital room is tiny – Julia, Annabel and I barely fit." I gave him a squeeze. "Thanks for offering, though."

The smell of roast potatoes and chicken wafted through the doorway and hung in the still air. "Dad helped us in case you were hungry."

Now that I could smell it, I was starving. Peter appeared in the lounge room. "Are you okay?" he asked as I came in.

I wasn't. Peter took my arm, leading me to the bedroom. "Viv, what's happened? What did they say?"

I couldn't get a single word to form on my lips, as tears fell and a numbness inflicted every cell of my body. I sobbed in Peter's arms, giving in to the one thing I swore I wouldn't do. Need him. "She has breast cancer," I finally managed. "She's in surgery now."

"Shit. How was she?" he said, helping me sit down.

"She was okay, but I know she was scared."

Peter sat beside me and pulled me into his arms. "I'm here for you, Viv. For all of you, whatever you need. I hope you know that."

I did, but I needed to hear it.

"Let's get something to eat and then I can drive you back to the hospital," Peter said.

"Thank you," I whispered. "With everything the way it is, I really do appreciate it."

"I know, and it's the least I can do." He smiled, taking my hand and leading me into the kitchen.

"You okay, Mum?" The fear in Adam's expression hurt.

"I'm fine, sweetheart. Please don't worry about me." I took in a deep breath, "Aunt Carrie has breast cancer and she's having surgery. We don't know much right now, but once they've removed the tumour, they'll have a better idea of what we're dealing with." I'd give anything to take away their worry. "Now, let's eat!" I declared with far too much enthusiasm. They saw right through me. They always did.

CHAPTER 14

David

Tom.kelly@yourperfectpic.com:

> *Hey Hun, I'm so sorry about Carrie and I'm so sorry I'm not there.*

How did he even know already? Anabel or Julia must have messaged him.

> *I know that things are hard for you right now and I'm sorry I haven't been in touch more, but I've been out of range and there's hardly any service where I am. Be strong, and whatever the news is tomorrow, just be there for Carrie. You guys all love each other so much.*

Why wasn't he here? I needed him here. I couldn't face finding out the results tomorrow without him.

I looked up from my phone, distracted by the sheets on the bed making a crackling noise as Carrie shifted position.

"She should start to wake around midnight," Nurse Annie said on her umpteenth visit. Earlier she had given each of us a pillow and blanket and turned on the television.

Note to self, nominate Annie for nurse of the year.

"Do you need anything?" she asked.

"I'm fine thanks," I said.

She left the room, and I returned to Tom's email. My eyes stung against the bright light of my phone in the dimly lit room.

> I'm beginning to regret my decision to leave, given everything that's going on. I hope you know that if I'd had any idea all of this would happen, I would never have gone. I did this for myself, but also for you. For us. I'll explain everything when I get back and I hope you can forgive me.

I sat upright in the chair. What the hell does he mean? I did it for us? Did what for us?

> I have to head back out to the country today, so I won't be in contact for a short time. I'll check emails when I can. Give my love to Carrie and the others.
>
> Tom xxx

"Viv?" Carrie was squirming in the bed.

"Hey, how are you feeling?" I whispered, stroking her forehead.

"Like a beaten egg, with cotton wool for a mouth," she muttered, licking her lips. "Can you get me some water?"

I poked my head into the hallway and signalled to Annie. "Can she have some water?"

She nodded, fetching a jug and glass and bringing it into the room. "How are you feeling, Carrie? What's your level of pain, from one to ten?" Annie asked.

"Twenty." She winced as she sucked on the straw Annie held for her. "Did they take it all, or just the lump?"

"They just took the tumour and some lymph nodes. You were very lucky," Annie said, touching her arm gently. "I'll get you some pain meds after I check your blood pressure."

She left the room again, and Carrie moaned and shifted in the bed. She looked uncomfortable, her face contorting in pain.

"What can I do?" I fussed. "Can I get you something?"

"No, it's okay. I just feel awful," she mumbled.

"Of course you do, you just had major surgery."

"No, I mean with all of you here."

Annabel stood up, changed position and flopped back down into the chair. She never even opened her eyes.

"We don't mind. You'd be here if it was any of us."

Carrie smiled. "I promised Tom I'd look after you until he got back, not the other way around."

"What do you mean?" I asked.

"Okay, Carrie," said Annie, returning. "I have your pain meds."

What was Carrie talking about? When had she promised Tom?

"You'll probably feel really sleepy after this," said Annie. "So, get some rest. Your sister will make sure." She flashed me a smile.

"What did Tom say?" I asked Carrie when Annie had left.

There was only a small window of opportunity before the medication took hold.

"Nothing, just that he loves you, and he wanted me to help him."

"Help him what? Carrie? Help him what?" But she was out. Bloody hell!

***

Tom had been standing at my front door, about to tell me something terribly important when the clanking breakfast trolley roused me from my sleep. Pain ripped through my neck and down my right arm.

"Bout time you woke up." Julia's raised eyebrow and sly smirk indicated I'd missed something. "We've been listening to you muttering for half an hour."

I wiped my lips and sat up in the armchair, pain searing across my shoulders. "What time is it? Where's my phone?" I asked, looking about.

"It's 8:30." Carrie's voice was hoarse and dry, but the colour in her cheeks had somewhat returned. "The nurse said the doctor will be in shortly, before his rounds." She covered her mouth in an attempt to hide her quivering lips.

"Carrie," Annabel gently stroked her arm, "just do the best you can. One hurdle at a time."

"Mrs Cameron, how are you doing this morning?" Dr Durbinder said as he walked in.

"Not too bad, but pretty sore. And please, call me Carrie."

I moved to her side, as did Annabel and Julia. Are we

preparing for bad news? It won't be bad news. Are we sensing it? My heart was pounding.

"Well, Carrie, the surgery went very well, you're very lucky."

Lucky? What a word to use at a time like this. I doubt Carrie was feeling lucky. Lucky is when you win five dollars on a scratchy or get an extra pickle on your burger, not when you've been cut open and had half your breast removed.

"We were able to remove the tumour and some of the surrounding tissue," Doctor Durbinder went on. "But we also had to take six lymph nodes from your armpit and upper arm." He pointed to the area. "I'm really happy with how it went, but we'll need to wait for the lab results before we know for sure."

"What will the results show?" Julia asked. Carrie was as bad as I was when it came to anything technical or medical. Julia was much better at that stuff.

"The tests will confirm exactly what type of Cancer we are dealing with and in turn allow us to better organise an appropriate treatment plan for your sister."

Treatment plan? Didn't she just have it all cut out? I looked at Annabel to see if she was panicking too, but she was concentrating on the doctor, and appeared to be chanting something under her breath.

"There will likely be a need for some chemotherapy and radiation treatment," the doctor explained. "How much will be determined by the test results."

"When will that start, doctor?" Annabel asked, between mantras.

"We should get the test results back on Monday. You'll need to stay in hospital for at least four to five days, Carrie, depending on your recovery, so I'll make you an appointment in my consulting rooms here for Monday afternoon, and prepare a referral to the oncologist."

The air in the small room was dense and hot. I could feel my cheeks burning as Carrie buried her face in her hands.

"Carrie?" Doctor Durbinder said, lowering himself onto the bed beside her. "I know this isn't easy, but believe me, in the scheme of things, this is all good news." He patted her blanket covered legs and warned us sternly to take care of her.

"We're here for you every step of the way," I promised. "Day and night. You'll be telling us to piss off before long."

"I tell you to piss off all the time now," she laughed through falling tears. "I'm going to be such an ugly baldie. You know how round my head is."

"Think of all the fun we'll have buying wigs and hats," Annabel said.

"I need to call Edward," said Carrie. "Jules, pass me my phone."

She did as Carrie asked. "I need to head off anyway, but I'll pop back later." Julia grabbed her keys and kissed us all goodbye.

"I'll come with you, Jules, I've got a Reiki client at ten," Annabel said.

Mum walked in with Edward. "I'm off too," I quickly added, "I better get home and sort out those boys."

Instead, I made a beeline for the cafeteria and a strong latte. Despite being brewed in a hospital cafeteria by a ninety-year-old volunteer, the coffee was hot and strong.

Chemotherapy. I only knew what I'd seen on television and in movies, but it was always awful. I don't want this for you, Carrie. I don't want you to have to go through this. I don't want you to die. My eyes stung, and the muscles in my face ached. I felt as if I'd aged 40 years in the past few weeks alone.

"Are you alright?"

I looked up to see who had spoken. A man sitting at another table was looking in my direction.

I looked behind me, but hadn't noticed that the cafeteria was almost empty. "Who, me?" I asked.

He nodded, waiting for a response.

"Yes, I'm fine. A million miles away, that's all," I smiled.

"Do you mind if I sit with you?" he asked politely.

Do I? Why does he want to sit?

"Sure, go ahead, but I warn you I'm not much company at the moment."

"Well, I'm not either, so we make a good pair." His eyes were red against his olive complexion and his chestnut hair, peppered with grey, was dishevelled, as if he had been running his fingers through it over and over. "My sister's having surgery this morning. She's been diagnosed with breast cancer," he said.

"That's awful, I'm so sorry. My sister had her surgery last night. For breast cancer too."

"Well, perhaps we were meant to meet today. How is she? If you don't mind me asking."

"She's okay. But she's scared, I think. We all are," I said, stirring my coffee.

"I know, I'm petrified." His voice seemed to catch on the words as his deep brown eyes filled. When he could, he continued. "Our parents died a long time ago, so it's just been me and Savannah for years. She's got two little ones." His eyes filled again. "They're only ten and seven." He wiped at his tears with a tissue, "I'm so sorry, I didn't mean to sit down and burden you with all of this."

"Let me get you a coffee. I could use another one too," I offered.

Poor man. I looked back at him as he ran his fingers as I suspected, through his hair with a shaky hand. That was one thing I had to remember; to be grateful for the fact that I had my three sisters and our parents, even though they drove me crazy. He had no family, but her.

"My name's, Viv, anyway, what's yours?" I said, handing him a cappuccino.

"It's David. Nice to meet you, Viv. It's a pity it wasn't under better circumstances," he laughed, offering his hand to shake.

It was a pity. Under different circumstances David's strong, but lean body and gentle manner would have appealed to me, but right now I just felt utter sorrow for him.

"And thanks for the coffee, you really didn't have to." His heavy eyes looked like they needed a good rest.

"You look as if you could really use one. I replied. "And I know the feeling."

A wide smile, revealing straight, white teeth, replaced the sadness on David's face. His square chin was dark with short stubble, and his green eyes soft, despite the obvious strain.

The vibration of my phone made a buzzing sound against the melamine table. It was Annabel:

Emergency coffee meeting about Carrie. Carmello's at two.

"Everything okay?" David asked.

"Everything's fine. My other two sisters, wanting me to meet them for coffee," I answered, rolling my eyes. "It was lovely to meet you David, but I better run." I stuffed my phone into my bag. "I need to get home and check in on my kids and organise myself before I have to head back here anyway."

David stood as I did. A gentleman. His gaze was penetrating, causing my cheeks to flush. My stomach had butterflies. What am I, a teenage girl?

"I hope everything goes well with your sister," I added.

"I might see you this evening then, when you come back. I'm sure I'll still be here!" Even with his smile, there was a sadness about him.

"You should head home for a while and rest while she's in surgery. That's what we did," I offered, patting his shoulder, "then you won't feel so exhausted when she comes out."

Was the patting too much?

"I might just do that. Thanks. I think I'll take the kids home and give them a break. Their father could use one, too. He's finding it pretty hard."

"Best of luck," I said from the doorway.

Although he was a perfect stranger, it felt odd to leave him there alone and sad.

"Viv," David called, heading down the corridor after me.

Had he felt it too? Like we'd connected. Oh crap, what do I say?

"David, I know we —"

"I'm so sorry to call after you, but as you were leaving, I noticed that you had your skirt on inside out."

What? I fumbled with the waistband, swivelling it to see the tag hanging from the back and the side seams exposed. How did I not notice?

"Well, thank you, David. I really appreciate you letting me know," I smiled, throwing in a nervous giggle to ensure he knew I was a complete nutcase.

"I thought about not telling you for a moment, I didn't want to embarrass you, but then I felt guilty. I'd want someone to tell me," he added, looking unsure if he'd made the right decision.

No, I think I would have preferred you didn't tell me so that I could have deluded myself into thinking that you hadn't noticed.

"Well, thank you again. Must run," I said, high-tailing it to the nearest bathroom.

I peeked from the bathroom door as David walked slowly back to the cafeteria.

***

"So, what's going on with you and Tom?" Julia asked when I took my usual seat and waved at Carmello to bring coffee.

"I thought we were here about Carrie? And anyway, what about Tom?" I fired back.

"Why is he saying that he went away for you, for both of you?" Annabel teased.

"Snoops! You read my email." I glared at the two of them.

"Calm down," Julia insisted. "Carmello's had enough of our carry-on lately. Anyway, it was an accident. Your phone fell on the floor while you were asleep and Annabel picked it up."

"Thanks Julia, blame me. You were the one that read it," Annabel returned sharply.

"You're both terrible," I declared. "You can't go around reading other people's emails. It's illegal or something. And there's nothing going on. I have no idea what he's on about, I wish I did. Carrie did say something to me last night though, when she was delirious, about promising him that she'd look out for me."

"Are you *sure* he's not, you know, in love with you?" Julia said. "You guys have been friends for decades." Julia shot Annabel a sly grin that she thought I hadn't seen.

They're not as devious as they think they are. They know something.

I decided not to tell them about the huge arrangement of roses that had been waiting for me when I got home from the hospital. The card read:

I'm thinking of you. I love you and I promise I'll be home soon. Tom xxx

"Anyway, we're here to discuss Carrie, so let's get on with it." I'd had enough of their antics for one day.

"We need to organise a roster for helping Carrie once she's out of hospital and having treatment," Julia said. She produced a notepad. She began drawing up columns.

"Well, I'm happy to take any shifts, and I'm sure Natalia will help out as well," I offered.

"My girls are heading in to see her tonight," said Annabel. "But Georgia's flat out with work, and Abbie lives so far, I'm not sure they'll be able to do too much."

"It's fine, if we add me and Mum, we should pretty much be able to put together a roster for each day," Julia said, jotting down notes. "Ava's almost settled into her new place, so she might be able to give a hand later too, but Jackson won't be back from Europe for another two months."

Listening to all the offers of help made me think of David. My family could be hard work at times, but I loved them, and no matter what, they would be there for me. I couldn't imagine being in David's position; to be facing losing the only family I had.

I needed to get over myself and stop being so self-absorbed. David needed someone. And I was going to help.

CHAPTER 15

The wedding of Erin & Jimmy (Warring Fathers)

"I'm on my way to a wedding and I'm late. What's wrong? How's Carrie?" I snapped at Annabel, who had called me three times today already.

"Carrie's fine. She's feeling pretty nauseous, but other than that, she's okay. Mum's here."

No wonder she's nauseous.

"Well, why are you calling me? *Again.*"

"It's nothing, I just wanted to let you know that Julia's coming here to stay with her tonight, so you don't have to," she said defensively, as if she was hurt by my irritation with her.

"Tell her thank you. Between weddings, kids and sorting out my life, I'm completely exhausted." I'd been making trips back and forth to the hospital all week and trying to manage everything else at the same time.

I felt bad for carrying on about my life when Carrie was going through chemotherapy and couldn't even hold down water.

"Sorry," I said. "I just meant that it's chaotic at the moment, but I'm happy to come whenever Carrie needs me. No matter what."

"Viv, everyone knows how hard you're working to keep everything together. Just because Carrie's sick right now, doesn't take away from what you've been going through either."

I appreciated Annabel's words more than I could tell her.

"Thanks Bel, but I know I sound like I'm whining, I don't mean to. Anyway, I'm late, so I'll call you later."

My phone sang out with its usual text message tone as soon as it hit the passenger seat. It was from David:

> Hi Viv, thanks for all the help and wise words over the past week, it's really helped me through. Can I pay you back with dinner?

How do you say 'as friends', without saying it? Since getting over my initial horror of the skirt incident, I'd met up with David for coffee on several occasions at the hospital. He was a sweetheart. Kind, considerate, a high school teacher. But once we spent time together, I didn't feel attracted to him. It was becoming apparent, however, that maybe he was feeling something more.

Friends have dinner all the time. Surely I could meet a man and just keep it platonic.

Tom and I have been friends for 20 years. Tom. He hadn't written since his last email, which obviously meant he was avoiding telling me what the hell was going on. Darcy, on the other hand, had called twice to see if I wanted to try another round of speed dating, only without the other dates. Peter was a whole other story.

But right now, I had Erin and Jimmy and their ridiculous fathers to deal with.

"Thank God you're here!" Jimmy said, hurrying to help me with my things. "I need you to help keep those two lunatics away from each other. Dad's already pissed Eric off by doing burnouts in his new Maserati outside their dealership this morning. He's left black stripes all over the road."

Exactly what I need – two idiotic businessmen who are more concerned about their car yards than their children. Poor Jimmy looked beside himself with worry.

"I'm on it, Jimmy. You just relax and go get a drink or something."

Here we go again. I had played intermediary numerous times for these two already, and today I was not in the mood. Just four more to go.

"Mr Canondale, how are you?" I smiled, dragging my signing table to the grassy area of The Blockade Community Centre. "Would you give me a hand?"

Jesse Canondale was the manly hero-type. The kind who loved to be needed by a woman, any woman. It wasn't the first time I'd used my feminine charms to distract him. My first meeting with Erin and Jimmy had taken place at a local pub.

"Neutral ground," Erin had explained, "where they'll both have to behave."

Jesse, Jimmy's father, and Eric Morgan, Erin's father, were sworn enemies and had been since high school days.

"He always thought he was the big man, even back then," Eric had explained at our meeting. "I stayed here in town and raised my family. I built my own business, from the ground up and we were doing just fine, until that useless wannabe," he pointed at Jesse, who was sitting at the bar, "came along and started throwing his money around and buying everyone off with his flashy look-at-me attitude. Then went and set up his dealership only a stone's throw from mine."

Erin looked over to Jimmy then back at me with desperate eyes.

"Let me grab us a drink and I'll have a quick chat to Jimmy," I said, heading to the enemy camp.

It was Jesse's turn. "I know they're in love and all, but of all the girls, in all the cities and towns, why did Jimmy have to pick *his* daughter?" Jesse complained, causing Jimmy to squirm on his bar stool. "I like Erin, she's a lovely kid, but her father is a complete imbecile. And I, for one, will never call him family."

"No one's asking you to call him family, Mr Canondale, but for Jimmy's sake, if you could just be civil for the wedding?"

He screwed up his face.

Where are their wives? Do they have wives? Surely they could talk some sense into them.

"What if I was to object on the day?" Jesse asked.

This man was testing my patience. "At the end of the day, as long as the two people getting married both give consent, then there's nothing anyone can do unless there is a genuine legal reason. The law is very clear. In fact, I don't even ask if anyone objects at weddings, because even if they did, it wouldn't matter."

Jesse took a swig from his pint of ale and crossed his arms, "Fine, I'll shut up, but don't ask me to shake his hand or anything."

"I have your word?" I said, holding out my hand to shake on it as Jimmy nodded encouragingly at his soon-to-be bride.

"Yes, I suppose." He shook, albeit begrudgingly.

I returned to a smiling Erin and handed her father a fresh pint. "Jesse has agreed to give his blessing and do the right thing for the sake of keeping the peace. Can I assume that you will do the same?" I asked, watching Erin wrap herself around her father's arm.

Eric looked nervously at his soon-to-be son-in-law and arch enemy at the bar.

"Dad? For me?" Erin pleaded.

"Fine, but you better promise me that even after you're married, you won't go over and work for them. You stay with me," he said sternly.

Was he kidding? These poor kids.

"Maybe Jimmy and I will start our own dealership and give both of you a run for your money," she teased.

"You wouldn't dare," her father scowled. He pointed his finger and made a face.

Now, as guests began to arrive and Jesse helped me with my table, he was smiling from ear to ear. "And how are you on this fine day?" He smirked, clearly pleased with himself and his efforts to upset Eric. It seemed that our agreement was out the window.

"Mr Canondale,"

"Please, call me Jesse."

"Jesse, I recall that you promised me that you would behave for the wedding. Eric promised the same." This was like dealing with pre-schoolers. "You know that if you cause any trouble, I'll have to ask you to leave, in front of everyone." I warned, pointing a finger and using my most assertive school teacher tone. Being a naughty boy was obviously his thing.

"Look, I know I got a bit carried away this morning, but I promise, best behaviour from now on." He held up his right hand to pledge. He was no boy scout.

"Well, you better,' I added sternly.

"And what if I don't, will you spank me?"

Eeeew, no! My fierce glare made its point. "C'mon, let's get set up before the bride arrives." Before I hit you with this chair.

Jimmy looked relieved to find everything ready to go and his father seated where he was supposed to be, no shotgun in sight.

"Thanks, Viv," he nodded, giving me a wink, "you really seem to know how to handle him."

Erin, radiant on her father's arm, appeared on the red carpet that led to her waiting groom. Eric glared at Jesse as they passed, and Jesse in turn looked at me. I stared him into submission. He tipped the wide brim of his hideous leather hat at Eric in a half-arsed apology. It was enough. Eric's hard face softened as he shook Jimmy's hand and kissed his daughter's cheek.

Thank Goodness. Despite the stress and the impossibly annoying people I had to deal with in this job, moments like this were often what made it all worthwhile.

What I didn't enjoy was the aftermath of my selfless attempts to placate the situation. When the ceremony finished and the guests had drawn towards the couple to offer them their congratulations, Jesse decided it was the perfect time to make his move. He slobbered on my cheek with a wet, open-mouthed kiss and whispered into my ear how much he'd like to tickle me with his moustache. Eew! I wiped away the slobber, and managed to get away from him. But he caught up again when I was packing up my stuff.

"Let me help you with all that," Jesse called.

"It's fine, I've got it," I said with a wave.

It was no use, he was already folding the legs of my table and picking up the two chairs. He loaded them into the boot, making space for me to put in my case and PA system.

As I leaned in, I felt his hand on my back. Yep, saw that coming. I'd played to his enjoyment of being dominated and now I was going to have to get myself out of it.

I spun around to politely tell him to shove off, but his face was only inches from mine. "Let's find a quiet place," he whispered, clicking his tongue back and forth.

Does he really think this is what every woman wants? An octopus, who can't keep his hands to himself – and at his own son's wedding?

"Jesse, I'm flattered, but this is not the time or the place for this, and even if it was, I'm not that type of person," I said, pushing him back to a reasonable distance.

"But honey, you're hot for me, I can tell."

Hot for him? I was a lot of things, but hot for him was not one of them. Grossed out by him? Yes. Disgusted by his childish and immature behaviour? Definitely.

"Right, Jesse, you need to go back over and be there for your son on his wedding day! You shouldn't be out here, trying to pick up their celebrant." This time I used my stern mother-hen tone.

"I love a woman who isn't afraid to get her man in line. I bet you're a rocket in the sack." He flashed what was obviously meant to be a suggestive smile, but was more like a filthy leer. He was NOT my man, in any way, shape or form.

"Go," I ordered, pointing toward the group who had already begun their family photos, "and no carry-on with Eric. I mean it."

I was good at this, maybe I could be a dominatrix. One that doesn't have sex or anything, just whips and beats men and orders them to make cocktails. I contemplated the possibility all the way to the soccer oval.

"How long have they got left?" I panted at Peter after running all the way from one side of the oval to the other.

"They're five minutes into the second half. We're up. Two goals to one," he said, handing me his water bottle.

"Oh, bugger. I wanted to get here by half time at least, but the bloody grooms fa—" No no no, that story doesn't need to be told aloud. And especially not to Peter. "Never mind, I'm here now. Go Adam!" I screamed.

Jack threw me a threatening look from his goalie position. I had a habit of getting carried away at sporting events and had been warned, on a number of occasions, that If I didn't contain myself, the boys would ban me from attending. They were eight at the time.

"Viv, any chance we can catch up for dinner tonight?" Peter said suddenly.

What? He'd caught me off guard, and I couldn't come up with a single reason why not as his eyes fixed on mine.

"Umm, yeah, I suppose so," I answered, even though my instincts were screaming at me to say no.

What excuse was there that would be plausible right now? I could be honest and say that it feels awkward and I don't know what I want. Or that I'm interested in seeing Darcy again? No, too hard. "What time?" Was what came out.

"I'll pick you up at seven." Peter looked far too excited for my liking.

This was a bad idea.

***

"It's just dinner," I swore, when Julia called to see if I wanted to join her and Carrie tonight.

"Edward's sick, so he's gone to stay with his son for a while. And Annabel's coming. She's helping Georgia organise a dinner party for her work colleagues, and she wants to get out before they arrive. We thought we'd order in."

"I promised Peter, I can't back out now."

"Fine, but remember what we talked about, Viv. Being strong and independent and not needing a man. Have you even used that 'toy' yet?"

"Julia, shut up! The thing is, Peter caught me off guard earlier and I didn't know what to say. I'm worried he thinks I'm going to forgive him, and that we can fall back into the same old rut." I hadn't forgiven him and, notwithstanding our little moment of weakness and familiarity, I wasn't sure I ever would.

"Listen, you just need to be careful. It's natural to think

that it's easier to end up back with Peter, where you don't have to worry about going on a date or waxing and plucking," she warned. "But you have to remember how you felt then and how unhappy you both were."

She was right. The affair and the betrayal were only the result of a long list of problems in our relationship. I'd hoped we could get things back on track, but what I needed from a partner when I was 20 wasn't the same as what I needed now and I assume it was the same for Peter. I wanted someone to talk to and spend time with, while Peter seemed to just want to do his own thing. I kept hoping that it would change as the kids got older. We'd have more time together and reignite the spark, but the good times were few and far between. I'd hung in there for the kids and because it was easier. It was hard to admit, but the affair was just the final blow.

"All I'm saying is if you do go back, make sure it's for the right reasons," Julia said.

My Call Waiting beeped. "I've gotta go, tell Carrie I'll see her tomorrow. Hello?" I said, answering the other call.

"It's me." The voice took a moment to register in my brain, "It's Tom."

"Tom! Oh my God. Why haven't you called? I've missed you. I hate you! What's wrong with you? I've been worried sick. You're not coming back, are you? Why haven't you even bothered to call me?"

"Viv, shut up for God's sake." He was laughing.

I'd missed his laugh so much. Tears filled my eyes, streaking mascara down my cheeks.

"I'm sorry I haven't called," he said. "I wanted to, but it's been difficult with work."

The note on the flowers - ask him. Ask him what he meant. "I got the flowers, thank you. Although I would have preferred a call. And by the way, I was a tad insulted that the flowers you sent Carrie were bigger than mine," I joked.

"Viv, I know the card was a bit cryptic, but I wanted to—"

The doorbell rang. Shit, Peter.

"Tom, hang on. Peter's at the door," I said, immediately regretting the words as they left my lips.

I covered the mouthpiece and called out to Peter. "Hi, let yourself in," I blurted. "I'm just on a call, won't be long. Get yourself a drink. The kids are out."

I ducked into the bedroom.

"Tom, are you still there?"

"Are you going out with Peter?" His tone had changed, "Viv, why?"

"He sprang it on me today, that's all. It's nothing serious, I promise. We're not rushing into anything. It's only dinner," I lied. I knew Peter wanted more. "Can you call me back tomorrow? I really want to talk. And I miss you."

"I miss you too, but I don't know if I can call again until next week. Please remember that you promised me no big decisions. I need you to keep that promise. I love you."

He was saying that a lot lately. "Okay, but call me as soon as you can. Or email or Skype or something, anything," I pleaded. I hadn't realised how much I missed the sound of his voice. "I need you," I said as he hung up.

"These are for you," Peter said, handing me a bunch of gorgeous, long-stem, red roses, "happy anniversary."

Shit! My mind raced. What was the date today? "I'm sorry, Peter, I didn't realise."

"It's fine," he lied, hurt filling his hopeful, brown eyes. "I've booked a table at Guaccio's."

That was a first. My heart sank. He was trying so hard, but deep down I really didn't know if I wanted to try at all.

CHAPTER 16

Just one of the clowns

"So, how did it go last night?" Julia asked.

I gave her a look to say that it hadn't gone well as I kissed the top of Carrie's head. "How are you feeling?"

"I'm fine, but stop using me as an avoidance tool. What happened?"

"Peter turned up—"

"Wait, wait for me," Annabel came running from the kitchen with a tray of coffee. She handed me a cup and plonked beside me on the couch.

"Peter turned up right as I was talking to Tom," I went on.

"What? Tom finally called?" Annabel exclaimed. "Did you ask him about the email?"

"Let her finish, Annabel," Carrie groaned, slapping her arm playfully.

"I was just about to ask him about the email when Peter rang the doorbell."

Julia threw her hands in the air and relaxed back against the couch. "Your life is like an episode of the friggin' *Bold and The Beautiful*, honestly."

"Anyway, I didn't get to speak to him for long and then Peter presented me with this huge bunch of roses," I paused for dramatic effect, "for our *anniversary*!"

"You forgot. Oh no, that's awful," Annabel said, covering her mouth while Carrie burst into laughter. "Poor Peter, that's so sad."

"Shut up, Annabel," said Carrie. "Have you forgotten what he did to her?"

"I know, but it's still awful, for anyone." Annabel was always considering the effect every action she took had on her Karma.

"We went to dinner and it was fine," I added, unsure whether to tell them everything.

"What? That's it?" Carrie knew there was more. "C'mon, give it up."

I sighed. "He took me to Guaccio's, which was lovely, and we chatted, but I was in the middle of saying something – I don't even remember what – and I noticed that he was looking over my head at the television."

I sipped my coffee, trying not to cry. It hurt, like it always had when I would try to talk to Peter or share something with him and he would pretend to listen. "I know it sounds petty, but I felt like that so many times in our marriage, especially towards the end. Nothing I had to say was interesting enough to keep Peter's attention. I always felt alone, even when I was with him." The words caught in my throat.

"Oh honey, it's okay." Julia put her arm around my shoulder. "These things are never easy and sometimes it's not until you leave a relationship that you realised all of the hurtful things that you excused."

"And then when he started chewing," I cried into Julia's chest, "it was driving me crazy. I think I've actually lost the plot. The way he chewed his food and sniffed made me want to throw myself across the table and strangle him," I sobbed. "I must be mad."

"Of course you're not," Carrie reassured me, "you've just outgrown him, that's all. You both need to move on."

"Carrie! Not everyone can be as black and white as you," Annabel protested. "Viv's been married to Peter for 20 years. These things don't sort themselves out in a few weeks."

"They do if you want them to," she argued. "If you face it and force the change. Viv's got other options." A grin formed on her lips. "There's Darcy the hottie, the sad guy from the hospital, and she's got Tom as well. Plenty to choose from!"

I lifted my head to look at her. "What do you mean I've got Tom? You said in the hospital after your surgery, something about promising him you'd keep an eye on me." I had her cornered.

"You've always had Tom," she shrugged. "And as for that night, I was delirious, how should I know?" Carrie had turned pale and took herself off to the bathroom.

"What are you wearing to Barbara's engagement?" Annabel asked.

Mum was making us go to her second cousin's daughter's engagement party – on a Tuesday night. I shrugged. "Who has an engagement party on a Tuesday?" I complained.

"Sometimes you have to wait months for a weekend booking. They probably just decided to take a Tuesday rather than wait. I haven't got time to buy them anything though, they're getting something from my cupboard." Annabel was a notorious re-gifter.

***

"I know it sounds odd being a Tuesday, but I've got my second or third or something-cousin Barbara's engagement tonight," I explained to Darcy when he called. I pushed further into the back of Carrie's walk-in robe so she couldn't hear me while she tried on dresses.

"As much as I'd prefer to see you, my mother would never forgive me." I huffed in an attempt to make it sound genuine.

"What about tomorrow night, are you free? I want to see you."

Silence filled the line as I mapped out the next 24 hours mentally. I had to do it. I needed this.

"Can we do Thursday instead?" I suggested. I needed a little more time.

"I'll text you my address. And, I'll make dinner," he whispered, adding a sensual element to his tone.

Crap. I can't do this.

"Viv?"

"Sure, Darcy, sounds great. I'll look forward to it."

Look forward to it? Ha, more likely make myself sick and paranoid about it.

"Who was that?" Julia asked peering over my shoulder, "Oooh, Darcy,"

"He's just what you need," Carrie smiled, "I hope you know that he's a playboy though. Just a bit of fun," she laughed, slipping on a dress, "I've known Darcy for a while, Viv, and he's not the relationship type."

"I never said I was looking for a relationship. I can do fun," I argued, flapping my hands about to somehow prove my point.

"I just want to make sure that you don't get attached and end up hurt, that's all." Carrie sighed, picking up another dress.

"Why don't you just stay in tonight, Carrie? You need to rest." I was worried about her pushing herself too much.

"I need to get out, Viv. I can't stand being cooped up here. Even if it is only as exciting as Barbara's engagement, it's better than being stuck here. And anyway, I'll be sitting down all night, how strenuous can it be?"

"Well only if you're sure. I know it's hard, but you do need to take it easy." I tossed an unsuitable blue halter-neck dress onto the bed, "I've got nothing to wear."

"Mum will be pleased you're coming, Carrie. She likes it when we're all together as a family, especially when her relatives are there. It's sweet really," Annabel said, entering with a dozen more dresses she'd brought with her. She had at least been able to keep her gorgeous and expensive designer labels, while everything else was sold off to pay debts during the divorce. I tried on another one that sucked me in so tight I couldn't breathe.

"None of us even like Barbara though," I moaned. She had always been a little dibber-dobber when we were kids, telling on us for everything. Most of the time we called her 'Hyena', thanks to the blood curdling, crazy sound she made when she laughed, that resembled some sort of primate mating call.

"I still can't believe that someone is actually marrying her," Carrie added, "imagine what he's like!"

"Be nice, Carrie," Annabel warned, "It's important to Mum, so we have to at least be pleasant."

Carrie had settled on a black pant suit. Dresses weren't her style.

"You lot ready?" Julia called from the front door. We have to get going or Mum will be after us."

Dresses on and looking respectable we piled into the car.

My phone chimed. It was Mum.

How long? Dad and I aren't going in until you girls get here.

I bet Dad's pleased. He'd be hoping we never arrive.

I hit reply: *Five minutes.*

Julia planted her foot on the accelerator before Annabel had even shut the car door. "Far out, Julia, you nearly took my leg off!"

It was going to be a long night.

***

Barbara looked like a big, blue meringue in her layered dress, made worse by ridiculously puffy sleeves.

Despite the colour scheme Barbara and Barry had chosen, they had at least shelled out for free booze.

"Have you seen the hideous ice sculpture?" Mum said, forgetting how to use her inside voice.

"Check out the kid," Carrie giggled, pointing to the sculpture.

"That brat that nearly knocked us over coming in, he's got his tongue stuck on the ice."

I poured a wine, filling the glass to the top. At least there's alcohol. Praise the Lord!

"Aunt Joan's trying to dance with the groom," Annabel whispered in my ear. By the time I spotted her, she was trying to dip poor Barry on the dance floor, while Barbara shooed her mother to get out there and save him.

The little brat, free from the ice sculpture, thanks to a cup of warm water, was now rap-dancing behind them and drew my attention away from the catastrophe. "Have a look at..." I went to say to Carrie, stopping mid-sentence when I spotted Kim.

The warm, wine-tingling feeling I'd been enjoying, turned ice-cold as panic set in. My heart pounded louder than anything in the room. In the far corner of the hall, to the right of Aunty Joan's frightening display, was Annabel's ex-husband Kim AND his girlfriend. I dug my fingers into the sides of my chair to steady myself and scanned the room. He was far enough away, but Annabel, or Mum, or any one of them would spot him eventually. I swallowed another mouthful.

Kim was the one thing in Annabel's life that had the ability to completely bring her undone. I kicked Julia under the table and gestured toward Kim. She knew as well as I did that when Annabel caught sight of him, she would explode.

"What's he even doing here? Julia whispered.

"I don't know. His girlfriend must be from Barry's side," I said.

"You better tell her now, before she sees him. Just tell her and we'll leave."

I turned to Annabel. "Annabel, I need you to listen to me

for a minute and promise me you won't react." Her bright smile faded. "Why don't you practise some of that tapping?"

"What?" she demanded, worry filling her voice.

"Promise me you won't react. Promise!" I insisted.

"I can't promise. I don't know what you're going on about yet," she said.

I held her hands tightly while Julia moved closer. "To the right of Aunty Joan, Kim is sitting at a table with some people. I tightened my grip as she pulled back and searched for them. "Just wait. He's with that woman, but remember where you are. Don't cause a scene," I warned, my voice slow and firm.

"That bloody sod!" Dad had spotted him.

"Dad," I let go of Annabel and grabbed his arm, "come with me." Nodding to Julia to take over, I led him to the entrance. "Dad, going off is only going to make things worse for Annabel. We're trying to keep her calm and this isn't helping," I said, my tone stern, "we need to go back in there, make our apologies and leave."

He was shaking his head defiantly, "I don't say much, Viv, but when it comes to you girls...I'll kill him," he spat, "that goes for Peter too. I don't know exactly what went on between the two of you, and I like Peter, but you just say the word and I'll have the bloody pair of 'em six feet under in a week."

Who the hell does he think he is, Don Corleone?

"Thank you, sort of. But Mum will be mortified if we go in and make a scene. Let's just get our things and get out of here. He doesn't even deserve our attention."

When Dad thought he was right about something, there was rarely any way to sway him, but this time he backed down. "Fine, but only because I don't want to have to listen to your mother go on about it for the next ten years."

"Thank you," I said, giving him a hug, "and for offering to murder Peter, I appreciate it."

"I'm going to make a pit-stop," Dad said, heading for the toilet, "meet you back at the table."

When I entered the foyer, I heard a commotion. And then I saw them at Kim's table. Mum was wet. Annabel was crying, Kim looked stunned and his girlfriend was being led away, drenched, by one of the waiters.

"What the hell happened?" I asked Carrie, who was standing by the door watching.

She smiled, but didn't answer. "Carrie? Are you alright?" Her face was pale and her eyes vacant. Something was wrong. Her legs seemed to weaken and I grabbed her arm to steady her, but her full weight pushed against me. Trying to hold her, I lowered myself to the floor with Carrie in my arms. "Mum!" I screamed as I guided her head gently onto the ground. I fumbled with my phone, trying to dial 000 as the others hurried to her side.

"Carrie! Carrie!" Mum shouted, trying to rouse her, but it was no use.

"I need an ambulance," I sobbed to the operator, "It's my sister, there's something wrong with her. She has Cancer and she's collapsed." I gave them the address and pleaded with them to hurry. I knelt beside her on the floor. "Don't you dare die," I wept, taking her hand.

When the ambulance officers arrived, they fitted an oxygen mask over her face before whisking her away. We piled into the car to follow. None of us spoke.

It was at least an hour before the doctor came out to the emergency room waiting area to see us. "She's okay, but resting. You can go in and see her for a few minutes, but it'll have to be quick."

"Is she alright? What happened?" Mum asked.

"She's just overdone it. Having chemo takes a lot out of a person and everyone reacts differently. Her blood pressure dropped significantly and she lost consciousness. She just needs a few days rest and fluids and her Oncologist will need to review her treatment plan. You can go in, but just two at a time until she's moved to a ward."

"You and Julia go first, Viv," Mum offered, squeezing my hand "We'll go after."

I nodded and followed the doctor with Julia by my side.

"She's in here," he said, pointing to a curtained cubicle.

"I'm sorry," Carrie rasped through the oxygen mask, "I don't know what happened."

I moved to her side and sat on the edge of the bed. "I know what happened. You pushed yourself too much. You're not invincible, you need to take it easy," I said.

She lifted her hand and pulled the mask away, "I have been taking it easy. I just can't stand being stuck in that house. I needed to get out."

Julia had moved to the other side of the bed. "Honey, I know it's not easy to be stuck at home, but you know what? It's only short-term. You're going to beat this and you'll be back to your old self in no time."

Julia's words seemed to provide her some comfort, but after tonight they did little to settle my nerves.

"Do you want me to call Edward?" I offered.

She shook her head, "I'll call him tomorrow. I'd rather speak to him myself."

I kissed her forehead and left the cubicle. Tears filled my eyes. There was actually a real possibility that we could lose her.

CHAPTER 17

The Wedding of Kimberly & Brad (Shorty shorts & Gym junkie)

"How did it go with Darcy last night?" Carrie sat up on the bed to scan my face and body language for signs.

There was nowhere to hide in her small hospital room. "Fine, sort of." Awful, weird, embarrassing.

"You know I'm going to find out anyway, so tell me. Wait, can we get some tea first, I can't get this metallic taste out of my mouth," she said, licking her lips and making a face. I helped Carrie to the bathroom, her arms thin as they linked with mine. I left her and went down the hall to make tea.

Why can't I seem to do anything to make it better? I felt so hopeless and scared for her.

When she returned, she rubbed her hands together like an evil witch in a fairy tale. "Right, now tell me every little detail."

I handed her a cup and curled up on the recliner. "Where's Julia today? Delay tactics were my specialty.

"She had to head home because Steve's flying back in for the weekend. Now get on with it!"

"Okay," Deep inhale. Long exhale. "Julia's been harping on at me about being self-sufficient, not needing a man, blah, blah, blah, and so I thought I'd give the new toy a bit of a test run, just to get me in the mood, you know?"

"You can't do that *before* a date."

Now she tells me. No one ever mentioned anything about there being rules.

"Well, how was I supposed to know that? I had no idea how well those things worked. It was like bang, bang, bang. One explosion after the other."

Carrie covered her eyes with her hands. Was my sex life really that horrifying?

"What happened with Darcy then?" she said. "Did you still go?"

"I had to. He was expecting me and he'd cooked dinner. Anyway, it was going fine. Awkward of course, because I'm so out of practice, but otherwise okay, until we moved to the couch and put on a movie."

"Yeah... And?" She propped herself up, stuffing a pillow behind her back, eager for the next tid-bit.

"So, he puts on this semi, kind of porn movie."

"What do you mean semi? It was either porn or it wasn't" she laughed.

"It was soft porn, lots of kissing and stroking, really crappy storyline. He snuggles up beside me, rubbing my hands and massaging my leg and stuff, but by then the bloody capsicum in the pasta was repeating on me and I kept getting this horrible taste. Of course, that's all I could think about, so I went to the bathroom and did a bit of a finger brush with some toothpaste."

"Is there any sex in this story?" She was growing impatient.

"Shut up, I'm getting to it. Anyway, by the time I came back he was completely naked, lying on a rug he'd dragged out, and not just a rug, a leopard skin rug, like he was bloody Fabio."

Carrie spilled her tea on the blanket from laughing and jiggling about. "Shit," she complained, wiping it with her sleeve. "So, did you make a run for it?"

"No, I was so stunned. He was completely naked", I said quietly, cupping my hands around my mouth.

"Why are you whispering? It's not like Mum's here," she said.

I shrugged and moved on. "So, he takes my hand and pulls me down onto the rug and starts kissing me and stuff, but it was weird. It felt different, not connected or something, because I've only ever been intimate with someone I knew or loved before."

"I know, but what happened next?" She pushed.

"He starts taking my clothes off and getting into it a bit, and then he says... I can't say it!" I covered my eyes.

"Viv, come on, what?" She wanted to hear the juicy bits.

"He went down, you know, there..."

"And?"

"...and then he said that he liked....a woman who was o'naturale!"

Carrie went into a complete fit. She's so going to tell the others.

"And what did you say?" She finally managed, holding her stomach and trying to breathe.

"Nothing, all I could think of was how much I'd been through to make it perfect and how much I'd bloody paid." I couldn't help but laugh too, "what the hell would he have said if I'd gone there before the wax?"

Carrie was gone. It was at least ten minutes before she could speak. I went out and made another tea while she rolled around.

"Okay, okay," she panted, inhaling deeply, "Did you get to actually have sex?"

"Eventually! Problem was, I couldn't feel a thing, stupid vibrator. I'm not sure if I fooled him with my moans, they were pretty impressive, but he finally gave up and decided to try a few other things."

Carrie's eyes widened, "Like what?"

I really wasn't sure I wanted to go into too much more detail. I'd given her plenty.

"Please, Viv. This is the best laugh I've had in ages!"

"Let's just say that he wanted to do a bit of role playing that I wasn't into. I've never even spanked my own kids let alone a grown man. Why do people like that stuff?"

"I don't mind a bit of role play. Nothing too weird," She grinned.

"Well, it's definitely not for me. The whole thing felt totally uncomfortable. And wrong. I want to feel something. I want to feel close to the person I'm with and have a connection with them."

"So how did you get out of it?" She had to know everything.

"I finally convinced him I'd hit the peak, so he thrusted

frantically with this ridiculous facial expression. Eventually he went off with a Lleyton Hewitt style, 'C'mon'. It was awful."

Carrie was looking at me with an expression I couldn't decipher. It was pity. Pity mixed with sadness and disbelief?

"At least you gave it a go," she said. "But maybe the casual thing isn't for you. Maybe you need someone that you're comfortable with, someone that loves you. Like Tom."

"What's going on Carrie? What do you know about Tom that you're not telling me?"

"Nothing," she said innocently. "I just think that once you realise you've outgrown Peter, and you've had a fling or two, you'll work out that Tom's everything you're looking for."

"We're friends Carrie, and we always have been. We don't see each other that way."

"Are you sure of that? Have you actually asked him how he feels?"

Why would I?

"Maybe you've never allowed yourself to see him that way, to even consider it because you were married."

No. I don't know. "There's been plenty of times over the years when we were having fun, or talking and messing about, and I wished it was like that with Peter. But there's no spark between me and Tom. I'm pretty sure I would have worked it out by now if there was."

"But how could there ever be a spark when you were so determined for there not to be?" said Carrie. "If you had looked at Tom through different eyes, eyes that were looking for a partner, maybe there would have been a spark."

Could there have been? I love Tom and there is no one in

this world I trust more than him, but what about attraction and chemistry?

"Stop confusing me. I've already got Peter to deal with, and now Darcy too."

"What happened to David, from the cafeteria?"

Shit, I'd completely forgotten about sweet David.

"It's all too hard," I said, getting up to pace around the room. "Peter's still sending me text messages every day, things with Darcy have escalated to this and I forgot to even respond to David last time, but we're just friends anyway."

"I'm not trying to make things complicated, Viv." The corners of her mouth turned upward to form a rare, gentle smile. Carrie wasn't often sincere. "I just want to make sure that you consider all of your options. Life's short and regrets suck, believe me."

I grabbed my handbag and gave her the bravest smile I could conjure, "I've got a wedding tomorrow that I need to prepare for, so I have to get moving." I said, kissing the top of her head. "I'll give you a call later."

I left feeling more confused than ever.

***

Kim and Brad were not the kind of couple I liked to work with. Not that I particularly enjoyed dealing with any couples these days.

The privately owned garden they'd chosen for their ceremony was deserted when I arrived. Brad couldn't seem to find his way out of a paper bag, let alone get himself dressed and to the venue on time.

The first time I'd met with them I had opened the door to find a teeny, tiny, skeleton of a girl, wearing shorty-shorts the size of a face washer, and her partner, who bore a frightening resemblance to The Hulk, in a super tight tank top.

"I'm a PT – that's Personal Trainer," Kim informed me before she even made it to my office. I quickly stuffed the chocolate wrappers strewn all over my desk into a drawer.

"We met at the gym," buff Brad said in his deep, 'He-man' voice, followed by a weird, nervous laugh.

"How exciting!" I responded, distracted by Brad's flexing pecs, which I'm sure he was doing for my benefit. "Take a seat."

"Yeah, Kimmy was helping me bulk up," he explained, thrusting his huge forearm out for me to admire. "Wanna feel?"

Umm, no. I smiled and moved on quickly. "So, tell me about what you're planning for your ceremony."

"Lots of flowers, white chairs, purple carpet runner and those huge umbrellas, I love them. Oh, and we've actually got a really big bridal party. Not big as in fat," she corrected.

God forbid!

"As in lots. Trust me they won't be fat. I've got them on strict diet routines." She tapped her stick thighs and crossed her legs, obviously pleased with herself.

"Yep," Brad cut in, "we've warned them, they'll need to weigh in each month and if any of them gain, they're out."

What the hell? Who would be friends with these people? Idiots who are likely to go off and create other smaller idiots who will one day be running the world.

"I've already paid the balance into your account," Kimmy beamed.

Great, just great, thank goodness they were far more concerned with their after-party rather than the wedding. Two appointments had been enough.

So, where the hell was everybody? I checked my watch and got out my paperwork. It was a 2:30 ceremony. Usually someone arrived at least half an hour before.

I sent a text message to Brad.

> *Hi Brad, just checking everything's okay. I'm at the garden, but there's no one here yet.*

I wasn't in the mood for this.

> Brad: *Yeah, sorry bout that. Kimmy must have forgotten to let you know that we changed the time. We're having it at 4 instead. Sorry. I'll be there about 3:30.*

For goodness sake! They managed to tell everyone else except the person actually performing the ceremony. The terms and conditions I provide to all my clients clearly states that if either of the parties does not arrive within one hour of the agreed time, I am well within my right to have them reschedule. If I had another wedding after this, then there would have been no option but to reschedule. But I didn't have another wedding and forcing the issue would only cause more trouble than it was worth. I wanted it out of the way. It would be worth the wait. I typed back:

> *Yes, obviously she forgot to mention it. I'll just wait here then.*

I hope he picks up on my tone.

Brad: *Smiley face*

Argh!

My phone chimed again, but this time it was David.

Hey, I didn't hear back from you, hope all is okay. Do you still want to catch up for a coffee? My shout?

I dug around in my handbag for a chocolate bar and stuffed it into my mouth. I was good at being married. Sort of. I knew what I was doing at least, and what was expected. Maybe it wasn't always great with Peter, but it was easy. We had sex (sometimes), we went to work, and we raised our kids. It wasn't all bad. I wanted that feeling of certainty again.

David again: *Please don't feel pressured. I completely understand if you're not up to it.*

Bloody hell. I want Tom. I want him here so I can moan and get him to help me understand what these men are thinking. What *are* they thinking? What am *I* thinking?

I responded: *Hi David, it's fine and I'm sorry for not getting back to you. Things have been a little crazy. Coffee sounds good. Let me know when you're free.*

David: *Tonight?*

Me: *Sorry, can't tonight. How's tomorrow? 10am at the cafe near the hospital?*

David: *Great. Looking forward to it.*

My head was starting to pound. I got out a pen and pad while I waited. Four columns, four men. Peter, David, Darcy, Tom. Darcy's not really interested in anything. Add him anyway. And Tom. Should I even add Tom? It's weird. Carrie's words had been festering in my back-brain since I left her. Well, just for argument's sake.

Peter:

Positives: 20 years, three children, comfortable, no pretending, less waxing and upkeep (bonus). Finances, families, no hidden personality traits.

Negatives: Cheated!!!!! Boring, sleeps all the time, cheated, chews loudly, cheated.

David:

Positives: Sweet and sincere. Seems genuinely interested. High school teacher so likes, and is probably pretty patient, with kids. Attractive.

Negatives: No vibe (sexually). Wore a brown cardigan!!! Too sweet (could get annoying). Made a slurping sound when he sipped his coffee. Crossed his legs oddly. Serial killer?

Darcy:

<u>Positives:</u> Hot. Chemistry/spark. Seems nice enough. Made good pasta. House/bathroom was clean.

<u>Negatives:</u> Bit into himself. Weird sex fetishes (that could get worse). Runs speed dating, so bound to cheat. Thinks he's Fabio.

Tom:
<u>Positives:</u>

I couldn't. Tom is Tom. He's wonderful and funny and sweet and he would never make a list like this about me. I felt like I was betraying his friendship by comparing him to the others on a self-indulgent, perfect-match list. There were so many positives to our relationship, but I knew alongside the positive list had to be a negative one, and there was only one thing – ruining our friendship. It wasn't worth the risk.

The light of my phone flashed as the high-pitched ring tone made me jump. It was Annabel.

"Guess what? Guess what?"

She didn't give me a chance to guess.

"I signed up to an online dating site and I've been talking to this guy for the last few days. He wants to meet. Ahhhh!" Her squeal came close to piercing my ear drum.

"Is he okay?" I asked, cautioning her with my mother tone. "Make sure he's not a serial killer or married or something."

"He seems okay, but you know what I'm like – as soon as I get there and talk to him, I'll get a feel for whether he's okay or not. And I'll ask my guides before I go."

Annabel's guides were her newest thing. Apparently if you

listened to your guides, they would always lead you in the right direction. Obviously, the guides allocated to me were blind drunk and mentally unstable.

"Is someone going with you? Don't go alone," I insisted.

"Yeah, Chrissy's gonna come, so I'm not by myself."

Chrissy was Annabel's new bestie and, although I thought it impossible, was even zanier than her. Between them they could tap their way to the looney bin.

"What do I say to him?" she asked. "I don't know how to talk to a man on a date."

And I do? My mouth only ever seemed to get me into trouble. "Just be yourself." No wait, that's not such a good idea. "Talk about how nice it is to meet him and ask him what he does for a living, what he's interested in. You'll be fine, just don't tap on him – or yourself."

"Oh, stop it, I'm not going to tap on him. Wish me luck. I'll come by the hospital on my way home."

"Good luck." My enthusiasm was fake and sceptical. He'd have baggage, like everyone else. He'd probably posted a profile picture from ten years ago and lied about how he likes to take walks and eat tofu. At least Carrie could laugh at Annabel for a change instead of me.

"Hi, Genevieve."

The groom's mum had crept up behind me. I'd met her once before.

"Hi, Angela, nice to see you again. How's it all going today?" I asked in my polite, speaking to an older person voice.

She rolled her eyes and lifted her hands. "Chaos. Utter chaos, honestly."

"What's happened? Is everything okay?" I asked. I wondered if someone had weighed in over their allowance.

"Oh, it's nothing major, just arguments over suit jackets and who has the rings, that sort of thing. I'm over it. I'll be glad to relax when we finally get to the reception."

"Well, here, you have a seat," I said, offering her mine, "and I'll go have a chat to the boys."

As Brad came around from the back of the house that sat on the gorgeous, heritage listed grounds, I abruptly spun around to face the other direction so he wouldn't see my face. What on earth is he wearing? Oh, if only Tom was here. C'mon, get it together. Don't laugh. Don't laugh.

"Hi Brad," I smiled, turning to face him. "All ready?"

"Sort of." He yanked on his vest before straightening his hot-pink tie. It was hideous. There was no shirt. Just vest and tie, not even a singlet. And it was white. I need to get a photo.

"Brad, beer?" The best man rounded the corner, followed by the other four goons of the bridal party. "How's it going?" he said in my general direction.

"Great, you all look... wonderful." Photos! I need to get photos.

I hadn't thought it possible for there to be anything more ridiculous than Brad and his goons, but when Kimmy finally arrived, she took ridiculous to a new level. Surrounded by her hot-pink bridesmaids, Kimmy was more orange than a fully ripe mandarin. As they approached, clashing sickeningly against the bright purple of the carpet runner, their orange-ness only increased in intensity. I scanned the faces of the groomsmen and the 50 or so guests, but no one looked anything other than impressed. Am I in an alternate universe? THEY'RE ORANGE!

"Hi Brad," Kimmy smiled, her bright white eyes and teeth glowing against her skin.

"You look gorgeous," he said proudly.

Gorgeous? Is he for real?

When Kimmy and her bridesmaids ripped off their tulle skirts to reveal hot pink shorty-shorts, it was over for me.

This was officially the most farcical wedding I had ever had the displeasure of officiating!

As I left the ceremony, I checked my messages. There was a text from Mum:

> Carrie's *been given the all-clear. We're on our way back to her house.*

Finally, some good news.

CHAPTER 18

We always have each other.

When I arrived back at Carrie's, Mum's car was still parked in the driveway. Great. I'd been hoping to avoid crossing paths with her for fear she'd launch into another lecture about how I should give Peter another chance.

"Carrie?" She wasn't in her usual spot on the couch. The family room was in darkness, with only the last rays of light coming through the window in sharp lines that bounced off the wall. Where are they? I could faintly hear the sound of water and muffled talking when I entered the hallway that led to Carrie's bedroom.

"Mum? Carrie?" The bathroom door was slightly ajar, steam vapours escaping through the opening. "Are you in there?"

"We're in here," Mum's voice came back, hollow and echoing.

"What's wrong?" I pushed back the door and gasped. "Is she alright?"

Mum sat on the floor with Carrie's wet head on her lap. Panic filled me as my legs shook beneath my weight.

"She's okay, just in a bit of shock, I think," Mum said in little more than a whisper.

I crouched down to stroke Carrie's head, but strands of her hair came away in my hand.

Her hair! Not her hair. I looked at the shower floor where the water was still running, and saw the matted hair clogging the drain.

"Oh, honey." What was there to say? I couldn't think of a single comforting word that would make any of this better. I turned off the shower and laid down and hugged her tight. "We'll get through this, I promise. You're not alone."

Tears streaked her pale face. "I don't know if I can do this," she sobbed. "I know I have all of you, and I'm grateful, but I feel so alone." She sat up, drawing her knees in close.

"Honey." Mum turned Carrie's chin to face her. "At the end of the day, every single one of us is alone. But we do have each other, we feel love and we support each other, even though each of us has a path and we walk it on our own. The best part though, is that we get to fill it with joyful occasions, loving people and happy memories. No matter how hard this gets, or how alone you feel, just know that we will all be here at any moment you need or want us to be."

Mum was actually helping; it was the second time in weeks that she'd stunned me.

"C'mon, let's get you back on the couch and I'll go get us some DVDs. Eighties style – *Breakfast Club*, *Pretty in Pink*, maybe *Fast Times at Ridgemont High*?" That was her favourite. "Some Italian takeout, and good coffee," I offered. There was nothing I wouldn't do to cheer her up.

Carrie nodded appreciatively, flicking the strands of hair from her fingers. My throat formed a lump and I tried hard to swallow it back. I couldn't cry, not in front of her anyway.

When I got in the car it spilled over like a pot brought rapidly to the boil. I cried until my eyes burned and my face ached. I picked up my phone and opened a new email to Tom.

> *Why aren't you here? I need you here. I'm barely holding it together.*

Then I pressed Send.

***

"He took me out into the side alley and kissed me!" Annabel proudly announced when she swanned through the front door and interrupted *Sixteen Candles*.

"What?" I laughed. She was jumping around like she had ants biting her backside. "Sit down for goodness' sake."

"Okay, okay," she agreed, falling into an armchair. "Massimo, the guy I met online—"

Massimo? I lifted an eyebrow. Ooh la la!

"—was actually pretty cute. We talked and talked. And guess what, he's into Reiki and massage too."

I bet he is.

"We got along *soooo* well, and then he asked me if I wanted to go for a walk, 'cause Chrissy was with us, but as soon as we got outside, he spun me around and started kissing me! It was fantastic!"

"I'm glad it worked out," I said with a smile. "Are you going to see him again?" I asked.

"I gave him my number. He already messaged me twice on the way home." Her face had lit up like a Christmas tree.

"Massimo – is he an Italian Stallion then?" Carrie joked.

"I don't know," Annabel blushed. "Hopefully, I'll get to find out."

"Excuse me, but I have to throw up," Carrie said, heading to the bathroom. "Not because of your story," she called back with a laugh.

"Listen," I leaned in close to Annabel, "Carrie had a bit of a meltdown today."

"Why? What happened?" The excitement that had filled her eyes disappeared.

"When I got here this afternoon, she was laying on the bathroom floor in Mum's lap. Her hair is falling out."

A gasp caught Annabel's throat and she recoiled. "Oh no, poor love. I can't believe she was laying on Mum's lap! That's a first."

"I know, but Mum was so good with her, I couldn't believe it."

"I can hear you whispering," Carrie declared. She barged between us and resumed her position on the couch. "I did have a bit of a meltdown, Bel, but I'm okay. It just took me a while to come to terms with the fact that it's actually falling out."

She was putting on a front. It was always easy to tell with Carrie. Her body language gave away how hard she was trying to convince us. Convince herself.

Later, I walked Annabel out to the car. "Can you message Julia and tell her we need to meet tomorrow at Carmello's at

11:30, to talk about what else we can do to help Carrie," I said in a low voice. "Mum will be here for the day with her."

"Has Edward even called? Is he coming back?"

"His son called and said he's got bronchitis, so I told him to pass on the message to Edward that she's fine and not to come home until he's better. I didn't want to say anything to Carrie, but it didn't seem like Edward wanted to call himself."

"There's no point in him calling himself anyway," Annabel said. "He can't hear on the phone and if he's got Bronchitis, he definitely needs to keep his distance."

"He'll be staying with his son anyway, so no need to worry." We were all worried. After Carrie's collapse she couldn't afford an infection as well.

"Okay, 11:30," she said through the car window, "I'll message Julia."

By the time I went back in, Carrie was asleep. I sat beside her, watching her chest rise and then fall, over and over again. Her lips looked thin and pink against her gaunt, pale face, the weight already falling off her quicker than it should. I pulled the blanket up to cover her chest and went to the spare bedroom. I texted the kids goodnight, but trying to sleep was hopeless. I needed to talk, I needed to hear another voice.

I hesitated before texting Peter.

Hi Peter. Are you still up? Sorry, I know it's late.

The reply came back immediately.

That's okay, I'm up. What's wrong?

> Me: *Nothing, just staying at Carrie's and*
> *things have been a bit hard today.*

I waited, unsure how to say what I needed to say. I texted again.

> *No matter what happens we'll still be friends won't we?*

My phone rang and I answered it quickly. "Hey, sorry, Peter, I'm just a bit emotional. I shouldn't have even messaged you."

Idiot, this was a mistake. It wasn't fair to him. He didn't deserve to be kept hanging while I tried to decide what I wanted out of life.

"Don't be silly, Viv. I'll be here for you until the day we die – whoever goes first," he joked.

"Peter, I need to be honest with you. Ever since, well, everything, I've been really confused. I don't know what I want and I don't know if we will ever be together again, but it's hard to just let you go too." I was crying.

"I wish every day that I could turn back time and change it," he said, "but I can't. And I know how much I've hurt you." His voice was soft.

Why did hearing his voice make me feel better, even though I couldn't bring myself to forgive or trust him again?

"Seeing Carrie like this has made me realise that life is short, Peter, and I don't want to let you keep trying so hard when I don't know if I can ever go back." I sucked in a breath. "I need to tell you that I've been seeing someone else." I braced for his response.

"I know," he said quietly.

What?

"It's okay. Of course, I don't love the idea, but I still hope, in my heart, that eventually you and I will find our way back to each other."

He knows? I can't think.

"I...didn't expect that. I don't know what to say. Thank you?"

"Thank me? For what? I just want you to be happy, Viv. I'd prefer it was with me, and I hope one day it will be again, but until then, I have no say in what you do with your life."

This counsellor he's seeing must be a magician. Maybe I should ask for the number.

"I appreciate that, Peter, more than you know," I said finally. "I'm so thankful that I can still call you. For some reason it was your voice I needed to hear tonight." I truly did feel grateful. It would be so easy to walk away, or make each other's lives miserable, but we still loved each other, despite our problems.

"Goodnight," I said.

"Night."

I hung up and pulled up the thin bed cover. "Please God, or the Universe, or whatever is up there, please let Carrie be okay. And please let me be okay."

I didn't realise the point at which I fell asleep, but it was swift, sucking me into a dream that played out more tragic than the reality I was escaping.

"Faster, faster," a weird, dream-state version of Darcy said, contorting his face into that same pained expression he had in real life. As my back slid around on the soft fur of the ridiculous rug, the front door swung open and Peter walked in.

"Really, Viv? Is he the best you can do? Sure, he's good looking, but he's a bit of a wanker."

Tom was there. "Yep, he is. What are you doing? You promised no big decisions or craziness while I was gone, Hun. I thought you'd wait for me." I swung my head around to see Tom sitting on a kitchen chair. He started to cry.

Why are they all here? I thought. Watching, like weird, dirty perverts?

I tried to push Darcy off, but my hands slid on his sweaty chest while he pumped away yelling "C'mon, C'mon."

Mum appeared in the doorway, followed by David close behind. I thrashed around, trying to get out from under Darcy.

"Get out!" I screamed at all of them. "You're driving me crazy. *Get out!*"

"Viv? Viv?" It was Carrie's voice. I scanned the faces in the room looking for her, but it was distant, far away. When I opened my eyes, she was sitting beside me on the bed. "You okay?" she asked, handing me a glass of water.

I sat up and leaned back against the cool bedroom wall. "That was the most bizarre dream I've ever experienced," I wheezed, still trying to settle my wired nerves.

"Viv, I think all of this – me, Peter, the others – it's taking its toll on you."

If the dream was anything to go by, she was definitely on to something. "I feel like my life is spiralling out of control, Carrie. I don't know which way to turn. I'm worried about you, and all these bloody men in my life are complicating everything. I can't help thinking that it would be easier just to go back to Peter. At least if I resumed my old life, as unfulfilling as it was, I would know who I am, where I stand."

"You realise that whatever was happening just then was only a dream, don't you?"

I nodded, even though it had felt more real than the conversation we were having right now.

"But I think you're right that this is all driving you nuts," she declared.

Gee thanks. Great pep talk.

"I think we should go away for a couple of days," said Carrie. "We can book a nice place, somewhere near water, and get away from it all."

Getting away was exactly what I needed. "When can we leave? I've had the urge to run away for weeks." I was already feeling the excitement building inside me. "Wait, I've got a wedding on the weekend. Can we go before?"

"Why don't we go on Tuesday? Mum's taking me to the salon to sort this out." She lifted and then dropped a clump of her hair. "I've decided to shave it off."

"Good for you," I encouraged her.

"We can leave after lunch."

"Yes, yes, let's do it! Leave it to me, I'll find somewhere nice," I added.

"Near water, like the beach or a lake or something," Carrie insisted. She got to her feet. "I feel like crap, I'm going back to bed. We'll sort out the details tomorrow."

This was fantastic. Natalia can keep an eye on the boys and make sure they get to school, and we can be back before the wedding on the weekend. Perfect!

I sat down at the small melamine desk in the corner of the spare room and switched on the computer. Lake or beach? Lake would be better – no sand or seaweed. What about a health spa? I looked at what was on offer. Yoga – I don't really love yoga, but I want to. Healthy food – that'll be good for Carrie. Focus – that would help me find my inner self, or is it inner child? No, I don't want to reconnect to my childhood. What does Annabel call it? Inner being, that's it.

I clicked on a few pages that looked more like camping grounds with hippies and candlelight. Definitely not. I clicked on another – 'Inner Wellness Luxury Retreat'. Perfect.

The website's pages were filled with images of two and three bedroom cottages nestled among large trees and fields of vivid green grass. The main house and eating area looked modern and spacious. This is it. This is the one! I clicked on the booking form and rustled in my bag for my credit card. We needed this. Carrie especially.

When the confirmation popped up, I squealed. I poked my head into Carrie's room, but she was fast asleep. I felt like I was high, I could have danced the Macarena if there had been anyone around to share it.

Then a thought occurred to me – Facebook. I had barely looked at it since the night Peter left. Keeping up with pictures of people's lunches and copious amounts of baby snaps had been pretty low on my list of priorities, until now. I needed a distraction.

Fifty-three notifications and four friend requests. Hmm. There were friend requests from Darcy – of course; Kimmy– no bloody way, she was annoying enough in real life. And too orange. David – oh, David's on Facebook, I didn't pick him for the Facebook type. I clicked *Accept*. The last one was John. Who's that? I clicked on his name to enlarge his profile picture. "Who the hell is that? John?" It was the boys' soccer coach.

Why is he sending me a request? For soccer maybe, to keep in contact? He'd sent me a text not long after seeing him at the bus station, to ask how I was doing. Is he interested in me? I shook my head. You are so damn full of yourself. Do you think every man on earth is after you? For goodness' sake, he's just being friendly and looking out for the boys. I needed to sleep, I was having back and forth conversations with myself.

Eventually the excitement of the retreat gave way to utter exhaustion, and my body slowly descended into sleep. This time, there was no dream, just deep, dark blackness.

CHAPTER 19

Truffles

*R*unning *a little late, sorry. Be there in 10,* I texted David.
I frantically pulled on my pants and fossicked around for a chewy so I didn't have to brush my teeth. I'd slept in, which was understandable given how much sleep I'd had lately, but I must have actually woken up and turned off the alarm on my phone. I had no recollection.

David replied soon after.

No problem, I was a little early so I got us a table. I'll order you a coffee.

Great, he had to be bloody early.

"Carrie!" I yelled, grabbing my bag and putting on my other shoe as I hobbled down the hallway. "I need my keeeeeeee..." With my shoe caught in the strap of my bag, I dropped to the floor with a thud and barrel-rolled into the kitchen, landing at Carrie's feet.

"Jesus, Viv, are you alright?"

"No!" I cried, tears filling my eyes as pain ripped through my left hip and shoulder. Carrie reached down to help me up.

"Ooooooh, that hurts," I howled, rubbing the area just behind my shoulder blade.

"What are you doing, you crazy person?" Carrie laughed, handing me a coffee.

I held my hand up. "I can't. I'm meeting David. And I didn't do anything, it was the strap of this stupid bag."

"Well, just be careful driving. You're clearly delirious."

"I gotta go." I gave her a kiss and managed to pass Mum without incident, as she came in through the front door. "Gotta go Mum, I'm running late," I said, pecking her cheek.

It was 25 minutes past our agreed meeting time when I got to the cafe.

"I'm so sorry," I said to David, who had chosen a quiet little booth at the very back of the dimly lit café.

"It's fine. I drank your coffee though, so we'll have to order some more." He beamed a sweet, white-toothed grin and got up to let me into the booth. "So, I'll order more coffee and something sweet?"

"That would be fabulous, thank you." What a darling.

The cafe was adorned with French-style furnishings including lovely old-fashioned coloured glass lamps, dark wood tables, and booths lined with an eclectic mix of floral and patterned material. But my attention was drawn to David, smiling politely as he chatted with the man at the counter. David had chosen black denim jeans today, with a casual deep blue shirt. Better, much better. If he'd worn the cardigan again, our friendship might have been over.

I got out my phone and messaged Annabel and Julia

Catch-up at two. I've got an idea.

"I've ordered a selection of mini cakes and truffles, I hope that's okay," he smiled, getting into the booth beside me.

Okay? Is the Pope Catholic?

"Of course, thank you," I said. "How are things going with your sister?" I asked without taking a breath. I hated uncomfortable silences. Peter would often ask me if I managed to take a breath when we went out or met new people.

"She's doing all right. It's hard to describe, but it's as if she's come to terms with where she's at, or something."

"I know what you mean." I remembered Carrie at that point. How can I tell him what may be yet to come? Don't, I decided, it might end up being different for them, his sister might have different treatment and not even lose her hair.

Instead, I told him about Carrie's treatment and how we had decided to make plans to go away for a few days.

"Oh, I've been to that place, it's fantastic." There was excitement in his voice as he offered me the plate of truffles the young waitress had placed on the table. "I went there for a week after my marriage broke down."

Marriage? He never mentioned he was married.

"It was years ago," he added, obviously noticing the surprise on my face. I was hopeless at hiding what I was thinking.

"What happened? If you don't mind me asking?"

"I don't mind, it was a long time ago now," he said. "We met and married young, and like most I guess, we worked too hard and didn't put each other first."

Was he a cheater? If he was a cheater, that'd be it for me.

"So, who left? Was it you, or your wife?" I had to know. I'm taking the truffles, if he's a cheater. I looked around for something I could tip them into.

"It was all a bit dramatic actually, but luckily, I had my sister. She was like my rock."

He still hadn't said. I scoffed down another truffle and waited for him to continue.

"I had a suspicion that something was up," David went on, drawing in a large breath as if to steady himself. "And one night I deliberately told her I was working late, but instead I came home. My friend – my best man actually – his car was in the driveway."

I held my breath in anticipation

"It sounds a little weird and stalkerish when I say it now, but I parked on the street and peeked in through the window to see what was going on, and that's when I caught them." His hands were shaking.

Poor David. "I'm so sorry," I said. I rubbed his hand and pushed the plate of truffles towards him. "I feel awful for making you relive that now."

"It's fine, I didn't expect it to affect me that much to be honest." He smiled at the waitress as she delivered our coffees. "Shall we get some more?" He took the last truffle and handed the plate to the girl.

YES! I love him!

"What about you?" he said, rubbing his fingers back and forth on the hand I had offered to comfort him.

"Similar story, but it was recent, and I'll end up a blubbering mess if I start. Do you mind if we leave that conversation for a later date?"

I couldn't talk about Peter to another man – except for Tom, of course, not yet anyway.

"Tell me about the retreat. What was it like?" I said. I tried to focus but I was carried away by the feeling of his fingers as they continued to make small circles on my skin. It was hypnotic. The sensation was making me feel as if my eyes might roll back in my head.

"It was exactly what I needed to recharge and refocus," he answered.

"Yes, that's exactly what I was hoping." I cleared my throat to regain my composure. I tilted my head and turned it sideways to stretch out my neck. It had been burning and aching along with my hip since I fell.

"Is your neck sore?" David asked, noticing my discomfort.

I nodded. "Turn around, I'll rub it for you. I was actually a masseuse before I was a teacher."

My eyes widened. He was full of surprises.

"Sorry, did I overstep?" he looked worried. "I know we don't know each other that well."

"No, no, not at all," I said quickly. I turned my back to him before he changed his mind. "I'm just surprised, that's all." I reached for the replenished truffle plate that had arrived, and eased back towards David. His hands gently massaged my tense shoulders making the hairs on my neck stand up.

"Anyway," he said, "at the retreat they have heaps of classes, and of course they teach you how to meditate to a level of utter contentment."

"Sounds fabulous," I moaned. His hands were amazing. He was amazing.

"They also have a fabulous workshop on relationships and the art of tantric sex."

Um, what?

"I know it sounds a little weird, but honestly, I highly recommend it. It really teaches you how to focus sexual energy and make it last for hours."

I'd never felt as turned on as I did right then, with a truffle in my mouth, and David's sensual hands on my neck as he explained tantric sex.

"More coffee?" The waitress asked, interrupting the moment.

David leaned around to check with me. "No, I'm fine thanks, I'm still drinking this one."

"What about some cake?" he offered. Removing his delicious hand, he cut me half a piece.

This is a man who knows what a woman wants.

***

"You look pleased with yourself," Annabel commented when I arrived at Carmello's. "Why are you always late?"

I'd ended up staying for lunch with David. "I do have a life you know," I shot back.

"What's this I hear about you and Carrie going away?" said Julia. "Just the two of you? Why can't we come?"

Annabel nodded in support.

"I never said that you couldn't come. Carrie and I talked about it very late last night and I told her I'd look into it."

"Well, I want to come too," Julia insisted.

Bloody hell. "Fine, as long as Carrie says it's alright."

"And why wouldn't she?" she demanded.

"I don't know, maybe she wanted some peace and quiet," I said.

"She wouldn't be taking you then, would she? You're more likely to involve yourself in some sort of catastrophe than me."

"I want to come too," Annabel chimed in.

For God sake!

Annabel's bottom lip shot out in a sad pout. "But I have clients this week."

"Never mind, next time," I responded, probably too quickly for her liking.

"So, when are we leaving?" Julia asked. She got out her over-sized diary.

Who uses an actual book for a diary these days?

"Actually, that's what I wanted to talk to you both about." I finally remembered why I'd asked them here in the first place. "On Tuesday morning, Mum's taking Carrie to the salon to get her head shaved."

Annabel gasped. "It's just so hard to believe."

"I know, but I was thinking we could do something nice for her, like check out some wigs or something," I said, looking at Julia, who was still scribbling in her book. "Julia? Are you listening?" She was irritating me today.

"Yes, I am, but I have a better idea that I wanted to run passed you both. How would you feel about shaving your heads too?"

Silence filled the space between the three of us. I've never even had short hair. I looked at Annabel who was stroking her brown locks.

"You know what? Stuff it, let's do it." It was so unlike Annabel to make a decision so quickly. "It's for Carrie, what's to think about?"

They were both looking at me. What if I looked hideous? "I still have three weddings. I don't know what my clients will say?"

"Do you care what they say?" Julia questioned.

Do I? I imagined Carrie's face. She was more important than my clients. The helplessness I had been feeling was overwhelming, this was our chance to really show her how much we loved her. "Stuff it, let's do it."

Annabel clapped her hands.

"Now, let's make a plan," said Julia.

"I need a coffee first," I said, trying to get Carmello's attention."

"What's this?" Annabel asked, picking up an envelope that fell from my handbag as I retrieved my purse.

"Forget it, I'm not going. I meant to chuck it in the bin," I said, snatching the bridal awards invitation from her, "I've only got three weddings left. Not to mention my behaviour at the last awards night."

"Don't you wonder though, if you're making a mistake? These couples keep nominating you." said Julia.

"It doesn't matter what they think any more," I countered. "I'm no good to them. They're better off with someone else."

"But you did care once, Viv," said Annabel. "You loved this

job before everything with Peter. You might have been a bit tired and needed a break, but to give it up forever?"

"Let's get back to Carrie. Shaving my head is enough to consider for one day," I said.

I'd been thinking a lot about my decision to give up being a celebrant. My constant irritation and negativity was unfair to people who were paying good money for me to provide an important service, not to criticise them and scowl. I wasn't the celebrant I used to be – not by a long shot. It wasn't fair to go on.

My phone beeped in my bag. It was David.

I had a great time today, hope we can do it again soon. X

He signed off with a kiss, what does that mean? I had fun. He obviously had fun. Don't over-think it. I wonder what he'd be like in bed. Sensual and slow. He'd take his time. Run those big, soft fingers in circles around every inch of my skin. His chest looked strong, but not muscly, under his shirt and I imagined it was hairless, smooth and silky.

"Are you alright?" Annabel said, snapping her fingers in front of me.

"Sorry, I was thinking about something."

"Obviously something good, by the look on your face," she laughed, "Carmello's coffee isn't that good."

"I had lunch with David, that's all. Nothing crazy. It was nice." I shrugged, attempting to throw them off another fishing expedition into my love life.

"Fibber," Julia called it. "Tell us, you have to." Both sets of their beady, demanding eyes were on me.

"Fine, it was better than I expected, and he's actually pretty great. We ordered truffles and he rubbed my shoulders, and then we ended up staying for lunch. That's it."

"That's it? That's plenty!" Annabel giggled.

"Why on earth was he rubbing your shoulders, in a café?" Julia asked. She sipped the last of her coffee and waved for a refill.

"I was complaining about my shoulder because this morning I fell over at Carrie's, so he offered to rub it. He used to be a masseuse though, he wasn't being weird."

Julia gave me the look. It was the same look she'd given me ever since we were kids and she knew that I liked a boy.

"Well, Massimo and I have been having phone sex and I have to say, I don't particularly enjoy it." I was grateful that Annabel had drawn the spotlight away from me, but her admission made me feel queasy.

"Phone sex!" I choked on the mouthful of coffee I had been about to swallow. "What kind of phone sex? Like text or video call?"

"Text messages mainly, that sort of 'what are you wearing' crap."

"Good for you," Julia slapped Annabel's leg.

"It's actually not that fun to be honest," she said. "You know I'm not good with words, and I just end up saying 'black underwear or I want to kiss you all over."

She looked sad. "I've even resorted to looking up love song lyrics and stuff on the internet for ideas. It's so stupid. I just want to *have* sex," she blubbered.

"Well, why don't you just text him that? Say I want you, I

want you to come over and make hot, passionate love to me right now." Julia was teasing, but she had a point.

"He's away at the moment, but as soon as he gets back it's on. Like Donkey Kong." She winked.

I winced at the lame reference. They were almost as bad as her painful repertoire of accents that she often whipped out at random moments. "I gotta go. Tuesday then?" I said, making a note in my phone calendar, like a normal person. "What if we meet here at ten and get to the salon before Carrie. That way we can be ready when she arrives."

"Perfect!" Annabel agreed.

"Yep, it's in the diary!" Julia said, closing her book.

Despite the good cause, I had a feeling of dread about shaving my head. Knowing my luck, my scalp will be horribly discoloured and look like a Brussel sprout or something.

CHAPTER 20

Truth or Dare

"Thanks, Peter," I said holding the phone to my shoulder with my ear while packing the last of my things. "I feel better knowing that you're around while I'm gone."

"I can't move into my unit until the end of the week, so any chance to get away from Mum's is a bonus," he laughed. "Plus, I'm looking forward to spending some time with the kids. Feels a bit weird to be staying in our room though."

"I know, but I do appreciate it, and the kids will too. Make sure the boys don't eat too much crap and that they get their homework done. I've left notes on the kitchen bench."

"Of course you have," he teased. He knew my obsession for making lists and writing notes, all too well.

I dialled Julia's number after Peter hung up. "I'm heading to your place now, so be ready. We have to pick up Annabel on the way."

Annabel had managed to rearrange her clients so that she could make the trip. How I had been deluded enough to think we were going to get away without them astonished me. "Can you quickly call her and tell her to be ready?"

"Will do." Julia sounded excited, upbeat. I felt like throwing up. Shaving my head had never been on my list of things to do.

"Annabel, Julia, Genevieve, it's so nice to see you all," Joanna, the salon owner, greeted us as we walked through the door. "Viv, I haven't seen you for ages, where have you been?"

"Long story," I smiled, determined not to get into it. Today was about Carrie.

"Well, come over here and take a seat. I think this is truly lovely what you guys are doing for Carrie. You had all of us blubbering in here when you called, Julia. Now, who wants to go first?"

I looked at Julia and gave her a poke.

She scowled back at me and raised her hand. "I guess I will," she volunteered, while Annabel and I both sighed with relief.

"We may not get you all done by the time Carrie arrives, so I'll get Jennifer to get the bubbly ready," Joanna said, pinning a cape around Julia's neck.

Joanna chopped away at Julia's shoulder-length strands while I covered my eyes. "I can't look," I giggled, peeking through the tiny gap in my fingers. Annabel was doing the same.

"Neither can I," Julia squealed, shutting her eyes tight.

When the buzzing of the clippers stopped, I peeked again. It was so short. The back of Julia's head was dark and covered in a short stubble.

"I've only done it on a number three," Joanna consoled her, flicking away the tiny hairs from Julia's neck with a soft, fluffy brush.

"Turn around and let's have a look," Annabel said, getting up from the couch.

Julia swivelled her chair around and waited for our reactions.

"It's actually not too bad," Annabel decided, running her hand over the bristles.

"I've brought an extra hat," I teased. "I'm only kidding, it doesn't look nearly as bad as I thought it would." She actually carried it off reasonably well.

"You're up next," Joanna smiled at Annabel, helping Julia out of the chair.

"Then you, Viv," Julia reminded me, plonking herself on the couch.

I could carry this off, surely. My stomach churned.

Joanna was halfway through Annabel's when Carrie and Mum entered the salon. Carrie's eyes widened and filled with tears the moment she set eyes on Julia's bald head. Jennifer had started handing out champagne glasses by the time Carrie had completely broken down.

"Attention everyone," I commanded, clapping my hands. "Today is a very special day, because it marks the first day of the next phase of all of our lives." I loved a dramatic speech. "Carrie, we decided that no matter how much you think this is a journey you have to walk alone, we will be here, side by side, through every single knockdown and every single triumph. So, if you have to be bald, then we'll be bald." I looked at Julia, with her bald head, Carrie with tears flowing down her cheeks, Annabel with half her head shaved in an eighties punk-rock fashion, and Mum, who was clearly overcome with emotion and already pouring another champagne. "We love you so much, and our heads will be a daily reminder of that. Cheers!" I toasted, raising my glass as the others followed.

"Thank you," Carrie mouthed to me as the buzzing of the clippers came to life again.

"I'm going to get mine done too, bugger it!" Mum declared after another champagne.

Annabel and Carrie both looked fabulous. Annabel had a great face for short hair and Carrie's pouty features stood out so much more without the distraction of her long locks. Mum, on the other hand, looked utterly ridiculous.

"Poor Mum," Julia whispered in my ear as we watched the horror unfold. She reminded me of a really wrinkly, ugly newborn baby.

"You're turn, Viv," Joanna announced, swinging the chair around to face me. "Take a seat."

"Wait, Viv," Carrie pleaded. "I really think you should consider just getting it short rather than shaved. You've got weddings coming up."

Relief flooded my pounding heart as Annabel and Julia glared at me.

"We agreed though. I really don't mind," I lied.

"Please don't," Carrie said. "I don't think your clients would appreciate it in their wedding photos, and it's not necessary."

"Cut and colour instead?" Joanna offered, holding up the palette of little hair swirls in dozens of different shades.

"Okay, if you insist," I beamed, unable to hide my relief. "What colour do you think?"

"Go short, and dark, like a deep chocolate brown. This one," Carrie said, pointing to a rich brown.

I hadn't been a brunette, my natural colour, in years. I'd been bleaching my hair blonde since my early twenties in an effort to hide the grey and look younger. It hadn't worked. "Yep, let's do it," I told Joanna, who had already begun snipping.

When she swung my chair back around, an hour and ten minutes, two lattes, and a donut later, my sisters' faces said it all. I looked bloody amazing. Ten years younger. Pangs of guilt poked holes through my veil of joy as I looked at their bald heads and Annabel and Julia's scowls. But it didn't last. I felt fantastic!

***

"Where on earth is this place?" Carrie moaned, looking in the street directory.

Who even has a street directory these days? "Julia, did you bring that bloody big thing?" I asked her.

"Yes, what's wrong with it? At least we'll know where we're going," she fired back in defence.

I pulled my phone from my pocket and hit the navigation icon. "Here, type in the address," I said, handing it to Carrie in the passenger seat beside me.

Annabel's phone message chimed its stupid 'Meet George Jetson' tone for the hundredth time since we got in the car.

"Annabel, that message tone is driving me nuts." I said. "If I have to listen to that for the next two days, I guarantee they will be charging me with justifiable homicide."

"Okay, okay I'll put it on silent," she laughed.

"Who is it, anyway?" Carrie asked, making Annabel squirm.

"It's just Massimo," she answered, shrugging.

"They've been having phone sex," Julia laughed.

Carrie's head shot around faster than I had seen her move in weeks. "What? Phone sex? Tell me!"

Annabel's cheeks had turned a bright red. "Thanks, Julia," she scowled, hitting her on the leg. "It's nothing. He's away and he likes to talk dirty in text messages."

Carrie was practically climbing into the back seat. "And what do you say back?"

"She writes lame stuff like, 'I like you. You are hot'." I was being mean.

"Is he texting you now? Sexy stuff?" Carrie asked, abandoning the GPS.

"Yes. And no, I'm not reading them out, Carrie, forget it." She locked her phone and put it face down in her lap.

"Just let me help you with the responses. C'mon, it'll be fun," Carrie begged.

Annabel wasn't convinced. "Fun for who? Me or you?"

"For both of us – and for Mossio of course, think how much he'll love it."

"It's *Massimo!* Fine," she relented. "I have no idea what I'm doing anyway. Only a couple though."

When I stopped at the lights, I picked up my phone and set the GPS myself, there was no getting Carrie back now. One hundred and 25 kilometres of listening to Carrie sex talk with Annabel's new man-candy. Not exactly the relaxing start I had imagined.

"Okay, write this." Carrie was rubbing her hands together gleefully. "Massimo, the very thought of your hot package is making me tingly. I'm imagining stroking your pounding chest as you push up against me and we move, thrusting in time. You're holding my hair, pulling it a little and I'm screaming for more."

Annabel's fingers were typing frantically, "Far out, Carrie, he's gonna have a heart attack."

We waited in silence for the reply until Annabel screamed.

"Read it, read it," Julia yelled at her.

"You read it," she squealed, throwing the phone at Carrie.

"Annabel I love this side of you! I had to pull over," Carrie read, putting on her deepest man voice, *"I'm looking at your profile picture. I'm imagining us standing in the shower, water falling all around us as I kiss you and drop to my knees—"*

"Okay, that's enough," Annabel cried, grabbing the phone back. "This is mean, and it's bad Karma. Anyway, there's no way I'm going to be able to keep this up later when you're not around."

Carrie slumped back into her seat. "You're no fun," she pouted. "How long until we get there?"

"About an hour and a bit, more if we stop to eat," I said, glancing at the GPS.

"Let's stop and eat, I'm actually hungry for a change. Must be all that sex talk," she teased Annabel. She couldn't help herself.

"Shut up, Carrie." Annabel threw a peanut, hitting her in the head.

"Hey!" Carrie retaliated with every piece of food she could find in the shopping bag at her feet, while Julia and I screamed at both of them.

I yanked the car into the driveway of the Roadworx Diner.

"Get out, you bloody pains in the arses. I need a break from your bickering," I ordered.

"I've got a sedative if you need to calm down," Carrie offered with a smirk.

She ran off as I lifted my fist in response.

***

When we finally arrived at the retreat, it looked exactly as it had in the brochure. Modern, luxurious and serene.

"Wellness Centre?" Carrie exclaimed. "You said we were going to a retreat!"

"It is a retreat, a wellness retreat," I replied, my tone defensive. "It's fantastic, and we have our own villa."

"It looks wonderful, Viv, good choice," Annabel said approvingly. At least someone appreciated my efforts.

"No phones? Are they serious?" Julia was pointing to a large sign that hung from an old, draping willow tree at the top of the gravel driveway.

No Mobiles Preferred
(Except for emergencies)

"Bloody hell," Carrie sighed. "Where have you brought us? To a hippie commune?"

"Just shut up and see what it's like before you start whinging. All of you." I dismissed their complaints with a wave of my hand. "Stay here and complain to each other while I go in and get our keys."

"Welcome, Genevieve. Party of four," greeted a man wearing a bright blue cravat, waving a clipboard at me. "You will be staying in 'Villa Revive'," he announced. "Dinner is at seven, and tonight there are a range of classes and therapies that you can choose from." He handed me a program the thickness of a magazine.

"Follow the gravel driveway around behind those villas." He pointed through the window to three cream-coloured units that stood side by side. "Yours is the last one on the left. Enjoy!" He smiled, jingling the keys.

"It's gorgeous," Annabel shrieked. She practically knocked me to the floor as I opened the door. "I claim this bed! Who's in with me?"

"It's three bedrooms, so you and Julia can share, seeing as you weren't even coming initially," I reminded them. There was no way I was sharing with either of them. Annabel peed about ten times every night and Julia had a terrible habit of talking, and even sometimes walking in her sleep. Sharing a bedroom with her for seven years as kids was bad enough.

"I'm gonna lay down for a bit. Give me a shout when it's time for dinner," Carrie said, closing her bedroom door. She looked exhausted.

While the other two unpacked, I made some tea and checked my messages. Tom!

tom.kelly@yourperfectpic.com:

Hey Hun, how's things? You sound stressed. I wish I was there right now to give you a big hug. I know you've got a thousand questions and we didn't really get a chance to talk, but I promise I'll be back soon. In fact, I'll be arriving home on 27 April. 4 Weeks!

There's so much I want to tell you, but it's hard in an email. Maybe it'll be even harder face to face, but I hope not. I've had a lot of time to think while I've been here, Viv, and I've come to some decisions.

I stopped reading. Decisions? What kind of decisions? He's going back over there after he gets back, I know it. He's met someone and he's leaving for good. I put the phone down on the bed and went to the kitchen. There was a bottle of wine in one of the bags somewhere. I tossed aside a hair straightener, toiletry bag and three bras. Why did I bring three bras?

Aha! I grabbed the bottle and a glass and closed my door. I didn't want to read the rest of the email. But I had to.

I promise I'll explain everything when I see you, but there's one thing I need you to know now. I love you. I know I've said that so many times over the years, but you never heard it the way I meant you to. I want you to hear it now.

I LOVE YOU.

Shit. *What?* No, he can't! I felt paralysed. Unable to move. Unable to process his words.

I always have and I always will. Viv, I'm scared that while I'm away someone else will see what I've always seen – an amazing woman, who loves books and chocolate and who smacks into things, but cares so deeply about everyone. A person who fails to see sometimes, when those she cares for are hurting her.

I know this is a lot to take in and it's unfair of me to do it like this, but I need you to know now. Not in four weeks, or a month, or a year. I've waited more than 20 years already, watching you, loving you and wishing you were mine so that I could treat you the way you deserve to be treated – with unconditional love and respect. I'm saying this because I wanted to give you some time to think about what I've said before we see each other face to face.

I hope you can forgive me for not being there for you through all of this. Please think about what I've said, and I'll see you in 4 weeks.

Tom xxx

I drained my glass and fell backwards onto the pillow. Why now? Why say this to me now? Just when I was beginning to get it together? Carrie knew about this! She's known all along. She's lucky she's got cancer. *Shit!* no, that's a horrible thing to think. Sorry God, Universe. *Arghhhhh.*

"Everything okay, Viv?" Annabel asked, poking her head into the room. "You're making weird noises.

Don't say anything. Think about it first. "I'm fine, just catching up on emails from some irritating clients. Sorry." I forced a smile. "We'll head over to the main room for dinner soon. I'll have a quick shower."

***

"What is this crap?" Julia screwed up her face and held her

spoon high so that the slop could fall back to the plate with dramatic effect.

"It's not that bad – if you hold your nose," Annabel said, picking up the menu. "According to this, it's Tofu stew."

"Stop it!" I cautioned them, "People are already staring at us."

It wasn't particularly surprising given that we looked like a travelling circus. Annabel was sporting the most ridiculous wig I had ever seen. It was red, shoulder length, and made up of hundreds of tiny braids attached to a thick black headband.

"You're not wearing that, are you?" Carrie had demanded before we left the villa. She wore it of course along with an all-in-one orange jumpsuit. Julia wasn't much better wearing Ugg boots with a leopard print dress.

"Viv, this trip was supposed to be about gorging on junk food and getting massaged by a hot Sven. At least that's how I imagined it," Carrie griped.

The room went dead silent, and dirty looks shot in our direction.

"Let's get out of here, I brought enough supplies," I said, getting up and hushing the others with my finger to my lips.

"Shit, Annabel," Julia hissed as Annabel's chair fell backwards with a crash. At the same time, her mobile phone sprang into a full volume ring.

"You can't have that in here," A cranky-looking member of staff bellowed, striding toward us with gigantic steps, her finger waving up and down.

"Run," Carrie giggled, grabbing my arm as we bolted to the door, giggling like teenagers, and followed closely by the other two bald-headed badgers.

"She nearly had you," I laughed, poking Julia as we ran side by side to our villa. "Reminds me of old times. Remember when you put me over the fence at that house to steal their cactus for our cactus garden? And then when I couldn't get back over, you left me there and went home?" I slapped her this time in response to her giggle. "You were such a bitch to me," I added as we fell in the door laughing and panting.

I rummaged in the bags that still sat on the tiled floor of the small kitchen, for anything that resembled junk food.

"Here, I brought some stuff," Julia said, throwing me a bag.

"Julia, I love you!" Carrie was pleased as she rustled through the loot, packed with all of her favourites: a mixed cheese pack, olives, salsa and chips, a bar of dark chocolate and three bottles of wine – two red and a sweet white as well as orange juice and fruit. We laid it all out in the middle of the lounge room floor, picnic-style.

"Let's play *Truth or Dare*!" said Carrie, with a witch-like cackle.

Annabel's worried eyes shifted from me to Julia and back to Carrie. She hated *Truth or Dare*. Carrie always made us play it when we were kids and Annabel would end up doing something awful or telling something she'd vowed not to.

"I don't know, aren't we a little bit old for that now?" she said. "Carrie, you're 45 for goodness' sake."

"Hey! I'm 42, *Julia's* 45. And anyway, you're only as old as you feel, Bel," said Carrie, flopping down onto a cushion.

"I'm in," Julia agreed, placing her cushion across from Carrie. Annabel reluctantly took her place while I got the glasses.

"Same rules as always," Carrie instructed. "You can't take a truth or a dare more than twice in a row and we each get two 'share' passes which means the others have to answer the same question or do the same dare. Use them wisely, girls." She broke out in an evil laugh and spun the white wine bottle.

"Genevieve," they sang in unison, clearly relieved when the bottle completed its rotation facing me.

Shit. I don't want to do a dare. It'll be something awful. "Truth," I winced as the word left my mouth.

"Right," Carrie said, leaning in. She was enjoying this. "Who is your fantasy man? The one you fantasise about when you're having really boring sex? Be honest," she warned, pointing her finger in my face. Annabel and Julia were both eagerly waiting with wide eyes.

I hated this game. "It would have to be Garek." He was a Polish boy I had dated briefly in high school, but he was hot. So, so hot.

"Who the heck is Garek?" Annabel whined.

"He's a guy she dated in high school. He was hot actually". Julia agreed, looking up at the ceiling as if she were recalling his image. "I can see that."

"Well, that's boring." Carrie wasn't impressed either.

"I want to use my 'share' card. Spill it, all of you. Carrie?" I said triumphantly. I had dodged her evil bullet and now it was on her.

"My fantasy sex person is Karen Hocking," she declared, without even batting an eye. "I had a fling with her about fifteen years ago. You remember, Julia?"

Julia nodded, but Annabel screwed up her face. "I honestly don't get how you could, you know, go there. Down there, I mean. With all that ... stuff," she squirmed.

Julia's snorty giggles were setting me off.

"Annabel, what stuff are you talking about?" said Carrie. "Are you sporting a few extra bits that the rest of us don't have?"

Annabel's face reddened to beetroot and she gulped a mouthful of wine.

Annabel never drank. This was going to get interesting.

"Got a kitchen sink down there, Bel? Maybe a colour TV?" Julia teased.

"Shut up! I just meant the bits and the cliforis and—"

I had to hold my stomach for fear it would burst as I rolled onto my back. "What the hell is a *cliforis*?" I laughed, hot tears streaming from my eyes.

"The bloody bit you tickle, you know the G-spot. Why is it called a G-spot anyway?" Annabel added, making us heave.

"It's clitoris, with a *T*, you dag, and they're not the same thing," Carrie managed to say, as Annabel began to laugh too. "How the hell can you reach 47 years of age and not know what your most precious body part is called."

"You are such cows!" Annabel scowled through smiling lips. 'Meet George Jetson' sang out from her phone as we tried to regain our composure.

Annabel poked her tongue out at us while opening the message. With an "*Eeeeek*" she threw her phone on the floor.

"What's wrong?" Julia asked, picking it up. "Oh my God!" She was hysterical again when she passed it to Carrie and then to me.

Given Annabel's apparent new interest in getting down and dirty, thanks to Carrie, Massimo had decided it would be a great idea to ramp up the phone sex with a close-up 'dick pic'.

My sides were ready to burst. It was ten minutes before any of us could speak.

CHAPTER 21

The Downhill Slide

The fan clanked and rocked with every rotation as I laid in bed. It seemed bound to drop and cut my head off at any moment. I don't care, let it. It would be easier that way.

Picking up the book I'd brought with me, I tried to read, but my brain ached and my thoughts were consumed with the email from Tom. I couldn't stay focused long enough for the words on the page to make any sense. I snapped it shut.

Movement in the kitchen. Someone was finally up.

"You look as bad as I feel," I said to Annabel, whose bloodshot eyes were heavy with bags the size of mountains.

"I only had two! This is why I don't drink," she sighed.

By the time we'd finished our game of truth or dare, Annabel had been completely out of it and poor Massimo had been bombarded with pictures of boobs. It was hilarious at the time, but probably less so in the sober light of day.

"What do you remember?" I questioned, hoping some of it would be lost somewhere in her subconscious.

"Not much after Julia dared me to be a horse, and then rode me through the garden."

Good, it was better that way. Annabel had made far too many horrifying admissions to deal with at this time of the morning. Knowing Carrie, they would be raised at a later time to make her squirm.

Carrie emerged from her room and grinned at me knowingly.

"Don't", I mouthed, warning her to leave Annabel alone.

"Yoga today?" Carrie looked a little better. She had some colour in her cheeks. The doctor had advised her not to drink excessively while having chemo. She'd stuck to orange juice and I was pleased that for once in her life she was doing as she was told.

"Are you up to it?" I asked, still worried that the added exertion would be pushing it.

"I actually feel quite good. I'll probably need a lie down later, but yoga and a tantric sex class sounds fabulous."

Annabel spat her tea into the sink "A what? Tantric sex class?"

"Yes, Annabel, and you're coming," Julia said, winking at me as she pulled her robe on. "You need to learn how to pleasure yourself, and Massimo of course. It'll be good for all of us."

She directed the last part at me. Why me? I'd been doing well in the man department lately. I was offended.

"We never did find out who your fantasy man was, Julia," Annabel prodded.

"It's Steve, of course. I don't need to imagine anyone else. Steve's hot, masculine, gentle but forceful, and he knows what I like. Our sex life is amazing."

Bloody Julia. Typical!

"But you must think about someone occasionally. Everyone does," I probed, determined to make her tell.

"Well, if I really had to choose, it would probably be Don Johnson, from his *Miami Vice* days, though. I loved those jackets he used to wear and his sleek style."

I put my fingers down my throat and pretended to gag.

"Annabel, you didn't tell either," Carrie reminded her.

"My fantasy man is Adam Levine," she said, placing her hand on her heart like a dreamy schoolgirl.

"Adam who?" Carrie questioned, lifting one side of her top lip.

"Levine, he's the singer from Maroon 5." Annabel whipped out a picture of him, naked, with only a hand covering his genitals that she'd obviously printed from the internet.

"Why are you carrying his picture around, you weirdo?" Julia laughed.

"Because it has my list of criteria on the back. All the things I want in a man." She said it as if such a thing was completely normal.

"Let me see." Julia snatched it from her hand and ran behind the couch, before she could grab it back. She read it out loud:

1. Muscles – not too muscly
2. Good hair – dark, flecks of grey, slick, longer on top.
3. NON-SMOKER
4. Tattoos
5. English accent

"English accent? Are you serious?" I laughed.

"Wait, there's more," Julia said, holding up her hand away from Annabel who was reaching across the couch trying to swipe it back.

6. Romantic and funny
7. Have a sexy side
8. Bow-legged

"What the hell is bow-legged?" said Carrie.

Annabel ignored Carrie's comment, "I want a guy who's trendy, dresses well, and smells good. You can all laugh, but if you ask, the Universe will provide. Focus on what you want and eventually you'll be led toward it, or it to you," she declared, managing to snatch the paper back from Julia.

"There's not a man on earth who could fill all those criteria," I said.

"I don't know," said Annabel. "Adam Levine comes pretty close, and David Beckham."

Carrie screwed up her face. "Sweetie, you need help."

***

I wasn't in the mood for meditation. My head was already swarming and silence was only going to amplify it. "Can't I just go back to the villa?" I moped.

"Viv, you need this more than any of us. C'mon, just try it. Let me do some tapping on you to warm you up to it," Annabel offered.

Great. I'd walked into that one. She was full of annoying encouragement as she tapped away on my forehead.

Julia and Carrie had already laid out their mats and taken their positions on the floor.

"Okay, that'll do," I said, pushing Annabel away and facing her toward her mat. "Go sit down."

The instructor, who just happened to be the same woman who told us off in the common room, led us deep into our inner selves. As I lost all train of thought, one image kept appearing over and over again. *Piss off, Tom. Piss off.* I tried to re-focus and banish his face from my mind, but it was hopeless; he wouldn't budge. I felt unbalanced in the darkness and opened my eyes to stabilise, but as soon as I closed them again, the face returned and so did the imbalance.

"I love you. I love you. I always have," Tom's lips mouthed, again and again like a record stuck on its revolution.

I don't know how I feel, I told his apparition. I love you too, but I can't risk losing you if it doesn't work. The truth was I didn't even know if I was attracted to him like that. I'd never let myself think about it before.

As I tried to push his image away, others joined in – Peter, David, Darcy. Annabel's tapping, Carrie's laughter, Julia's sex talk, all swam around in my head, making me dizzy.

In the silence, beyond the inner sanctum of my thoughts, there was a noise, a rustling and then a "Pfffffft".

My eyes shot open and locked on Annabel to my left, who was already red-faced. "Sorry," she called out, "that wasn't what you think it was."

Carrie and Julia's horrified faces stared back at me. Everyone in the room was looking at us again.

"It was just my pants moving against the plastic mat," she said re-enacting the motion to prove her point.

As I watched her shifting her backside along the mat, my intense inner monologue was shattered and an overwhelming urge to laugh took hold. Carrie was struggling, as she and Julia giggled and wriggled about trying to stay quiet.

"Shut up," Annabel waved angrily, making it so much worse.

"If you can't be quiet, you'll have to leave," the mean-faced instructor called out, allowing everyone a second opportunity to glare in our direction. Carrie had already managed to crawl to the door, dragging her mat behind her. Tears streamed down her cheeks with a snort escaping every time she met mine or Julia's eyes.

There's no way I'm going to a tantric sex class with any of them.

"Bloody hell, Annabel," Julia said once we were all outside, "what are you trying to do? Kill us?"

"I didn't even fart, honestly. It was the stupid mat." She was upset. "Why does this kind of thing keep happening to me?"

"It doesn't. It happens to Viv usually," Carrie kindly added, striding across the lawn toward the villa. "That woman is such a cranky bitch. C'mon, let's find something fun to do. I'm glad we got out of there anyway."

"I vote we go to the lake and relax in the sun for a while," I said. Water had always been a soothing force for me.

Julia grabbed the remainder of our snacks and we hit the tree-lined walking trail that led to the lake. The trees rustled in the warm breeze, old and tall and full of stories. I ran my fingers along the rough bark of the trunks and watched the different species of birds as they tweeted and played happily in the leafy canopies above. The air felt as if it was opening all of the tiny air sacs in my lungs.

"What's going on with you?" Julia asked.

The unexpected question stopped me in my tracks. "Nothing, why?"

"There's obviously something bothering you, Viv. Tell me."

How did she know? I'd been smiling, laughing, doing all the expected things. "No, nothing, I've just got a lot on my mind."

"Here, sit down," she ordered, pointing out a patch of grass as the other two walked on ahead and found a spot near the water. "Tell me what's up, maybe I can help."

Why was I so scared to tell her? She might help. No, it's too complicated. It all sounds ridiculous.

"Hello? You still with me?" Julia waved her hand through my gaze which had fixed on the water.

"Yes, it's just complicated. I don't even know where to start." Tears were already welling in my eyes. I opened Tom's message and handed her my phone.

"Oh," she said when she had finished reading, "I didn't realise he felt so strongly."

"Neither did I, and now I don't know how to handle it."

"Well, how do you feel about him? Can you see yourself with him?"

"I can see myself with him in every way except romantically, or sexually. I love him, we finish each other's sentences, I know what he's thinking ... but I never let my mind wander to that place, you know, imagining us together." The tears refused to stay away no matter how much I willed them to.

"Do you want to try? Give it a go with him?" She asked.

"I don't want to lose him as a friend, Julia. If it doesn't work out, what then?" I sighed. "And then there's Peter and David."

For once Julia had nothing to say. She shrugged and looked to the lake as if hoping to draw some inspiration from its beauty.

"I'm scared I'll make the wrong choice, and once it's made, there'll be no going back."

"Then don't make one yet. Try not to overthink it. Put it in the hands of fate or whatever. What does Annabel call it – the Universe, or—"

"Her 'guides'," I corrected.

"Why don't we just relax and try to enjoy all this while we're here. You can revisit it all once you get home. Don't ruin your relaxation time by obsessing about all these men! They'll still be there tomorrow."

As always, she was right.

"C'mon, let's have a dip," she said, pulling my arm and running ahead. "Hurry up, slow coach."

"The water's bloody freezing, I'm not going in that," I moaned, dipping in a toe. I preferred to look at water, rather than get in it. I hated the beach too. "I'm gonna lay down here." I spread my mat on the luscious green grass of the bank and drifted into sleep.

Light and sounds danced all around my head as I soaked in the warm rays of the sun and breathed in the freshness of the air. It was perfect. The elusive relaxation I had been searching for finally enveloped me, until a buzzing sound and Annabel's high-pitched scream brought me crashing back to reality.

I slapped at the buzzing mosquito, waiting for my eyes to adjust to the sunlight. They fixed on Annabel, who was clawing her way through the water in an effort to reach the bank.

"I felt something! I felt something slimy!" she squealed. I sat up and swatted another mozzie that was trying to attack my forehead.

"It's a lake, Annabel, it was probably a little fish or something," Julia said, pulling herself up on the bank.

"Julia, stop!" Carrie yelled. "Don't move."

Annabel's ear-piercing scream sent Julia into a blind panic as she burst into tears and barrel-rolled onto the grass in an effort to remove whatever was on her.

"I said stop, not throw yourself on the ground," Carrie yelled at her again. "Calm down!"

It wasn't easy to calm down once Annabel had declared Julia had a leech stuck to her butt.

I swatted more mozzies that buzzed around my face. Where are they all coming from? Caught up in Julia's plight, I had failed to notice the swarm of mosquitos that were now sucking on my arms, legs and face.

"Shit! Shit!" I hollered, springing to my feet and running circles on the lawn while the swarm buzzed around me.

"What the hell is she doing?" Carrie looked like she was ready to throttle the lot of us. "Viv, what the hell are you doing?" she hollered.

"Mozzies, I'm being attacked by fucking mozzies!" I screamed, running at full pelt down the glorious path that had led me to this festering hellhole. I made it to the villa and stripped off on the porch before jumping in the shower.

"Are you okay?" Annabel called through the bathroom door when they got back, minutes behind me.

"No! I'm covered in the bloody things, Bel." Ever since I was little, I was the one who was always eaten by mozzies while the others happily played.

"You've got sweet blood, cause you're a sweetie," Dad would say to make me feel better when the swollen bites would leave me looking like I had a horrible disease.

"I've probably got some calamine lotion in my first aid bag," Annabel offered. A moment later she called through the door. "Can I come in?"

"Yes," I sulked, wrapping myself in a towel and sitting on the lid of the toilet.

"Jesus, Mary and Joseph!" she muttered, screwing up her face. The other two appeared at the door, seconds later.

"Oh my God, Viv, you look terrible," Julia winced, dabbing my swollen forehead.

"You look like Herman bloody Munster!" Carrie added, just to make me feel worse.

I stood in front of the mirror. The skin on my arms, legs and face felt tight, but the sight was far worse. I gasped in horror as my reflection revealed the swollen bites that covered my forehead, cheeks and chin.

"Argh! That's it. ENOUGH!" I cried, shaking my fist at the ceiling. You fucking bastard of a Universe, Mother Nature, whatever, I've had it! I dare you. I DARE YOU to mess with me again. This is it, you got it. IT! No more!"

The three pairs of wide eyes that were staring at me, didn't blink.

"I'll get you a drink," Carrie offered, finally breaking the silence and returning with a full glass of white wine while Annabel and Julia worked on covering the welts with lotion.

"At least you didn't have a leech sucking on your backside," Julia said. "Carrie had to pick the friggin' thing off, and another one that had crawled up under my T-shirt." She shivered at the memory.

"I told you there was something in that water, but no, no one believed me," Annabel gloated.

I stared at the white bathroom wall through a haze of steam that lingered from the hot shower. I wondered if this is how it felt to be locked up in a lunatic asylum.

CHAPTER 22

Laughter is the best medicine

"Seeing as we didn't get to do the Tantra class last night, I want to do the 'Laugh yourself healthy' session today before we leave," Carrie announced.

I groaned and dropped my toast back on the plate. I'd lost my appetite. "My entire body is itching and driving me nuts, Carrie, and you were completely exhausted last night, we were worried. You need to rest."

"I was really tired, that's all. You try having as much chemo as I've had and see how you feel." She was pulling the cancer card, there was no getting out of it. "I'm sick and I need to laugh myself healthy. And so do you. And you," she pointed at me and then at Annabel. "We could all do with trying something positive. That's what we came here for."

Laugh yourself healthy. How ridiculous. The last thing I felt like doing right now was laughing.

I felt more like beating the hell out of something. I needed a 'punch your way to happiness' class.

"I'll give it a go," Annabel said.

Of course she would. This sort of thing was right up her alley.

"It starts in half an hour. I'm getting in the shower," Carrie called from the hall.

I dropped my shoulders and went to my room to change, but ended up reading Tom's email again. Just come back, Tom. Please come back.

My phone buzzed, it was David.

> Hi Viv, just wanted to say that I hope you're having a good time. Really enjoyed our coffee, hope we can do it again soon.

He didn't deserve to get mixed up with a head case like me.

"Come on!" Carrie called from the front door, "we'll miss the beginning."

"I can't believe you're making us do this, Carrie." She didn't care about our wellness, she just loved to torture us.

"I think it'll be fun," Annabel said, but quickly added "sort of" when I glared at her.

"Stop whining and move it," Carrie ordered as I stood on the porch of our villa, watching the three of them cross the lawn to the gathering area.

I followed, dragging my feet. "It's weird. What will they even be laughing about? It's completely stupid," I growled.

"Your face should be enough to get us all going." Julia had to have her two cents' worth.

"Me? Have you not taken a look at this one?" I said, pointing at Annabel who had covered her bald head with a ridiculous beanie that had eyes and pink rabbit ears.

"Hey, I love my hat, shut up," Annabel shot back, pretending to be hurt by my comment.

The small group of about fifteen, were gathered under a gigantic mop-top tree.

"Welc—" the instructor began to say before she realised it was us and promptly stopped.

"Shit, it's that cranky cow again," Carrie whispered. "Don't they have any other instructors in this place?"

Her narrowed eyes fixed on each of us in turn, warning us to behave or else. How can you disrupt a laughing class anyway? Sheesh. The instructor didn't look like the kind of person who laughed very often.

"Alright, let's get laughing," Nasty said, opening her frowning mouth wide, and allowing a horrible cackle to resonate through my head. Others followed, making sounds that I feared might attract the wildlife, to see what all the commotion was. Annabel was already bobbing up and down and throwing her head back as she cackled like a Banshee.

"C'mon, Viv," Julia pushed, goading me with crossed eyes and fish lips.

The nasty instructor took it up a notch and started bending over and standing up swiftly with bursts of hilarity. I swapped mortified looks with Carrie. How could they embarrass themselves this much in public? Carrie tried to join in, bending her knees and letting out the most pathetic and awful attempt at a laugh I had ever heard. She looked like she was trying to lay an egg. When she met my eyes and saw my utter shame for her, we both fell into a fit of laughter. Real laughter.

"Well done," Nasty said while we heaved and choked. *We're*

laughing AT you! I wanted to yell, but the sight of the whole lot of them – their big, gaping mouths and ridiculous expressions – only made me laugh harder.

***

Beside me in the passenger seat, Carrie turned the radio up to full. "I love this song," she yelled over Pharell, who was singing about how damn happy he was.

Despite the laughing class, and Pharell's insistence, I didn't feel happy. Going home meant facing everything and everyone, and I didn't feel ready. Not yet. I needed to think. Away from everything, my sisters included. I could barely string a single thought together with all this racket.

Unable to hear anything above the noise, I hadn't noticed the police car following with its siren on and headlights flashing.

"Shit, there's a cop behind me with his lights flashing," I said, straightening up. "Is he pulling me over?"

Julia and Annabel were already staring out the back window.

"Um, yes, I'm pretty sure he is, and he looks kinda mad," Julia said.

Panic flooded my brain. What do I do? Stop, you have to stop. Where? there's nowhere. It's a highway. Keep going, find somewhere.

"Viv, pull over, he's waving his arms about," Annabel insisted, her tone urgent.

I ignored her. No, find a proper spot, a safe spot, that'll be better. I kept driving.

"Viv, this isn't *Thelma and Louise*. Stop the bloody car before he calls in backup and starts shooting at us. He knows we've seen him. *VIV!*" Carrie screamed.

"There's nowhere to pull over safely," I shot back, "I can't stop here, there should be a safety lane up ahead. When I found it, I pulled in and wound down my window as the officer walked up to the car.

"Ma'am, why didn't you stop when I signalled you?" he asked, obviously frazzled. "I've been following you for five minutes."

"I wasn't concentrating, I'm sorry."

Carrie pinched my leg and frowned at me. Shit, I shouldn't have said that. "I mean, I was concentrating, just not on what was behind me. You know, not looking out the back window."

"Didn't you hear the siren?"

I shot Carrie an evil look. "This one," I said, pointing to her, "had turned the radio up full blast and was singing at the top of her lungs."

"Are you alright? You don't look so good." He was staring at the welts all over my face and arms with a curious expression.

"She's fine," Annabel decided to interrupt, "it's just mozzie bites. She was attacked."

"You're very lucky that I didn't call it in as a chase, I wasn't far off... Annabel? Is that you?" The officer asked, leaning in the open window.

Annabel was mid-bite into a Snickers bar, "Hmm? What?"

"It's me, Gerry Bradbrook. From high school." He put his notebook back in his pocket.

Yes! I flashed Carrie a sneaky, hopeful glance.

"Gerry, of course, hi. Wow, a cop, that's hot. Not hot,

awesome, I meant to say awesome," Annabel fumbled, covering her mouth while Gerry blushed.

This is good. C'mon, Annabel, bring it home.

"This is crazy," Gerry said, shifting nervously from his left foot to his right. "I always wondered where you ended up."

"Yep, here I am. In this car. Running from the police on a highway," she laughed, flipping her hand casually in the air.

Carrie rolled her eyes in frustration.

"So, what have you been up to, Gerry?" Julia interjected to distract him.

"Well, I'm a cop, obviously. I was married, but I'm not anymore," he said, winking at Annabel.

"What a coincidence. Annabel's divorced, too," I declared, feeling her foot penetrate the back of my seat.

"This is kind of embarrassing," Gerry confessed, his cheeks flushing, "but I had such a crush on you through high school."

"Hahahahahaha. Hahahahahahah. Hahahahhahaa." Annabel's third bout of laughter was one too many. She always laughed like a crazy person when she was nervous.

"You two should go out sometime," Carrie quickly intervened.

"Um, I'd love to. Would you be up for that?" he asked Annabel.

"Of course, yeah, sure," she replied as a piece of nut flew out of her mouth and landed in Julia's hair. "I'll give you my number." She smiled, tugging on the bunny-eared hat that still covered her bald head. Gerry took his notebook out again, and Annabel recited her number as he wrote it down.

Now put away the notebook Gerry. Please. I looked at Carrie and Julia, whose eyes were fixed on the book too. *Put it away. Put it away.*

Gerry tapped the top of the book with his pen and tucked it back in his pocket. "Have a great day, ladies. Don't have that music too loud," he warned, pointing his finger at Carrie who flashed her sweetest smile in return.

We were off, without a ticket. Go Annabel!

***

Peace and quiet, finally. When I got home, there was no Peter, no kids, no sister. The boys would still be at school and Natalia was either at work or classes. I put down my bag and laid on the bed. The scent of Peter's aftershave escaped from the pillows as they squashed beneath my head. I loved his smell. He always chose the best aftershave, even though he rarely spent a lot on anything else. That was probably what attracted that young girl to him. Stop it. Don't go there. Not now.

I ignored my ringing phone and curled into a ball, dragging the covers on top of me. My eyes stung and my head throbbed. I fell fast asleep until Peter's voice woke me.

"Viv, wake up. You have to wake up." He was insistent, pushing the hair from my squinting eyes.

"What time is it?" I mumbled, closing them again.

"It's six in the evening. There's a couple here, an older couple, who say they have an appointment with you."

My eyes flung open and my heart rate increased to a sprint. "Shit, I forgot," I said. I jumped from the bed and smoothed my T-shirt. "Stall them. Make tea or something."

"What the hell happened to you?" Peter was staring at my red, blotched face.

"Mozzies, now go, quick. Tell them I'm organising their papers and I'll be out in a minute. Make sure the boys aren't lounging around in their underwear," I added.

"They're in their room. I'll make tea. By the way, your hair looks great."

"Dee Dee, Max, how are you?" I said, casually swanning into the room. "Before you ask, I had a bit of a run in with some mosquitos, but I'm fine."

"Oh, you poor dear," Dee Dee comforted, sipping her tea and reaching for a Tim Tam.

I threw Peter a thankyou nod and arranged the paperwork on the kitchen table. "Let's get started then."

Dee Dee and Max were sweethearts. They were probably one of the nicest couples I'd had in a long time. I actually liked them.

"Luvvy," Max began, his voice shaking, "I know that this may be somewhat of an unusual request, but would there be any chance, I mean would you mind if we," he said, taking Dee Dee's wrinkled hand, "got married here?"

Here? As in here at my house? It wasn't uncommon for celebrants to do weddings in their back yards for couples who were only having a short ceremony with a few witnesses. It wasn't always practical to book a park or venue for a ten minute ceremony. I'd done several at home in my early career, but I hadn't had one here in years. Peter was pointing to the back yard.

"Our back yard's not too bad, Max, but it's not ideal. Are you sure?" I asked.

"We're really not sure if anyone, other than our two friends who are the witnesses, will even come," Dee Dee explained through teary eyes. "Our families aren't happy about it, you see."

"Is there a problem? A reason they're upset?" I asked. Dee Dee seemed like she wanted to get it off her chest.

"Well, my wife only passed away four years ago," Max went on, while Dee Dee took her hanky from her purse and dabbed her nose. "And my son feels that it's too soon for me to marry again. He thinks Dee Dee's using me. Having it here will be neutral ground, you see."

What would she be using him for? Sex? Or to get all his non-existent money. Max had already told me that they each had their home, but nothing else. He would rather see his father alone and miserable than risk what he thinks he might inherit!

"I told Max I would be happy to sign a paper to say I don't want anything of his," Dee Dee said, "I have enough."

My heart ached for them. These two were the most romantic and sweet couple I had ever encountered. They were in love. Real love. The kind that saw past all of the material things; that knew the road ahead would be difficult and fraught with ill-health and challenges, but worth every second that they were afforded the luxury of enduring it together.

Max patted Dee Dee's hand and gave her a gentle smile. "You'll be doing nothing of the sort. If he comes, he comes, and if he doesn't, too bad."

"Good for you, Max! In my experience you can't please everybody so you may as well please yourselves. Be happy. Make your own choices." I felt quite philosophical, but realised I wasn't taking my own advice. I looked up at Peter who met my eyes.

"I'm hoping my children will come," Dee Dee went on, "but I'm not sure. My son is interstate and my daughter is not happy about me getting married at all. She thinks I'm ready for the old people's home. She has some issues." She lowered her voice as she said the last part as if the walls might gossip.

Jesus, what had these two bred? Nasty, greedy, self-absorbed human beings. I felt like calling them all and giving them a piece of my mind.

"How many will there be at most? If they all end up coming?"

Max looked at Dee Dee who was counting her fingers. "Maybe ten?" She said with a shrug.

"That sounds about right. A couple of our grandchildren are happy for us and have said they will be coming," Max said, clearly happy that someone was on their side.

Thank goodness, "Okay, well you're very welcome to do it here. It's a short ceremony and given that you'll only have a few guests, it's not a problem for me."

They both nodded, "Are you sure you wouldn't mind? We'd hate to put you out." Dee Dee said for both of them.

"I don't mind." I smiled, "It's settled then. I'll see you Saturday week."

"Do you need me to help?" Peter offered as we watched them pull out of the driveway, "I can mow the lawn and tidy up out there. Make it look nice?"

I appreciated the offer. "That would be great, thank you. I don't even know how to start the bloody lawnmower, and neither do either of your sons," I teased.

"I have to get going, but I'll come back and get my things later if that's all right?" Peter said.

"No problem." Our exchange felt almost normal, but completely alien at the same time. We were discussing the usual things, things we'd been discussing for years. Lawns, kids, who was going where, doing what, but there was a false pleasantness about it, a fear of saying the wrong thing or upsetting the status quo. It made the exchange feel unnatural somehow, almost forced. For now, it would have to be enough. Peter was being nicer than he'd been in years and there was no point looking a gift horse in the mouth, even if that gift horse came with baggage.

CHAPTER 23

Face off

"You've done a great job out here," I said, handing Peter a beer. He had come over on Saturday and Sunday, and it was the third day in a row he'd arrived straight from work.

"It's coming together really well," he said. "I'm just gonna get a few pencil pines to line the fence, and tidy up the back garden section, and then it'll be perfect for Saturday."

"I really do appreciate it, Peter. I'm so glad that we can be like this and not all crazy, tearing each other's throats out." I had been a bit crazy and throat-tearing initially, but what's done is done. There was no undoing it. In fact, Peter and I were actually getting on better than we had in years.

"I wanted to talk to you about your unit," I said, pulling out two of the outdoor chairs and offering him one. "I'm happy for you to take whatever you need to set yourself up. We've got more than one TV, the extra fridge in the shed, and plenty of bed linen and kitchen stuff. Take whatever you need, it's only fair."

"Yeah, I might need to round up a few things, but you know Mum, she's practically filled the spare room with stuff for me to take."

"Of course she has. A glory box!" I teased. I knew exactly what he meant. These little exchanges and shared understandings were the most poignant. The single line that one of us could say and the other would understand exactly what it meant. The sight of something I hated, that Peter would immediately know to move or get rid of. The facial expressions that indicated we didn't like someone or the taste of something. They're not easily re-created with a new partner. They take years, decades even, to develop.

"Well, I want you to know that I'm happy for you to take whatever you need," I said getting up. "I'll be in my office, so call out if you need anything."

I sat at my desk and turned on the computer. It was time to respond to Tom.

tom.kelly@yourperfectpic.com:

Dear Tom,

Sorry that I haven't responded, but you kind of shocked the hell out of me. Even now, I honestly don't know what to say. I've always known that you loved me, but I didn't know you felt like that. This is hard for me to say, so I'm just going to say it. I don't know how I feel. I love you, of course, you are my very best friend, but I don't know if I love you like that. Carrie insists that maybe I haven't felt a spark between us because I've shut myself off from even entertaining the idea, but I'm not so sure.

Maybe there just is no spark. I want to be completely honest with you before you get back. I'm seeing someone else – it's only new and casual at this point, but I think I sort of like him.

And Peter is still around and all of this is actually really confusing and hard.

I knew exactly what Tom would be saying as he read this. He'd be pacing back and forth, upset with me for not cutting Peter loose when I had the chance. He was adamant that Peter didn't deserve another chance.

I know what you're thinking right now, but honestly Tom, Peter has changed. You wouldn't even recognise the way he is now, and the truth is, I'm not ready to let him go completely. I'm not saying we're getting back together, or that we're not. I actually don't know what I'm saying. Anyway, what I really wanted to tell you is that I appreciate what you said and I'm sorry that I didn't realise before, but I don't know if I feel the same. I just don't know. Our friendship means everything to me and I can't wait for you to get home.

Viv xxx

I read it over twice more before I pressed *Send*. For some reason my stomach cramped as I watched the *Message sent* notification appear on the screen. Had I made myself clear enough? Why was everything so damn hard? Was I just stringing all three of them along? Then what? Wait for two to get sick of me and see who's left? They'll probably all get sick of me. I would.

I leaned back in my chair and concentrated on a picture I had pasted onto the vision board Annabel had forced me to make. It was a quote by one of her favourite authors, Louise Hay. The words were set to a backdrop of a blue swirling tunnel, with a woman walking through it alone and toward the light at the end. The words read: *You have been criticising yourself for years and it hasn't worked, try approving of yourself and see what happens.*

Approving of myself. Is that even possible? How could I approve of the way I was treating people? I hadn't been totally honest with any of them and as for my clients, it was my marriage that had fallen on hard times, not theirs. Most of the people I dealt with were just starting out their lives together and deserved to feel all of the excitement that came with that. Perhaps if I learnt to stop inflicted my misery on others, approval would follow.

There was a knock at my office door.

"Viv?" Peter called.

I quickly closed my email and opened the door.

"Thought you could use one of these," he said, handing me a large latte. "You look like you've got a lot going on in there." He smiled, tapping my forehead.

Despite his failings, he knew me well. He'd known me since I was a teenager. "Thanks, Peter. It's exactly what I needed. The kids will be home any minute. Stay for dinner?"

His eyes lit up. "Sure, that'd be great."

Peter closed the door behind him. I sipped the hot liquid gold and relaxed into my chair. My shoulders were aching from holding them tense as I wrote to Tom.

My phone beeped, it was Carrie.

Treatment going well and I'm feeling a bit better. Meet at Carmello's Sunday at 2?

Carrie had been in for another round of chemo the day after we got back from the river and this time she'd been violently ill for three days. I texted back.

I'm so glad you're feeling better. Sunday is great.

***

Dee Dee and Max arrived 20 minutes earlier than I had expected them.

"You two look wonderful," I said, meeting them in the front garden as they waited for others to arrive.

"Thank you, dear," Max smiled, his cheeks turning pink, "It's just an old suit. One I had in the cupboard." He smoothed down the flaps of the jacket with open palms.

"I really like your dress, Dee Dee." She had chosen a cream-coloured slip with a full lace overlay which looked stunning on her.

"Here they are," Dee Dee said, patting Max's shoulder.

Two cars full of Max and Dee Dee's family pulled into the driveway. I scanned the faces, trying to place the dissenters of the group. It was fairly easy to tell based on their miserable expressions.

Yeah, you don't want it to happen, I thought, but you're

too scared not to come in case you get written out of the will altogether. It made my blood boil as I summoned my sweetest smile and led them through the side gate, to the backyard.

Dee Dee stopped in her tracks as soon as she saw what Peter had done to the yard. "This looks wonderful, dear. I hope you didn't do all of this just for us. We'd feel terribly guilty if you did."

"It needed to be done anyway," I assured her. "Having your ceremony gave us the little push we needed."

Dee Dee looked as if she was about to cry.

"Come through." I waved to the others who were still making their way around. We needed to get this going before Dee Dee messed up her face powder.

"My granddaughter and grandson are coming, but they'll be a bit late. They said to start without them as we have a lunch booking after this," Max explained, taking his spot beside the satin covered signing table I had set up on the lawn.

"Of course. They can find their way around the back when they get here," I said, arranging the documents and signalling the guests to gather in close.

Dee Dee joined Max beside the table and took his hands. In the few moments between arranging everyone and beginning the ceremony, I watched them standing there, eyes on each other, as if there was no one else in the world. They knew they didn't have the blessing of the people who watched on, and they knew their time together would be shorter than most who took these vows, but I watched their love move between them, freely and without reservation. Dee Dee cared nothing about whether her dress was wrinkled, or if the guests were oohing and aahing, or if her song had been played loud enough, as most brides did. Max hadn't turned up reeking of alcohol or being jostled by his groomsmen. There was only the two of them. Complete, content in each other's love, and happy.

Pull yourself together, I scolded myself, wiping a tear from my eye. This is their day, not yours.

"Welcome everyone, to this ceremony we are about to celebrate between Dee Dee and Max. We are here not only to witness their commitment to one another, but also to wish for them the blessing of experiencing every happiness that life has to offer," I began.

The displeasure of the man I assume was Max's son was evident in his screwed up nose. Ignore him. It's not bothering Dee Dee and Max, so why should it bother me?

"As you exchange your vows, I ask you to now please join hands and repeat after me. We'll start with you, Max."

My attention was momentarily drawn to the side gate as the two grandchildren arrived. The young man and woman tiptoed over to the others and watched on.

"I ask all present ..."

"I ask all present," Max repeated.

"To witness that I ..." As I said the words I looked at the girl who had just arrived. Where have I seen her before? My mind searched its inner filing cabinet for a connection, while Max continued.

"Maximillian John Carradine."

I loved Max's full name. It sounded even better said aloud.

Where have I seen that girl? She noticed me staring. She seems to have recognised me. Shit. Where from?

I suddenly lost my train of thought. The look on the girl's face, as recognition washed over her, was enough to trigger the memory of where I had seen her. At Peter's work Christmas party.

***

"You're joking!" Julia exclaimed, her eyes wide.

"What the friggin' hell did you do?" Annabel didn't cuss too often, but this was clearly an exception.

Returning from the bathroom, Carrie took her usual seat and looked at us with confusion. "Hey, Viv. I only went to the loo, what did I miss?"

Julia filled her in while I waved at Carmello for coffee and signalled two fingers for a double shot.

"I hope you flattened her," Carrie said, smacking her hand on the table. "God, I wish I'd been there."

"I'm glad you weren't. And I've got a bone to pick with you later," I said, giving her a knowing look. She looked away; she knew exactly what I was talking about.

Carmello appeared with the coffee much quicker than usual; Carrie's loud slap on the table reminding him of previous outbursts and the fact that we couldn't be trusted.

"So, what happened?" Julia prompted. "What did you do?"

"As soon as I realised it was her and that she knew who I was, I couldn't even think. I stopped dead in the middle of Max's vows! I thought I was actually going to faint."

Annabel's hand covered her mouth. "You didn't faint though, did you?"

"No, but I came close. My bloody legs started shaking and I had black spots flying around in my vision. My first thought was to find a weapon. I actually started scanning the yard, looking for something, but the only thing nearby was a plastic rake."

Annabel gasped. "Please tell me you didn't hit her with a rake."

"I was so close, but poor old Dee Dee was looking at me with tears in her eyes as Max was saying his vows, and you know what? Despite how rattled I was, I couldn't ruin it for them."

"Are you serious?" Carrie laughed, her disbelief apparent in her tone, "you actually kept going?"

"Yes, and I was very proud of myself. I felt so sorry for Dee Dee and Max. They didn't deserve to have their day ruined."

"What happened then?" Julia asked, sipping her coffee.

"I managed to get through the ceremony. I was shaky, but I got through it. She wouldn't make eye contact with me at all, so after the ceremony I just went straight over to her and asked to have a word."

"You didn't!" Annabel said, her eyes wide.

"And what did the child have to say for herself?" Carrie butted in.

I turned my full attention to her. "Well now, Carrie, that's where you come in!"

Her smug grin, full of triumph and pride, gave me the answer I already knew.

"What?" She protested.

"Well, she said that someone called and left a message saying that if she ever messed around with a married man again, she'd better watch out. She thought it was me!"

"Carrie, you didn't" Annabel questioned.

Carrie remained quiet.

"Anyway, I told her what a nasty piece of work I thought she was and I made her look at our family photos on the wall and pictures of the kids to make her feel bad."

"And what did she say? Did she say how it happened?" Julia probed.

"What could she say? She claimed that they hadn't meant for it to happen, it progressed blah, blah, blah, pretty much the same crap Peter said. I had to laugh though because she said," I put on my best teenage girl voice "'you know, he was never going to leave you or anything and anyway, like, it wasn't like I was going to run off with some 50-year-old man or something. It wasn't like that.'"

Carrie clapped her hands with glee as Annabel laughed and Julia slightly choked.

"You have to tell him that," Carrie insisted, "he deserves to know that the child called him a 50-year-old!"

"Are you okay though?" Annabel asked, patting my hand, "that would have been traumatic and scary."

It was. I was petrified, but I had been spurred on by adrenaline and a few quick gulps from Peters shed stash of Jack Daniels while the family forced smiles for a photo.

"I'm actually okay. In fact, I feel better. A lot better." I had been reliving the moment I would face her over and over and now that it was done, it was a relief. "I feel as if a huge weight has been lifted off my shoulders and at least I know that the way Peter said it all happened is true. Not that it really matters now anyway."

"It does matter," Julia corrected, "you may not think so right now, but it will matter in the long run."

"What does she look like? Is she skanky?" Annabel asked, leaning in as if I were about to reveal a big secret.

"Yep. She's 22, or something, and had on heels she could hardly walk in."

Annabel gave an understanding nod, "I'm starting to think these men are all the same. Can't see past a firm set of boobs."

Carrie nodded in agreement.

"Anyway, I want to share my news," Annabel beamed, "I'm having dinner with Gerry tomorrow night."

"Fantastic, that's so exciting!" I congratulated her. Gerry seemed like a nice guy and Annabel deserved someone good.

She relayed details of their plans while I dug into the abyss of my handbag for my beeping phone. "Far out!" I cried, frustrated, tipping the contents onto the table. "Where is my damn phone?"

Carrie plucked it from the mess and read the message. "Um, okay," she grinned. "Not really sure how to respond to that."

I grabbed the phone and read the message. It was from David.

Thanks for a wonderful time last week. Hope you enjoyed your time away. Wondering if you might be free to catch up for dinner? I can't wait to see those gorgeous nipples of yours.

"What?" I looked at Carrie who had a smile that stretched from one side of her face to the other, while Annabel and Julia exchanged confused looks.

The phone beeped again, and then again within seconds. It was David.

Noooo, I'm sooo sorry. Dimples. Dimples. Stupid, rotten auto-correct. I swear I typed dimples.

And his second message:*I did not mean to write that word. This phone stinks!*

I texted a reply: *Don't worry about it.Canyou do Wednesday? Same place? Can't wait to see your nipples too, lol.*

Tuesday is great. Thank you!

"I wanna see," Julia pouted, reaching for the phone. She turned it so that Annabel could read it, too.

"Oh dear, poor guy," Annabel giggled. "I would have died if I wrote that. Does this mean you two are dating?"

"Not dating, really. He just asked me if I wanted to get together again." I tried to explain, but I wasn't sure I even knew what it was we were doing. Were we dating? "Peter's been wonderful lately too. I'm so worried about hurting any of them."

"Well, I have some news too," Julia announced, "Steve and I have started having Skype sex!"

Who announces something like that at a cafe? At the top of their lungs? I picked up the menu and hid behind it.

"Viv, for goodness' sake. So what? He is my husband."

"Julia, the whole cafe doesn't know that," I scolded her, lifting the menu back up.

"Oh, get over it." Carrie cupped her hands around her mouth and sang, "Julia's having Skype sex, Julia's having Skype sex."

It was worse than kindergarten.

CHAPTER 24

Chicken Cacciatore

Only two to go. Two more weddings left in my booking list. Freedom from the loving looks and sickly sweetness was now within reach, beckoning and teasing me with possibilities. So why did I feel so uneasy?

"Mum, can you tell Natalia to help me get the chicken on? She said she would and now she reckons she's too busy," Jack griped from my office doorway.

We had recently drawn up a cooking roster for during the week, which had been totally unsuccessful to date. The main point was to try to get the boys to learn some skills. I was worried that their future partners would despise me for allowing them to be so hopeless with household duties.

"Mum," Natalia was at the door. "I've already told him what to do, he just can't be bothered," she complained, her exasperation apparent. She had mothered them both over the years, always looked out for them in the playground, but her patience was being tested lately.

"Jack," I said, meeting him in the kitchen. "Natalia can't keep guiding you through. Grab the iPad, look up the recipe, and follow it," I smiled, handing him the device.

He took it and screwed up his face at Adam who was grinning from the couch.

"It'll be your turn tomorrow, Adam, so wipe the smirk off your face," I warned when he poked his tongue out at me.

I went back to my office, determined to start on the mountain of paperwork I had to get done, but I opened Facebook instead and clicked on Tom's profile. I missed his face so much. I looked through his pictures, not realising how many of them had me in them, at least in the background. There was one that a friend had taken of the two of us sitting across from one another in a booth of a dingy-looking pub. I remembered that we had been discussing the merits of the food van that arrived when the drunks spilled out at closing time. Tom had been arguing for the pulled pork bun with slaw, while I had declared that the barbecued ribs with baby potatoes was the best. What I hadn't realised at the time, was the two of us and how connected we were. It was like we were the only two people in a room that actually was packed to the rafters.

I closed the page. Work. Do your work. Opening my email, I clicked on the first; I'd read a few lines before realising I'd opened Peter's account.

> *Hi Peter, Please find attached a quote for the cape and mask that you requested for your costume. I can hold it for 7 days, but you'll need to pop in and pay the deposit if you want us to hold it for the 26th April.*

The 26th? That's the date of my last wedding, Charlotte and Barton's charity Masquerade Ball. He wouldn't! Would he? Why? I quickly closed the email, afraid that he'd be able to tell that I read it.

I went back to Facebook and messaged Annabel.

> *I accidentally saw an email of Peter's and apparently, he's hired a masquerade outfit for the 26th. I have a wedding which is a masquerade ball on the 26th!!!! You don't think he's planning to come and surprise me or something do you?*

> *Really?* Annabel replied. *Maybe. He says he wants to get you back, maybe this will be his grand gesture or something???*

> Me: *No one even knows this is an actual wedding. I have to pretend to be a guest for the ball. He can't just pop out from somewhere and do something dramatic!*

> Annabel: *Maybe it's not even for the same thing. Don't jump to conclusions. Come up here tomorrow and I'll muscle test you.*

I collapsed into the back of my chair and groaned. Why can't she just offer normal advice like everyone else? Annabel liked to muscle test everyone to find out the answers to questions. She would make you hold an arm outstretched. She would then ask a question like, "Do you like chocolate?" while pushing your arm down. If it held it was true. Then she would ask you a real question and repeat the action to see if the answer was true or not. It was such a load of bull.

I typed my response:

I'll think about it. Bit busy tomorrow. Enjoy your date tonight and don't be too naughty.

Annabel: *I'll test myself for you. Call you in the morning*

Testing herself was even more ludicrous. Whatever, it was better than anything I was coming up with. Maybe she could work out where my life is going at the same time.

"Mum, dinner," Jack called from the kitchen. The upbeat tone in his voice was promising.

"This looks great, darling," I complimented him on his efforts. "You've outdone yourself."

Jack smiled triumphantly as he dished up his Chicken Cacciatore. It was completely delicious.

Unfortunately, by three am it became apparent that despite its deliciousness, there had been a fatal error in his preparation. The boys took turns in the laundry toilet, while Natalia and I took turns hugging the bowl in the bathroom.

Drastic times called for drastic measures. I had no choice. I crawled back to bed and called Mum. She arrived within the hour, and immediately began the clean-up mission as I floated in and out of consciousness. When I woke, it was three o'clock in the afternoon. I reached for my phone on the nightstand and messaged David.

I'm so sorry, but I can't make dinner tonight.

Just the word made me want to vomit as I held the phone shakily above my head to type.

> *Unfortunately, I ate some undercooked chicken and have ended up with food poisoning. Raincheck?*

David replied a moment later.

> *Thank Goodness! Not that you have food poisoning, but when I first opened the message, I thought you were cancelling because you had time to think about my previous autocorrect fail. I'm actually going to be away for a couple of days, but get together when I get back? Get well X*

My arm collapsed. I had never felt so sick in my entire life. I rang the bell Mum had thoughtfully placed beside the bed and summoned her. She appeared in the doorway.

"All okay? What do you need?" she asked, sitting on the side of the bed. She was thoroughly enjoying being so terribly needed, but I was grateful whatever the motive.

"Some cold water, and maybe a cup of tea or something?" I groaned. "My stomach's hurting from being so empty."

"I made the kids some tea and a dry piece of toast, which seemed to help. I'll fetch you some. Shall I put the telly on?" she said, pushing the button before I could answer.

"Who's with Carrie today?" I managed. Talking was making me feel sicker.

"Annabel stayed there last night and said she'd spend the day. Don't worry, it's all sorted." She waved away my concerns with a flick of her hand. If there was one thing my mother was good at, it was taking charge when everything fell apart. If there was a catastrophe or something serious, she would swoop in and take charge, whether it was invited or not. On most occasions it was appreciated, but every so often she would go too far and piss people off. Right now, she was a Godsend.

***

"Hey, how're you feeling?" Peter asked, poking his head through the door. "Can I come in?"

I rolled onto my side and pulled the pillow up behind me. "Sure, of course. Have you looked in on the kids?"

"They're okay, still not out of bed either, but your Mum said they're a lot better today than yesterday," he said, handing me the cup of tea he'd brought in. "Poor Jack, he feels pretty bad though. I told him it might have been the chicken itself, rather than his cooking, just to ease his mind."

"Oh, poor thing. As soon as I can actually get up, I'll talk to him. I do feel a bit better today," I said, wincing as the hot liquid filled my empty stomach.

"Your Mum told me what happened with..." His voice trailed off, but I knew who he meant. Thankfully, he had the good sense not to say her name.

"You know what? I'm glad I had the chance to have it out with her, but honestly, Peter, what were you thinking?" I said, screwing my face up to convey my distaste. He didn't answer as his head fell and his eyes focused on the floor.

"I know it's a big ask," he said, breaking the uncomfortable silence that had filled the space between us, "but I was wondering if you'd consider coming to see the counsellor with me on Monday, like I mentioned to you before? She'd like you to come along if you're willing."

See the counsellor together? I did want to meet her, but I couldn't keep giving Peter false hope and letting him think that we might get back together.

But would it be giving him false hope? Maybe it wasn't false. It hurt my brain too much to think about and I was beginning to think that a life of celibacy was a better choice.

"Can I think about it? I can't seem to manage anything right now, let alone any big decisions."

"Of course," he smiled, "and I want you to know that *I* know, that even if you come, it doesn't mean all is forgiven or we're getting back together."

He was reading my mind.

"Your mum told me to tell you that Carrie called. She had her treatment this morning and she was fine. Only some slight nausea, but nothing too bad. Julia said she'll stop by later to see you."

"Thanks, can you tell Mum I might try a piece of toast now. I need to get moving again. I've got so much to do. Would you mind bringing me the computer?"

I added more pillows to prop myself higher against the headboard of the bed, ignoring the wave of nausea that rose in my throat.

Peter returned with the computer, followed by Mum with the toast, giving me a sly wink behind Peter's back. She just couldn't help herself. I ignored her.

"Thanks, both of you." I truly felt grateful and lucky. It was fine to pretend not to need anyone, but the truth was, I did. I needed them all.

I opened up the laptop and took a bite of the toast, chewing it until it was practically liquid before swallowing, for fear it would revisit me later. Other than four new wedding enquiries and hundreds of 'free offers', including one that alerted me to the fact I had just won 50 million dollars in some unknown country's lottery, there was nothing. Nothing from Tom.

I opened Facebook in the hope that he might have posted something or messaged me, but my hopes were dashed again. My private inbox popped up with Annabel's ridiculous profile picture of her dressed up as a fairy. A bloody fairy! She had more costumes than the rental shop and wore them at every opportunity.

> Hi, how you feeling? she asked.

> Me: A bit better, but still crap. Now I know how poor Carrie feels, except she has to put up with it constantly.

> Annabel: She's not too bad today. She was tired when we got back, so she's asleep now. Had my date with Gerry!!!!

> Me: And???

> Annabel: It was freakin amazing! We have so much in common and we talked and talked. He even said he's thought about me, he actually said dreamed (lol) about me since high school!

Me: *Really? Was that in a really sweet way? Or a weird, creepy stalker way?*

Shut up! Annabel replied. *In a good way. We were so in sync, I even muscle tested him to see if he was telling the truth and he was.*

I cringed. *Mmm, and he was still interested after that?*

Yes, he was! You won't believe it, but he actually told me that now we've finally found each other, he never wants to let me go. So there! And we're going out again tonight.

Me: *Well, have fun. Be careful. Remember that you don't know him that well yet.*

Annabel: *Yes, of course I will. You know me, I'll be checking out everything. Get better. Speak to you tomorrow. X*

The problem was I did know her, and Annabel's idea of checking out everything was making sure his arm didn't fall when she asked him if he was a serial killer.

I closed Facebook and opened up my client files. The wedding of Anastasia Kontidis and Rocco Fiorito had come to be known as, 'Romeo and Juliet' or 'The Italian and The Greek'. These poor kids were destined to fail if their families had anything to do with it. Rocco's family weren't dissimilar to the Corleone's of *The Godfather*, while Anastasia's five brothers and strict Greek father posed their own threat. After many months of fighting, and the pair being forbidden to see one another, Anastasia went off to work one morning and ended up giving birth to a healthy baby boy, much to the shock and horror of everyone concerned.

"I hid the pregnancy easily," she had told me, holding on tightly to Rocco. "I knew that if they found out they'd kill him." She gave Rocco a sweet smile and he responded with a kiss.

Rocco continued with the backstory. "With the baby here, they had no choice but to allow us to get married, so here we are. Although, I can't promise the wedding won't end in an explosion of some sort or another," he joked.

I wasn't so sure it was funny. According to Anastasia, the engagement party had ended with six police patrol cars and a paddy wagon required to break up a fight that had started over who was going to win the World Cup soccer match.

I prepared their ceremony and sent it to print in my office. I needed to get up. My legs were sore and ached when I swung them off the bed to stand up. I felt sick. I sat back down and waited until it passed before trying again.

Natalia's door was slightly open when I peeked in. She was fast asleep. The boys were both in bed, Jack watching a movie on his laptop and Adam playing video games. "How are you two feeling?"

"Like the shit on the bottom of a marathon runner's shoe," Adam answered as I swallowed back the urge to wretch.

"Thanks, Adam, a simple 'I feel crap' would have sufficed. Jack?"

"Not bad, Mum. Guilty more than anything. I'm so sorry if I did this. I swear I'm never cooking again."

"I'm never eating anything you cook again anyway, so don't worry about it," Adam insisted.

I gave Adam my warning glare and turned my attention to Jack. "Honey, we don't know what it was, so there's no point worrying about it. Get some rest."

"You're up," Mum smiled, clearing the junk mail from the kitchen table for me to sit. "Wasn't Peter just wonderful with the kids? And you!"

Where's the Scotch? Give me Scotch.

CHAPTER 25

The wedding of Anastasia & Rocco (The Greek & the Italian – Romeo & Juliet)

To the displeasure of both families, Anastasia and Rocco had settled on the gorgeous Solero winery for their wedding. A ceremony in the large, thriving garden would be followed by a five star reception in the main dining hall. Anastasia's family had, of course, been pushing for their local Greek Orthodox Church, with Rocco's family insisting on the wedding being held in their catholic parish. A civil ceremony at a winery seemed, to the couple, like the perfect compromise to piss them all off.

I pulled into the carpark an hour earlier than I would usually arrive, determined to make sure I was ready before the two hundred guests began to arrive. I set up my documents on the table in the garden and headed inside to find the function organiser.

"I've got Emergency Services on speed dial in my mobile, ready to go," the young woman assured me. She looked more petrified than I was.

How do I get myself into situations like this? They had sounded so sweet initially; I should have known there would be some disaster to follow.

I peeked in at the main dining hall as it was being prepared for the wedding reception, inhaling deeply to taste the damp, woody, fruit flavour that seeped from wine barrels that lined the back wall and foyer.

Dozens of round tables filled the space under crystal chandeliers, made even more impressive by the draping that hung loosely from each corner of the ceiling. The white satin lengths met together in the middle, beneath a stunning, low-hanging chandelier.

More money than sense. Typical. I'd been around Greeks and Italians enough to know what they were like when it came to weddings, and this couple had two families throwing money at them in an effort to outdo each other. As I took in one last, fragrant breath, I heard voices from the adjoining room.

"Rocco, there's still time. You don't have to do this."

It was a woman's voice. His mother?

"You can still marry Melina, she won't care that you have a baby."

"But I'll care that she has a moustache thicker than mine! Mama, please, not today, I mean it. If you can't be happy for me and Anastasia, then leave, all of you. Anyone who is not happy for me today, leave. Now!"

The woman ranted, swapping between Italian and English,

"Okay, okay," she eventually conceded. "I put on a smile, we do it your way."

The beep of my phone bounced off the stone walls with double the normal volume. Shit! I took off back to the garden before anyone came out.

The message was from David.

> Hi Viv. I was supposed to be back by now, but I've had to stay on for a few meetings after this boring conference. I know we were going to have dinner, but I wondered if you might be my date for a ball? Sounds tacky, I know, but it's a charity thing my cousin is throwing. Anyway, it's on the 26th at the Santino Centre and I'd love you to come. Let me know?

I swiped through the calendar on my phone to the date confirming what I already knew. Charlotte and Barton's surprise wedding Ball thingo. I didn't even know what it was really. A charity ball? Secret wedding? Fundraiser? Cheap-arsed way to get out of paying for a huge wedding? The last one was probably correct.

I had to get more details.

> *Is your cousin's name Charlotte or Barton?* I texted back.

> *Yep, Charlotte. Do you know them?*

I couldn't tell him how it was a surprise.

> *Not personally, I know of them through the charity. I'm already going though, so I'll see you there?*

David: *I would have loved to take you as my fat, but save me a dance?*

Why would he love to take me as his fat?

David: *DATE. Shit! It was supposed to say date. I'm getting a new phone.*

I smiled. *No worries. Yep, you should definitely get a new phone.*

I put my phone away. For now, I needed to concentrate on getting through this wedding and making it out alive.

"Hey, how are ya?" Rocco said, giving me a nod.

"I'm fine, thanks. You look fabulous," I said, giving him a nod back and gesturing to his sleek, black suit and gold tie. One by one, his seven groomsmen appeared and gave me the nod. My neck was beginning to hurt.

"Everything all set?" Rocco asked, shifting nervously from foot to foot and looking over his shoulder at five-second intervals.

"Rocco," I forced him to focus his attention on me, "everything is going to be fine. Anastasia will be here in about ten minutes. The ceremony only goes for about 30 minutes and you two will be off enjoying yourselves as a married couple within the hour."

A calmness settled on his tense shoulders. "Yep, you're right. I just wanna get this over with and finally show 'em all."

My heart felt heavy for their struggle. They were so determined to be together, risking a wrath that the most seasoned, hard-core *Mafioso* would be wary of. It was no wonder he wanted it to be over.

The crowd had gathered in, filling the seats and the entire garden area. Greeks on one side, Italians on the other. I felt as if I was at an international soccer match.

The roar of Harley Davidson motorcycle engines filled the grounds. "Here they come," I said, ushering the boys into position, while hidden behind a wall, the bride and her party got into single file. A slow familiar tune, "Ave Maria", began to play as one by one the bridesmaids appeared and stepped onto the carpet. When the music changed to Andrea Bocelli, Anastasia appeared on her father's arm, cradling her newborn son.

The second Rocco's eyes met hers, the sound of his breath catching in his throat unexpectedly filled my eyes with tears. I felt privileged to be a part of this moment, as it etched its perfect beauty in Rocco's memory forever. The tension that had filled the crowd, fell away.

"Welcome everyone, to the wedding of Rocco and Anastasia. The Giving Away of the bride is a tradition that has been around for centuries. It has a long history dating back to Roman times where the bride's father or elder brother would have had the responsibility for her care and protection. This responsibility then passing, on the day of her marriage, to her husband.

Today, while times have changed, we can still take meaning from this form of giving away ceremony. Today, as a woman is not property to be given and taken, it is used more generously as an opportunity for the relationship between a father and his daughter to be publicly acknowledged.

It is also an opportunity for the families and friends of the couple to show their support and acceptance of their union." I accentuated the word 'acceptance'. "Since you are all here, we may take it that this is a representation of your love and support and invite Nikos to speak on behalf of all present. Who, then, presents this woman to be married to this man?"

Her mother rose to her feet and together they answered, "We do."

"And with whose blessing does this man come today, to stand beside this woman?"

Rocco's parents rose. "With our families blessing."

Thank goodness for that. It was risky putting those words in, but it was important to Rocco and Anastasia. Forcing a public display of support from both sides would bind them to their promise. If it had gone badly, my back-up plan was to run to the car and hide.

Anastasia kissed her father's cheek and passed the baby to him. Her hands were shaking as she took Rocco's, but their faces radiated pure happiness. They'd made it. The fight was finally over.

***

"Are you okay, Mum? You look as white as a ghost," Natalia asked, placing her hand on my forehead.

"No, actually. I wasn't sure I was going to get out of that alive," I said, fumbling with the kettle.

"What?" Natalia was looking at me like I was mad. "From the wedding?

"Yes – two hundred Greeks and Italians, most of whom looked like they'd been in training for the muscle Olympics, and who, I might add, despise each other."

"Okay, that doesn't sound good." She took the kettle from my hand, insisting I sit down. "So, what happened?"

"In the end it was fine, though one of the fathers actually joked about making me an offer not to lodge the paperwork."

"I'm surprised you didn't run into any of Dad's buffoon cousins," she laughed, handing me a cup of tea.

We'd never had much to do with Peter's family. His mother had fallen out with her two siblings long ago, but refused to ever say what it was over. We were thankful, they were all awful.

My phoned beeped and vibrated on the table. A message from Julia.

Guess what??? I'm going to be a Nanny!

I turned the phone to Natalia so she could read it.

"As in a job, or is one of them having a baby?" she asked.

I was thankful she was confused too. I dialled Julia's number. "You're getting a job as a Nanny or one of the kids is having a baby?" I said quickly, before she could get a word in.

"Oh shut-up. Ava's pregnant! We're so excited. I'm not going to be called Grandma though. I refuse. What do you think about Nulia or Janny?"

"What the hell is a Janny? It sounds like something you wear to bed," I laughed.

"What? What's wrong with it?" She sooked.

"No, I think Granny, or Grandmother, suits you better. I'll be sure to tell the others," I teased.

"Don't you dare! Carrie will have a field day coming up with nasty names. Listen, Ava and Luke want to have a celebratory dinner on Thursday night at Carmello's, can you and the kids make it?"

"I can, but I'll have to check with the kids and let you know, Granny!"

"Piss off." She hung up on me before I could repeat it.

"Dinner Thursday night at Carmello's," I said to Natalia. "Now, I'm going to crawl into bed and watch telly. Order pizza?"

Natalia was already checking her calendar. "Thursday's good. Go lie down, I'll call you when the food's here."

I turned on the TV and climbed into my bed. The evenings were growing cooler with each passing day and I shivered beneath the thin bed cover. I pulled my imitation mink blanket from the trunk at the end of the bed and wrapped myself in it. I was asleep in seconds.

The smell of the pizza Natalia had left on my bedside table was invading my unconsciousness, and causing my already disjointed dream to take a psychotic direction. Pulling myself from the clutches of a pizza-eating Freddy Kruger, I rolled over and switched on the lamp. Five am, great. No point getting up this early. The pizza looked good. I took a slice and flicked through the channels. Who would have thought there would be such a wealth of shopping and religious instruction so early in the morning?

***

Bronwyn Bardon, the counsellor, worked from home.

"Shouldn't we knock?" I said to Peter as he opened the front door.

306 - SUSAN MURPHY

"No, you just go in and wait in the lounge room. She'll come out when she's finished with the client she's with now."

The woman who had managed to turn my husband from a disconnected, unfeeling wanker into a caring, considerate human being that I actually liked, appeared to live like a pig.

"I feel like cleaning up in here while we wait," I whispered with a screwed-up nose. "How can she have people coming and going here with all this mess?"

The lounge room was piled with clutter in every direction, and the kitchen bench was even worse, with dishes piled into a tower in the sink.

"Look at this! She's just left her purse out here, open. And all her bills." My voice had gone up an octave.

"Shhh!" Peter laughed at my disapproval. "Don't worry about it. So what if she's messy, I'm not here for her to give me cleaning advice."

"But how can you trust the advice of someone who is so disorganised she can't even keep her house tidy?"

"Because she's a fabulous counsellor, that's why. Sit down and read a magazine or something."

"I would if I could find one under all this crap," I sulked.

How can she live in this pig-sty? And happily let others see it? Maybe that's how she tests her patients. Leaves her purse out to see if they'll take anything. What if they did? It wouldn't exactly be helping them which is what she's meant to be here for.

"Peter, how have you been?" Bronwyn smiled when she came out, extending her hand. "And you must be Genevieve. It's great to finally meet you."

She was much nicer than I had anticipated, although a little masculine. I had imagined her with blonde hair in a high bun and navy-blue suit, but 'Bron', as she insisted I call her, was short in real life, with brown, unruly hair and preferred black pants and a black top.

She led us into her office. "I'm so glad you agreed to come along Genevieve. I really think it will benefit Peter, and you too, I hope. I'm sure all of this has not been easy for you either."

"Definitely not," I spluttered through a misplaced, nervous giggle, adding an eye roll for dramatic effect.

"I have been working with Peter," she continued, "through some of the issues that he felt may have led to his affair and other problems. Part of that process has been about owning up to the choices he made. That can be a difficult thing, but part of that is about facing the people he's hurt and having the opportunity to apologise."

Okay, why is she looking at me? She's waiting for me to say something. So, say something.

"Of course, yes," I nodded, shifting in my chair.

"Go ahead, Peter, look at your wife and give her your apology."

Why? Why do we have to look at each other?

I met his eyes as he began, but couldn't hold them without grinning. Not because it was terribly funny, it wasn't. But because whenever something was serious or uncomfortable, my natural instinct was to smile and laugh. I picked at my nails instead.

"I'm not really good with words, but, Viv, when I first met you, you were just a young girl. I fell in love with your sweetness and your innocence and how much you cared about everyone and everything. I loved our life together and, deep down, I thought we'd be together forever. But when I started to lose my way, call it a midlife crisis or something," he laughed nervously. "Instead of turning to you like I should have, like I wish I had, I turned to others and made really bad decisions. I know that I've hurt you so much and ruined your faith and trust in me. If I could take it back, I wouldn't hesitate to erase the last few years and re-do them. I hope one day you can forgive me."

Tears were streaming down my face, but rage was bubbling inside, heating with every word.

"Genevieve, how does that make you feel, hearing Peter's apology?"

Stay silent. If I started, it was all going to pour out like an overflowing septic tank. I opened my mouth to speak, but closed it again. Don't do it. Not like this. Wait until you're calm. I shifted in my seat, unsure what position would make me less likely to spill over. Arms crossed. Uncrossed. They were watching me.

"Um, how does it make me feel?" A crazed cackle and snort escaped before I could stop it, followed by a vicious hair flick. "I feel..."

Peter leaned back in his seat, sensing the coming storm, as Bron put her pen to paper.

"... fucking cheated, lied to, and ripped apart at the seams." Let the shit storm begin. "Once again, this is all about Peter. Everything has been about Peter. 20 years and this is what it's all come to? It's been all about Peter from the day we met." I spat. I sucked in another breath and launched again. "I can't stop think-ing about all the times he was texting on his phone, to her, while we were all together. I feel sick. No – disgusted and embarrassed. No – humiliated. I'm so fucking stupid. All of that time I was still trying to get his attention, wondering what I was doing wrong." My crying had become a high-pitched screaming. "Fuck! Why? Why did you do this to us? And now, Carrie's got cancer, Tom's gone, the kids will be leaving soon enough. What's left? What's left for me after all of the hard work I've put in? Nothing! No twilight years with my husband, travelling the world, eating pastries and enjoying being free, just sadness and regret for everything that could have been." I collapsed into sobs.

Wait, I remembered something else, "And now look," I pointed my finger ferociously at Peter. "He's suddenly the kind of husband I've desperately wished he would be, but it's all been tainted by all this crap."

I'd barely noticed that Peter was crying and Bron had turned white. She hadn't written a single word on her page.

I snatched the tissues from her desk and wiped my face. See, I should have kept quiet. Now they both look like *they* need therapy.

"Viv," Bron said gently, "I'm sorry to have put you through that. I didn't realise your emotions were still so raw. I think that maybe you need to get some counselling separate from this before we move forward. You're clearly dealing with a lot. Perhaps you wouldn't mind if I referred you to someone?"

I nodded, refusing to look at either of them.

"Why don't you pop out to the waiting room while I finish up with Peter."

I got up and headed for the door. When I closed it behind me, I let out the breath I'd been holding and took in a long, deep one to replace it. My chest was tight and my head aching. Bloody hell, I hadn't expected that. I hadn't even realised I was carrying around so much anger and resentment. I sat back down in a clear spot on the couch and opened Tom's last email. I hit Reply.

I know it's only two weeks until you're back, but I need you so much right now. Wish you were here. X

I closed the message as the office door opened. Peter's eyes were still red and his face much sadder than when we went in. I'm such a bitch. He wanted me to come so he could apologise and I end up screaming the place down. Fantastic. Happy now?

"Peter, I'm so sorry," I said when we got in the car. "I really had no idea that I was going to react like that. It just all...spewed out."

"Viv, it's fine. And you're right, it has been all about me. It's just not easy to hear it out loud. Bron said we'll go over everything next time, once I've had a chance to absorb it all."

I couldn't stand the sad look on his face. At least it might deter him from coming to the ball. Terrible, why do I think things like that? Karma will get me for being so mean.

The ride home was filled with an impenetrable silence. Neither of us spoke. I didn't have a clue what to say after that outburst. I got out of the car and came around to Peter's window. "I am sorry," I said again. "I hope you understand."

"I do, and I'm not giving up. I still think that you and I can make it work. It just might take some time."

CHAPTER 26

The last supper

"Guys, hurry up, we're going to be late for dinner," I yelled from the front door. The boys were never ready on time for anything unless it was soccer.

"I'm ready, Mum," Natalia said, joining me at the front door. She looked beautiful.

"I love the way you put your hair up." I investigated her messy bun. "I wish I could do something like that."

"I'll show you," she promised. "Let's get in the car. And turn it on, it'll make them move faster," she giggled.

By the time we arrived, we were fifteen minutes late. "Come in, come in," Carmello welcomed us at the door. "These boys have grown so much. Still playing soccer?" he asked, sweeping his foot across the floor as if to kick a ball.

"Yes, and don't get them started, we're already late," I said.

"You boys come over and see me after, so we can talk about the cup teams," he nodded to a very eager Jack and Adam. Natalia was already at the table.

A glowing Ava, accompanied by her partner, Luke, were standing at the head of the table.

"Congratulations," I squealed, hugging them both awkwardly with a jiggle.

"Late as usual!" Julia teased.

"Hi, Steve," I said, giving him a kiss and deliberately by-passing Julia. "How does it feel, soon-to-be grandfather?"

"I don't mind being Grandad or Pop, but Jules is struggling," he laughed, putting his arm around her.

While Carmello served our mains and the wine flowed end-lessly, the chatter and laughter around the table was wonderful. We hadn't been all together like this for a long time. It was special, almost perfect, but I felt Peter and Tom's absence from my side. There hadn't been a get-together in 20 years that one, or the other, wasn't a part of.

"Viv? Are you okay?" Annabel asked, sliding into the empty seat beside me.

"I'm good. It's just nice to have us all here together like this. It's nice to remember what's really important. So much has happened lately, Bel, it's mind-blowing."

"I know," she said, oddly avoiding my eyes. There was a dis-comfort in her voice, as if she was holding something back.

"What's-" I was cut off by Dad, who was standing and com-manding everyone's attention by tapping the side of a glass with his knife.

"Attention," he called with a wide grin. "As the head of the family, I've decided I'd like to say a few words."

We all exchanged bewildered looks. Here we go.

"I just wanted to congratulate my darling granddaughter,

Ava, and of course, Luke – you're lucky to have her mate - on the wonderful future addition to the O'Reilly clan. Even if he or she won't carry on the name, it'll still have the blood and honour of being an O'Reilly."

Carrie groaned loudly, which led to Dad nudging her arm to shut her up. They'd been replaying this scene since I was born. Dad loved nothing more than to tell anyone who would listen how the O'Reilly's are a superior race, smarter and stronger than anyone else, while we – mostly Carrie – pretended it was all rubbish. We didn't think that really. Dad had instilled in all of us a deep sense of Irish pride that would never diminish, no matter what name we took.

"Your grandmother and I are very pleased to have our first great-grandchild coming into the world," he continued, "and I thought that perhaps it would be a good thing if we could be grandparents together."

What was he on about?

Natalia was looking at me, I was looking at Carrie, and she looked at Julia. Mum was looking at all of us, and the boys were looking at their phones.

Grasping a chair, Dad reached into his pocket and retrieved a small, black velvet box. He lowered himself, slowly, very slowly, to one knee, clutching the chair for support as Mum's hands covered her gaping mouth.

"Will you do me the honour of becoming my wife? Again?" he asked, holding the ring box in front of Mum.

They can't stand each other. A ten-day cruise had barely seen them both come back alive! What was he thinking?

"Yes, of course," Mum cried.

What was *she* thinking?

Julia's stunned eyes met mine, mirroring their horror. Annabel, on the other hand, was clapping excitedly.

I'm going to slap her. We'll all suffer if they end up in the same house.

"Won't we all make gorgeous taffeta bridesmaids?" Carrie smirked, already making the situation worse.

Yuk. She was right. Mum will definitely make us be bridesmaids and wear some horrid peach taffeta number.

Natalia found our distaste amusing. "Mum, be happy for them. It's sweet."

Sweet? Sweet is delicious ice-cream. Sweet is a lovely couple falling madly in love. Sweet is not two old farts who can barely stand the bloody sight of one another, torturing their children by deciding to re-marry!

I looked at Carrie, who was winking at me with pleasure. My stomach turned itself upside-down and my head grew faint as a thought, more horrifying than anything that had come before, made its way into my consciousness. Dad confirmed it.

"Of course, we'd like you to do the ceremony, Viv." He beamed.

Julia spat lemonade onto her lap as a satisfied smile spread across Carrie's face.

Annabel was on her feet, tapping the same glass Dad had used to deliver his terrifying blow. What the fuck now? I couldn't take any more. Julia, who had not yet managed to say a word, shot me another fearful look and tightened her grip on Steve's arm.

"I have some news, too," Annabel squealed, clapping her hands like a seal.

Please say you've won the lottery so you can buy an island to hide me from all of this, I prayed.

"I know it's fast, but Gerry has asked me to marry him too!" Her voice had risen to a shriek.

Marry him? They've only had three dates.

"She's gone mad," I mouthed to Carrie, who had descended into a laughing fit.

Ava sprang from her chair. "I have to throw up. Sorry, not because of you... this, I mean," she spluttered, running for the bathroom with one hand on her belly and the other covering her mouth.

"Who's Gerry?" The boys' attention had finally been coaxed from their phones by all of the excitement.

"Your new uncle, apparently," Carrie answered before I could say anything. Not that I had anything to say.

What the hell was there to say?

***

The weekend hadn't eased the trauma of Thursday night's dinner revelations. With a heavy feeling in the pit of my stomach, I pulled into Carrie's driveway. We'd decided to meet at her house for our Sunday coffee catch-up instead of Carmello's. Carrie had been feeling a bit nauseous and wanted to stay in. Smile. There's nothing wrong with faking a bit of happiness for Annabel. There's no point saying what you really think, it'll just upset her, I told myself. Who was I to pass judgment on what's right or wrong, anyway? I had married plenty of couples who had found each other on the internet, after only having met in person once or twice.

When I walked through the door, I could see Carrie already rolling her eyes at whatever Annabel was saying. Julia was at the kitchen counter.

"Hey, Jules," I said, leaning in for an air kiss. "How did you recover from the other night?" I hadn't spoken to her since the dinner. I'd assumed she'd gone into hiding.

"Hmm, it was a bit of a shock. Thinking of Mum and Dad getting married again is frightening," she said, her body shuddering at the prospect.

"I'm changing my phone number because Mum's gonna drive us all nuts with her incessant complaining about Dad," I said. "Maybe they'll keep their own places. Let's convince them to live separately." It was the perfect idea. If they continued to live apart, things wouldn't have to change that much.

We joined the others on the couch.

"Good, now that you're all here," Carrie announced.

"I suppose you're getting married too?" I teased.

"No, quite the opposite actually. I'm getting divorced."

"Oh, Carrie. I'm so sorry," Annabel comforted her. "What happened?" She pretended to pat Carrie's arm, but she was tapping, I could tell.

Pretend to be sad, I reminded myself. All this pretending was exhausting.

"Dick, Edward's son, called and said that given the circumstances, with me being unwell, he thought it best that his father move in with him permanently. He said he thought it was best for everyone and that Edward felt the same way. Apparently he's also taken up with Dick's mother-in-law."

"Hun, that's awful. What a Dick." Julia smiled at her clever wit. "Are you okay?"

"I'm fine. I had a feeling, and I'm glad he's found someone. Our relationship was nothing more than patient and carer in the last few years, you guys know that." Relief was evident in her voice.

"Who would want to date Edward?"

Did I say that out loud? Julia's glare confirmed that I did.

"Dick's mother-in-law has dementia, so I think they'll be perfect for each other. Edward is terribly forgetful these days and he'll be happy to have someone just to sit with on the couch. We've met her a few times and she's honestly really sweet. Anyway, I've moved on," Carrie grinned, with a casual wave of her hand.

"What do you mean by that?" I asked. There was always more to everything Carrie said.

"I've met someone else. One of the oncology nurses at the hospital." She sipped her tea as if that was the end of it.

"Don't you dare act like that's all you're going to say," Annabel warned, "Spill it, right now!"

"There's nothing to spill. She's amazing and we're in love."

"She? It's a woman?" I choked, sucking a mouthful of coffee down my windpipe.

Annabel's interest had turned to quiet contemplation, while Julia was, as usual, unaffected by the revelation.

"What's her name?" she asked, without even the bat of an eye.

"Annie, and she's gorgeous," Carrie beamed. She looked happier than I'd seen her in a long time.

Why was I even surprised? She'd never made a secret of

swinging back and forth between men and women. Carrie deserved to be happy, and I felt happy for her, until the sudden image of her snuggled up to an old grandma made me wince.

"She's not old, is she?" I asked, unsure I really wanted to know.

"No, actually. She's my age, a year younger, in fact. "You met her, when I had my operation.""

Sweet nurse Annie!

"That's great news, Carrie. We're so happy for you. Aren't we?" Julia directed her stern eyes at me and then Annabel.

"Yes, of course. It's wonderful," we both answered, talking over the top of each other.

The ringtone of my phone was a welcome distraction. I didn't recognise the number.

"Hello, Viv speaking."

"Hi, Viv, this is John, from soccer." His voice sounded shaky. "I hope you don't mind me calling, but I really need a favour."

A favour? What kind of favour could I possibly do for John?

"My mother passed away on Friday, and the funeral is this Wednesday. I was wondering if you might possibly officiate for us? The celebrant the funeral home had organised was awful."

A funeral. This week? "Oh, I'm so sorry to hear that, John. Can you hold on and I'll check my calendar?" I needed a minute to think. Three sets of questioning eyes were on me as I held my hand over the phone and looked at the ceiling.

Charlotte and Barton's wedding on Saturday. I needed to prepare the ceremony and get a costume. Argh, a stupid costume! If I prepared tomorrow, I could meet with the family Tuesday night, do the funeral Wednesday, and shop for an outfit Thursday. *Bloody hell!* Just say no.

"Of course, John, I'd be honoured to. I'll give you a call tonight to organise a time to get together and go over the details."

"What was all that about?" Carrie asked when I hung up the phone.

"The boys' soccer coach's mother died and he wants me to do the funeral on Wednesday. I haven't even got time to scratch myself as it is this week, but I couldn't say no."

"You never can, Viv," Julia said. "I think it's about time you learnt how."

"Here, let me do some tapping on you," Annabel said, grabbing my wrist.

Just what I needed. I deeply and completely loathed my inability to never say no!

I suffered through ten minutes of tapping and affirming responses, before I finally managed to escape. Driving home, I still felt overwhelmed and out of control, despite "deeply and completely accepting myself". Julia was right, I said yes to everything and always ended up getting myself into a stressful mess.

Without even thinking, I pulled into the carpark of our local Catholic parish church. I hadn't been to church for years, but for some reason, divine intervention I decided, my subconscious led me there.

I opened the wooden door and entered, dipping my fingers in the water and making the sign of the cross. How could I not find peace in here? It was quiet, dim and calm. My buzzing anxiety lifted with every step I took toward the altar. I sat in a pew and stared at the stained-glass windows, feeling something – Connection? Warmth? – for the first time in a long time.

"Hello?" I hadn't noticed a man approaching. "My name's

Father Jacobs. Can I help you or are you just here for a visit?" Father Jacobs' wide smile was cheerful and friendly.

"Visiting. Actually, that's a lie, I don't even know why I'm here. I was heading home and I ended up here, somehow."

"That happens a lot, actually. People are heading somewhere else, but end up being drawn to the Church, needing to connect to something bigger, to feel cared for."

That was exactly how it felt. "I feel disconnected, as if I'm in a frantic tailspin that has no end and no direction. I don't know how to get it back on track," I told this complete stranger who smiled back reassuringly. "I feel as If I'm going to lose my mind."

Why was I telling him all this? For some strange reason he didn't seem like a real person, more like an entity of enlightenment.

"Modern life often makes us feel this way," he said. "Even me, but it helps to give it over to God. When you realise that the control is not in your hands, you have no choice but to simply trust that things will work out how they're supposed to. Trust the fact that there is a bigger plan for all of us. Including you."

His words were having an affect on me. Are we really in control? Is there a bigger plan for me that won't be affected no matter how much I worry about it or try to force it?

"Thanks, Father. I think I really need to give over control to someone else right now. I've never been terribly religious, but I like the idea that someone, somewhere is looking out for me."

"The Church hasn't always made it easy for people to place their trust in it, but if you were led here today, then it was for a reason. I hope it brings you some comfort."

It had. I was glad I came.

CHAPTER 27

Fanny Marie Hooper

*T*en weddings and a funeral! Hugh Grant, eat your heart out.
I pulled up outside John's gorgeous, two-storey mansion, not far from Carmello's. He'd definitely come out relatively unscathed after his divorce from Josie. I'd never warmed to her. She rarely came to watch the kids play soccer, but when she did, she dressed as if she'd stepped straight out of one of those *Housewives of Wherever* reality shows.

"Hi, Viv, thanks so much for doing this," John said, leading me through the white marble hall into the dining area. "Everyone, this is Viv, the celebrant."

Seven people sat around the twelve-seater timber dining table. Each said hello in turn, except for one. John had warned me that his brother, Archie, had some "issues".

"He was a drug addict and alcoholic for many years," he'd explained. "It ended up damaging his brain, so he might behave strangely."

Fabulous! I took a seat at the head of the table and unpacked my case. "This is a difficult time for everyone, but my role is to work with you through the process of putting together a tribute for..."

John jumped in, "Fanny Marie Hooper."

I nodded. "Would you mind introducing yourselves, so I can understand who is who? I'll make some notes, if that's okay," I added.

The family members each introduced themselves in turn, and relayed their relationship with Fanny. She was clearly a much loved woman. My conversation with Father Jacobs played in my mind as I listened to stories of Fanny's strength, wisdom and determination.

I wonder what my family would say about me if I died? They'd probably make jokes and talk about all of my disasters. They'd love that.

Annabel had suggested some years ago, during one of my "lost" phases, that I write the kind of eulogy I'd want for myself and then use that as a guide for living my life. I'd thought she was nuts, but now, sitting here, it didn't seem like such a bad idea. I'd want people to say I was warm, caring and always gave of myself. That I laughed a lot and brought joy to others.

"Archie might be a bit rowdy on Wednesday," John warned when he walked me out to the car. "He doesn't handle stuff like this very well and he gets pretty loud. I apologise in advance, but if you could just ignore it and carry on, no matter what he does, I'd really appreciate it. Thanks again."

I smiled and got in the car. What the hell was Archie likely to do? Panic was setting in. Give it over to God or the Universe, or whatever. Control is not in your hands. Que sera!

***

"She looks peaceful," the funeral director said to John and his sister, "like she's sleeping."

She does bloody not. She looks dead. I placed my papers on the raised podium, tucked away in the front corner of the room, beside Fanny's open coffin. I hope they planned to close the lid after the viewing. I'd never had to stand on a raised podium before, and while I'm sure Fanny was lovely, I didn't fancy looking at her dead body for the next hour.

Archie approached the door on his sister's arm. Here we go. Deep breaths. Remember what John said – keep going, no matter what.

Archie yanked at his tie. "Fuck, no, John," he cried when he saw his mother in the coffin. "I don't want her to be dead." He picked up her lifeless wrinkled hand.

Eeeew. Put it down. I almost gagged at the thought of touching that cold skin, but his distress was so raw, I couldn't help but feel for him.

Fanny's sister was at her side as well as three of the grandchildren. Despite my unease, their grief was moving. They had loved her, and she them. She was the matriarch of their family.

"John, she's not dead!" Archie hollered, stepping back from the coffin. "Look, she's crying."

I was pretty sure my heart had actually stopped beating in my chest as I leaned toward them to see over the top of John's head.

"Look, look, see for yourself. Jesus, man, get her out of there," Archie wailed.

"Archie, calm down," John demanded, taking his arm. "I assure you, she's gone."

"Well, why the hell is she crying? Look," he insisted, pointing at her lifeless face.

John leaned in to look, and for the briefest of moments fear swept over his face. "No, look," he assured Archie when he realised, "it's because Aunty Maude was leaning over her and a tear dropped onto Mum's face." He pulled Archie in to see and dabbed it away with a tissue. "She's gone mate, I promise you."

I excused myself and darted for the bathroom. Calm down, I chanted over and over, until it finally began to sink in.

When I got back to the room, the seats were almost full, and Archie had planted himself on the floor beside the coffin.

"On behalf of the family of Fanny Marie Hooper, I would like to thank you all for being here today and sharing in this celebration of her life," I began. "Before we begin, it is important to the family that rather than this be merely a funeral for Fanny, that this truly be a celebration of the person she was and the memories she has left us with."

My eyes were fixed on Archie, analysing his every move in anticipation of cutting him off at any sign of an outburst. He wriggled about on the floor, his expression flitting between utter sadness and disbelief. The photo montage the family had prepared was what finally pushed him over the edge.

As photos of them as children and Fanny in her younger, happy years brought most to tears, Archie broke into a loud wail, as he rolled around on the carpet.

"No, Mum," he cried out. "Who's gonna make me scrambled eggs?"

Not one person in the room, other than me, looked even remotely bothered by Archie's behaviour. I felt like launching off of the podium to cover his mouth and shut him up. But every pair of eyes remained on the screen. The photos of Fanny and the life she had led, were heart-wrenching and beautiful. If she was my mother, I'd pause the pictures until he shut up so we could actually hear the music and have a chance to mourn her.

When the montage was finished and the eulogy had been read, the coffin was closed, allowing the family to lay a flower on top in final tribute. John laid his and stepped over to speak to me quietly. "Thanks so much," he whispered. "You were wonderful and especially with Archie. We were really worried that he'd carry on, but he wasn't too bad."

Wasn't too bad? Clearly, they were used to his behaviour and had come to accept that this was just how it would be. It was lovely that they were so willing to love him no matter what.

"That's nice of you to say, John, but it was actually really nice to have the privilege of saying your mum's final words."

He leaned in and kissed my cheek before excusing himself to return to his family. I left them to grieve, but I felt uplifted, more than I had after a ceremony in a long time. Being in charge of the final, formal words of dedication that would be said about a person's life, felt valuable and rewarding. Having the family say their thanks and knowing that I was able to do justice to a person who was dearly loved in this life, was much more meaningful than sending two people – who were destined to annoy each other for the next few decades – off into marriage.

I hopped in the car, leaving the family to eat tiny sandwiches and reminisce.

Funerals. I could be good at this.

***

"I'm completely dreading this stupid ball wedding," I groaned to Carrie, who looked up at me from the concoction she was pouring from her juicer.

"Why? It sounds like so much fun. You can be secretive and anonymous. I'd love it."

"Well, maybe you should go instead. For one thing, I have absolutely nothing to wear, and secondly, David will be there, and possibly Peter. Disaster!"

"David's a bit of a problem, but at least you'll know someone there and not look like a complete loner. He'll be the perfect cover until the surprise is out in the open. Anyway, you don't even know if Peter's coming." I'd explained the debacle to her.

"But what if he does? And I'm there with David?" I grumbled into my cup.

"You're not going to be there with anyone!" She was getting annoyed with my incessant whinging. "You're not dating David, are you? And you're not with Peter either. Stop obsessing. You never know, you could go home with someone else by the end of the night."

"Ha! I've got enough on my plate, my eyes will be firmly on the floor. Behind my mask. I hate masks. Everyone's going to look completely scary. I hate not being able to see faces."

"Anonymity can be a wonderfully seductive thing," she smirked, raising a suggestive eyebrow. "Let's go shopping. I could use some retail therapy, and we'll find the perfect outfit."

I wasn't convinced, but agreed anyway.

"I think something in a deep red, corseted, with a full skirt," Carrie decided when we pulled up outside the 'Dress It Up' costume shop.

Sounds awful, I thought.

Inside, she pushed me toward the change room and returned with two dresses and a handful of masks. The first one didn't even come close to meeting at the back, and the second was green!

"I'm not wearing green, Carrie, forget it," I declined, handing it back through the door, "I'll look like a giant insect."

The store owner's eyes narrowed at my remark. "There are plenty of lovely colours over here," she suggested, her tone sharp as I quickly closed the door to hide.

Three more dresses landed over the top of the cubicle door. "Here, try these, they're much nicer," Carrie insisted, taking the others.

"This one's not bad," I called. "Come have a look."

"Not too tight," she said, spinning me around. "Bit of cleavage, but not too much. I love it. It's perfect! Now try these." She handed me the hideous, painted half faces.

"Who puts half a face on a stick? It's ridiculous," I complained, holding them up with no enthusiasm.

"Stop it! Here, let me do it." She snatched the mask and fitted it properly onto my face. "Not bad."

It was actually better than I thought. Hiding wasn't such a bad idea. I could hide from Peter and David, and everyone else.

I stripped off the dress and handed it to Carrie to hang up. "Go put this one on order, and tell her I need to pick it up by Saturday morning at the latest."

"Yes, sir," she saluted and headed to the counter.

After I'd dressed, I walked out to meet Carrie at the front of the shop. "I'm starving, let's get lunch."

"Have you thought about what you're going to say to Tom when he gets back on Sunday?" Carrie asked casually, as if she was barely interested.

My insides churned at the sound of his name. "I have no idea. Everything he's said in the past few months has been cryptic and confusing and now, with the whole 'I love you' thing, I don't even know what to say to him."

"But you do love him, don't you?"

"Yes, but I love you, and Peter, and the kids, and the dog!" I was getting exasperated. "I don't know if I *love* love him."

"Would you be willing to give it a try? See if there's anything between you?"

"I'm scared, Carrie. If it doesn't work out, what then? And I don't know how I feel about Peter, or David."

"Do you want my honest opinion?" She was going to give it to me anyway. "I think that your time with Peter has passed. You'll always love him, but it's over. And as for David, he's nice and all, but I can't see you ending up together."

I'm glad she was so sure of everything. "Someone wise –" There was no way I was going to tell her it was a priest, "– recently told me that sometimes we have to give control over to a higher power, so that's what I've decided to do. I can't think about this anymore, it's completely doing my head in. I feel like a nervous wreck." I took a bite of my pizza sub.

"That's actually not bad advice," said Carrie. "Just take it as it comes and see where it leads you, but promise me you'll stay open to every possibility."

"I promise," I said through a mouthful of bread.

After lunch, I crossed the mall to the hairdresser's and made a booking for Saturday morning. I should be charging Charlotte and Barton for all this extra money I had to shell out for this wedding.

"Here you are," Carrie said, tapping my shoulder, "I found Julia."

"Got time for a quick coffee?" Julia suggested.

There was always time for coffee.

We walked to the food court and slotted into the bolted down chairs. "Have you thought about what you'll do after, if this is your last wedding?" Julia asked.

"It might not be the last, you've got Annabel and Mum and Dad yet," Carrie smirked.

She was loving this. I made a face at her. "Actually, I think I've made a decision," I declared.

"Well...what is it?" Julia prompted.

"I'm still giving up weddings, but instead, I've decided to be a funeral celebrant."

I hadn't expected smiles all round, but the two screwed-up faces weren't very encouraging.

"Why the hell would you want to do that?" Carrie coughed. She dabbed her mouth with a tissue to mop up the coffee she'd dribbled.

I shrugged. "It's actually much more rewarding, and I feel like I can make a difference. Do something good, you know?"

"Well, if that's what you want to do, then I say go for it," Julia encouraged me. "The change of focus might really do you good. You can always swap back later if you change your mind."

"It's your funeral!" Carrie laughed, pleased with her joke. "At least you know that people are always going to die, so you'll never run out of business."

CHAPTER 28

Red Velvet

"I'm in the shower!" I screamed as the water turned hot. The boys always managed to run the kitchen tap just as I was getting under the shower. Red raw skin was the last thing I needed. Preparing for this stupid ball was causing me enough anxiety.

I hoisted one foot up on the glass so I could reach the bottom of my leg with the razor. There was a time limit, approximately three-to-four seconds before it slid back down the glass to the floor and I'd have to start over.

Peter's possible appearance was playing on my mind. I should just call him. Make up a reason and find out what he's doing.

I got out of the shower and pulled on my slip. I was dreading the heavy dress and bodice, leaving them until the very last.

I went to the bedroom and grabbed my phone, dialling Peter's number. "Peter," I began, trying to sound casual. "I'm heading out tonight, I have that ball I told you about a while back?"

"Oh yeah, surprise wedding or something, isn't it?"

He said it as if he hardly remembered. He's covering.

"It might be a late night," I went on, "and I just thought that if you're not busy you might pop in and check on the boys? Natalia's working."

That sounded suss. The boys stayed home by themselves all the time and Peter knew it. Crap, I should have thought of something better before I called.

"Um, okay," he said, sounding confused. "I'm actually going out too, but I can call through before I leave?"

He's going out, I knew it! "Oh, no that's fine then. What are you up to tonight?" Silence filled the line. "Sorry, I didn't mean to pry."

"No, it's fine, it's just one of the boys I work with. He and his wife are both celebrating their fortieth. Just at home, nothing special."

Aha! Liar! If it's nothing special, at home, why does he need a fancy-dress costume and mask?

"Okay then, don't worry about the boys, they'll be fine. Have fun," I said, hanging up quickly before he could ask any questions.

I was convinced. He was going to turn up at the Ball.

Jack poked his head in the door. "Me and Adam are heading over to the oval to kick the ball around. Have fun tonight," He smiled.

"Thanks Honey. I've left some money for pizza on the kitchen bench."

When the front door closed, I picked up the dress, if you could call it that. It felt like a suit of armour. I stepped into it and tugged until it was high enough to put my arms through the holes. How the hell was I going to do it up? I tried to lace the back while the dress was on, but I couldn't see the laces. I reversed up to the mirror, but it was hopeless. I dropped the dress back to the floor and did it up, but of course, then I couldn't slide it up over my backside. I attempted to put it over my head, but the lacing, once done up, refused to budge over my boobs.

I stomped my foot like a spoiled child and threw myself face first onto the bed. How did women wear this crap? They had servants to dress them, that's how!

I picked up my phone and called Annabel, she lived the closest.

"Are you at home?" I demanded without even saying hello.

"Yeah, why?"

"Cause I have to get to this Ball to do that surprise wedding and the stupid dress that Carrie made me get won't go on!" I hissed.

"What do you mean it won't go on?"

"It literally won't go on! What do you think I mean? It's got lacing at the back and I can't do it up. Natalia's left and the boys aren't back yet. Can I quickly call through your place on the way?"

"Of course, come now."

I hung up, gathered together the documents and packed them into my case, running through a checklist in my head. Ever since forgetting the ceremony documents I was paranoid of a repeat. I hitched the dress up with the back gaping, stuffed my makeup bag and phone into my handbag and ran out the door. Getting in the car was the next drama. The full skirt of the dress was so big I could hardly feel the accelerator. I hiked it up as much as I could until I had a gigantic pile of fabric on my lap.

"Too bad," I shouted at the dress as I reversed, tyres screeching, out of the driveway. How wonderful it would be to add 'late for the biggest wedding event of the year' to my list of recent disasters. I thought of my eulogy, they'd love using that one. It wasn't until I was on the main road that I realised the petrol gauge was on empty. Without a word, not even one starting with F, I waved my fist at the sky, much to the amusement of a car of young hoons that had pulled up alongside me. I'd obviously provided them with their evening's entertainment as they mimicked me by waving their fists at God too. I poked out my tongue and planted my foot on the accelerator.

I wasn't going to make it to Annabel's! I pulled into the petrol station and adjusted the dress enough to locate my feet and place them on the ground. With a heave, I swung out of the car with the back of the dress gaping.

What are you all looking at? I flashed them all a 'piss off' smile and filled the tank. Peter used to fill the cars up. I hated putting in petrol and always drove it to the last drop.

"Off to a fancy dress, I hope," the attendant joked. Clearly she was a comedian.

"No, why do you ask?" I smiled back, enjoying watching her face turn red as her manager shot her a warning look.

Annabel was waiting when I finally pulled up her driveway. "Geez, Viv, what on earth have you done? This is all in knots at the back," she complained, tugging at the bodice.

"I know, I know, just get it undone, I need to get there."

"Okay, okay," she griped, getting a fork, "but I don't want to ruin it."

"What are you doing with a fork? Are you planning to eat the laces?" I moaned. "Get a move on!"

"No, the prong can get into the knots and pull them out. Here, stand still," she hollered while I wriggled about trying to look. "Is David still going tonight? Do you think you'll go home with him?"

I could hear the smile in her tone. "I'm not thinking about anything right now except getting there on time."

"Done!" She declared, pulling the laces in tight and tying them. "Now get going. And good luck."

"Thanks," I called through the window as I took off. I had five minutes to make a fifteen-minute drive.

***

The Santino Centre looked amazing. I had attended functions there before, but never anything like this. Charlotte and Barton had explained to me at our meeting how they planned to transform it into a medieval castle, themed on some television show they loved, but I had no idea of the lengths they'd planned to go to.

Gigantic Styrofoam pillars, made to look like stone, were placed at intervals throughout the room, while low-hanging draping adorned the entire ceiling, blocking out much of the overhead light. The dark hall was instead lit by large candelabras, set along the walls every couple of metres, blazing with at least a dozen candles each.

Two hundred or so guests – all dressed in medieval garb and

masks – were already wandering about, making their bids on silent auction items or finding their seats at lavishly decorated tables. They'd even managed to find goblets and quaint antique beer steins.

"Welcome everyone," a voice boomed throughout the room, bringing the guests to a halt. I ran for the nearest dark corner.

"Hi," I said to numerous masked people who were also hiding in the dark spot. One face had a large toothy grin painted on it like the Joker from Batman. I shuddered. A room full of faces that didn't move or give anything away was horrifying.

Charlotte and Barton were standing side by side on the stage. Charlotte was speaking. "Thank you all so much for being here tonight for such a worthy cause and one that is dear to all of our hearts."

What was their cause? I couldn't even remember. Was it babies? Or small babies or something?

"Many of you here tonight have either had a premature baby or know someone who has."

Ah! *Premature* babies.

"The work that the NICU does is beyond compare, and we hope to show our support and appreciation with this fundraising event. Tonight, we will be bringing you an evening full of fun, festivities, sword fights and jousting, but we do ask of you, one thing. As you enjoy all of this fun and frivolity, remember the children, and dig deep into your pockets – or chequebooks – so that we can truly make a difference. Oh, and there will be a big surprise coming up for you shortly to get the ball rolling."

That was my cue. I made a run for it across the dance

floor and up the half-dozen stairs to the stage curtain. Charlotte waved and signalled for me to meet her at the back.

"Viv, yay, you're here. We are so excited. It's come together so much better than we expected," she cheered, doing a happy shuffle.

"It truly looks amazing," I congratulated her as Barton returned from the stage.

"Thank you, Viv. And thank you for agreeing to be a part of this. This means the world to us. The NICU were there for us with both of our babies who were born very premature, and finally we're able to give something back." Barton said, pulling Charlotte in close.

How cynical am I? I thought. Ridiculing these people, making them out to be greedy weirdos, when they're actually kind and decent human beings. They stood for something. Which was more than I could say for myself.

"Get yourself a drink from the bar. We were hoping to get started in about 30 minutes, if that's okay with you?" Charlotte asked.

"It's perfect, and I could use a drink. I'll see you back here in about 25." Drink. Bar. Must find it.

"Scotch on the rocks, thanks," I said to the bartender. "Actually, make it a double?" I didn't usually drink before a ceremony, but in this instance, I could make an exception.

Where was David? How the hell were you supposed to find anyone in this place with all these stupid masks? I scanned the room, admiring some of the fabulous costumes. Long flowing dresses, some with tight bodices, and others that draped all the way, like silk, to the floor. There were men dressed in armour

338 - SUSAN MURPHY

and others like noblemen, while some had gone for the easier peasant look. My eyes stopped on one man, dressed impeccably in red velvet and carrying a shiny, silver shield. He was leaning against the far wall with one leg lifted behind him, resting on it for balance. His mask wasn't one of the evil smiling faces, it was serious, but gentle. It looked as if he was staring in this direction, at me, but it was hard to tell.

I downed the last of my drink and looked for him again, but he was gone. Never mind, it was show time. I grabbed my bag and headed for the stage.

As I entered the stage door, the man in red velvet rushed by me, bumping me slightly and stopping to see I was okay. He didn't speak, but I felt as if I knew him. Was it Peter? He was too tall and not the same build as Peter. Maybe it was David, but why wouldn't he have said something? I shrugged it off. I had done so many ceremonies in my years as a celebrant, I often passed ten people a day that I could swear I'd seen before. When you speak to a crowd of a hundred or more on a regular basis, some of the faces etch themselves into your memory.

"Ready to go?" I asked a very nervous-looking Charlotte and Barton, who were pacing the stage.

"All ready. Mum's just bringing our girls up and then let's do it!" she said, squeezing Barton's hand and fixing her wildly excited eyes on his. "We'll all get into position, and then the curtain will go up. The mic's already set for you, Viv, so if you can just call everyone's attention that would be great. Eeeeek! This is really happening!"

When the curtain went up there was no need to call the

attention of the room. Mouths gaped as excited squeals rang out from every corner of the room.

I announced. "The little surprise that Charlotte and Barton have for you tonight is that they have decided there would be no better time, no better place, and absolutely no better friends to share with them as they pledge their commitment to one another in marriage."

The room erupted with applause and whistles. They had kept the secret well. A lump formed in my throat as people gathered in toward the stage, tears streaming and mouths cheering.

They fell into awed silence as Charlotte and Barton made their vows to one another.

"Every love story tells us," Barton began, "that we may believe we have loved, we may believe we have lost, but true love comes only once, and you, my darling, are my soul mate to eternity."

Charlotte was crying when she began. "Barton, despite what I thought I knew, I realised when you kissed me for the very first time that I had not experienced true love, love that was destined and always meant to be."

The support of the room, the love of their family and friends, and the way they held their children throughout the ceremony was like nothing I had ever experienced. It was almost over-whelming.

This is what it meant to do something for others, this is what it meant to be surrounded by love.

The cheers erupted again as I presented them for the first time as "Man, Wife, Mum, Dad, Daughter, Son and Friend." They had wanted it that way. I remained on the stage and packed up my papers as they descended on the crowd to the outpouring of congratulations.

The man, the one I had seen before, wearing red velvet, stood at the back and watched on, his mask still firmly in place.

He was definitely looking at me.

CHAPTER 29

All along

After being forced into participating in a round of the Italian dance, 'The Tarantella', I retreated to the bar for a refill while the jousters took to the stage.

I scanned the room again for any sign of David, or Peter, or the man. It couldn't be Peter. He was definitely too tall. David had to be here somewhere. Surely he'd seen me on stage, unless he was late.

Leaning against the far wall, in the same place he had stood earlier, I spotted red velvet. I'll just go over, say hello, casually, as if in passing. I grabbed the Scotch the bartender had poured me and made my way in his direction. He was distracted by the jousting, but when he spotted me approaching, he headed straight for the exit doors and into the foyer. I followed, but by the time I reached them, he was nowhere in sight.

Bugger! It was Peter or David, dressed up to look different and unrecognisable. It was one of them concocting some ridiculous romantic plan, I decided. It had to be. Peter? A romantic plan? Ha! Although, he'd been so different lately, so maybe. But the man was too tall, I was sure of it.

I tried to picture Peter and David's height compared to mine, holding my hand above my head to where I roughly thought they stood, but instead managed to draw the attention of a woman passing by.

"Are you alright? She asked, as if I might be having some sort of problem.

"Fine, no, fine, thank you," I smiled, hurrying back to the bar. It was safe at the bar.

"Would you like to dance?"

The mask that I turned around to see was only moderately scary.

Why not? Couldn't hurt, but then I halted abruptly when the awful memory of the awards night flashed through my mind.

Confused eyes peered at me through the slits of the mask. What the hell, just keep control.

This one definitely wasn't Peter. Long hair, blue eyes, and much thinner. It wasn't David either. He was taller and broader in the shoulders. Argh, these masks were ridiculous. When could we take them off? It was impossible to read or judge people without seeing their faces.

I followed the stranger to the dance floor. Maybe it was better this way. Harder to be judgemental. Maybe I could actually like someone without even seeing their face first.

Charlotte and Barton's words replayed in my mind as I twirled back and forth in the stranger's arms, and puffs of grey smoke filled the air around us. He flung me out again, and with only a brief release of my hand, it was another masked man who drew me in, closer this time. The red velvet man.

He held my left hand tightly in his and cradled my back with the other. His smell had already carried me away to some fantasy place when his lips pressed hard against mine. In my mind the entire room had fallen silent as I prayed for it to never end. Who it was, or why, fell away into nothingness. I couldn't think of anything but his lips, I couldn't think at all.

When he finally pulled back, I felt faint, dizzy, like the women I ridiculed in romantic movies who looked at men while batting at them with adoring eyes. He took me by the hand and led me off the dance floor.

I didn't care where we were going, I didn't care why, I just wanted him to kiss me again. He pulled me against his body, pressing his lips to mine again as he swept me into the dark alcove behind the deserted office stairs.

Beneath his suit, his body was hot. He felt wild, uncontrolled, but then he slowed to a stop, holding me back to look into my eyes. I knew them. I knew his eyes. He lifted his mask as I stepped back from him.

"Are you disappointed?" he asked, worry furrowing his brow.

I didn't answer.

"Did you hear what the groom said before?" he asked. "About there being only one true love, a love that was destined and can't be avoided? Well, for me that's you. I had to do it this way."

I felt behind me for the stairs and sat down. "I don't understand. You're different. You even look different." I could barely string my sentences together, my mind was moving so fast trying to make coherent thoughts. I wanted to jump up and hug him and tell him how much I'd missed him, but slap him senseless at the same time.

"I'll explain everything, I promise, but I need to ask you one thing." He sat beside me on the step. "Did you feel anything? And if you did, will you come with me now?"

Tom's familiar hands were holding me tightly as they had done so many times in the past. Only they felt different now. They felt intense and passionate.

I hesitated. "But you've been gone for three months."

"I know I have, and I'm sorry. But if you felt anything at all and you're willing to consider it, I've booked a suite across the road at the Marriott. Carrie brought your things up to the room so that if you decide to come with me, we can go there and be alone to talk. I'll understand if you say no, but I had to take the risk, once and for all."

My heart was pounding. I hadn't felt something, I'd felt everything. Every ounce of his love, every moment of his longing, and every regret for the years he'd wasted not being honest. I felt more than I'd ever felt before, with anyone.

I looked into his pleading eyes. They knew everything about me. Every embarrassing secret, every bad habit and vice, yet they still loved me.

He'd lost weight, at least 20 kilos, and his hair was short. A dark shadow of stubble covered his chin and cheeks, his face rugged and handsome.

"Yes, I'll come."

Without a second's pause, he lifted me from the step and kissed me again, "I love you," he breathed, taking my hand and leading me out the door.

A light rain fell on our faces as we crossed the busy street and into the foyer of the hotel. We kissed in the elevator and inside the room, where a dozen or more candles burned in glass jars.

"I'm sorry," he said, "I had meant for us to come here to talk, but your sister set everything up."

Carrie! She'd known all along. I knew it!

Tom turned on the light and quickly rounded up the candles. I watched him as he blew them out and set them on the small desk. How had I not seen it before? His eyes, soft and gentle, his face, handsome and strong, his unfaltering dedication to me. He was beautiful and perfect and my heart ached at the thought of him feeling he had to better himself for me. He loved me exactly as I was, and yet he felt the need to change himself to make me see him.

I turned the light off before he could blow out the remaining candles that now only partially lit the room. I led him to the bed, cupping his face in my hands. "Why?" I pleaded, "Why did you do this?" Tears filled my eyes and fell to my cheeks.

"Please don't feel that way," he answered softly, gently kissing my face. "You, Genevieve, make me want to be the best I can be. I've loved you since that very first day, first moment, first second in that book shop, and I have despised myself ever since for never having the courage to fight for you."

I stroked his face, feeling the pain emanating from his heart.

"I knew things with Peter weren't going well and I made a decision to finally declare my love for you no matter what, but I didn't feel like I could do that, like I was worthy of you without being my best. You deserve my best. I had organised the trip, and there was some work involved, but only for the first few weeks.

346 - SUSAN MURPHY

I spent the rest of the time at a fitness retreat. I was determined to come back the kind of man that deserved you."

"But why would you do that? Why didn't you just tell me?" I cried, desperate to understand if he thought I was the kind of monster that couldn't love someone for who they were.

"When you and Peter actually broke up, I was going to cancel the trip so I could be here for you, but Carrie knew about my plans and she literally made me go ahead with it. It tore my heart out to leave you, but I wanted so badly to make this happen." He wiped at my tears with his hand.

I confessed. "When you didn't respond to my emails, I thought you'd found someone over there."

"Coming back to you was the only thing on my mind. Every day."

I put my arms around his neck and fell backwards so that he fell with me onto the bed. We laid silent, staring into eyes we'd looked into a million times, but never with true honesty. They were honest eyes, for the first time in more than 20 years.

"Is this weird for you?" he asked as I silently searched his face for all of the things I hadn't allowed myself to see.

"I thought it would be, but it feels as if it was all there anyway, without the kissing," I laughed.

"I wish I'd had the courage all those years ago." His eyes fell to my neck, "maybe we could have had this from the beginning." There was regret in his voice.

I lifted his face so that his eyes were level with mine. "Do you think we could have had this if we hadn't been friends first? I truly believe that everything happens in the order that it's meant to. I was supposed to marry Peter. I was supposed to have my three, beautiful children, and we were supposed to find each other at this point in our lives. I don't regret a single thing."

He leaned in and kissed me tenderly. We were lost in the moment, in each other, until it became increasingly apparent that the damn dress was not going to come off.

By the time I was flat on my face with Tom kneeling over me, his teeth desperately trying to untangle the impossible knot Annabel had tied, every ounce of romance that had filled the candlelit room was gone. When the knot finally came free, our utter relief gave way to hysterical, desperate, unbridled passion. I yanked my arms from the clutches of the evil dress, kissing him with a fierceness I didn't know I possessed, while Tom tugged and pulled at it to release me. We fell onto the bed, propelled by decades of lust, love and desire. It was hours before we emerged from each other's arms.

"It's hard to believe we're really here. I don't think I've actually let it fully sink in yet." He smiled, kissing me gently.

"We've got a lot of time to make up for," I grinned. "I need to message the kids and let them know I won't be home."

"I'm gonna have a quick shower and get us something to eat," Tom whispered in my ear.

I watched him as he walked to the bathroom. He was so much thinner, toned and gorgeous. Was I that shallow? Surely it wasn't his weight that stopped me from being attracted to him.

You know what? Stop it. Stop being so damn hard on yourself. Whatever the reason – Peter, marriage, life, kids, friendship – it didn't matter anymore.

I searched for the phone in my handbag. There was a message from David.

Hi, Viv, I'm sorry to say I'm not going to make it tonight. Managed to reverse into someone as I pulled out of my driveway. Catch up soon?

As friends it would have to be.

While Tom showered, I sent the kids a message and one to Carrie.

I knew you were up to something! I knew it! You bugger, you knew all along. But I love you for it xx.

My Facebook icon was showing fifteen notifications. I clicked on it to see Peter tagged in his cousin's fancy dress fortieth birthday party.

He had lied about where he was going, but it was probably to save any awkwardness because I wasn't invited.

Telling him about this would be difficult, but given his new found tolerance and understanding, I knew it wouldn't ruin him, or our relationship.

Telling the kids would be harder, but no harder than if I had dated someone else. They loved Tom and he loved them. He'd been part of their lives, our lives, since the day they were born.

Telling my sisters would be... Wait, I'm sure they already knew!

Everything was exactly where it needed to be, where it was supposed to be.

I was beginning to sound like Annabel.

THE END

***

Want a sneak peek of *Confetti Confidential, Annabel's Wedding?*

CHAPTER 1
12 Weeks
***

With twelve weeks until her wedding, Annabel was glowing. Not because she was a beautiful soon-to-be bride, but because she'd had a fake tan trial that had gone horribly wrong.

'It'll settle down, don't worry about it,' I consoled her. 'At least you know to go with the much lighter shade for the actual day.'

Annabel's pout turned to a grin. 'Shall we stop in at the bridal store and have another look at my dress?'

'Alright,' I agreed. I would rather have headed home, but gave in knowing that it would cheer her up. She was orange after all. The problem was that I'd seen the dress so many times already that a few nights ago I'd even had a dream about it. It was more of a nightmare given that the dress had chased me with its coat-hanger still fixed into the shoulders like some kind of killer garment.

'What are you smiling at?' she asked as we made our way into the store.

'I was thinking about the first time we came here. We had so much fun that day with Harry.' Boutique Bridal was only the second store we had visited during our hunt for the perfect wedding dress for Annabel, but we didn't go any further. Harry Rosen, a famous wedding dress designer, had been visiting the store that day to update his collection and turned the fitting into an exclusive party. We sipped champagne and laughed while Harry fitted Annabel in different styles from his range until finally, she found the perfect one.

'It was a fantastic day, wasn't it?' Annabel pulled on the dress the shop assistant had brought out and proudly pirouetted in the ivory and lace gown she had finally settled on. She'd surprised me by choosing the gorgeous, straight, full-length piece, but then ruined it, at least in my opinion, with a puffy short-sleeved bolero. It wasn't to my taste, but it definitely screamed Annabel. My big sister and I had never shared the same sense of style.

'You look amazing,' I said, eyeing her up and down, 'or at least you will, once the tan settles.'

'I'm so excited, Viv. I can't wait to marry Gerry. Do you think the weather will be okay?'

The pair had opted for a May wedding, which was risky. I'd warned them that the weather can be unpredictable at that time of year, especially since they had chosen the twenty-third, but the falling autumn leaves and cooler days were exactly what they wanted. They would say their vows in the sprawling Adelaide Botanical Gardens among piles of red and brown leaves, and lush green grass that sprawled as far as the eye could see.

'The weather will be fine,' I assured her, 'and even if it's not,

Tom said he'd organise a couple of those giant umbrellas to be on hand, just in case. Don't let it worry you.'

'I'm so proud of my girls for offering to organise the wedding set-up, although I'm worried it'll be too much for them. They're really happy for me and Gerry, but I also want them to enjoy it.'

Annabel's daughters, Georgia and Abbie, had done us all a huge favour by taking over the organising of the ceremony and reception as well as overseeing it all on the day. The less Annabel had to worry about at the moment the better. My nieces were great at this stuff. Annabel had nothing to worry about. 'They'll be fine, and they'll have plenty of helpers. They want to do it for you guys and I think it's lovely.'

'That reminds me, we're meeting with the celebrant next week and I want you to come along. Just to offer some suggestions. Would you mind?'

I nodded. When they first got engaged I'd thought they would want me to do the wedding, but when Annabel insisted that I be a bridesmaid along with Carrie and Julia, I was ecstatic. That was until she took us shopping for our dresses. We fought for five hours straight over colours and styles. Carrie wanted something black and long, Julia wanted something 'flowy', and I wanted something A-line to assist with making us look slimmer than we actually were. Eventually, Annabel threw her hands in the air and admitted defeat. She decided to make the decision herself and ordered something online. What arrived was a frightful pink number with a frill along the bottom. We all hated them, including Annabel.

'Fawn's a fairly new celebrant, so I just want to make sure everything is right. She's lovely, you'll like her.'

'No worries,' I agreed. I had intended to go anyway. Fawn was probably as lovely as Annabel described, but I'd seen enough 'nice' celebrants who were new and unfortunately had no idea what they were doing. I wanted to offer some suggestions about some of the personalised wording for the ceremony.

I noticed that Annabel's excitement had slowly faded and given way to something else, an expression I couldn't quite decipher. 'What's wrong? Is there something going on with you and Gerry?' I asked.

'No, nothing like that.' She hesitated and turned away from me. 'It's Gerry's son.' Her smile faded altogether. 'I'm just not sure about him. I'm worried that he doesn't like me.'

'How could someone not like you, Bel?' I asked, giving her a squeeze. 'Tap on him or something until he comes around.' Annabel quite honestly believed that Reike and the Emotional Freedom Technique (tapping) that she practised could solve everything.

She laughed nervously, but I could tell it was upsetting her. She climbed up on the dais for one last look at herself in the dress, leaning close to the mirror.

'Stop that looking into your soul stuff, Bel, and just trust the fact that you love Gerry and he loves you. This is right and everything will be perfect.'

'What are we doing about the hens' night?' I asked, changing the subject.

She moved back and the beaming smile had now returned. 'You'll have to ask Julia and Carrie, they banned me from any of the planning. Not that I mind, I've got enough to deal with, but please don't let them do anything awful.'

'I'll do my best,' I said, raising my hands to suggest that the blame not be laid with me if anything did go awry. 'I'll give them a call and find out. Carrie might be leaving soon, so we need to get it sorted before then.'

'I can't wait to meet the little guy. Carrie said his name is Niran and it means eternal. I love it.'

We were all keen to meet the toddler that Carrie and her partner Annie were about to adopt. Annie had already started the process when they got together, and it didn't take Carrie long to decide that she wanted to be a part of both of their lives. They were just waiting on the green light to go to Thailand to collect him.

'Now, what about your wedding night?' I asked, rubbing my hands together in anticipation of the details. 'What are you wearing for that?'

Hopping off the elevated platform, Annabel was trying not to laugh. 'I've got something nice.' Her cheeks had already turned pink.

'"Nice" like you'd wear to Mum's birthday? Or nice like we saw in that shop Julia took us to?'

'Shhh,' she giggled, the sound instantly transporting me back to our younger years when my big sister was always chasing some boy or another. 'It's nice, okay? A matching set, all white and frilly. It even has suspenders.' She whispered the last part. Even now after a marriage, two children and an engagement, talk of sex still embarrassed her.

'Woo hoo,' I teased.

'I still have those edible knicker things too,' she confessed.

I laughed at her admission, but I had to give her credit. I was sure she'd have eaten them within a week. 'Why didn't you try them out with Gerry?'

'I don't know. I ate the bra and just kept the pants hidden away. I was thinking about using them on the wedding night too, although it's kind of a bit gross. What if Gerry's not into it?'

She'd eaten the bra. I knew she wouldn't have been able to keep herself from scoffing it. 'He'll be into it, Bel, trust me.'

After Annabel made the final payment on the dress, checked on the alterations for the bridesmaids' dresses, and organised yet another fitting, we finally left the shop and headed home.

I could smell the aroma of bolognaise sauce from the driveway.

'How was your day?' Tom asked when I kissed him. The taste of the red wine he'd been drinking tingled on my taste buds.

'Fine, nothing terribly exciting. Another fitting for Annabel's dress. Are the boys here?'

'No, they're staying at Peter's. Jack called and said they'd be home during the week to catch up and have dinner.'

The boys spent a lot of time with their father these days, which was great for them, but difficult for me. They'd become so much closer to their dad over the past year and it had done all of them good. They were often off fishing on Peter's boat, or catching a game on weekends, and he was more responsible about their school work than I could have hoped. Seeing Tom and I together as a couple had been an adjustment for everyone, but Peter had accepted it and never spoke poorly of either of us. I missed them dreadfully, but I could see how much they were enjoying time with Peter.

'Is there wine for me?' I asked, searching for the bottle.

Tom took a glass from the cabinet and held it out to me while he poured. 'Well, I have some news. I've been nominated for an award for one of my photos. You know, the ones of the people playing chess in the park? I submitted it to a local government art competition.'

'That's fantastic news!' I kissed him again and hugged him tight. Since his return from England, Tom had been concentrating on establishing himself as a serious photographer. He still opted to do a few weddings here and there, but he'd been concentrating mostly on what he liked to call 'grass-roots' photography. Real-life shoots that involved photographing people in 'real' situations, sitting on benches, or just in a moment.

'When is the award ceremony? I need to make sure I mark it on my calendar now.'

'It's in a couple of weeks. It's a Thursday so it shouldn't be a problem.' He turned back to stir the pot that was wafting a delicious aroma that filled the kitchen.

'Do we get to dress up?' It felt like ages since I'd put on something nice and had my hair done.

'They're sending a formal invitation in the mail,' he replied, lighting a candle he'd placed in the centre of the table. His romantic nature wasn't showing any signs of diminishing with time as it often did in relationships. Tom was as attentive and thoughtful as he'd always been.

My phone buzzed in my pocket. Julia.

We need to get together and organise the Hens. I was thinking we could have it here at my house. We can get some waiters, drinks and 'entertainment'. What do you think?

Sounds good, I typed back, not wanting to get caught up

texting back and forth. *Let's get together with Carrie during the week and make a plan.*

I turned my attention back to Tom. 'Did Natalia call?'

'No, she hasn't.'

'I'm getting worried, Tom, it's been four days.'

He laughed, then quickly apologised when he realised I was wounded. 'She's twenty, Viv, and she's with her boyfriend in Italy. Give her a break. She'll call.'

I huffed because he was right. I was proud of my amazing daughter and how fabulously she was living her life, but also a tiny bit jealous. She and her boyfriend, Jude, had both applied to study overseas for the first semester of the year, but from my conversations with her, they were having the time of their lives exploring the city and finding tiny, perfect little eateries to study in.

'Promise me that after this wedding is over, we'll go to Italy and France,' I begged. 'I've wanted to go forever.'

Tom turned from the sauce and put his hands on my shoulders, massaging them gently. 'I know, and I'm all for it. Let's give Annabel her big moment and then we can start planning. We can spend a few weeks, maybe even a month, sightseeing and travelling around.'

Excitement pulsed through me. 'I want to be sipping a latte in Rome by August,' I declared.

It was strange to be thinking about taking this trip with Tom. For twenty years I had been dreaming of taking a holiday to Italy, but it had always been with Peter by my side. The thought of going with Tom brought so many more possibilities. Tom

loved art and history and he'd want to see everything and experience all the little things that other tourists wouldn't notice.
Peter would have preferred to eat pizza and see a soccer match.

'So, looks like we're alone.' Tom's smile widened as he turned
the hotplates to low and took my hand. He kissed me gently as
he pulled me into his arms before guiding me to the bedroom.

Even though we'd been together romantically for a year, in the
bedroom we were still discovering each other. It was the one part
of ourselves we hadn't shared in our long relationship as friends
and it was new and exciting. Tom had always been a caring and
loving person, but as a sexual partner, he was deep and intense.
But even in those moments when we were connected spiritually,
mentally and physically, I still needed more of him. I craved to
know him more, be closer. It scared me. I wondered if he felt it,
but I couldn't ask. Instead, I pulled him in tighter so that the
feel of his warm skin against mine would ease the desire.

An hour later we were stuck with gluggy spaghetti and
slightly burned bolognaise.

'What's wrong? I know it's awful,' Tom said, noticing the
discomfort on my face.

'No, it's not that. My stomach's playing up. I think it's all
the wedding plans and worrying about Natalia. I feel anxious
about the wedding for some reason, like something's going to go
terribly wrong.'

'It's not. You need to relax.' He stroked my arm gently.

'I know, but if something does go wrong it'll probably be
because of me. I'll fall over or step on Annabel's dress or something. You know what I'm like.'

Tom laughed and took my plate from the table. 'Go and have

a bath and find your happy place. Stop stressing about things that haven't even happened, and aren't likely to happen.'

I took his advice and settled into a tub full of warm water surrounded by scented candles. I imagined a forest with chirping birds to help my mind relax, but there was still so much to organise for the wedding, how could anyone relax? Instead, I made mental lists while I soaked.

1. Bridal party dinner: Annabel wants Chinese, maybe King Tao's? Pick a date and see if everyone's available. Should we even have one? Maybe we could just skip that.
2. Help her organise thank you cards for bridal party.
3. Invites need to go out next week.
4. Hens night: A hotel or apartment? Topless waiters? Maybe one stripper. Not a full strip, just down to jocks. Annabel would have a heart attack if he was naked.
5. Night before wedding: Are we staying at Annabel's? Games and dinner? Spa treatments?
6. Wedding day: Hair at 7:30. Breakfast. Makeup. Car picking us up at 1pm. Ceremony at 1:30. Photos. Reception from 5pm. Bring thongs for dancing.

When I climbed out of the tub an hour later, Tom had made me a cup of peppermint tea and put on one of my favourite movies, *Crazy, Stupid Love*.

'Thanks,' I said, hugging him, 'this is exactly what I needed. When he brought out the block of dark Rum and Raisin chocolate, I squealed and scoffed a row, while he started the movie.

Everything was perfect. I wanted to allow myself to feel

grateful for the point at which life had delivered me, albeit kicking and screaming, but I couldn't shake a feeling of foreboding that had begun to burrow itself deep inside of me. Ever since the night of Charlotte and Barton's charity ball wedding, when Tom swept me off my feet, I'd been feeling lucky. Maybe lucky wasn't the right word, it was more like a sense of contentment, as if the planets had aligned and the timing, for once, was perfect for things to end up exactly as they were meant to be. Some days I would sit in the back garden, sipping a cider and watching all the colourful birds in the overhanging fig trees that all but consumed our yard. Tom would be reading the paper or fighting with the lawn mower and we were happy. Even when he was doing mundane things like cooking dinner, I could feel his love for me. It seemed to fill every space we inhabited, without consuming or overpowering it. It was right. And perfect.

I'd loved that feeling in those first weeks, but as the months had passed, a familiar doubt had begun to creep in. There was no escaping it. It was hereditary, my Irish genes just wouldn't let me be. I knew, inherently that something just had to go wrong.

I tried to ignore the nagging feeling as I watched Tom fiddling with the remote control. How could I be so lucky? After everything I had been through, the turmoil with Peter and a harrowing time with Carrie being sick, I really did feel eternally grateful for the place it had brought me to. Without it, all of it – good and bad – I wouldn't be here. Not with Tom, or like this.

I cuddled into him and tried to shake it off. I needed to learn to see change as an opportunity to grow, and be grateful that no matter how crazy life got, or how out of control and overwhelming things sometimes felt, we would have each other.

I had no idea what was coming.

Confetti Confidential, Annabel's Wedding - coming soon.